LOST

ROADS

LOST ROADS

JONATHAN MABERRY

A Novel of the Rot & Ruin

WITHDRAWN

SIMON & SCHUSTER BFYR

NEW YORK LONDON TORONTO SYDNEY NEW DELHI

Also by Jonathan Maberry

THE ROT & RUIN SERIES

Rot & Ruin

Dust & Decay

Flesh & Bone

Fire & Ash

Bits & Pieces

THE BROKEN LANDS SERIES

Broken Lands

THE NIGHTSIDERS SERIES

The Orphan Army

Vault of Shadows

Scary Out There

Mars One

SIMON & SCHUSTER BFYR

An imprint of Simon & Schuster Children's Publishing Division
1230 Avenue of the Americas, New York, New York 10020

For information about special discounts for bulk purchases, please contact Simon & Schuster
Special Sales at 1-866-506-1949 or business@simonandschuster.com.
The Simon & Schuster Speakers Bureau can bring authors to your live event.
For more information or to book an event, contact the Simon & Schuster Speakers Bureau
at 1-866-248-3049 or visit our website at www.simonspeakers.com.
Book design by Laurent Linn
The text for this book was set in Chaparral Pro.
Manufactured in the United States of America
First Edition
2 4 6 8 10 9 7 5 3 1
Library of Congress Cataloging-in-Publication Data
Names: Maberry, Jonathan, author.
Title: Lost roads / Jonathan Maberry.
Description: First edition. | New York : Simon & Schuster Books for Young Readers, [2020] |
Series: Broken lands ; book 2 | Audience: Ages 14 up. | Audience: Grades 10–12. |
Summary: "After losing her mother, Gabriella 'Gutsy' Gomez continues her journey
to save those infected with the zombie plague, all while having to defend her home from
the Night Army, who's back and even stronger than before"—Provided by publisher.
Identifiers: LCCN 2019056479 (print) | ISBN 9781534406407 (hardcover) |
ISBN 9781534406421 (eBook)
Subjects: CYAC: Zombies—Fiction. | Survival—Fiction.
Classification: LCC PZ7.M11164 Lo 2020 (print) | DDC [Fic]—dc23
LC record available at https://lccn.loc.gov/2019056479

This is for Viet Mai, Tammy Greenwood, and Aleta Barthell,
the 2017, 2018, and 2019 recipients
of the Jonathan Maberry Inspiring Teens Award,
presented in my name by the
Canyon Crest Academy's Creative Writing Club.
It's a tad surreal to have an award named after me,
but it's a great pleasure to give it to teachers and educators
who are out there truly making the creative experience
for teens a more effective and magical one.
I celebrate you all!

And—as always—for Sara Jo!

ACKNOWLEDGMENTS

Special thanks to some real-world people who were willing to enter the world of the living dead with me. Thanks to my agent, Sara Crowe of Pippin Properties. Thanks to my brilliant and talented assistant, Dana Fredsti.

LOST
ROADS

PART ONE

NEW ALAMO

If we don't end war, war will end us.

—H. G. WELLS

GABRIELLA "GUTSY" GOMEZ WAS SURE EVERY SINGLE thing—living or dead—was trying to kill her.

This was the world and that's how it was.

IT STARTED LIKE THIS.

A bunch of them in a classroom at Misfit High. Gutsy and her best friends, Spider and Alethea. Gutsy's adopted coy-dog, Sombra. Karen Peak, head of town security. The two old teachers, Mr. Urrea and Mr. Ford, known to everyone as the Chess Players. The California Kids—Benny Imura, Nix Riley, Lou Chong, and Lilah—who'd arrived in town just as an army of ravagers and shamblers was attacking. Two grizzled and scarred old soldiers had shown up as well—Benny's older half brother, Sam Imura, and special ops agent Joe Ledger. Grimm, Ledger's massive and heavily armored mastiff, lurked nearby.

All of them there in that room. With a monster.

Captain Bess Collins.

She was the one who'd run a hidden military base near New Alamo. She'd overseen the lab that used the citizens as lab rats for bizarre medical experiments. She had allowed Dr. Max Morton and his team to systematically inject various unsuspecting townsfolk, including Gutsy's own mother, with deadly diseases so they could study the reanimation process. They said it was to try and save the world, to find a way to control or destroy the parasites that created *los muertos*. To restore some intelligence to the newly risen dead. To remove the aggression that made the shamblers want to kill and devour.

Monsters doing monstrous things to fight other monsters.

That was how it started.

Captain Collins admitted all of this now. She admitted that her team had made terrible mistakes. They had experimented on wounded or dying soldiers and accidentally turned many of them into murderous thinking zombies—ravagers.

She admitted that everyone in New Alamo was expendable if the end result was a cure.

And she told them about their worst failure: Years ago the team at the lab had found the original infected person, a brutal mass murderer named Homer Gibbon. He had not become a shambler and could somehow control the other undead. Gibbon had been terribly mangled in a car accident during the initial outbreak. Soldiers had collected what was left of him and brought him to Collins's lab, where she and Dr. Morton had stitched Gibbon back together like a pair of Frankensteins. They'd experimented on him, but had badly underestimated how dangerous and powerful he was.

Homer Gibbon—the Raggedy Man—had escaped.

It was he who'd sent an army against New Alamo.

It was he who'd sent an even larger force toward Asheville, where the fledgling American Nation was trying to rise from the ashes of the old United States.

It was he who was going to sweep across the face of the world and devour all living things.

Captain Collins told them all of this.

And then, as if fate wanted to cruelly punctuate her words, screams tore the air.

The dead had come back to New Alamo.

Gutsy and her friends had only won a single battle. The war for the right to survive—to *live*—was just beginning. They knew this now.

FORD RUSHED TO THE WINDOW AND STUCK HIS HEAD
out, ear cocked toward the east gate, but then he frowned and
turned back. "God . . . it's coming from the *center of town*."

Urrea crowded in next to him. "By the hospital, I think.
Please, no . . ."

Gutsy snatched her crowbar from a desktop and dashed
for the door, Sombra at her heels. Everyone followed. Gutsy
yelled over her shoulder as she ran.

"Someone watch her."

"I got it," said Chong, and he wheeled around back to the
classroom.

The rest ran.

As they exited the school, the sounds of the screams were
horrific, and gunfire cracked through the hot afternoon air.
Small arms, rifles and shotguns.

"I don't understand," gasped Spider. "How can there be
this big a fight *in* town?"

No one had an answer, and they all ran harder.

As they rounded a corner, they saw a terrible fight in
progress—not at the hospital but across the square by the
livery stables, which had been used to store the many enemy

dead until they could be taken out by the cartload and burned.

Just ahead, a gang of ravagers poured out of the stable, each of them armed with axes, pitchforks, and sledgehammers that they swung with terrible efficiency. People were down, clutching broken arms or shattered faces. Blood from open wounds splashed ten feet high on the walls. A couple of residents were firing handguns as they backed away, but they were almost immediately overrun. There were more attackers than there were bullets.

"*Ravagers!*" Gutsy cried.

"I thought they'd checked them all from the attack," gasped Nix. "All the dead ones were silenced, weren't they?"

Lilah reached the melee first and leaped into the air, swinging her spear in a glittering arc that cleaved through a ravager's wrist. He shrieked and dropped his ax, then Lilah crashed into him, knocking him backward. She reversed the spear and swung a short, devastating blow to the killer's temple that dropped him like an ox in a slaughterhouse.

Gutsy and Benny split right and left and Nix came up the middle, her gun in both hands as she fired careful, spaced shots. The ravagers were not quite *los muertos* but they were no longer human, and it was very difficult to kill them. Head shots, however, took everything down, human, inhuman, or in-between.

Sam Imura moved past Gutsy with his sniper rifle in his hands. The weapon was a precision instrument designed to kill from great distances, but Sam proved that it worked close-up. He shot, pivoted, shot, pivoted, shot. Each time a ravager went down with a black dot on forehead or temple.

Then Captain Ledger reached the fight and he drew his

katana so fast that the weapon was nothing more than a whisper of silver. He and Sam peeled off and ran toward the hospital on the far side of the square, carving a path of destruction. Gutsy stared at them. Ledger, Sam, and the California kids were all warriors. She and her friends were not. There were no samurai or special ops soldiers or trained fighters in New Alamo. Just ordinary people.

Watching them did not make her feel diminished or foolish or helpless, though. For Gutsy, it had the opposite effect. She saw how experienced fighters worked. There was a clear science to it, a practicality, and she was all about that.

Gutsy hefted her crowbar and felt coldness run through her veins. Some of it was fear. Some of it was a kind of rage. She and her friends had learned the terrible art of killing on the wall, and that meant they were not helpless.

A ravager rushed out of the stable and swung an ax at her, but Gutsy ducked low and smashed her crowbar into his kneecap. His leg buckled, dropping him onto the injured knee—and Gutsy hit him in the head, making him fall back and drag a second ravager down. A third attacker swung a shovel at her, but Gutsy twisted away, and the blade missed her face by inches. She recovered and smashed the ravager in the throat, but the blow was badly aimed and did little damage. The man simply staggered away without falling.

"Move!" yelled a voice, and Gutsy evaded again as Alethea's baseball bat—Rainbow Smite—whistled past and took the same ravager on the point of the chin. The man spun like a top and fell bonelessly to the ground.

Then Gutsy pushed Alethea out of the way of a ravager with a pitchfork, parried the weapon with her crowbar, kicked him in the knee, and then smashed the killer's skull. He fell, broken and still.

Spider used his *bo* to drop another ravager, and for a few minutes there was furious fighting as more of the monsters came out of nowhere. The whole world seemed to be defined by pain and blood and violence. The defenders, shocked and terrified though they were, fought like wildcats.

There was a brief moment's respite as the last of the ravagers on that side of the street went down, though pockets of battle raged all around them.

"This is impossible," yelled Mr. Ford as he and Urrea came limping up. "The crews couldn't have missed this many of them . . ."

It was Nix who answered; she'd fought her way to the open doors of the stable and had a good angle to see inside as she jettisoned her empty magazine and slapped in a new one. "Look!" she cried. "They're coming up *out of the ground!*"

It was true. Inside the barn there were at least a dozen ravagers, and more were climbing out of a ragged hole in the dirt. Horses in their stalls screamed and kicked, and halfway down the line Gutsy's own horse, Gordo, was rearing and slamming his massive hooves against the bolted door.

Gutsy turned to look across the street, where more of the ravagers were in a fierce battle with people outside the hospital. Could all those killers have come from this one tunnel? It chilled her to think the whole town might be riddled with hidden entrances.

The ravagers in the stable saw the cluster of teenagers and grinned like ravenous wolves. One of them bared yellow teeth that had been filed to wicked points. "Fresh meat!"

It jolted her to hear one of them speak. Had they always been able to do that? The thought made them somehow more terrifying. More like evil people than victims of a disease.

"Pair up—watch each other's backs," Benny yelled as he waded in, his sword moving too fast to follow. Nix moved with him, her small freckled hands rock-steady on the handle of her pistol.

Gutsy estimated that at least thirty ravagers were in the streets among the crumpled and bloody bodies of the men and women who'd first been attacked. Mr. Cantu, one of New Alamo's tomato farmers, lay staring at the sky with sightless eyes. Sofia Vargas was slumped against a wall with most of her throat gone. Others, too—some so badly mangled that they couldn't be easily identified. As she watched, Mr. Cantu suddenly twitched, his slack hands spasming into fists and then opening wide. He sat up, eyes still staring and totally blank, but his mouth snapping at the air as if trying to bite the smell of blood.

Movement out of the corner of her eye made Gutsy whirl around as a ravager rushed at her with a big farming sickle in each dirty hand. But Alethea moved to meet the attack, bashing one sickle away with such a powerful blow that it shattered the ravager's arm. Then she hit the killer with three very fast blows to the face and head. He fell at her feet. Alethea's tiara was slightly crooked in the nest of her hair, but she raised Rainbow Smite and gave a wicked grin.

THE FIGHT WAS DREADFUL.

In one of those odd moments where things seemed to swirl around them as if they were the calm eye of a storm, Gutsy and Alethea locked eyes. No matter what else happened now or in whatever lives they would have, both knew that they'd crossed into a bigger version of the world. Or maybe it was in that moment the two fifteen-year-olds realized with bittersweet clarity that they weren't the little girls they'd once been. They weren't grown women, either, but they were closer than ever to the people they would become.

They fought and fought . . .

And then there were no more ravagers inside the stable— only broken bodies lying in rag-doll heaps. Dead for real now. Dead forever.

Gasping, her heart aching in her chest, Gutsy staggered to the stable door and looked outside.

Captain Ledger and Sam were finishing off the last of the ravagers. Dr. Morton was overseeing the triage of the wounded, tailed by an armed guard. Morton was as much a monster as Collins, but he was the only doctor left alive in New Alamo, and they needed his medical knowledge and his understanding of the zombie plague. The guard was there to keep him from running, but also keep him alive. A lot of people in town would love to kill the man for his crimes, but they, too, needed him. When this was all over, Gutsy wondered how long the doctor would last. She certainly had no sympathy. Not a trace of it.

The doctor met Gutsy's gaze for a moment. She saw fear there, and some anger. And a mix of other emotions she couldn't easily define. But he turned away and busied himself with work.

Spider spat on the ground as he passed him. Alethea did too. Gutsy did not, but in her thoughts she was doing awful things to the man. Truly awful things.

Closer to the hospital entrance, the Chess Players were silencing both injured ravagers and reanimated citizens. It was brutal, soul-crushing work. A single ravager was still on his feet, but he was running away. Sam Imura raised his rifle and, with an almost casual nonchalance, put a bullet in the back of the killer's head.

And then it was over.

The fighting, at least. Not the pain, the loss. The horror.

Everything became unnaturally quiet. Gutsy wasn't even sure she was breathing. It was like a painting of carnage in a book; everything seemed flat and two-dimensional. There was death everywhere. Gutsy later learned that some of the killers were not ravagers but what Benny called R3's. Fast living dead. There were none of the slow shamblers around. They hadn't been part of this attack.

More than two dozen citizens of New Alamo lay dead or so badly wounded that they would die soon. There were nearly twenty others with lesser injuries, but of those, five had bites, which meant that within a day or two they would die too.

All around the square people were weeping, children screaming. Adults screamed too, as they came out of hiding to discover the fate of their loved ones.

Gutsy heard someone gag and turned to see Alethea bend over and vomit into the street. Gutsy, not knowing what else she could do, pulled the sweaty strands of Alethea's hair out of the way. Then she patted her friend's back and handed her a crumpled handkerchief. Alethea dabbed at her mouth, nodding thanks. She was pale and haggard, and her eyes were jumpy.

"Hey . . . ," soothed Gutsy. "Hey, now. You okay?"

Alethea pasted on a totally false smile that faltered and fell away. "I . . . I don't know how much more of this I can take, Guts," she said.

"I know," Gutsy agreed.

She and all her friends seemed to teeter on the edge of a black and bottomless pit filled with terrors. A hole where there was no light or hope. No trust, either. That had been smashed to splinters by the betrayal of Dr. Morton and the evil of Captain Collins.

She bent and kissed Alethea's cheek. "It'll be okay," she said.

Her friend shook her head. "Don't lie to me."

Gutsy had no response to that. She offered a meaningless smile and rose, waving for Captain Ledger and Sam Imura to come over to the barn so she could show them the tunnel.

"Someone get me a lantern," said Ledger. Gutsy took one from the wall and handed it to him. Sam covered Ledger with the rifle as he leaned down into the tunnel mouth. Everyone crowded around to see.

"Look," said Spider, pointing, "they got it all shored up with boards."

"No way they dug that since the attack on the wall," said Gutsy.

"Nope," agreed Ledger. "Makes me wonder if this is the only tunnel, too." He glanced at Benny. "Go tell Karen about this, okay? Have her start a search."

"On it," said Benny, and he ran outside.

"What if there are, like, fifty of these things?" asked Spider. "What if they're all over town?"

Ledger shook his head. "If there were a lot of them, we'd all be dead right now. No, I think this might be another of the Raggedy Man's experiments. First he hits the wall with a big force, then he tries this ninja stealth stuff."

"Yes," said Sam. "He's learning a lot about the town, too."

Ledger nodded. "We're going to have get the walls repaired. Right now a couple of nearsighted gophers could invade this place. In the meantime, I want to see where this goes."

"You're too big," said Lilah. "I'll go." She handed her spear to Nix, drew her automatic, checked the magazine, then dropped into the hole.

Ledger handed his lantern to her. "No heroics, kid. You look and you come right back. If you run into anything nasty down there, give a yell."

Lilah's reply was a sour little laugh, and then she was gone.

There was a scuffling sound, and then Lilah came scrambling out of the hole. Ledger helped her out and she sat, panting, on the edge of the opening, brushing dirt out of her hair.

"It's about sixty yards long," she said in her ghostly whisper of a voice, "but it connects with a bigger tunnel that I think was some kind of old drainage system. The bigger part is brick-lined. Old. And there were some places where it looked like the drainage tunnel is caved in. Seems like they had to clear it out to finish this one."

"If I had to guess," said Benny, "they were digging this out so they could invade the town from inside at the same time they hit the walls. The cave-ins must have slowed them down."

Nix nodded. "Lucky break for us."

"Doesn't feel that lucky," said Spider. "They killed a bunch of people today."

"If these tunnels had been finished in time," said Sam, "they would have killed everyone."

Alethea gave a loud, derisive snort. "So . . . this is us being lucky?"

"This is us still being alive, kid. Take the wins where you can." Ledger turned to Gutsy. "You know anything about the old sewer system? How big it is? Where it goes? Anything?"

"No. But Karen would."

"I'll go ask her," said Spider, and hurried out.

"In the meantime," said Gutsy, "I think we should go back and ask Captain Collins a whole lot more questions."

"Yes," said Sam, his dark eyes glittering.

Lilah retrieved her spear and ran her thumb along the wicked edge of the blade. "I volunteer to ask."

KAREN PEAK AND SPIDER ARRIVED BEFORE THEY COULD leave the stable. Gutsy brought her up to date.

"There's only a couple of drainage tunnels big enough to crawl through," said Karen after thinking about it. "One is definitely collapsed. That happened when Billy Cantu and his crew were digging up the streets to lay down new sewer pipes. They didn't even know about the other tunnel and smashed through it. Since it was old and not in very good shape, they filled that section in after they laid their pipes. The other one that Lilah found goes way, way back to when there was an old Catholic church here in the late 1800s. Runs about four hundred feet, but it's not tied into any of the modern plumbing. I can check the maps to see if there's more, but I don't think so."

She knelt at the edge of the hole and lowered the lantern.

"I don't think there's more of these," she continued. "But I'll have some guys check. They can drive some rebar down to see if they hit anything. Can't spare too many people, though. Everyone's either helping with the wounded or working on the walls. We're really stretched thin."

"Got to be done, though," said Sam.

They all moved out into the sunlight. There were screams from people in agony and moans from people in despair. The street was splashed with blood, red and black. Here and there bodies were covered by sheets. Karen asked, "You going back to talk to Collins?"

"Yes," said Gutsy.

Karen turned and stepped close to Ledger. She looked up into the soldier's hard, scarred face. "I don't care what you have to do to get those answers, but *get* them. You hear me?"

"Loud and clear, sister."

The head of town security nodded, then turned and hurried back to the hospital.

"She must be in hell," said Sam. "Blackmailed into helping Collins and Morton . . ."

"This whole place is hell," said Alethea, and no one even tried to contradict her.

As they walked back to the school, Gutsy fell into step with Nix.

"Was it worth it?" she asked.

Nix frowned. "Was what worth it?"

"Leaving your home in California. Was everything you went through worth finding out what was out here? Those reapers and all this mess?"

Nix walked half a block before answering. "When you go looking for the truth, you can't expect it to be all sunflowers and puppies. The world is the world. I, for one, do not want to live in ignorance."

Gutsy nodded, accepting the practicality of that.

"Tell you what, though," said Nix, a smile blossoming on her freckled face. "It isn't all bad out here. It's dangerous, sure, but we've seen so much that's beautiful along the way. Not every person we meet is a psychopath or a monster. We've met *good* people out here. Friends."

"Like Captain Ledger and Sam Imura?"

Nix gave Gutsy a sidelong look. "Sure. And other people, too. When the world's this messed up, maybe you have to go a long way from home to meet your *real* family. Not blood kin, but what my mother used to call 'soul family.'"

"What's that?"

"The family you *choose* for yourself. The ones who've been through enough stuff to understand someone else who has scars."

She didn't ask Gutsy if she understood what that meant, and didn't water it down by explaining that she wasn't talking about physical scars. Nix was making a judgment call that Gutsy *got* her. Which she did.

They smiled at each other.

Soul family.

Up ahead, Benny suddenly jerked to a stop. "Wait . . . something's wrong," he said sharply.

The front door of the high school stood open, and there was blood smeared on it.

"Chong!" screamed Lilah, and bolted forward.

The others drew their weapons and ran after her.

THEY FOUND ONE OF THE TWO TOWN GUARDS JUST inside the front door. Alethea gagged and turned away, her face going gray. Spider stood with huge, unblinking eyes.

The man had been hacked to pieces.

Lilah merely jumped over him and tore down the hall, screaming Chong's name.

They found Chong on the floor, half in and half out of the open classroom doorway. He lay still and silent in a pool of blood.

Lilah flung her spear down with a harsh metallic clang as she dropped to her knees beside Chong. Her hands were everywhere, checking for the wound that killed the boy she loved.

"You're not allowed," she said in a weirdly high-pitched voice of panic. "You're *not allowed.*"

Her face was livid with stress and her eyes bright with tears. Lilah's hands were everywhere at once. Spider and Alethea knelt by her.

Ledger moved past them, pointing his gun down the hall. There had been a terrible fight. Broken weapons, smashed glass, and plaster from damaged walls littered the floor. Several of Chong's arrows were buried deep in door frames or lying on the ground, the barbs coated with dark and polluted blood.

"Sam," he said, "on me."

The sniper fell in to Ledger's rear left corner, and the two of them moved along the hall with quick, quiet steps, shifting their weapons toward open doors, covering each other as they took turns entering and clearing the classrooms.

Gutsy, Benny, and Nix crept behind the two soldiers. Ledger sent Grimm ahead and Sombra immediately followed, but even the dogs moved cautiously. The hall had an ugly vibe to it, as if it were a battery that could store anger, pain, and violence. Gutsy felt that whatever happened here was over, but her nerves did not accept that assessment.

When they rounded the corner at the end of the hall, they found the second guard. The man stood over a pair of dead ravagers, but he swayed as if half asleep, his eyes looking nowhere. His body was streaked with red, but the blood around the bites on his face and throat was already turning black. Gutsy could see the tiny, threadlike worms wriggling in it.

"Oh, no . . . ," she said. It was Abdul, a leather worker from town who worked three nights a week for Karen Peak. At least, that's who and what he had been. Now he was a shell, a vehicle for hunger and pain. Abdul raised his hands toward them and opened his mouth in a moan of bottomless need.

"I'm sorry, brother," said Ledger, lowering his pistol and drawing a heavy knife. The blade rose and fell, and Abdul collapsed into the only kind of peaceful sleep afforded to anyone in this broken world.

Gutsy turned away, heartsick. Abdul was one of the nicest people she knew. Kind and funny. And now gone, with all of his laughter and talent and life stolen from him. Not by Ledger but by Collins and all the scientists like her who'd done this to the world. Gutsy wanted to cry. She wanted to take her crowbar and smash Collins to pieces.

They moved on, finding more bodies of the ravagers, each with a head wound. Gutsy frowned; there was something odd about them. Some still had weapons clutched in their cold hands, and others had weapons near them, but they didn't actually *look* like ravagers. Two of them were dressed in regular pants and shirts. No chains or any of that.

"*Los muertos*," murmured Gutsy. "But . . . how'd they get in here?"

No one answered.

They reached the classroom, and Ledger waved the teens back as he and Sam went in fast. There were no shots, no yells. Nix and Gutsy exchanged a look and then entered the room. It was a complete shambles. Chairs were overturned, a desk had been flipped over and used as a barricade. The ropes used to bind Captain Collins lay cut and discarded.

And there were seven bodies on the floor. Sombra sniffed one and recoiled from the slack flesh, snarling and scared. The hair stood up all along his spine. Six of the dead had arrows stuck in eye sockets, foreheads, or temples. Chong, with his steel-tipped arrows, had fought like a demon.

The other ravager had been killed more crudely, clearly beaten with a folding chair.

"She's gone," snarled Benny, and kicked a metal trash can halfway across the room.

"Come on," growled Ledger, and they went back to where Lilah and the others were clustered around Chong. Gutsy had been afraid of what they'd find there, but Chong's eyes were open. They'd propped him against a wall, and he looked around with the glazed eyes of someone who'd just come out of a deep, deep sleep.

Benny rushed to his friend's side, but Lilah shoved him back. "He doesn't need you pawing at him," she barked.

Ledger tempted fate by kneeling to examine Chong, ignoring lethal stares from Lilah. Then he sat back on his heels.

"The kid okay?" asked Sam.

"The kid," said Chong in a weak voice, "is decidedly *not* okay."

"Looks like a concussion and a pretty nasty laceration," said Ledger. "Can't tell if your skull's fractured, though, so you're going to have to take it real easy for a while."

"Oh, bummer," said Chong. "I was planning on doing jumping jacks and standing on my head."

"Don't do that," began Lilah, then colored as she realized he was joking.

Chong just gave her a wan smile. Then he looked around. "What happened? I . . . can't remember much."

They told him about the attack in town. Chong looked horrified and saddened by the carnage.

"What happened *here*?" asked Ledger.

Chong's face clouded as he picked through tangled memories. "I heard a sound. A crash, like a broken window. Abdul went to look, and then suddenly there were a bunch of zoms running down the hall."

"Running?" echoed Nix. "Fast ones? Like R3's?"

"I . . . guess," said Chong, frowning. "It's a little blurry."

R3 zombies were one of several recent mutations the kids from California had fought. The R3's had been exposed to experimental compounds that were intended to accelerate the life cycle of the parasites and essentially burn the infection out. The problem was that before that happened, those zoms became faster and, in many cases, smarter. Gutsy wondered if this was similar to what Collins and Morton had used on the soldiers who'd become ravagers.

"Weird thing is," said Chong, "there seemed to be two different kinds of zoms, and I don't think they liked each other all that much."

"What do you mean?" asked Benny.

"Well . . . there were the ravagers like the ones we fought at the wall, all leather and chains. But there were some in regular clothes. Just people, you know? Except they were totally out of their minds. Actually raving and yelling."

"Yelling what?" asked Gutsy.

"Just yelling. Not any actual words, just howls. Like people who are so angry they can't even form words. These . . . yelling ones . . . they attacked two of the ravagers, but the ravagers put them down. It's nuts, I know, but the ravagers seemed to be scared of them."

"You must have seen it wrong," said Alethea. "Ravagers aren't afraid of anything."

Chong shrugged. "Maybe. I did get hit pretty hard, so honestly I don't know what's real or not."

"And maybe you saw what you thought you saw," said Sam. "There are bodies back there dressed in street clothes. I didn't see any obvious bites on them, now that I think about it."

"Yeah," agreed Ledger, looking uneasy. "And their skin color was close to normal."

"Wait," said Spider. "Do regular people turn into ravagers, though? I thought those guys were all soldiers who'd been experimented on."

"At this point," said Ledger, "I don't know. You got yourself a whole bunch of strange zombies down here in Texas. More mutations than I've ever seen. Tell you what, though— until now I haven't been all that worried about the ravagers, because I figured, how many can there actually be? But if your average citizen can turn into one of them . . . Well, that's a special kind of scary, isn't it?"

"Yes," said Spider, "it is."

"HOW DID CAPTAIN COLLINS ESCAPE?" ASKED BENNY.

Chong's face turned bright red, and he couldn't meet anyone's eyes. "I . . . well . . . I guess I . . . um . . ."

"You let her go?" roared Alethea.

Lilah immediately got up in her face, but Alethea did not back down. Nix cut in between them and pushed them apart.

"He had to," she said, then cut a look at Chong. "Didn't you?"

Chong nodded, then hissed because nodding really hurt. "Yes. Ouch. Yes."

They all understood it, even if they didn't like it. Chong had been fighting a gang of fast ravagers or mutated shamblers. In a close-quarters battle, even a good archer wasn't likely to win. Collins, however, was a tough military officer— and, despite being a vile murderer, she was alive, and their enemies were monsters. The battle lines were clear.

"She was incredible," said Chong, his voice almost colored with admiration. "She grabbed a folding chair and just went ape on them. I went out in the hall to use my bow, and just as I got the last of them . . . *bang*. Next thing I know I'm waking up with you guys."

"You're lucky she knocked you out instead of taking a second to cut your throat," said Sam, which earned him a glare from Lilah.

Then she shifted her anger to Chong. "She could have *killed* you, you stupid town boy."

"Pretty sure she tried," observed Chong.

Alethea raised her hand. "Permission to, like, totally kill her the next time we see her."

"Granted," said Chong. He rubbed his head.

"Do we have any idea where this . . . this . . . ," Nix began, fishing for an appropriately vile word and instead giving her word choice enough venom to kill a scorpion, ". . . *woman* . . . might have gone?"

"Not anyplace around here," said Spider. "No one in New Alamo is going to help her."

"And the base is destroyed; there's nowhere to go," said Gutsy.

"We can use the dogs to track her," said Ledger. "My guess is she went to ground somewhere in town. There are a lot of empty buildings. She's going to need rest, food, and supplies. Then she's going to have to sneak out of here as soon as it's dark. There may be other bases around, and she'll—"

Gutsy suddenly shot to her feet. *"Oh no!"*

"What's wrong?" Ledger demanded.

"God, I think I *know* where she's going," Gutsy cried, and then she was running. Sombra uttered a sharp bark of alarm and leaped to follow her. Ledger gave Sam a look, and then ran to catch up.

THERE WAS A STEADY FLOW OF REFUGEES COMING IN from the Broken Lands. Some were alone and half-crazed from seeing everyone they knew and loved slaughtered; others were family groups. One group of a dozen older teens and young twentysomethings had come in just after the big fight at the gate. Their camp had been down by the Rio Grande and had been overrun. Only they had survived.

Karen Peak welcomed them and, like the others before them, sent the young survivors to see Mr. Martinez, who was in charge of housing.

"I'm no Realtor, but I guess you kids can take your pick," he said, gesturing to a row of homes inside the east wall.

"No one lives here?" asked the tall young man who acted as the spokesman for the group. He was nineteen, but his face was weathered and his eyes looked ancient. He wore a cowboy hat over long blond hair.

"No," said Martinez. "Any house you see with a red ribbon on the door is free for the taking. Sad truth, kids, is we lost a lot of good folks in this part of town. You'll have to deal with anything they left behind. Clothes, pictures, and all that. We don't have enough people to clean all these houses out."

"That's no problem," said the young man.

Martinez managed a smile. "It'll be a comfort to us all to have some new faces around here. Some new life, if you take my meaning. Lot of older folks in this part of town, so having you kids here is great. Say, I never did catch your name, son. . . ."

"Trócaire," said the teen with a genial smile.

"Wow, that's a mouthful."

"It's Irish," he said. "My parents moved here when I was four. Just before the plague. And this is Ténèbres." He indicated a thin girl, a year or so younger than he was, whose long black ponytail stuck out through the opening of a red baseball cap.

"Happy to meet you, Teeny-breeze," said Martinez, mangling it.

"This is great," Ténèbres said. "Thanks. I hope we're not inconveniencing you."

"No, no, just the opposite. Great to have you." Martinez smiled and held his arms wide to indicate all of New Alamo. "This is your town now."

He left them there and walked back to the town hall to fetch the next group.

"Our town," said Ténèbres.

"Yes," said Trócaire, smiling. "Nice to know."

MR. URREA TAPPED MR. FORD ON THE SHOULDER. "I don't like the look of this."

They stood together near the entrance to the hospital, taking a short break from helping tend the wounded. The two old teachers were bent from exhaustion but straightened as they saw Gutsy and the California kids race past, with the soldiers out in front and the dogs racing alongside. The whole bunch of them vanished into the building.

"God," said Ford, "*now* what?"

Gutsy was the fastest of all of them and burst into the hospital ahead of Nix and Benny.

Karen Peak was in the hall talking to a nurse, and yelled as they blew past. "What is it?" she demanded. "Did you find another tunnel, or—?"

"Collins got away," cried Gutsy without breaking stride. "Not sure if she left town yet, but we think she might want to take Morton with her. Do you know where he is?"

Karen hurried to keep up, talking as she ran. "He finished his triage work, so he's either in his office or out back having lunch. When he's not working, we're keeping him under guard and away from people."

"Smart," said Gutsy.

They raced through the hospital, which was still crowded with the injured and the dying. The sound of weeping filled every corner of the suite of treatment rooms and echoed down the corridors set aside for intensive care and recovery.

The only relative quiet was the research wing, where senior staff had offices next to various small labs and storage rooms. It was also where Dr. Morton's office was. The bulk of the research data was stored there, and the entrance to the military access tunnel was hidden behind a false cabinet.

The hallway leading to Morton's office was empty.

"Where are the guards?" asked Karen, but from the note of despair in her voice she already knew. There was a splash of bright blood on the outside wall of the doctor's office.

Everyone drew their weapons, but Sam and Lilah took the lead, each of them ready for anything. Ledger and Grimm were behind as they cautiously opened the office door, fading left and right to avoid possible gunfire.

There was none.

The two guards were inside. They turned toward the intruders, moaning piteously and reaching with dead hands.

"No . . . please, not again," breathed Spider. He looked sick and turned his face away.

"I'll do it," said Lilah, hefting her spear. A moment later both of the *los muertos* lay still and forever silent. Alethea took two lab coats down from pegs on the wall and covered them.

Benny hurried to the big cabinet in the far corner. Gutsy

followed, watching as Benny pulled the doors open, her crowbar raised, ready to strike if there were more *los muertos* in there. The cabinet was a fake, hiding the entrance to a flight of stairs leading down to an underground passage that ran beneath the walls and far out into the desert. Benny and his friends had come through that tunnel and hidden door during the assault on the town. Now, Collins, Dr. Morton, and the others who were part of their twisted research project used it to get in and out of New Alamo.

The doorway and the dark mouth of the stairway were empty. Both dogs, however, growled down into the shadows.

"She went that way," said Benny, pointing to a few drops of blood on the top step. He started to follow, but Sam's strong hand shot out and caught his arm.

"If she's down there, she'll kill you," said the sniper.

Benny took half a pace back. "We can't just stay here."

"You can," said Sam as he unslung his rifle. "Hunting is more my thing."

Benny studied his half brother for a moment, then nodded.

"Okay, Sam, you take point," said Ledger. He clicked his tongue for Grimm, and the three of them went down the stairs into the black mouth of the tunnel. Gutsy listened but didn't hear them make a single sound. Not even the big armored dog.

They all waited, weapons ready. The office became unnaturally still and quiet. Time seemed to hold its breath as if in fear of the next moment. Karen Peak had her pistol out, but Gutsy could see her hands tremble. The woman was on that ragged edge between violent anger and total exhaustion.

"There's one good thing," said Nix, breaking the silence but speaking in a hushed voice. When the others looked at her in surprise, she said, "When we first came here, there were ravagers and zoms in that tunnel. We dealt with them. But since then there doesn't seem to have been any more."

"So?" asked Karen. "They dug a whole new tunnel under the barn."

"Sure, but this is a bigger and better one, and yet the ravagers didn't use it."

"You're right, Nix," said Gutsy, brightening. "Maybe the Raggedy Man doesn't know about this one. We might have lucked out here."

"'Luck' is a weird word to use," said Spider.

"With you on that," agreed Benny.

"Luck's relative, I guess," said Gutsy. "Maybe we'll never know the exact reason the whole horde didn't try to use the tunnel. But we can be glad they didn't."

"No joke," said Benny. Then he glanced in the general direction of the school. "Still don't get how the ravagers got to the school without anyone seeing them in town."

"Same for those ones Chong said were yelling," said Nix. "The ones in street clothes. Where'd they come from?"

No one had an answer to that. Gutsy exchanged a look with Alethea, who raised her eyebrows.

"Gosh," she said, "another mystery. Fun times."

A few minutes later, Ledger, Sam, and Grimm returned, and they did not look happy.

"She's gone," said Ledger. "Killed both guards stationed at the far end of the tunnel. Head shots. Took their weapons and spare ammunition. At a guess I'd say she forced them to move the cases of canned goods we stacked to block the door. Maybe promising to let them go if they cooperated, but . . ."

Alethea snorted and leaned on the knob end of her baseball bat. "So what if she's gone? Maybe the ravagers will get her. It's not like she has anywhere else to go. The base was blown up, right? She can't go there."

"Where else is there?" asked Spider.

Ledger shook his head. "Not exactly sure. There are weapons caches out there somewhere. Sam's been trying to figure out where. Or . . . who knows, she could be hoping to make it all the way to Asheville."

"Isn't that where *you're* from?" asked Gutsy.

"Only kind of," said Ledger. "It's the capital of the American Nation, and there are lots of people there. No doubt Collins has some friends there too. If so, they're keeping a low profile; I don't who they might be, and that's weird, because it's the kind of thing I *should* know." His mouth tightened, and his eyes seemed to go hard as polished stone. "If I ever get back to Asheville, I intend to find out who knew about what was going on down here. I'm going to pin some people to the wall and get some answers; you can count on that."

"We don't know if that's where Collins is going, though," said Sam.

"He's right," said Gutsy. "There could be another base somewhere else. Or another lab."

"At this point, anything's possible," said Ledger darkly.

"Why are we talking about this?" asked Benny. "Let's go get her."

"I'm for that," said Gutsy, and Alethea made a nasty sound of agreement.

"Well . . . that's the other thing," said Ledger heavily. "Collins took one of the quads and slashed the tires on the other machines. She smashed some stuff on each of them. Stuff I don't know if we can repair."

"Oh no . . . ," breathed Nix.

Benny gripped Sam's arm with sudden desperation. "*Which* quad did she take? Did she take the blue one? God, please, please, please tell me she didn't take the blue one."

"Why?" asked Alethea. "What's so special about the blue one?"

"That's Chong's bike," said Nix in a very small voice.

"So?"

"It's the one that had his extra medicine in the saddlebags." Nix turned pleading eyes toward Sam. "Chong has some with him, but he left the rest down there for safety because . . . well . . . we weren't planning on staying all that long. It wasn't the blue one . . . was it?"

They all looked at Sam. He closed his eyes and nodded.

Interlude One

The Hated

SIX YEARS AGO

THE BOY DIDN'T HAVE A NAME. NOT REALLY.

In his earliest memories he was always called "Boy." If his parents had ever given him a name, it was lost when they vanished. The boy couldn't recall a single detail about them. Not voices, not faces. He had been unloved forever, and only barely cared for. Less generously than a stray dog would have been treated, and usually much worse.

He fell in with one group of people after another. Some were killed by the gray people, the biters, the dead. Some died from diseases that swept through whole camps. Many were slaughtered by gangs who raided refugee settlements and took whatever they wanted. One day they came and took all the children.

The years that followed were an obscenity that his mind refused to hold on to. He ran away nine times and was found each time. There were fists and whips and worse.

Then the raiders were themselves raided and butchered by a bigger group. And another. And another. He was passed along with the others. With a dwindling few.

Until the people in black came along and killed the killers.

At first the boy thought he had been saved. Truly saved,

because these killers wore angel wings on their chests, and they spoke of faith and church and god. But they were not there to save him. No.

They beat him and tied him up along with hundreds of others. More children, and some adults, were added to the long, tethered lines of prisoners as they moved across the blighted face of the world. At first they called him Little Sinner, because of what had been done *to* him by other people. But because the boy kept trying to escape, and searching for him took time and a lot of effort, they gave him a new name.

They called him *the Hated*, or merely *Hated*.

And Hated he became.

"Come here, Hated."

"Do this, Hated."

"Kneel and pray for forgiveness, Hated."

When the captives numbered one thousand, the people in black—reapers, they called themselves, soldiers of the Church of Thanatos—began a pilgrimage. All of the prisoners were to be taken to a place where they would meet and be judged by a man called Saint John. Even the reapers feared—but also loved—the saint.

The pilgrim-captives all looked like scarecrows: emaciated and starved, bruised from countless beatings, numb from loss. They were like the gray people except that the dead felt no pain and had no awareness of their lot; the sinners were all too aware.

They staggered along from Texas to Wyoming, through lands blasted by bombs and blighted by strange diseases. From one wasteland to another, following a beaten trail that many bare feet pounded flat over countless travels. They marched in long lines, bound front and back with rope tied around their waists, links in an awkward chain of staggering bodies. If anyone fell, they were cut from the line and left to bleed out with dozens of bloody red mouths cut into their skin. The ropes would be retied, the line tightened, and the march continued.

There was a girl tied directly in front of Hated. He ached to know her real name but did not dare ask, because conversation of any kind was punishable by beating. A second offense meant being cut from the line and left like a scrap of meat. In his mind he called her Leafy, because one morning several small autumn leaves got caught in her long hair, and they stayed there all day. He watched them dance as she walked.

Over the terrible days of that pilgrimage he created scenarios in his head about how he could escape and save Leafy. How he could get a tree branch—or maybe steal a knife from the guards—and open red mouths in *them*. Tear them into carrion meat and slash the bonds holding Leafy. Even if he had to die while doing it.

Dying *for* something would be wonderful. To save Leafy, to make sure she escaped, and to stand fast and kill enough of the guards to erect a mountain of safety between them and that beautiful girl.

Then they would forever after speak of the Hated with dread rather than contempt. And when Leafy remembered him, it would transform him into something possessing wonderful new meaning. She would learn his name. Not "the Hated" but something else. Maybe she would give him a hero's name.

On a day when the reapers said they were nearing the

end of the journey, he decided that he had to act. During a rest break he'd found a piece of broken shell and hid it in the waistband of his torn trousers. As the day wore on, he quietly and secretively began sawing at the rope around his waist. One single stubborn strand at a time.

The line of stumbling figures moved out of the brilliant sun and into a valley of shadows created by a bleached billboard and a rusting big rig truck. The shadows were inky black, and that's when he made his move. He took a firmer grip on the shell and ferociously cut at the rope. The last strands fell away.

Before anyone knew what was happening, he rushed the closest guard. He slashed with the shell with such unbridled force that it cut like a razor, opening a screaming red mouth below the guard's chin. The Hated turned as a shower of red splashed him.

The prisoners began screaming. Leafy too. In the shadows he could see only her outline, but her scream was there, filling his ears, filling the world. The sound of it drove him deeper into his rage. He ran past her and attacked a second startled guard. This time it took four cuts to drop him. Then the Hated tossed away the piece of shell, knelt, and tore the knife from the guard's twitching fingers. Although he had never once held a fighting knife, it felt oddly familiar—as if it *belonged* to him. As if the weapon completed him in a way he could not understand.

He should have lost that fight. He knew it. The guards knew it. And everyone watching knew it. He was a prisoner, a sinner. He was nothing. A hated thing with no training.

And yet . . .

He never quite knew how many of the guards he'd killed. Six? Seven? Even the toughest of them fell back in fear and surprise as he came charging. He was covered in red and shrieked as he fought. He yelled at Leafy to run, but she did not know that name. She stood with the others, staring in shock at the monster he'd become.

The prisoners did not join the fight. They did not run. They didn't say a word. Even those who screamed had fallen into silence.

The Hated turned as another guard fell, looking back to see where Leafy was. But he was out in the blinding sunlight now, and she remained in darkness. There were a dozen uninjured guards left, and they formed a ring around him, closing in, their blades ready to tear him apart.

"*STOP!*" cried a voice so sharply that everyone froze. The reapers turned and immediately knelt, pressing their fists to their chests as a figure came walking out of the shadows and into the sunlight. It was a tall man, very slim and wiry. Like all of the reapers, he was dressed in loose black clothes, with dark red streamers tied to his wrists and ankles. On his chest was a beautifully rendered chalk drawing of angel wings, and his shaved head was covered with elaborate tattoos of thorny vines.

He stopped a few feet from the Hated. Although handles protruded from sheaths on his belt, thighs, and wrists, he held no weapon. And he stood well within striking range, as if he had no fear of the sharp knife in the Hated's bloody hand.

He was older than the other reapers, but seemed to hold more power than all of them put together. His eyes seemed older still, and there was a strange sadness in them despite the kindly smile on his lips.

"What is your name?" he said. It was a question no one had ever asked the Hated.

It was so unexpected that the Hated could not at first answer it.

"H-Hated," he finally managed. The name came at last. Ugly to his own ears.

"No," said the man. "That is not your name."

He took a step closer. The Hated could have killed him right then.

Except that he knew he couldn't. Not *this* man. The truth of it seemed to burn hotter than the sun.

The man reached out very slowly and touched the Hated's cheek. It was a gentle act, an alien thing. No one was kind to him. No one had been, except a few random strangers here and there.

"You are not hated, my son," said the man. "You are loved."

"Wh-what . . . ?"

"You have opened red mouths in these others, and in doing so released them to be with god. You have shown them such kindness and mercy."

The Hated did not know how to reply to that. He lowered his knife, having nearly forgotten that he held it.

"From now on, to all in my hearing," said the man, raising his voice, "and to every believer of the true faith of Lord Thanatos—praise his darkness—you will be Brother Mercy. This I have said, and thus it is so."

And, to the Hated's complete surprise, the guards all lowered their knives and yelled it out.

"*Brother Mercy!*" they cried. Over and over again, and soon the prisoners picked up the words, chanting them, turning them into a prayer. The Hated could feel his shame and emptiness die. He could *feel* the Hated crumble into dust and blow away.

From then on, he was Brother Mercy.

He raised the knife again, offering the weapon to the sad-eyed man.

"Oh, no," said Saint John of the Knife, "keep it, Brother Mercy. You will need it."

PART TWO

THE ROAD
TO ASHEVILLE

The sound of snow in trees makes silence,
makes the poem in my pocket
sing through the holes,
the loose change of angels,
all those fallen lights
into the world we came
in on sound, the stranger cadence
of wave, and drum.
And our inner work is to never stop
hearing ourselves for the rest of our lives
when everything conspires
to drown the silence of us out.

—ANNE WALSH, "GRIEF IS THE THRONE WE ALL SIT ON"

MORGIE MITCHELL SAT IN THE SADDLE OF THE rumbling quad and studied the farm. The sun was low in the sky, and this looked like a good place to spend the night.

Despite being with Riot, Morgie felt very alone. Benny and the others had gone off to warn the people in the small town of New Alamo—which they'd learned about from a dying soldier—while Morgie and Riot continued on their way to Asheville. Since leaving their friends behind in a forest near the ruins of Harlingen, Riot and Morgie had followed Route 77 north, planning on using it to skirt the radioactive wasteland of Houston. From there they would merge onto Route 90 and head east.

This farm was along the way, and it reminded him a bit of home. Unlike the carefully tended fields back in Central California, this place was clearly untended. Abandoned. The acres of soy had grown wild over the years and been invaded by a thousand kinds of weeds. Young scrub pine and wild maple trees stood alone or in clusters, their boughs crowded with birds.

Beside him, his on-again-off-again girlfriend, Riot, squinted beneath a flat hand held above her eyes. She was thin and wiry, with a bandana that hid most of the wild roses and thorns tattooed on her shaved head.

"It's pretty," said Morgie.

Riot didn't respond to that, but instead pointed. "Zom."

Morgie followed her finger and saw a thin figure walking slowly and clumsily along a gravel road that ran from a big farmhouse. A boy, dressed in pajamas that were so ravaged by weather they were barely more than rags.

"I see him."

As the zom tottered closer to them, Morgie saw that he was wrapped by creeper vines, as if he'd stood for so long that they'd grown all over him. He'd seen that before, and it made him sad. It was such a lonely and terrible thing. Waiting forever.

"We better git before we get bit," said Riot, and gunned her engine. The roar of the quad motors—a sound rare and unnatural in all this tranquility—had almost certainly triggered the creature from its lonely vigil.

Morgie scanned the overgrown fields of the big farm. "Don't see any others. The house looks to be in good shape. Be nice to sleep indoors."

"Glad you ain't ending the day without at least one good idea," said Riot. Lately that was the kind of thing she said. Little digs. Once upon a time she'd joked like that, but now neither of them was smiling. Certainly not at each other.

Morgie winced but turned away to keep it from showing.

He loved Riot, but wasn't sure she was capable of returning it. Not really. Even Riot admitted that she was damaged goods. After all, she'd grown up as a reaper—as Sister Margaret—in the Night Church. During those years she'd been physically and verbally abused by Saint John and his senior reapers. She was emotionally scarred in ways Morgie could never really understand. Before meeting up with Benny, Nix, Chong, and Lilah in Nevada, Riot had never lived in a town. She'd never had a loving family, and had no idea at all what a normal life was like. In that regard she was much like Lilah—though not as distant and strange. Nix told him it was huge that Riot could fit in at all, or that she could love anyone ever.

Morgie tried to be an adult about it, to be understanding and accepting and patient. But Riot's words still hurt.

Sticks and stones will break my bones, but words will never hurt me.

The old schoolyard rhyme never made sense to him. Of *course* words could hurt. They punched faster and smashed harder than any physical weapon. Morgie was a good fighter, but one of Riot's comments could slip through his guard and draw blood.

He suspected that Riot was on the verge of breaking things off completely, and maybe by insulting him she hoped he'd be the one to leave first.

Fat chance, he thought. Stabbing words or not, he loved her. He just wished he knew how to be *in* love with someone like her.

She snapped fingers in front of his face, startling him. "Hey, Earth calling Morgie Mitchell. You even in there?"

Morgie growled something and tried to swat her hand away, but she pulled it back too quickly.

"Let's go," he mumbled.

"I'm already gone," laughed Riot as she zoomed away down the hill.

Morgie lingered a moment longer, slowly gunning his engine. "Yeah," he said. "I know."

THEY STAYED THE NIGHT IN THE OLD FARMHOUSE.

They worked together to clear the place—checking each room and closet for lurking zoms—and found nothing. They cooked a meal in silence, ate in silence, and went to bed in separate rooms on separate floors.

He sat up for hours, weary beyond words but unable to sleep.

Morgie understood heartbreak. He'd been in love with Nix his whole life, and had nearly died trying to protect her from Charlie Pink-eye and the Motor City Hammer. But Nix only ever had eyes for Benny.

Then he'd met Riot and fallen very hard for her, intrigued by her exotic looks, her complex history, her humor, and her strength. She'd even loved him, too. Or said so.

Now, though, that love was fading into a dusty nothing that matched the entire landscape of the world.

He sat up, staring out through a crack in the shutters at the endless field of stars. Remote and cold. He couldn't touch them, either, and they were indifferent to him.

Sleep finally took him, and he fell a long way into bad dreams.

In the morning, exhausted from that kind of night, he helped repack the quads, and they continued on. There was a long way to go, and he was sure he was going to feel every inch of every mile of the journey, knowing he could not catch up to Riot in any way that mattered.

PART THREE

NEW ALAMO

No man chooses evil because it is evil;

he only mistakes it for happiness, the good he seeks.

—MARY WOLLSTONECRAFT

ALETHEA SIGHED HEAVILY AND SAID, "AM I THE ONLY one who's starting to think we're all cursed by witches?"

"I like witches," said Spider vaguely.

Gutsy shook her head. "No. This is just cause and effect. And some bad decisions. Chong should have kept his drugs with him all the time."

"Sure," said Alethea, "go tell that to Lilah. Bet she'll appreciate the criticism. She seems like a very understanding kind of gal."

Gutsy almost said, *Well, it's what I would have done.* Then something occurred to her.

"Hey," she said, touching Nix's shoulder, "maybe we're panicking over nothing. Karen's daughter, Sarah, is infected too. She gets regular medicine from Dr. Morton to keep her from turning. Maybe he has a stash of it somewhere."

"*Had,*" said Ledger sourly. "You saw his office. He's missing, presumed either dead or with Collins."

"Okay," said Gutsy, "but there still might be a supply of pills somewhere."

Everyone brightened and even smiled, but then Spider raised his hand. "Guys, I don't want to be a downer here," he said, "but I seem to remember someone saying that the pills were made at the base, and that Morton only brought in some at a time."

The brief bubble of elation burst at once, and if anything, everyone looked even more stressed and scared than before.

Gutsy cleared her throat and attempted to inject some optimism into the moment. "We should have asked Doc Morton if there's *another* base or lab anywhere around."

"What we should have done," said Karen bitterly, "is kept him on a leash. God, my daughter could die because we didn't think this through."

"We're all in shock," said Gutsy. "And I'm afraid we're acting like it. Making bad decisions."

Ledger shot her a quick appraising look, then nodded. "You're right. What makes it worse is that Sam and I should have been calling the shots here. This is what we do."

"*Used to do*," said Sam.

"Doesn't matter. This is on us," insisted Ledger. "And being clumsy ends right now. We need to find Morton, and if he's dead or gone, then we need to find someone in this town who can step up and figure out a way to make those pills. Do you have a pharmacist?"

"Sure," said Karen. "Manny Flores."

"Okay, then he's our fallback. But first things first: Collins or one of her cronies was here. Someone had to have seen something."

"I'll go find Manny," said Karen.

After she left, they began grilling the staff in that part of the hospital. When that yielded nothing, they tried outside.

One of the nurses on break pointed to the alley at the back of the building.

"He went down there," she said.

"Was he hurt?" asked Ledger.

"Morton? No, I don't think so. But I heard someone tell him there was an injured kid. Not sure if there was a bite or not, but the doctor took his bag. Danny was with him."

Danny was the guard assigned to the doctor.

They all headed to the rear of the hospital and down the back alley, but there was no one in sight. Then they heard the cries, filled with hopeless agony.

Sombra and Grimm bounded forward, and everyone else ran after. They rounded a turn that opened into a small cement courtyard that was used as an informal break area. Plastic chairs were scattered around as if a storm had swept through. They saw Danny and Morton locked in an awkward embrace, moving together in a graceless and terrible dance. Danny's clothes were slashed and soaked with blood. His eyes were vacant, his mouth smeared with red as he tore at the doctor's shoulder with a snarling, hungry mouth.

SAM DREW A KNIFE, BUT GUTSY GOT THERE FIRST. SHE swung her crowbar in a fast, tight arc and caught Danny on the temple, knocking his head sideways, breaking the connection of the bite. The zombie staggered and Gutsy struck again, this time with more raw power and precision, and shattered the back of the guard's skull. The creature sagged and then toppled over, his face and limbs settling into a terminal slackness.

Morton dropped to his knees, clamping a trembling hand to his torn shoulder, weeping, pleading, begging for help. He had smaller bites on his face and neck and even his scalp, and his eyes were feverish and jumpy with blood loss and shock.

As they all variously knelt or stood around him, Gutsy felt such a deep conflict tearing her up inside. On one hand, this was the man who'd carried out Collins's orders to infect Mama with a deadly disease. This same man was responsible for half the bodies buried in Hope Cemetery. By any measurement he was a monster, a hateful and callous murderer. He was evil.

At the same time, though, he was powerless. His strength and his ability to do any additional harm had been bitten away. Even if there were a doctor left in town who could operate on him and repair the damage to nerve and vein and muscle, Morton was doomed—and he knew it.

Captain Ledger crouched in front of Morton, forearms resting on his knees. "Well, ain't you a sight, Doc. This is a case of irony literally biting you. If we didn't need you, this would be funny."

Morton whimpered.

Ledger used his knife to cut some cloth from Morton's lab coat, then folded it and pressed it to the man's shoulder. "Hold it in place, Doc; you know the drill. It's not that bad. None of these bites are. No major veins or arteries. Bet it hurts, though, and later I'll find some time to get all weepy about that."

"Hey, guys," called Spider, who had knelt by the dead guard, "this is weird. Danny's been stabbed. There's not a single bite on him."

"He's right," said Sam.

"Well, ain't this a pickle, Doc?" murmured Ledger. "Looks like somebody knifed Danny and then sicced him on you. Isn't that interesting as all heck? Tell me—did Bess Collins come to pay you a social call?"

"B-Bess . . . ?" stammered Morton, confused. "How c-could she? She's locked up. N-no . . . it wasn't her."

Ledger frowned. "Who did it, then?"

"I don't know. Two strangers. Teenagers, I think." Morton hissed as pain shot through him. "They wore hats and had cloths over their mouths."

Ledger studied him. "Curiouser and curiouser."

"Collins must have more of her goons in town," suggested Benny. "She must have sent them."

Ledger tapped Morton's chest. "You got something to say about that?"

"How would I know?" whined Morton. "They didn't exactly come here to make speeches. They had knives, they . . . they killed that guard and knocked me down. I . . . I must have blacked out for a few seconds. I woke up when he—*it*— attacked me." Tears ran down his cheeks, turning pink as they passed through smears of blood. Morton shook his head. "It all happened so fast. I didn't even see them leave. They were strangers. I never saw them before."

Gutsy came over and squatted down next to Ledger. "How many people does Collins still have in town? Who *else* is part of all this?"

Morton licked his lips, then winced as he tasted blood. "I don't know. Some. I never wanted to know names. They're just . . . just . . ." He didn't finish the sentence, clearly uncertain how to make it sound as bad as it probably was. "Please . . . help me."

"If you want help, Doc," said Ledger casually, "you have to earn it. Tell me why Collins wanted you dead."

"I don't know," he wailed, but when Ledger only smiled and made no move to get help, the doctor drew a breath, and in a more controlled—though bitter—voice, said, "From the way you're talking, it's clear Bess got away. If so . . . then maybe this was her cleaning up loose ends. Maybe she was mad because I talked to you. She has to know that I would. I won't take the fall for her or anyone. Not after what she made me do. Not after what happened to the town. I'm not a monster."

"Yes, you are," said Gutsy coldly. "You killed my mother."

Morton could not look at her. "I did what Bess made me do. You can't say no to her. Not her. You have no idea what she's really like. She's more terrifying than anything out there. What choice did I have? I . . . I . . . oh God, it's all falling apart. *Look at me.*"

"Yeah, yeah, yeah," said Ledger. "Look at you. Can't begin to tell you how eaten up with sympathy I am. Oops—'eaten up.' Sorry, unintentional pun. Funny, though."

"Please . . ."

"If Collins was cleaning up loose ends, then that means she was afraid of something you might tell us," said Ledger, "and I find that real darn interesting. Now, we got a couple ways we can play this, Doc. I figure you have about six, seven hours of what we can both agree will be screaming agony. Then you make that *very* interesting transition to being what my friends in California like to call a 'zom.' Then, you have all the time in the world to wander around going bitey-bitey. Personally, I think it would be fun to lock you up in a cell and keep you as a pet. Would you like that, Doc? New Alamo's zombie mascot. Truth to tell, there would be a bit of justice in it."

Spider made a sick sound, but Ledger pretended not to hear.

"Help me, for God's sake," wheezed Morton.

"Why don't *you* help *us*?"

Morton's eyes seemed to sharpen at that. "What do you mean?"

"Well," said Ledger, "as I understand it, you infected Karen's daughter, Sarah, which is some evil stuff right there. Makes me want to do very bad things to you while you're still alive to feel them. No, don't you dare look away. You look me in the eye when I'm talking to you."

Morton did, but Gutsy could see how much it cost the doctor. She fished inside her heart for a splinter of pity, and surprised herself by finding it.

"You've been giving Karen some drugs for Sarah," continued Ledger. "Something to keep the Reaper Plague from spreading. That's the only reason Karen hasn't put a bullet in your brainpan. Those same drugs could keep *you* alive. Am I right?"

"Yes! The RZ16 pills. That's what I need. Get me to my office. I have some. I *need* them, before it's too late!"

Gutsy heard Benny gasp, but beat him to the punch with the obvious question. "How many of those RZ16 pills do you have?" she demanded.

"Enough," said Morton quickly. "There's enough for me to keep working. I can still be of use. I'm the only doctor left, and—"

"Slow down, sparky," said Ledger. "How many is 'enough'?"

"Thousands of capsules. Enough for me." He flinched as he looked at the faces of the people gathered around him. "And I can make more."

"Wait a minute," snapped Gutsy. "You can make as much of those pills as you want?"

"Yes. But you need to get me back to my office so I can—"

Gutsy made a sudden lunge, but Ledger shoved her back, and then Spider was there, pulling her away. Gutsy fought against the hands holding her, yelling so loud that spit flew from her mouth. "You could have given those pills to everyone who ever got bitten. All those people who got hurt on the wall. Everyone who was hurt today—you could have saved them all! Why didn't you? What's *wrong* with you?"

Morton whimpered, bleeding, sobbing, defeated and terrified. "I'm sor—" he started to say, but Ledger grabbed a fistful of his shirt and pulled forward with shocking force.

"Doc," said the soldier quietly, "if you say you're sorry, I'm going to let Gutsy have you. I'll *hold* you for her."

The doctor flinched but said nothing. Ledger shoved him back against the wall.

Gutsy was breathing hard, but she stopped fighting, and Spider slowly relaxed his hold. She nodded to him but continued to glare hatred at Morton. She got to her feet and moved to stand close so her shadow fell across the doctor's face. Ledger pivoted on the balls of his feet and glanced up at her.

"Do you know what's going to happen now, Dr. Morton?" asked Gutsy. "Right now, we're going to take you to your office. You're going to show us where these RZ16 pills are. You're going to tell us everything we need to know in order to get the right dosages to everyone in town who's been bitten. *Everyone*. You want to know who'll be the *last* person to get those pills?"

Morton stared at her.

"Then," continued Gutsy, "you're going to tell the hospital pharmacist how to make those pills. You're going to make sure it's done right and that there's enough for everyone, for as long as they live. That's the way you get to stay alive. If you mess this up—if you don't do everything you can to help us—then *I'm* going to kill you. I'm going to make it hurt, and I'm going to make it last a long, long time."

"God . . . Gutsy . . . ," murmured Alethea, shocked.

Gutsy didn't look at her friend. She didn't look at anyone except Dr. Morton. The world around her seemed to be made of ice.

"Do you understand me?" she asked.

Morton said nothing. He sat there, weeping. Ledger leaned close.

"The lady asked you a question," he said. "If I was you, I'd give her the answer she wants to hear."

THEY GOT MORTON TO HIS FEET. BENNY AND SAM took an arm each and half walked, half carried the doctor down the alley and into the hospital, following Gutsy and trailed by everyone else. Nurses, techs, orderlies, and the many wounded stared in fear and confusion. There was no sign of Karen, and Gutsy figured she was still looking for Manny. It hadn't been more than a few minutes since she'd left them, after all.

Gutsy walked alone, aware of the looks her friends gave her. Even Benny seemed surprised by her threat to Morton. Nix, on the other hand, caught Gutsy's eye and gave her a single nod. Everyone understood, but Nix seemed to truly *get* her.

Sombra trotted beside her, throwing nervous looks around. The coydog's devotion softened Gutsy's heart, but only a little. Rage was a furnace inside her chest, and she knew that at the rate things were going, it was going to consume her. Ever since Mama died, the rage and pain seemed to define the whole world. It made her envy the dead.

They reached Morton's office, but before they got to his door, the two dogs began growling again.

"No more," whispered Spider. "Please, no more . . ."

But, of course, there was more.

This was the world, and that's how it was.

The door to the doctor's office stood ajar. Ledger waved everyone back and clicked his tongue for Grimm. The dog looked into the room and then sat. No growls or tension.

Ledger stood behind him, sighed, cursed softly, and lowered his gun.

They went inside. Every drawer, every closet, every container in the large office had been pulled out, turned over, emptied onto the floor. There were some capsules there, but they were crushed—stamped into ruin. Bottles of powders had been smashed. Water and a few noxious chemicals had been poured over the broken capsules, ruining everything.

"No!" wailed Morton. He pulled free, and they all watched as he lurched around the room, pawing at the debris with bloody fingers. Then he dropped to his knees, buried his face in his hands, and began to cry with deep, racking sobs. "Gone . . ." they heard him say in a broken voice. "All of the RZ16, all of my store of ingredients . . . *gone*."

Gutsy was unmoved by his grief, knowing it to be totally selfish. There was no chance at all Morton was grieving for the loss of drugs that could help Sarah, or Chong, or any of the wounded, except in that saving them was likely to earn him some clemency. And some drugs. She walked over and, ignoring his injuries, hooked him under the armpits and hauled him to his feet. Gutsy shoved him against the desk, took a strong handful of his shirt, and pressed the tines of her crowbar under his chin. No one made the slightest move to stop her.

"Tell me you can make more," she said.

"THEY'RE REINFORCING THE WALLS," SAID TÉNÈBRES.

She and Trócaire walked along the inside of the rows of stacked cars, watching as men and women worked with chain hoists erected on sturdy pipe scaffolding. Through the open gates they could see teams of horses dragging more of the wrecked cars into the town.

When New Alamo had been originally fortified in the awful months after the dead rose, it had been surrounded by walls of stacked cars, and direct access to the town gates had been via long corridors of more stacked vehicles. The idea was to create a kind of chute or funnel that would make it easier to see anyone approach. That strategy had failed during the big attack, though, because the dead had simply swarmed through those corridors. The town walls had walkways on top from which townsfolk could shoot or hurl rocks, but the corridors were too remote and too long to man in that way. Now there were teams of people tearing down and repurposing the crushed cars.

The couple stopped to watch for nearly half an hour, sometimes holding hands.

One of the workers, a heavyset woman wearing a hijab,

walked past them to a rain barrel, filled a plastic souvenir mug to the brim, and drank it all down. She wiped her mouth, shook out the cup, and hung it on a hook by the barrel. Then she noticed the two teenagers and gave them a nod.

"You're new," she said. "Refugees?"

"Yes," said Ténèbres, "and happy to be here."

The woman nodded and followed their gaze. "Wall's going to be stronger than ever, don't you fret. We're going to make that wall so darn high and so darn thick that no one's ever going to get in here again."

Trócaire grinned. "Glad to hear that."

The Muslim woman pulled a pair of heavy canvas work gloves from her back pocket. "You kids looking for work?"

"Yes," said Trócaire. "We'll do anything. Delighted to."

The woman nodded and pointed to a tower of scaffolding on which sat a huge crane. "We're about to start building higher levels. Don't suppose you know how to use a boom crane?"

"No," said Ténèbres, "but we're fast learners."

"Good. Lot of folks don't like working that high up. If you care to volunteer, we'd be grateful to have you."

"Then count on us," said Trócaire.

THEY MOVED TO A CONSULTATION ROOM.

Spider went out and brought back a nurse to dress Morton's wounds. She was quick and efficient, but the scowl on her face made it clear she hated giving him any comfort. Manny Flores, the hospital pharmacist, was also brought in. Ledger told him everything.

"The doc says he can walk you through some steps to make more of the drug we need," said the soldier.

Flores gave him a brief two-count of a stare, then turned to Morton, took a notebook and pen from the jacket of his lab coat, and said, "Tell me."

Morton spoke fast, and Flores took furious notes. Gutsy stood with her friends and the California teens and listened, but much of the conversation shot completely over her head. Morton, gasping with pain and racked by desperate fear, spoke in a rapid-fire stream of technical terms, and Flores's questions were equally niche.

The nurse wanted to give Morton a shot for the pain, but he snarled her away. "I need my head clear, dammit."

At that, the nurse threw down the syringe and stalked out, throwing over her shoulder a hope that he died screaming.

"Really feeling the love here in your little town," said Benny under his breath.

"We're known for our charm," said Alethea with a wicked smile.

Finally the pharmacist stopped writing and frowned down at the complex notes, then hurried out of the room. Ledger squatted once more in front of the injured physician.

"I was able to follow some of that, Doc," he said mildly, "and what I heard was more of a stopgap measure than an actual treatment. You wouldn't be trying to pull something, now, would you? Because that would be mighty unfriendly, and—I have to admit—I'm already feeling a tad cranky."

"No," said Morton between gritted teeth, "it's the best I can do for now. I don't have the right compounds to make a batch of the kind of pills we need."

"That's not the answer any of us want to hear."

"Listen to me, you Neanderthal," growled Morton, "do you think I *want* to die? Collins knew what she was doing when she came in here. She knew I had key ingredients locked up because I didn't want anyone else to know about them. I made what I needed for Sarah after hours when the pharmacy staff was gone for the day. There was enough here to last for three months. Now there isn't."

"How much does Sarah have at home?" asked Gutsy.

Morton's eyes shifted guiltily away. "Karen gets a week's worth at a time. She was here four days ago, so . . ."

Spider made a sick sound and kicked a file cabinet. Morton flinched, then groaned as pain from his torn shoulder rippled through him. He eyed the syringe of painkillers. Ledger picked the needle up but didn't use it.

"Talk first," he said, "feel better after. You were saying, Doc?"

"If we cut the doses for one of the kids, maybe then we'll have enough for me—"

There was a rasp, and suddenly the tip of Benny's sword was touching Morton's throat.

"Doc," Benny said softly, "you are going to want to be real careful about how you finish that sentence."

Morton blanched. "I'm telling you, we don't have enough of the right materials here. The main chemical stores were at the base. If I turn and reanimate before someone can get more of the materials, who will make more pills?"

"You're going to die anyway," said Gutsy. "The base is destroyed; I saw it burn."

Morton gave her a scathing look. "Site B." He said it as if everyone should understand. When all he saw were perplexed expressions, he repeated it. "*Site B.* You need to go to Site B."

"Stop saying 'Site B,'" growled Gutsy, "and tell us what it is."

"And *where*," added Benny.

Morton looked disgusted, as if everyone in the room was mentally deficient except himself. Then he gave the full and correct name for Site B. "It's the Laredo Chemical and Biological Weapon Defense Research Facility. It's where they sent all the bioweapons after the international accord. They were all supposed to be destroyed, but, hey, let's face it—that stuff was too valuable to be incinerated. We stored it instead. With *tons* of weapons."

Ledger turned to Sam.

"The cache," said Sam.

"Well, golly, golly, golly," said Ledger. "I think it's Christmas morning."

"Don't start hanging your stockings too fast," said Morton sourly. "The parasites and chemical samples are there, but the process of making the pills takes time."

Ledger leaned in a little. "Exactly how much time?"

THEY WENT BACK TO THE SCHOOL, WHICH HAD MORE or less become the headquarters of their bizarre group. The Chess Players, their work at the hospital done for now, joined them.

They broke the news to Chong about his missing quad and its store of drugs, and about the destruction of the supply in Morton's office. Chong's response was to sink down to the floor, lean his head back against the wall, and close his eyes. Lilah threatened to kill Morton, but that was hollow. They needed him. So instead she wept and held Chong. Benny sat beside him, holding his best friend's right hand, and Nix lay on the floor, her head on Chong's thigh.

Gutsy and her friends stood apart, clustered together in a sad and angry silence. Spider knelt down and began petting Sombra, who whined softly.

The Chess Players, Captain Ledger, and Sam Imura were clustered around a desk, poring over maps to try and determine the exact location of Site B. Morton, who was no soldier, had only a general idea of where it might be.

"It could be here, here, or maybe here," suggested Mr.

Urrea, pointing to spots that were within a day's wagon ride from the destroyed base.

"Could be farther out if they're using jeeps," said Ledger. One of the surprising things Morton told them was that the base had a large number of functioning vehicles. Jeeps, Humvees, and trucks of various sizes. The fact that no one in town had ever seen one suggested that the vehicles were used carefully, and never close to New Alamo. "That increases their operational range; and Collins did leave here on a quad."

Gutsy came over and said, "I don't think it's that far away. When Collins and her Rat Catchers came to the cemetery, they were on a wagon—no jeeps or any of that stuff. And if they switched to something with a motor after they left, I'd have heard it. Sound travels forever out in the Broken Lands."

"Maybe there's another tunnel entrance out there," said Benny. "Somewhere closer to the cemetery. And one big enough for a wagon and horses."

"A tunnel to where, though?" asked Nix. "To the base that was destroyed? Or to this Site B place?"

"Unknown at this time," said Ledger.

Sam tapped a couple of spots with an emphatic finger. "These two places line up with rumors I've been hearing about weapons caches. They're both within half a day's ride on horseback, and I think we should try them first. Collins said that the Raggedy Man is coming with his army, and I'm not sure we could stop even a small attack, let alone a massive assault. Whether we find Collins or not, we need those guns."

"More important," said Ford, "if that Site B place is of a decent size, and if it's well hidden and well protected, then we might be able to evacuate everyone there."

"The ravagers destroyed the main base," countered Urrea, "and that was protected."

"Sure, but maybe that was a sneak attack. We wouldn't be surprised."

"I like it," said Ledger. "It's better than staying here. Besides, I'm not all that keen on making any kind of last stand in a place called 'Alamo,' you dig?"

"Well, speaking of ambushes," said Urrea, "if Bess Collins gets there first—or is already there—wouldn't she be expecting us? Wouldn't she be preparing to defend that place herself?"

"I wish you hadn't said that," muttered Ford.

"No, he's right," Ledger told him. "But she's one person. More scientist than soldier. Sam and I have some experience with infiltrating hidden bases."

"A bit," said Sam, giving a rare smile.

"We still need the chemicals for the drug," said Nix.

Ledger nodded. "Let's hope that one of these spots is Site B. It'll be one-stop shopping."

"When do you want to leave?" asked Gutsy.

Ledger smiled. "Thanks, kid, but you're not going. None of you are. This is for me and Sam to do."

"Hey, what just a darn minute—" began Alethea, but Ledger held up a hand.

"Just listen. If Site B is the kind of facility I suspect it is, then we need to come at it quick and quiet. We can't hit it with a frontal assault. Even if we won, we'd take losses doing it. Sam and I will head out first thing tomorrow."

"Why wait?" asked Ford.

"We need time to get there and scout the location. We'll

have to go most of the way on horseback and then walk in the last couple of miles. All of that's going to take time, and there isn't enough of today left," said Ledger.

"I don't like it," groused Urrea.

"You don't have to like it, brother. You just have to accept it."

Sam nodded. "Before we go, I think Joe and I should walk the town with Karen and give what advice we can on how to fortify. We know some dirty tricks."

"Yup," said Ledger. He turned to Ford and Urrea. "And you two old farts can make yourself useful preparing food and supplies for a possible evacuation. Benny, Nix, Chong, and Lilah can help. They've been through enough conflicts to have good ideas. Listen to them. And as for you three," he added, looking at Gutsy and her friends, "you know the town and the people. Spread the word. Get them ready. Be smart. Don't panic anyone, but also don't soft-sell this. If the Night Army hits before we get back, New Alamo will fall. Be ready to get out. That means taking a lot of supplies into the tunnel. Maybe stocking some in that car wash at the entrance. Oh, and make sure people have carts, strollers, anything with wheels. That'll make it easier to take more food and water. Be sure those things are in good shape. Grease the wheels. You know what to do." He directed this last to Gutsy, who nodded.

"And one more thing," said the soldier. "There has to be someone in this town who used to work on cars. Find them and see if they can figure out how to repair the quads."

"Okay," said Gutsy dubiously.

"Joe, what if there aren't enough chemicals at Site B?" asked Nix. "Or you can't get in?"

Ledger turned to Max Morton. The old soldier gave him a very cold and ugly smile. "The doc here is going to do his level best to make sure what we have lasts. That means he gets *his* pill last, after everyone else gets a dose."

"That's insane," cried Morton. "If I'm sick, I can't work—"

"Then make sure there's enough drug to go around."

The room was unnaturally quiet.

"Good," said Ledger after a long moment. "You all have jobs to do, and I need you to do all of them."

THE GROUP BROKE UP.

As they were filing out, Gutsy approached Benny and his friends. "Don't any of you know how to fix those quad things?"

"Not me," said Benny. "Never been handy with tools."

Nix also shook her head. "We all know a little bit of routine maintenance, but . . ."

"But what?" demanded Gutsy, appalled. "You mean you came all this way and only *one* of you knew how to keep those quads working?"

Nix and Benny looked deeply embarrassed.

Gutsy wanted to scream at them. Stuff like this made her so mad. All it took was some common sense and a little planning. Why was it people so rarely thought ahead? With what she carried with her every day she could clean and dress a wound, start a fire, purify water, catch and clean a fish, sharpen sticks, build a small shelter, collect dew, and a dozen other useful things. And that was just her walking-around gear. If she was going to drive a machine all the way across the country, Gutsy would have made sure she knew how to take a quad apart down to the last bolt and washer and put it back together again. She'd have brought replacements for all of the key functions.

Now, though, did not seem the time to make a speech about preparedness.

Ledger overheard the conversation and came over. "Y'know, guys, Gutsy here makes a good point. You four are idiots."

"Hey," said Benny, but without emphasis. "Look, we left in kind of a hurry. We thought you were in trouble and came out to . . . you know . . ."

Ledger stared at Benny until he shut up and looked down at his shoes. Chong gave his friend a slow, ironic pat on the shoulder.

The old soldier glanced at Gutsy. "How old are you?"

"Fifteen," she said, immediately defensive. "Why?"

He smiled. "Because this isn't the first time I thought you were the smartest and most mature person in the room."

Gutsy felt her cheeks burn, but somehow managed to keep normal. More or less. "Okay, well, I, um . . . I'm going to, um, start asking around to see if anyone used to be a mechanic."

And with that, she fled.

TRÓCAIRE FOUND TÉNÈBRES ALONE, SITTING ON A kitchen chair she'd pulled close to a window. He came up behind her and placed a gentle hand on her shoulder and stood, watching.

Two men were pushing a quad along the alley between this street and the next. A big red mechanic's toolbox jiggled on the seat. A young boy followed behind, pulling a wagon that was piled high with engine parts.

"Well," said the young man, "isn't that interesting?"

Ténèbres shivered. "I'm afraid," she said.

Trócaire bent and kissed the top of her head. Her skin was cool. She reached up and took his hand and gave it a fierce squeeze.

"Now, come along," he said. "We have work to do."

ALL DAY AND WELL INTO THE EVENING GUTSY LOOKED for a mechanic. So far she'd asked a hundred people about fixing quads or motorcycles, and all she'd gotten were head shakes. Sombra trotted along, quiet but very much there for her.

It was close to nine at night when they headed toward the south side of town, where some of the older residents lived.

"Hey," said a voice, and Gutsy turned to see Captain Ledger and Grimm walking across the street toward her. "Any luck?"

"Not yet."

They walked together for a while, stopping to ask the same question, getting the same answer. Suddenly a voice cracked through the air.

"Captain Ledger!"

They turned to see Karen Peak come running toward them. She looked exhausted to the point of near fainting. And the look in her eyes made Gutsy want to cover her ears so she wouldn't hear more bad news.

"I just came from the hospital," Karen said in a quick, ragged voice. "Morton said he thought there might be some small amounts of the right chemicals at the hospital after all.

He said that he just remembered. Whatever. There were some notes he wanted, too—step-by-step instructions for making the pills. He told Flores to get all of that from a locker in the maintenance room. Before you ask, no, we didn't know that he had other hiding places. The locker was a dummy. Dial one combination and it opens like any other locker; dial a special combination and the whole thing swings out and there's a safe built into the wall. Morton gave Flores the combination because there are special files in there. The most important stuff, actually."

"And you're going to break my heart and tell me that Collins got to the safe first," said Ledger.

The wretched expression on Karen's face was enough of an answer.

Ledger spent a few moments looking up into the nighttime sky. "Well, life is a juicy little peach, isn't it," the captain said after a while.

"How bad is all this?" asked Gutsy.

"Bad. With the formula, Morton thought he might be able to thin out the mixture to make the pills last longer without diluting the medicine's effect. But it's a really complex process. Dozens of steps, very precise measurements . . ." She shook her head in despair. "He said that without the formula it might take too much time, and . . ."

Her voice suddenly broke, and Karen's facade of professional control dissolved into a mother's terrified tears. She covered her face with her hands and leaned her head against Ledger. Gutsy stood by, feeling clumsy and helpless. She wasn't all that close with Karen, but her heart broke for her. Sarah was an innocent in all of this, and Karen—as her mother—

was helpless. The two dogs whined louder and nudged Karen with their wet noses.

Ledger gave Karen a gruff hug and then gently pushed her back. "Show me that safe," he said. "Gutsy, you keep looking for a mechanic. I have a feeling that quad is just about our last, best hope."

Ledger and Karen hurried off, Grimm trotting along behind.

"Well," said Gutsy to Sombra, "I guess it's up to us to perform an actual miracle here."

Sombra wagged his tail. Gutsy smiled and gave him a piece of dried goat, which he chewed greedily.

Gutsy ran from house to house, from store to church to workshop, asking everyone she met in the hope of finding at least one person who still remembered how to fix motors.

Instead she found *two*: Jose Santamaria, who looked like he was a thousand years old, and a sixtysomething man wearing a faded tie-dyed shirt. She'd seen the second guy at town fairs, playing guitar and singing old songs about love and peace. His name was Sunny-Day Ray.

"Actual working quads?" gasped Sunny-Day.

"Well, damaged ones," said Gutsy, almost apologetically.

"Most things that are broken can be fixed," drawled Jose. The two mechanics grinned at each other, and Gutsy wondered how long it had been since either had found a reason to smile. They ran off to get their toolboxes, then Gutsy led them back to the hospital and down into the tunnel. They were absolutely delighted to encounter machines that had—until Collins's sabotage—worked. They fell on the quads like hungry vultures.

There was the one quad in the tunnel, and two more were hidden in the car wash. Gutsy gathered the other teens—her friends and the California kids—and it took about a gallon of sweat apiece to bring the other two quads down to where the mechanics were working. Sunny-Day Ray and Jose seemed not to notice whether the teens were there.

So, they all left.

Gutsy said goodbye to the others and headed back home to wash and put on some fresh clothes. The ones she'd been wearing were stained with soot and blood. As she and Sombra walked through the town, she could feel waves of depression crashing down over her. They darkened the night sky even more.

Inside and along the walls, fires burned in oil drums set at regular intervals, and there were whole battalions of bottles filled with any kind of liquid that would burn, each with a piece of rag stuffed into them, ready to light and throw. It was the best line of defense they had left, because most of the ammunition in town was gone, used in the battles. It made Gutsy wonder if that was part of the point of the two attacks. If there was even one more raid, they would run out of bullets, and probably use up the store of firebombs.

What had Collins said? Something about the Raggedy Man having the largest army in the history of the world. If so, then he could afford to keep throwing his troops at New Alamo until all the town had left for defense were clubs and knives, and those would not stop a wave of thousands of shamblers. That, Gutsy knew, was the logic of an undead general. Even Captain Ledger with his sword or Sam Imura with his sniper rifle could not take down enough of them to stop *los muertos* from wiping New Alamo off the face of the planet. There were not enough bullets, not enough blades, not enough human physical strength left to stop an army of billions. It chilled her to the bone.

"This is how we're going to lose," she told Sombra.

The coydog, being only an animal, wagged his tail, happy to be spoken to. Gutsy knelt and wrapped her arms around the battered dog and held on for dear life.

Then a soft voice spoke out of the shadows.

"We're not going to lose, Gutsy Gomez."

She jerked her head up, and through the tears in her eyes Gutsy saw a slim figure dressed in soiled clothes, with hair that was ratty with grime and dried sweat and a face streaked with dirt cut by dried tear tracks. It was a beautiful face, though.

So beautiful.

"Alice."

Alice Chung came into Gutsy's arms and they clung to each other. Sobbing. Holding on for dear life. Gutsy kissed Alice's hair and face and hands.

"Alice," she said, repeating the name over and over.

PART FOUR

THE ROAD TO ASHEVILLE

But I've a rendezvous with Death

At midnight in some flaming town . . .

—ALAN SEEGER, "I HAVE A RENDEZVOUS WITH DEATH"

"YOU THINK BENNY AND THE OTHERS ARE OKAY?" asked Morgie as they packed their gear onto the quads after another night in another empty house.

Riot answered with a shrug.

"We made the right choice, though, didn't we?" Morgie prodded. "Splitting from the others like this? Going to Asheville?"

Another shrug.

He sighed and changed the subject. "Okay, so I did the math on the trip, and it'll take us about thirty-two more hours at top speed to get there."

Nothing.

"But we'll probably have to go slower. So it could take as much as fifty hours all told. With rest stops and all, that's at least a week."

Not a word.

"I was bitten by a zom last night and turned into a flesh-eating ghoul," he said.

Riot flinched and cut him a look, but when she saw him grinning, she gave a scowl that was as dark and threatening as a storm cloud.

"Just checking to see if you were listening to me," he said.

Riot stared at him for several seconds, saying nothing. Then she went back to packing her quad. Morgie sighed and stopped talking. They left a few minutes later.

They drove in silence, Riot way out in front. As they made their way north, Morgie focused instead on the landscape and wildlife. They passed small herds of zebras, and another of wild horses. The latter made sense because of all the abandoned horse ranches they passed; the zebras must have come from a zoo. There were carcasses and bones, too. It was getting easier to recognize the difference between zombie bites and marks from the claws and fangs of living predators. Probably a lion or tiger, he figured.

A camel walked slowly along the roadside, and Morgie smiled at it until he got close and saw that it was deformed. Not a zom camel but something equally disturbing—a mutant. Maybe it was radiation, or perhaps chemicals from a tanker truck or train; but whatever it was, the camel was hideous. It had one normal eye, but the other was a darkened pit over which flies crawled. Instead of two nostrils it had five, and its mouth was filled with jagged teeth and what looked like stunted tusks. It smelled of feces and sulfur. Morgie gunned his engine and left it behind.

A lot of the plants were mutated, too. Trees whose trunks were twisted as if writhing in slow pain as they grew. Carnivorous plants with small rodents and geckos caught in the clutches of sappy leaves. Butterflies as large as doves but with stingers like scorpions.

And yet in the midst of all of this were flowers of incredible beauty. Perfect roses, fields of daisies and brown-eyed Susans.

For nearly two miles a pack of dogs ran alongside Morgie's quad. They were ordinary dogs, many of them dangerous-looking, but they did not snarl or snap; instead they seemed to run for the sheer joy of it. It made him smile, and when they stopped running he turned to look back and saw them standing in the road, tails wagging.

Ahead Riot was slowing, allowing him to catch up. She cut her engine near a faded billboard for a local airport, and he pulled up beside her. Riot took out her binoculars and studied another herd of zebras.

"What is it?" he asked.

"Heck if I know," she said, handing him the glasses. "Something sure ain't right over yonder, though. Take a look."

Morgie took the binoculars, and for a split second their fingers brushed. It sent an electric shock through him, and he looked at her. Saw her glancing back. He wanted to believe that he saw some lingering love among the hatred and sadness there. But Riot turned away and pointed where she wanted him to look.

"I saw blood on a couple of them. Looked more like injuries than them bleeding from sores."

"Yeah," agreed Morgie. "They're pretty skinny, even with all this grass to eat. Maybe they're sick. Radiation or something. Predators go for the weak and sick animals, right?"

"Maybe," said Riot slowly. "They're acting pretty calm. Can't be anything hunting them right at the moment." Then she added, "But if there's something hunting *them* out here, then *we* need to know about it. Wouldn't be all that funny if we dodged a bunch of zoms and then got eaten by a pack of lions."

Morgie braced his elbows on the handlebars to steady his view. Now he could see the blood, but it made him frown. Predators usually came up at quarter angles, slashing at the rear legs to hobble deer or horses or other big grazing animals. However, all of the blood he saw was on the upper necks of the zebras. Then the tight knot of animals shifted enough so that a bloody carcass on the trampled grass became visible. The movement also allowed Morgie to see their faces.

One of the zebras, as if sensing that it was being observed, raised its head from the thick grass and looked directly their way. The binocular lenses were powerful, and now that he was braced, his view was rock-steady.

"Oh . . . my . . . *God*," he breathed.

The faces of the zebras were smeared with bright blood. It wasn't theirs. On the ground, now partly visible, was a tawny African lion.

It was dead.

The zebras were *feeding* on it.

THE OTHER UNDEAD ZEBRAS RAISED THEIR HEADS. One by one, looking to where the first one was staring. It was a scene that was at once terrifying and bizarre.

"Please tell me I'm not really seeing what I'm seeing," said Riot slowly.

The herd of undead creatures suddenly broke into a trot and then a gallop, thundering across the field toward them.

"*Move!*" cried Morgie.

They turned on their quads and hit the gas. The wheels spat dust and dried grass as they bit the turf, and then the two machines were hurtling down the road. The pack of animals were running every bit as fast. They did not move with the slow and uncertain gait of human zoms but galloped at full speed.

The road snaked around. They could drive fastest on the blacktop, but the zebras were cutting toward them at an angle that would let them catch up before the road straightened out. It forced Morgie and Riot to leave the road and cut across wild pastureland in order to keep ahead. The ground was uneven, filled with rocks and gopher holes, and choked with brush.

"We're not going to make it," yelled Morgie as he gave the

quad all the gas it would take. He willed it to lift off, to fly.

His heart sank as he thought of all that he'd been through, everything he had suffered and experienced, the dangers he had faced growing up in a town surrounded by the dead. Morgie Mitchell had survived all of that, and now he was going to die in a terrible, painful, and absurdly stupid way: eaten by freaking *zebra zoms*.

A sound burst from his mouth, interrupting the flow of despairing words.

As the zebras drew so close their big yellow teeth snapped at the fenders of his quad, Morgie burst out laughing. Then he gave it more gas and sped away, leaving the creatures in a swirl of road dust.

Thirty feet ahead, Riot turned to see if Morgie was still behind her.

She saw his face. Saw that he was laughing.

"Boy's crazier than an outhouse owl," she said.

And then she was laughing too.

THEY REACHED THE STRAIGHTAWAY SECTION OF THE road a hundred feet before the zebras caught up. The engines roared in defiance as Riot and Morgie gave them all the gas they could devour. The machines shot forward, and soon the gap was two hundred feet. Three hundred . . .

Morgie's speedometer told him he was going a little above forty miles per hour, near the quad's top speed. Riot had an identical machine. The zebras were losing ground very slowly, which suggested they were running at better than thirty-five miles per hour—as fast as a racehorse, and these creatures could not tire. But the quads could run out of gas.

They whipped past ancient billboards advertising things that no longer had meaning. Bail bondsmen. Politicians running for office. Internet providers. And a dozen different kinds of fast food. One of them was a hamburger chain that promised to "Feed You on the Go!" That kind of irony he did not need. After all, Morgie and Riot were the fast food on today's menu.

Then Morgie saw a different sign:

KLEBERG COUNTY AIRPORT

TWO MILES

There was art on the billboard that showed a single runway and a cluster of small buildings. Morgie whooped and waved his arm at the sign. Riot glanced at him and then at the billboard, and she nodded.

Three of the zebras were outrunning the others, closing the distance with every step.

Morgie and Riot raced for their lives. The quads burned along the road, and the monsters followed. But the road was becoming harder to navigate. Hulks of dead cars and broken sections of asphalt made them zig and zag, wasting speed. Morgie risked a look back. The main herd was nearly half a mile back now, but three of the zebras were no more than thirty yards behind him. How they were able to run so fast was beyond Morgie's understanding.

The airport was so close now. They could see a big chainlink fence—the heavy kind, with stout pole frames and a wide gate on wheels. It stood open, and beyond that they could see planes and buildings.

As they rushed toward it, Morgie had an idea. Wild, crazy, possibly suicidal, but he knew he had to try.

With the fast zebras closing in, Morgie and Riot shot through the open fence and onto the airfield. Morgie slowed a little, letting Riot zoom ahead. As soon as she was well ahead, he jerked his handlebars to one side and throttled hard, sending the quad into a tight right-hand turn. The tires skidded, creating massive dust clouds as they fought the forward momentum and tried to grab the road in a new direction. The animals tried to turn with Morgie, going for the closest prey. They stumbled and collided. Their confusion gave Morgie time to correct his angle and regain speed, and soon he was racing along the inside of the fence. The zebras regained their balance and chased him, ignoring Riot. The rest of the herd was coming, but there was time. How much? Ten seconds? Fifteen?

Morgie circled, glancing back to make sure the three fast zebras were still following only him. One of them was lagging behind, stumbling a bit, and he figured it must have injured itself during the collision.

"Come on," growled Morgie as he shot out into the open field again with the animals in thundering pursuit, and turned in another wide circle, praying that the creatures couldn't learn from their mistakes. He cut the wheel again, fought for balance, and shot forward, bisecting his own arc. The sudden turn caused another collision, and he grinned as they tumbled over one another while he drove back into the parking lot.

Morgie hit the brakes, sending the quad into a skidding, sliding, screaming sideways turn just inside the opening in the fence. He leaped from the quad, tore his bokken free, and grabbed the sun-heated metal of the gate's upright pole. The dead zebras screamed at him and charged as Morgie threw his bulk against the wheeled gate. The old metal, pitted with rust and disuse, also shrieked. The single wheel on which the gate rested creaked like door hinges on a haunted house. But it began to move. He nearly had it closed when he ran out of time.

Morgie whirled and brought his bokken up in a two-handed grip. It was a sturdy piece of polished oak. Twenty-eight inches long, heavy and powerful. As the first zebra jumped at him, trying to smash him down with cracked hooves, Morgie threw himself sideways, twisted as he fell, rolled, and was back on his feet in a second, pivoting, raising his wooden sword, stepping in to put mass behind the blow. And he struck.

The bokken hit the zebra just below the knee of its left foreleg, and the cannon bone exploded inside the dead flesh, sending a reciprocal shock through the weapon and into Morgie's hands. He gritted his teeth as he ducked the biting mouth and swung again, aiming for the other leg. The movement changed the angle of his swing, and the sword instead crunched into the long pastern bone. Again there was a big, wet crack, and, as Morgie backpedaled, the zebra's legs buckled and the thing went down.

Morgie had no time for a killing blow, though, because there were still two other zebras approaching. He ran around the quad, making the first zebra turn sharply to follow, and then put a foot onto the saddle of the machine and leaped over it, slashing down with all his force. The bokken hit the zebra behind the ear, high near the spine, and the animal staggered. As Morgie landed, he instantly pivoted and struck above the knee of the left foreleg. The animal fell.

Now there were two crippled zoms on the ground, screaming with hate and hunger. The third limped forward with increasing fury. A sound of thunder made Morgie wheel, and he saw that the rest of the herd was rushing toward the small gap left between gate and fence. If they hit it, their weight would slide the gate open again.

He ran for it, dropping his sword, grabbing the gate pole, and shoving. The thing did not want to close—as if it enjoyed taunting him with only a lie of safety—but Morgie Mitchell was very strong and very scared. He forced the gate to clang shut, and then he dropped the security cuff in place a split second before the herd hit the chain-link wall.

The whole length of the fence bowed inward, and every scrap of metal it was made of screeched in protest.

But then the animals rebounded, falling, collapsing, howling in frustrated fury.

Morgie dove for his bokken and came up with it just as the limping zebra lunged forward to bite him. He bashed the thing's head to one side, kicked the closest leg, and then brought the weapon up and down in a series of crashing, crushing, splintering blows.

It collapsed and lay silent.

Morgie staggered over to the others and silenced them.

Then he stumbled backward and sat down hard on the ground by his quad, his bokken falling with a clatter to the asphalt. He dragged a forearm across his face to wipe sweat from his eyes, and when he looked at his hand he was not surprised to see that it shook badly.

He was vaguely aware of the roar of Riot's machine getting closer. She slowed to a stop five feet away but didn't dismount. Instead she looked from Morgie to the dead creatures to the frustrated herd outside. And back again.

"Well," she said very softly, "glory be. Ain't you something?"

Morgie smiled, nodded, and then turned away to vomit onto the ground.

Interlude Two

Brother Mercy

SIX YEARS AGO

AUTUMN WAS BURNING OFF, AND A STIFF WIND PRO-
claimed winter's advent with frosty insistence. Leaves skittered past the wiry saint and the lean, wolfish boy.

"Honored one," said Brother Mercy, "tell me about god."

The question pleased the older man, but they walked a
dozen paces before he made a reply. Saint John laid his palm
flat over the angel wings on his chest. "Our god is the only
true god. He is Lord Thanatos—all praise his darkness—who
was the son of Nyx, goddess of the night, and Erebus, god of
darkness. Although they were his parents, he grew in power
and was soon more powerful than them and all other gods.
He rules all of time and space."

The saint paused as a hawk screamed in the air far above
them. They both stared up but did not see the bird.

"There have been some people," continued the saint,
"who heard the song of our god in the whispering shadows and in prophetic dreams. Long before the gray people
were blessed with endless life, these prophets took up their
knives and opened red mouths in the unholy. They were
reviled, hunted, imprisoned, even executed. Called madmen

and serial killers, but those were the words of sinners who did not understand. I was one such man."

"You . . . ?"

"Oh yes." Saint John sighed and shook his head. "Prophets are never understood or accepted in their own countries. They chained me, beat me, and sentenced me to death." He smiled now. "As if death was a punishment."

They both laughed at that. A squirrel squatted on a tree branch, munching an acorn, watching as the two men in black strolled past.

"God was always moving in our lives, though," said the saint. "My first proof of this was that the sinners put me into a cell with another prophet. A greater one. A man of perfect vision and extraordinary power."

"What happened to him?"

"When that time comes, I will take you to meet him. My heart tells me that you and he will have much great work to do together." He paused. "We will speak more of him another time. For now, just know that I spent much time with him before I was sent to another kind of prison, and escaped from it just as the gray people awoke and the glory of god's plan filled my mind. I strolled through burning cities, reveling in the beauty of the new age that was dawning. God led me to a church of a failed faith, and there, hidden behind the altar, I found Mother Rose and twenty-seven angels."

Brother Mercy already knew this part from the daily religion classes all reapers had to attend. A favorite story was about how Saint John discovered a group of orphaned children who'd fled from a gang of sinners of the worst kind. A woman named

Rose was running from the same savages, and they caught her outside of the church. Saint John intervened on her behalf, sending the men into the darkness. Together, he and Mother Rose, along with those children, founded the Night Church. Brother Peter, the strongest of the little angels, became the first reaper. Brother Mercy loved Peter as the truest hero of the faith.

"It is the beauty of our religion," said the saint, "that with the simple perfection of our sanctified knives we can cut the perversion and sinfulness from the flesh of the infidel, and in doing so release them into the infinite peace of nothingness. The physical world belongs to the gray people now. That was the purpose of the plague. Our lord called all of the living to shuck off the bonds of the flesh and join with the eternal darkness."

"So . . . our purpose in life is death?" ventured Brother Mercy, still trying to sort through it all.

"Yes," answered the saint.

"But *we* are alive."

Clouds drifted across the sky, and as they passed in front of the sun their shadows painted the landscape. "We are alive," agreed Saint John, "but only as servants. It is our task to seek out any heretics who persist in being alive; they blaspheme with every breath."

"But we fight to stay alive," said Brother Mercy. "Doesn't that make us sinners too?"

"*We* are not sinners," assured Saint John, laying a comforting hand on Brother Mercy's shoulder. "Many of our brothers and sisters *were* sinners, but since kneeling to kiss the knife they have become god's chosen reapers in the fields of the world. We must bear the burden of life until the sinners have all been sent into the darkness, and then we shall join them."

PART FIVE

NEW ALAMO

"With fire and sword the country round

Was wasted far and wide,

And many a childing mother then,

And new-born baby died;

But things like that, you know, must be

At every famous victory."

—Robert Southey, "The Battle of Blenheim"

GUTSY GOMEZ STOOD ON THE HIGHEST POINT OF THE wall looking down into the town. Alethea and Spider were with her, and so was Alice. She and Gutsy held hands. Sombra sat like a gargoyle, leaning out to sniff the air. They were all pale and haggard from horror and sleeplessness.

But they were all alive.

The walls of stacked automobiles that ringed the town were broken in places—burned, blown apart, pulled down, fallen. Many of the homes and buildings inside the town had burned down, and only desperate actions by brave people had kept the whole of New Alamo from being destroyed. Smoke still curled up from piles of rubble.

Worse than that, below them were row upon row of corpses. They lay wrapped in sheets or tarps or whatever was handy. Killed during the two battles and silenced by friends and neighbors.

"How many is it now?" asked Alice.

"Too many," said Alethea.

"Three hundred and eighty-six," said Spider.

Gutsy didn't ask how he knew the exact number. Spider counted things. It helped him to quantify the world, to contain it with facts and figures. Gutsy could relate. She always wanted to understand how things worked. And why they worked. And in thinking that, she realized that she was trying to shift away from how big and monstrous that number was.

Three hundred and eighty-six people. In history books, the phrase used to describe the number of people killed in battle was "butcher's bill," and that hadn't made sense to her until now. There had been fewer than half that many dead at the end of the fight, though. The rest had succumbed to mortal injuries and bites.

They stood together, watching the teams of ordinary people they knew—a seamstress and a tomato farmer, a potter and a farrier, a schoolteacher and a kid from her own grade—work as undertakers. Moving from body to body, making sure each had been spiked in the back of the neck. Wrapping them in shrouds. Binding the corpses. Lifting them onto carts. They worked in a strange silence, and—apart from having to end her own mother's unnatural life—it was the most horrible thing Gutsy had ever seen. The worst thing any of her friends ever saw.

Sombra whined softly and used his wet nose to push against her thigh.

"I should go home," said Alice.

"Yeah," said Spider, "I heard your mom was hurt this afternoon. Is it bad?"

"I haven't really had a chance to see her," admitted Alice. "Mrs. Frye from next door is taking care of her until I get back. Don't think it's too bad, though, or Mom would have said something. She hurt her hand."

"Come on," said Gutsy, "I'll walk you home."

They left the others on the wall and climbed down, walking hand in hand without either realizing they were doing it. The awareness crept into Gutsy's mind, though, and she nearly let go out of some awkward reflex. A few days ago, Gutsy was tongue-tied and clumsy even *talking* to this girl, and now they held hands as if they'd been together forever. Somehow, in the midst of a terrible battle, she and Alice had become more than a thing.

They'd become a couple.

It sounded weird in Gutsy's head, because she was sure everyone was staring at them in surprise or disapproval because Alice was so amazing and a catch by any standard. Gutsy did not consider herself to be even remotely in the same league. Not by a million miles.

When they reached the end of Alice's block, Gutsy stopped.

"Look," she said, "maybe we should say goodbye here."

"Why?"

"Well . . . your mom . . ."

"My mom knows I'm like you, Guts."

Gutsy blinked. "She does?"

"Sure. I told her weeks ago."

"Wait—*weeks*?"

Alice kissed her. Then leaned back a few inches, her eyes searching Gutsy's as her fingers traced a soft line down her cheek.

"If you don't know that I've had a thing for you for a while now," Alice murmured, "then you haven't been paying attention."

Gutsy smiled. "I've been paying attention about some

things," she said, and kissed Alice. The world went away for a long, sweet time.

Then a cart stacked with shrouded bodies rumbled past pulled by two horses, startling them, breaking the kiss. The reality of that cart seemed to hook the awkward beauty of the moment and drag it through the mud. When Gutsy glanced at Alice, there was no trace of a smile left on that lovely face.

"I'd better get home," Alice said. "I want to see how Mom's doing."

"I—"

Alice silenced her with another kiss. Quick and light, and then she turned and walked the rest of the way home. Gutsy watched her go, aching to run after her. Hating that the moment was spoiled, and afraid that there might not be many moments like this for them.

Sombra leaned against her and whined softly, offering and needing comfort in equal measure. Gutsy bent and scratched his head. "You'd probably have been better off if you went feral and stayed out in the Broken Lands. You picked a real winner when you adopted me."

Sombra wagged his tail anyway.

"MOM," SAID ALICE SHARPLY AS SHE PEELED BACK THE bandage and gaped at her mother's hand, "you didn't tell me it was *this* bad. God. You need to have them set your fingers."

"I'm fine," Mrs. Chung insisted. "It's just a sprain."

Her mother's hand was swollen and had turned a violent purple. The fore and ring fingers jutted out crookedly, each slanting at a forty-five-degree angle from the big knuckles.

"Come on," said Alice. "I'll take you over to the hospital so they can—"

"No," said Mrs. Chung sharply. "They've got enough to worry about over there. It's nothing."

"It's *not* nothing. What if they heal like that?"

"I can soak them in cold water. It'll be fine."

"No, it won't," said Alice, getting scared and angry. "If you won't go to the hospital, then I'll set them myself. You know I can do it."

That sparked an argument that rose into a yelling match. Mrs. Chung was like that, always hating anyone to make a fuss over her. Alice won the fight, though. The clincher was when Mrs. Chung tried to prove the injury wasn't as bad as it looked and attempted to make a fist. Her resulting scream got the neighbor's dogs barking furiously. Alice sat back in her chair, arms folded across her chest, head cocked to one side. She sat like that, in a stony silence, until her mother sighed and nodded.

Alice went and got a tongue depressor from her first aid kit, a flexible bandage, and a thin leather belt, which she held out.

"What's that for?"

"For you to bite down on."

"Don't be ridiculous."

"Mom, you tried to make a fist and screamed loud enough to kill birds in flight. Setting those fingers is going to hurt a lot worse. Use the darn belt."

"Don't be fresh."

"*Bite*," growled Alice, holding out the tooled leather belt.

Her mother glared at Alice for ten long seconds. Then she took the belt and put it between her teeth. Alice took a breath, steadied her mother's wrist with one hand, and with the other took each finger one at a time and pulled sharply. The broken bones came apart, and when she released, they snapped back into place.

They were both glad Mrs. Chung had the belt.

THE FOLLOWING MORNING GUTSY HEADED OVER TO
the Cuddlys' place to see if Alethea and Spider were up yet,
but ran into Joe Ledger along the way. He came striding across
the street with his massive combat dog trotting beside him.

"Hey, kid," the old soldier said amiably. "You going anywhere in particular?"

"To see my friends."

"Can it wait?" he asked. "I'd like to talk with you."

"Um . . . sure . . . ?" she replied. It came out as a question.

"Let's walk." He set off without waiting, and she hurried
to catch up. "Listen, Gutsy, Sam and I are going to be heading
out in a few hours. We should already have gone, but Sunny-
Day Ray said they might get one—or possibly two—quads
working. If there's a chance of that, then it's worth waiting
a bit. If nothing else, it'll give us more options if Site B isn't
where we think it is."

"Okay," she said, seeing the logic.

"In the meantime, I'm trying to get all of the facts straight
in my head about what's been going on in this crazy town of
yours. I know most of it, but there are some gaps, and I have
some questions."

"Like . . . ?"

"Like, you went out to the base the night of the big attack, right? You saw it burn. But do you know if anyone from the base escaped?" asked the old ranger. "Any soldiers? Any lab staff, maybe carrying equipment cases?"

"If they did," said Gutsy, "I didn't see them. Why?"

"Just trying to figure out how those nonmilitary folks we saw at the school got turned into ravagers," said Ledger. "If that's what they were. I checked them again, and neither had bite marks of any kind."

"They could have died some other way," said Gutsy. "Everyone who dies—"

"—comes back as a zombie, yes. We all know that. But whoever they are, they must have died very recently. There was absolutely no sign of decay."

Gutsy thought about it. "Maybe they were from one of the little camps out in the Broken Lands. Before the ravagers began attacking everyone in the area, there were a whole bunch of settlements. Some big, with fifty or more people, but most pretty small. Families, groups of loners."

Ledger nodded.

"Or," Gutsy continued, "they could have been from the base. Not soldiers but something else—scientists or lab techs. Like that."

"That feels more likely to me," said Ledger. "Even so . . . something about them gives me a bad feeling. Can't quite put my finger on it."

"I know," said Gutsy. "Chong said they were fighting the ravagers. What does that mean? If they're not shamblers and not ravagers . . . what does that leave?"

"Beats the heck out of me, kid. We have a lot more questions than we have answers."

"Well, if anyone who wasn't a ravager got out of the base, I didn't see them. It was pretty crazy, though. Mostly I saw ravagers heading toward town. I ran back right away to warn people."

Ledger nodded. "And by doing that, you probably saved everyone."

"Not everyone," said Gutsy bitterly. "A lot of people died."

He stopped and turned, fixing Gutsy with a hard, blue-eyed stare. "But *all* of them would have died if you hadn't. Focus on that, kid. That's the patch of sunlight in all this."

"Kind of hard to see anything sunny right now."

"You will." Ledger sighed. "Well . . . I hope so, anyway."

They exited through the east gate and walked onto the battlefield. Parts of the big walls of stacked cars had fallen, and most had burned to blackened shells. The heat from those fires weakened the metal of the cars, and the walls now swayed and creaked ominously. Teams worked with pulleys and levers to reinforce the barriers with fresh cars dragged in by mules. It was grueling, backbreaking labor.

And it was slow.

Gutsy looked along the sections that had been repaired and then at the much longer sections that were still undone. The hot morning suddenly felt very cold. Sombra raised up on his hind legs, paws against one of the cars, and whined, as if even an animal could see the danger here.

"God . . . ," she breathed.

"I know," said Ledger.

"It's taking too long."

"I know." He tapped her arm. "Come on."

They walked out into the fields on the other side of the rows of cars, picking their way through one of the many new gaps. Out there she saw so many dead *los muertos* that in places it was hard to know where to step. Thousands of them.

"The ravagers used to be soldiers, right?" Gutsy asked. "So, this whole thing was what? Them just following the Raggedy Man's orders?"

Ledger nodded. "That's what Collins said."

"This may sound weird, but even though I had to fight them and, you know . . . *kill* them . . . I don't actually *hate* the ravagers. And definitely not the shamblers."

A ghost of a smile flickered over Ledger's face. "Why would you? They're driven to kill because of parasites that hot-wire their brains. That's not evil any more than a mosquito or lion is evil. As for the ravagers, it's harder to say if they are evil or still being controlled by the parasites. Maybe not so evil, then, as damaged and directed. The Raggedy Man seems to be able to control what the parasites do, so he's *definitely* evil. He was a serial killer before being injected with the plague."

"Collins and the Rat Catchers are evil, too," said Gutsy.

"Sure they are," said Ledger, "but they don't think so."

"Oh, come *on* . . ."

Ledger ran fingers through his gray-blond hair. "Listen, kid—people don't wake up one day, look in the mirror, and say, 'Hey, I think I'll be evil from now on.' Doesn't work like that. They have a view of the world that may be skewed from another perspective, but it makes sense to them. Sometimes it's greed, and I've gone up against a lot of those types. Criminals, corrupt politicians, heads of multinational corporations.

A lot of harm was done in pursuit of money back in the day. Forests destroyed, the air polluted, the climate damaged . . ."

"How's that not evil?"

"I didn't say it wasn't evil, kid; I said the people who did it didn't *see* it as evil. There's a kind of mind-set that makes some people think that they're entitled to do whatever they want. Maybe because they're already rich, or because they think other people shouldn't have the same rights as them, or . . . well, there are a lot of messed-up rationalizations. There was one guy, a showman, who said that there was a sucker born every minute, which implied that if someone was gullible enough to be suckered, then it was on them and not the person trying to con them."

"That's nuts."

"Sure. But it's how some people think. It's their justification, and it keeps them from admitting to themselves that they're bad. Remember, most hatred is born from fear."

"Collins doesn't seem to be afraid of anyone."

"Oh, she's afraid. Her fear is all wrapped up in her need to save the world," said Ledger. "On some level she thinks everything she's ever done—every life taken, all her moral crimes—will be washed clean if she comes up with a cure. Might happen that way too. Bess Collins could become the most important person in the history of humanity. And people like you and your friends won't even be a footnote in the history books."

They walked through the battlefield for nearly five minutes before Gutsy could find any words that fit in her mouth.

"I hate that she could win. I want to kill her for what she did to Mama."

Ledger studied her. "What if she actually *does* find a cure? Will you still want her dead then?"

Gutsy had no answer to that.

They walked in silence through the field of the dead.

SPIDER WORKED ALL MORNING, HELPING WHERE HE could, looking for more things to do, more places to be. Everywhere in town there was more to be done. Homes to repair. Food and supplies to be salvaged from destroyed buildings. Bodies to be buried. Old and injured people to be taken care of. Animals to be fed.

He dragged Alethea with him, and by noon they were staggering with weariness, covered with dirt and blood, gasping for air, but there was still so much.

They shuffled wearily down the street, heading back to the hospital, having just escorted an injured mother home to the empty house where her husband and eldest daughter would never return. The woman was as silent as a stone, her eyes barely blinking, her dark skin gone sickly yellow with shock. Then the two teens left her there in the wasteland of her life.

Alethea glanced at her foster brother. "You okay?"

Spider shrugged.

"No, seriously," she persisted. "You've been acting weird all morning. I mean weird-*er*. Don't make me have to check you for bites, now. I swear to God I'll—"

"We killed people," said Spider. His voice was nearly empty of anything except breath. No tone, no inflection. A dead voice.

"No," said Alethea, "don't even try to go there. We put some of *los muertos* down. That's all we did."

"We *murdered* those soldiers."

"Who? The ravagers? Sorry, honey—they might have been soldiers once upon a time, but all they were last night were *los muertos* in leather and chains."

"They could speak," said Spider. "They could think. They could remember who they were, and we *killed* them."

Alethea gave a stubborn shake of her head. "Nope. No way. Those freaks were halfway to being *los muertos*, and, okay, maybe they weren't brain-dead shamblers, but they're not *alive*. They're not people anymore."

Spider flinched at her words. "How can you say that? Even the shamblers were people once. And it's not like what happened to them is their fault. And now they're dead because we killed them. I never wanted to kill anyone. Never."

He shook his head and lapsed into a dangerous silence. Alethea tried to touch him, to give him reassurance, but there was no response at all.

When they were six blocks from the hospital, Spider abruptly turned and walked into the mouth of a shadow-darkened alley.

"Hey," called Alethea. But she saw him drop his fighting stick. Saw him sink down into a low crouch and wrap his arms around his head. She saw his body shudder as the sobs—still unheard—tore through him.

Alethea pawed at the tears forming in the corners of her eyes.

She straightened her tiara and went into the alley, knelt down, and pulled Spider into her arms.

Interlude Three

Brother Mercy

FIVE YEARS AGO

"WHAT PATTERN DO YOU WANT?" ASKED THE TATTOO artist, Sister Ambrosia. "You look like someone who'd like thorn bushes, or maybe wasps. Something with some edge, am I right?"

Everyone in the Night Church had their heads shaved and scalps tattooed as a sign of faith and humility before god.

Brother Mercy glanced at a group of women seated on stools a dozen yards away, waiting for their turn with another artist. Leafy was among them. They had not spoken at all in the thirteen months since Mercy had fought the guards to try and save her. Girls and boys were kept apart until they had taken the full reaper vows and underwent the tattoo ceremony.

Leafy—now known as Sister Sorrow—already had her tattoos outlined: hummingbirds dipping their long beaks into the open mouths of lilies, datura, and honeysuckle. She sensed him watching and looked at him, giving a shy, brief smile.

He felt his face grow hot, but in a good way.

"Brother . . . ?" prompted Sister Ambrosia. "I can give you anything you want. Bugs, birds, fish . . ."

"Leaves," he said.

"What kind?" asked the tattoo artist.

"Dead ones," he said, remembering that sacred autumn day. The leaves in her hair had been withered, but all the more beautiful for that. It was as if death's holy hand had touched her that day.

Sister Ambrosia looked at him, then over to Sister Sorrow, and then down at her tools. She wore a small and knowing smile that Brother Mercy did not see.

PART SIX

NEW ALAMO

You have to keep your mind as wide-open as your eyes, because almost nothing is what it seems.

—TOM IMURA

THEY ALL MET BACK IN MR. FORD'S CLASSROOM
around ten that morning.

"Okay, campers, here's where we stand," said Captain Ledger, taking charge of the meeting.

Gutsy, Alethea, and Spider sat in a clump of chairs by the window. Benny and his friends were still clustered protectively around Chong against the opposite wall, as if their closeness could somehow protect him from reality. Ford, Urrea, Karen, and Sam sat on folding chairs between the camps of teens. Grimm and Sombra were asleep, back to back, in a broad patch of golden sunlight.

"Sam and I are going to be heading out soon," Ledger began. "My hope is that we can work out some kind of deal with Collins—maybe even give her a pass to walk away in exchange for a crap-ton of the stuff we need to make more drugs, and enough weapons to stand a chance against the Night Army. Anyone have any objection to that plan?"

Alethea raised her hand. "It sucks."

"I know it sucks, but do you have any objection to trying it?"

"No," she said, adjusting her tiara. "You have my permission to proceed."

Ledger grinned. "Some good news: Jose and Sunny-Day Ray fixed one quad by scavenging parts from the other two. It means that there's only one that'll work, but it runs. Kind of. They warned me that it has to be kept under thirty miles an hour to keep the engine from going kaflooey. Don't even ask me how they found tires that fit. The tires are patched and nearly bald, but we have a working quad, so let's not look a gift horse in the dentures."

"Thank God!" cried Urrea, and Ford nodded, his hand over his heart.

"The downside is that the suspension is shot, and there are some other issues that make the quad a poor choice for two big men with a lot of heavy weapons and gear to piggyback on it," said Ledger. "Which means we have both lost time and need to go by horse. The only upside is that if Collins is where we think she is, it's not that far away, and she's unlikely to have moved on."

"That's a big 'if,'" said Urrea.

"It's what we have." Ledger's face clouded. "And . . . that brings us to some news none of us are going to be happy with. The good news is that Manny Flores has made a batch of the drug. What's bad is that it's not full potency. Best estimates are that Chong, Sarah, and Morton have less than a week before . . . well . . ." He let the rest hang and threw a weak, consoling smile at Chong.

Everyone automatically glanced in Chong's direction, and then over at Karen. Gutsy felt her heart sink in her chest.

Less than a week.

"This does leave us with a few options," Ledger continued, and the others all looked suddenly, desperately hopeful.

"Option one is we send Chong back to California on the quad, because there's a lot more of the drug there."

"Not a *whole* lot," corrected Chong. "It's one of the reasons I came along on this trip: Asheville has the biggest supply, but it might also be threatened by the Night Army. We have a lot more back home than what's here in New Alamo, but not an endless supply. Much as I'd normally volunteer to go back and get the drugs, I think I'll stay here."

"Wait—why?" asked Benny. "It's a good plan."

"No, it's not," said Chong. "I mean, c'mon, look at me, Benny. I can't walk down a set of stairs without throwing up. I get double vision and headaches. Much as I would love, love, *love* to go back home and never leave again . . . do any of you really see me driving all that way?"

"Chong's right," said Nix. "It's a bad plan. He'd be in a ditch half a mile down the road. No offense."

"None taken," said Chong.

"How far is it to your town?" Gutsy asked. "How long would it take?"

Urrea raised his hand like a kid in his own class. "On good roads, it's sixteen hundred miles. Sixty-six hours at twenty-five miles per hour. If you take into account sleep, bathroom breaks, clearing debris from the roads, and avoiding and/or dealing with *los muertos*, figure closer to ninety. With everything going right, that's four days at eighteen hours driving per day."

"It won't be anywhere near that quick, though," Benny said, looking thoroughly stressed. He explained the big detours they'd taken to avoid nuclear strike zones and areas polluted by chemical spills. "I think it would be closer to a hundred twenty hours. That's five days easy, maybe six."

"Six lucky days, sure," said Nix. "We didn't have a lot of lucky days on the way here. Whoever went would get there just as the pills ran out here."

"Might be quicker than that," said Ford, "because now you know the safest route."

"Safest, yes," Nix said, "but not the quickest."

Gutsy raised her hand the way Urrea had and waited until everyone looked at her. "Can I say something?"

"Sure, kid," said Ledger. "We're open to all ideas right about now."

She looked directly at Benny. "When you told me about your trip here, you said you had a radio of some kind. What did you call it? A walkie-talkie?"

"Kind of," said Benny. "What we have is a satellite phone, which has a better range than a walkie-talkie, but it stopped getting a signal a while ago."

"Yeah," Ledger said morosely. "I found it in your saddle-bag and tried it, too. Not a ghost of a signal. We're way out of range."

"Oh," said Gutsy, deflated.

"What'd you have in mind?" Benny asked.

"Well . . . ," she said uncertainly, "I thought that if some-body drove back, they could try calling along the way until they got through, then maybe someone from your town could drive out to meet them. And bring food, fuel, and a big bag of pills. That way, whoever we send could turn right around and come back."

They all looked at her.

"But if the phone isn't working, then . . ."

Ford asked, "Excuse me, but how can we be out of range of a satellite?"

"I was just going to ask that," said Urrea.

"But you're old and slow."

"I'm only thirteen years older than you."

"Sure," said Ford, "but let's face it—they haven't been good years."

Ledger, amused, said, "Satellites aren't built to last forever. A lot of them had their electronics fried when the nukes went off. EMP waves go up as well as down. We probably lost eighty to ninety percent of the satellites over North America right there. Then we have natural failures like onboard computer navigation or systems failure, collisions with space junk, old age, whatever. The American Nation has managed to establish intermittent uplinks with four satellites, two in regular orbit and two geostationary. Problem is that they're not linked, because they belonged to different telecom companies. Only one is military, and it's a weather satellite we've piggybacked off of to bounce calls around." He paused and looked around. "Is *anyone* following me on this?"

"Clinging on by my fingernails," admitted Urrea.

"Gist is that it's not easy to make a call," said Ford.

"Nearly impossible from anywhere in Texas," Ledger agreed. "We managed to get calls from Asheville to the base we had in Nevada and to the Nine Towns in Central California, but that's about it. And that's spotty. Clouds, rain, whatever—it all mucks it up, and you have to wait for the right times of day for the orbiting satellites to fly through the right zones in order to sync up with the ones in fixed orbit."

"That's a problem. What's a solution?" said Alethea.

"Are you saying we *can't* do it?" asked Gutsy.

"No, not from here we can't," said Ledger, "but your idea is pretty darned good, kid. If someone drives to California with the sat phone, I can give them a list of times and ranges where it might be possible to access the signal and make a call." He paused. "It's a gamble, though, and if it doesn't work, then . . ."

"Then they can't get back in time," said Chong.

Ledger nodded.

"But if it *does* work," insisted Gutsy, "then someone from your town could come out here with the drugs. It would cut the time in half."

"Best-case scenario," Ledger said thoughtfully, "is that Solomon Jones back in Reclamation sends the pills, and maybe a group of his Freedom Riders and my own rangers by air."

"Air?" asked Spider, puzzled.

"We have a bunch of helicopters," explained Ledger. "Of all the aircraft that were downed by the EMPs after the nukes were dropped, they were the easiest to repair. The American Nation has a fleet of them. Hundreds. Chinooks, Black Hawks, Apaches—the lot. And we have a bunch of Osprey tilt-rotors. There's one in New Haven, which is south of Reclamation."

"Surely the range is too far for helicopters," said Ford.

"Sure, but we have refueling depots all over the place out there. In California, Nevada, and elsewhere along the route from there back to the capital in Asheville. Not saying they'll send a bird to deliver pills, but Solomon likes these kids, and he's a good guy. Bet you a shiny nickel that's what he'll do."

"If whoever goes can make a call," said Benny.

"Yeah," said Ledger, and despite his words, there wasn't a lot of optimism in his tone. "If."

There was a long moment of silence as they all thought about that.

Then Benny stood up. "I'll go."

"No," growled Lilah, jumping to her feet. "*I'm* going." She said it with enough lethal intent that Benny held up his hands, palms out in a no-problem gesture.

"I can ride with you," he said in a placating tone. "Watch the road. We can switch off driving to make better time."

"No," said Nix, "I'll go with Lilah. And before you say anything, Benny, just think about it. If the quad can't take a lot of weight, then who's best? Lilah is about one twenty. I'm *maybe* a hundred. We're not carrying a bunch of heavy machine guns and grenades and all that assault stuff. Two pistols, my sword, and Lilah's spear, and some food in a trailer pod."

"But . . . but . . . ," began Benny. Then he stopped. "Okay. For the record, I hate this plan."

"Noted," said Ledger. "Let's do it anyway. And I mean right now."

Chong carefully got to his feet and walked over to Gutsy. He wrapped his arms around her and gave her a long hug. "Thank you," he said softly.

"Okay, okay, enough," growled Lilah. She pulled Chong away, turned him to face her, and jabbed a finger into his chest. "We'll get back as soon as we can. In the meantime, you are *not allowed to die*. Do you hear me? You. Don't. Die."

His smile came close to breaking Gutsy's heart. It was filled with love and compassion. It was clear that all Chong—sick, dying Chong—cared about was not breaking Lilah's heart.

If there were better reasons to cling to life, Gutsy couldn't think of them.

"WE HAVE WORK TO DO," SAID TRÓCAIRE.

The other refugees—now thirty-four of them—nodded and got to their feet. They were all dressed for the jobs they'd gotten since moving to the town. Waste removal. Light construction. Gravedigging.

Trócaire hugged each of them and whispered their names before releasing them. Ténèbres gave them radiant smiles as they went out, alone or in pairs.

When they were all gone, Ténèbres and Trócaire stood together in the open doorway, watching the sun fall pale and dusty through the smoke from the corpse pits.

"I love you," she said.

Trócaire did not reply. Instead he watched a teenage girl and a battered mixed-breed dog walk along the street. He shivered.

"What's wrong?" Ténèbres asked, frowning.

He licked his lips. "I . . . I don't know, exactly. Just got a weird feeling."

"Why? Because of that girl?"

Trócaire nodded. He leaned out to watch the girl and

the dog walk away. "You know that old blues song? I forget the title, but there's a line about 'bad luck and trouble.' Yes," he said, nodding again. "Bad luck and trouble. That's what she is."

JOSE AND SUNNY-DAY RAY DOUBLE-CHECKED THE quad, and Karen made sure the girls had more than enough food. The trailer pod held extra gas cans. Sam took a few minutes to sharpen Nix's sword, giving it a razor keenness. Ledger went over list of spots where they had the best chance of making contact with the satellites.

Benny and Nix then went a few yards away to hold a brief and very private conversation. There was a lot of hugging and kissing, too. Seeing the sweetness between Nix and Benny made Gutsy yearn to see Alice.

They were all gathered outside the exit of the tunnel, which emptied into the Texas Rose Car Wash, a single-story cinder-block building squatting just off a main highway. The morning was clear and bright, the sun just above the horizon and a few cotton-ball clouds scattered haphazardly in the west.

From the outside, the Texas Rose looked like any other abandoned building in the Broken Lands, with cracked pavement, grimy windows, and dead cars and old bones tangled in the weeds.

"I passed this place a hundred times," said Gutsy. "I never knew."

"Kind of the point of a secret entrance," Ledger said dryly.

The captain went over the functions of the satellite phone in detail, despite both Nix and Lilah assuring him that they already understood how it worked.

"I don't care," he said, and continued his lecture. Gutsy paid a great deal of attention, though, because she found the device fascinating. Ledger had Nix demonstrate the method of making calls, and each time she pressed a button there was a burst of harsh static. He also double-checked that the solar charging panels from Benny's backpack were working. When he was completely satisfied, he stepped back, folded his arms across his chest, and frowned. It was the first time Gutsy had seen him look truly worried.

Lilah hugged Chong for a very long time, kissed him, hugged him again, and then pushed him back. "I mean it," she warned. "Don't die."

"Staying alive," said Chong. "Got it. Top of my to-do list."

Lilah gave a stern nod and then stalked to the quad, snapping her fingers for Nix to follow. Nix, amused, shrugged and went to climb onto the back; however, Gutsy ran up and pulled her aside. She bent close and spoke rapidly in Nix's ear. The little redhead listened, then looked up at Gutsy, smiled a great smile, and nodded. Then she climbed onto the back of the quad. Lilah started the engine and drove off without another word. Nix looked back until they were out of sight, lost in dust and distance.

"What was that all about?" asked Benny, but Gutsy just shrugged.

"Maybe nothing," she said. Benny started to say something else, then let it go.

The sound the machine made was so strange to Gutsy. Machines were rare in her world, and those that worked were usually clockwork, steam-driven or hand-cranked. She shook her head.

"So loud," Spider said, mirroring her thoughts. "How did people deal when there were machines like that all over? Cars and planes and all that?"

"After a while," said Ford, "we stopped hearing all of that noise."

"Really? That doesn't seem possible. Or smart."

"Possible, yes. Smart . . . well, we didn't have zombies back then."

"Must have been nice," said Alethea.

Urrea sighed. "I don't know; there's a lot to be said for silence."

They watched the dust blow away. When the road was clear, there was no sign of the two fierce girls on the noisy little machine. Silence reclaimed the morning. Gutsy looked south to where sunlight gleamed on the fenders and glass of the cars that made up the walls of New Alamo. From this distance, which was close to two miles, the town looked whole, and she so wanted to accept that lie.

"Now we wait," said Benny. "Swell."

"No," said Sam firmly, "now we find Site B."

He went into the tunnel, and almost everyone followed except Ledger, who stopped Gutsy with a light touch on her arm.

"That satellite phone idea was pretty brilliant," he said.

She shrugged. "Not really. I'm just trying to be practical, I guess."

"Trying and succeeding, kid, which makes you pretty formidable."

"For a kid, you mean," she retorted. "That's what you keep calling me."

Ledger grinned and sat down on an ancient wooden chair that was in one corner of the room. "Oh, heck, I call everyone younger than me 'kid.' Don't mean it as a slight. No . . . what I meant was that you're formidable as a *person*. Age has nothing to do with it. Makes me wish I'd met Mama Gomez, because my guess is you got a lot from her."

Gutsy said nothing. She shifted uncomfortably because she hated compliments and never knew how to react. Ledger gestured to another chair and she sat, perching on the edge.

"You remind me of myself when I was a kid," he said. "You see, I had some very bad things happen to me when I was about your age. Someone I loved was hurt, and I couldn't do anything to help. All I got to do was bury her."

"That's . . . horrible," said Gutsy. "I'm so sorry. But why are you telling me this?"

"I saw you with Collins before she escaped. You have a lot of control, but there is a whole lot of rage, too. Bess Collins killed your mom. She killed a lot of people you knew. You want revenge, but that can't be your main goal in life. It can't be what drives you."

"Oh, I don't know, Captain," Gutsy said tartly. "It seems to me that revenge is a pretty practical game plan."

He gave her a cold, appraising look. "Sure, kid, and that's how it feels sometimes. I've gone after revenge a bunch of times, and even got it more than my fair share. Maybe it balanced some cosmic scales, but I'm not so sure if it ever did me any real good."

"You're alive."

"Sure. And almost everyone I ever really loved is dead," he said. "My wife and kid. Gone. My whole family. Gone. Ever since the dead rose, I wake up every morning and beat the crap out of myself for not having been in the right place at the right time to stop all this from happening."

Again, Gutsy said nothing.

"You have friends here," said Ledger. "Alethea and Spider love you. And you have that girl, what's her name?"

"Alice."

"You have Alice. If you let yourself get twisted up inside because of a need to find and punish Collins, you could lose all of that."

"What am I supposed to do?" Gutsy demanded. "Just let Collins go?"

"Let me put it this way," said Ledger. "We're in a war, so sure, we have to be warriors. If we, as warriors, want to not only survive the war but have a place waiting for us when the battle is done, then we have to fight for the living, not the dead. If anything, that shows how much we love those who've passed, because we are not throwing our lives away on a gesture that the dead can't care about."

He took a breath and let it out as a crooked smile formed on his lips.

"You have a great poker face, kid. I can't tell if I'm reaching you at all or just wasting my time."

Gutsy rested her hand on the doorjamb of the entrance to the tunnel.

"I hear you," she said. "And I appreciate—"

The glass windows of the car wash exploded inward toward them in a shower of glittering shards as dozens of howling figures crowded in.

Interlude Four

Brother Mercy and the Strike Team

FOUR YEARS AGO

BROTHER MERCY LED THE RAID. IT WAS HIS FIRST TIME as the leader of a reaper strike force. Being one of the soldiers in previous raids was different. Frightening. But also exhilarating, because he knew that both Saint John and god were watching.

Now it was different.

Now he was in charge, and neither Brother Peter nor Saint John were there to guide him. Now it was Brother Mercy who was in charge. Fifteen years old and in charge of forty reapers, some of them three times his age. Many of them much more experienced in combat.

The young reaper stood in the shadowed entrance to an old shopping mall. Outside, dozens of heretics labored in geometric fields that once had been the landscaped green spaces scattered throughout the parking lot. They laughed and talked among themselves, unaware there was any danger. Brother Mercy and several key reapers had come here as refugees and joined the community. They were being trained to farm. Everybody was welcome here, but everyone had to work.

That was fine, thought the young reaper. He had come here to work. To do his god's work. He didn't mind a little physical labor in the meantime.

Brother Mercy's hand trembled as he drew his long knife. Sweat chilled his body despite the heat inside the mall. He licked his lips, which had gone dry. With his free hand, he raised a silver dog whistle to his lips, took a deep breath, and blew.

From the woods all around the mall, a sound rose up in response—a deep, awful, enormous moan of hunger. Rank after rank of the living dead broke from the tree line on the far side of the parking lot. The farmers saw them and screamed, dropping their sacks of fruit and baskets of vegetables, and they ran for safety.

Straight toward the mall entrance. Toward Brother Mercy.

Brother Mercy allowed the heretics to get very close before he spoke two words to the reapers clustered behind him.

"For god," he said. And the knives of the reapers flashed.

The day turned dark with a beautiful shade of red.

PART SEVEN

THE ROAD HOME

No passion so effectually robs the mind of all its powers
of acting and reasoning as fear.

—EDMUND BURKE, On the Sublime and Beautiful

NIX AND LILAH DROVE OUT OF SIGHT.

To Nix it felt weird. She could actually feel herself leave the energetic connection she usually felt with Benny. It was strange and unsettling, like stepping out of the world she and Benny had shared for so long. The last time they had been physically distant from each other for any length of time was when Charlie Pink-eye and the Motor City Hammer had kidnapped her. It was only a couple of days before Benny helped her escape, but it was their longest time apart.

Not that they had been glued at the hip. After the reaper war, she'd broken things off with Benny, needing to explore who she was. She still saw him during that time, and continued to train with him and their friends, learning a lot of deadly skills from Captain Ledger. Later, when they started seeing each other again, it was more on her terms. Or on even terms, with Benny growing into his own confidence and not *needing* her.

The trip from home to New Alamo—all those long miles on the quads—gave Nix a lot of time to think. About life. About her future. And about Benny. She knew she loved him, but was no longer so sure that romantic love mattered all that much to her. She knew that the battle with Charlie and the Hammer, the search for the airplane, and the reaper war had completely warped the process of growing up for all of them. They were so much tougher and more experienced than sixteen-year-olds should be. At least as far as what she always expected life to be like at that age. At the same time, she was mature enough to know that she wasn't yet mature. Not completely.

Nix had no real idea what that meant. Maybe it would mean she needed to spend time alone again. Maybe for a long time.

She turned to look back and saw that New Alamo had become merely a glint of metal and a smudge of smoke, lacking any details.

Lilah drove, pushing the quad as fast as she dared.

She tried to feel the machine as if it were an extension of her own body, just as—in combat—she felt the spear as an extension of her arm. Lilah wanted it to be strong, to be capable, and willing to blow past its own limitations. The engine's growl was reassuring, but every time she goosed the speed past twenty-five miles an hour, it shuddered. As if it were afraid of going too fast. Or afraid of what was waiting out there, standing between them and saving Chong.

Lilah knew it was stupid to think of the quad as anything more than a dumb machine, and the shudder as more than leftover damage from what Captain Collins did.

That did not change how she felt. Not one bit.

"Come on," she told it, speaking low so Nix wouldn't hear. *"Come on."*

The machine tried.

Lilah believed that because she needed to believe it.

"Come on."

Seated behind her, Nix heard the words, knowing full well that she was not meant to. It hurt her heart. Lilah was so strong, so skilled, so dangerous that it was easy for most people to think that she was this invulnerable goddess of combat. The kind of hero who went joyfully into every battle and lived for whatever kind of bloody conflict was coming next.

Nix knew Lilah. She knew about how the Lost Girl became lost. She'd been part of group of refugees, had seen her mother die giving birth to Lilah's sister, Annie. Had lost all of those people and then she and Annie wound up in the fighting pits of Gameland, a horrific place where children were forced to fight zombies so corrupt people could place bets. The sisters escaped, but Annie was murdered in the process. When she reanimated, Lilah had been forced to silence her sister forever. The Lost Girl became lost indeed. For years she hid in the mountains and spent her days hunting evil men like the ones who'd captured her and Annie.

It was Nix and Benny who found her. Together with Benny's older brother, Tom, they had destroyed Gameland. They took Lilah back to their town, where she met and fell in love with Chong.

However, neither revenge on her sister's killer nor the love and support she found in Mountainside could bring Lilah all the way back from the remote places where her mind lived.

What Nix understood and Lilah probably knew subconsciously was that this love was built as much on fear of abandonment as it was on true affection. Maybe the Lost Girl believed that if she lost Chong, who else could ever love her as much or as freely?

As they drove, Nix's mind wandered from Lilah to the troubles they were running from. Or was it toward? Her perspective seemed askew.

Nix thought about the name the people in New Alamo used instead of Rot and Ruin. The people here called it the Broken Lands. That almost made her laugh, because everything and everyone was broken in one way or another.

All the king's horses and all the king's men couldn't put Humpty together again.

The rhyme jangled in her head like notes played on an out-of-tune piano.

Yeah, she thought. *That's all of us.*

Lilah tapped her with an elbow, and Nix turned to follow her pointing finger. Ahead was a patch of smoke. Dark and oily, rising in a slow column into the blue sky.

Nix leaned close and yelled, "You think that's the hidden base?"

"Has to be."

"Don't get too close," Nix warned.

Lilah pointed with her spear. "Look, over there . . ."

A thousand yards from the smoking crater of what had been the base was a group of tattered figures. Lilah slowed and stopped so they could both study them through binoculars.

One corner of the exposed base was relatively undamaged, and several zoms milled around, pawing at flickering fire or curls of smoke. They all wore the burned tatters of military uniforms, and a few still had helmets and holstered sidearms.

"Are . . . are they zoms?" asked Lilah. "Or people from the base who managed to get out?"

Nix studied the figures. "I don't know. . . ."

One of them must have seen her movement and raised his head. He stared at the two girls. She could see him peering through the haze. Then the zom did something Nix had never seen one of the dead do before: he used the flat of his palm to shade his eyes. Then the dead thing raised his other hand and pointed *directly at them*.

"He's still alive—" Nix began, but then her mouth fell open in shocked silence.

The zom opened its mouth, not to moan with hunger but to utter an ear-splitting howl of inhuman hate.

And then it leaped like an ape onto the pile of debris and began climbing madly toward them. The girls flinched in horror and surprise. Lilah got to her feet and gripped her metal spear, while Nix backpedaled and whipped her sword free of its scabbard. The zombie climbed faster and faster, still howling—and now others joined it. They jumped onto the chunks of stone and pulled themselves up the twisted metal struts. First only a handful, but soon others came running out of the inner compound, out of what was left of the base. Ten more. A dozen. Twenty. More and more of the dead soldiers. They saw the figures on the edge of the crater, and the sight drove them to madness. They climbed over one another, kicking and snarling, howling with insane rage.

It wasn't anything either of the girls had ever seen. It was wilder and yet somehow more dangerously focused even than the R3 zombie mutations they'd fought in Nevada the previous year. And it was stranger than the ravagers. This, they both knew, was some *new* mutation. Maybe it had been caused by the mix of all those chemicals and biological samples down in the base. Maybe it was something else entirely. All Nix and Lilah knew was that if those creatures got out of the pit, they were both going to die. Quickly and very badly.

This was a fight they could not win.

Lilah drove off as fast as she could. The wild zombies chased them. They were so whipped up into a frenzy that they slashed at the air with their fingernails, bit at the plume of dust behind the quad, and chased the girls for miles.

And miles.

And miles.

PART EIGHT

THE ROAD TO ASHEVILLE

My first wish is to see this plague of mankind, war, banished from the earth.

—GEORGE WASHINGTON

MORGIE AND RIOT WERE MORE ALERT AND NERVOUS as they continued on their way—partly because the zebras had totally freaked them both out, and partly because everything seemed to be getting stranger. Wilder mutations in animals, insects, and plants. Strange clouds of chemicals that hung almost unmoving in the air. Rain that came in squalls and burned on their skin.

Morgie was jolted out of his troubled thoughts when he saw Riot, who was a quarter mile ahead, suddenly slow and pull over onto the shoulder of the highway. He stopped next to her. They were on the entrance to an overpass that crossed Texas 111. He turned off his engine and joined her over by the guardrail.

Below them, covering the whole of the road, was a gas station for big rigs, with huge white tank trucks and some scattered buildings. Everywhere, sprawled like broken dolls, were bodies. All around them, and splashed on every possible surface, was blood. Red and black. Human and zombie. Buzzards and crows pecked at the human corpses, and flies swarmed around the zoms. They could see small creatures—rats and lizards—scampering in and out. It was a frenzy of savage appetites.

"What happened here?" asked Morgie.

"Let's go look," Riot said.

Together they climbed down from the overpass toward the scene of the carnage. The birds, animals, and insects moved. The sluggish breeze toyed with torn strips of clothing. Everything else, though, was still.

Still as death, thought Morgie, appreciating the old simile for what it really meant.

They went all the way down and moved together through the mass of bodies, each of them angled to watch half the area, trusting the other to do the same.

Morgie's sneakers crunched on shell casings, and he stooped to pick one up. Sniffed it and then handed it to Riot. She smelled it as well, and looked around with the critical eye of someone who has seen slaughter many, many times.

"How long ago?" asked Morgie. "Last night?"

"This morning," said Riot. "Dawn or a little later. See? Some of them bigger pools of blood ain't dried yet."

Morgie straightened. "Seeing a lot of shell casings. Pistol, hunting rifle, and shotgun."

Riot gave him a troubled nod. "How many living people, you reckon?"

"Has to be twenty or thirty," Morgie said, looking around. It wasn't always easy to tell regular corpses from those of freshly turned zoms.

"And at least three hundred zoms," observed Riot. "I don't see any guns."

"Yeah," said Morgie, frowning. "You think the people won and then grabbed all the guns before they left?"

"Maybe," said Riot, but there was doubt in her voice.

"That soldier Benny talked to said something about the Night Army," said Morgie. "Kind of wonder if this was them."

Riot squatted down beside one of the dead humans. It was a woman of about thirty, with brown skin and a head cloth stained with blood. Riot gingerly lifted one of the woman's hands, fighting the stiffness of rigor mortis. The arm only bent slightly, so she leaned close to peer at it, then indicated that Morgie should take a look. He knelt and saw a lot of dark specks against her skin.

"Powder burns," Riot said. "She was firing a gun. Look at all the shell casings around her. She died hard."

They moved among the dead, seeing more evidence of the fight and what had killed each of these people. Head or spine trauma in every case. Any who'd died in other ways would have turned to zoms long before now. But there was something strange about some of the corpses.

"Hey," said Morgie, pointing to the face of a short, heavy Asian man. "Look at his face."

"It's a burn," said Riot. "So what? Could have been from that rain."

"I don't think so," he said. "We both got soaked. It hurt and all, but it didn't do this to us." He pointed to a white woman wearing camo pants and a T-shirt with similar burns on her face, neck, and upper arms. "See? And that woman over there? Same burns. And this big guy right here."

"Yeah, I see."

"You know what I'm *not* seeing? Burns like that on any of the zoms. Not the ones that look like they zommed out a long time ago."

"You're right," said Riot. "It's only on people who look like they died in this fight."

They moved through the battlefield again, this time looking for the same kinds of burns, and finding them on nearly every person. Some extensive, and others only a little.

"Doesn't look like the burns happened *during* the fight, though," said Morgie. "Nobody's clothes are singed."

"Whatever it is," said Riot, backing away, "I don't like it. Let's get the heck out of here."

THEY REACHED THE TOWN OF SCHULENBURG THAT
night and slept safely but uneasily in the storeroom of the
Potter Country Store. They'd hoped to find some old, pack-
aged food that hadn't been looted, but the store looked to
have been stripped down to bare shelves and floorboards.
They pushed empty refrigerated-food cases in front of the
doors, ate a meal of cold rabbit Riot had killed and smoked
days before, and sat up late, both of them unable to sleep.

Morgie didn't start any conversation but willed Riot to
say something. After two hours of silence, she said, "Ain't a
soul in this town. Not one."

"I know."

"You got any theories on that?"

Morgie shrugged, then realized she couldn't see that in
the utter darkness of the locked office. "They didn't all wander
off," he said. "Sign outside town said the population before
the plague was over twenty-eight hundred. Some of them
would have been living people who got out. Some would have
zommed out and gone wandering off. But there should still
be a bunch here, roaming around town or just standing and
waiting. You thinking ravagers, maybe?"

Riot frowned. "Maybe. Or disease. Or it could have been reapers. We—I mean, *they* had strike teams this far east."

Something occurred to Morgie. "You know, these ravager guys seem to be doing just about the same thing the reapers did. You think there's some kind of connection?"

Riot thought about it. "I . . . don't really know. Saint John and my mom had a lot of plots going on. They had scouts everywhere. Who knows what they were cooking up?"

"Yeah," said Morgie, "but *Night* Army and *Night* Church . . . ? Two big armies using zoms as shock troops? Come on . . ."

Riot stared at him for a while, then shivered and looked away.

Eventually they fell asleep. In Morgie's dreams the zoms had somehow shrunk down to the size of ants, and in the middle of the night they crept in through his ears and nostrils and open mouth. Once there, they began eating him from the inside out. He could feel the thousands of tiny mouths biting him, tearing at his veins and muscle tissue and tendons. And he could feel the infection of their bites flooding through his blood, polluting him, killing him without the mercy of permanent death.

He woke in absolute darkness, slapping at his skin with furious hands, gasping and on the very edge of screaming. Then he realized it was a dream and shoved a fist into his mouth to stifle the shriek.

Morgie sat there, quivering, sweating, telling himself that it was only a dream. Even though it felt like something far more real.

"LET'S GET OUT OF HERE," MUTTERED RIOT AS THEY finished packing the next morning. "This whole place gives me the heebie-jeebies. I'd be right happy to lose this town in my rearview."

"Yeah," Morgie agreed as he bent to pick up his gear. He suddenly turned aside as a massive belch erupted from his stomach. It seemed to come out of nowhere, and was so big it actually hurt. "Oh jeez . . . I'm so sorry . . ."

Riot laughed. "Wow. They could probably hear that all the way back home."

Morgie mumbled more apologies as his face flushed with embarrassment.

Suddenly he belched again. Only this time he felt his breakfast rush up hot and acidic from his belly. He threw up behind the fender of a rusted car.

"Damn, boy," said Riot. "You dying on me here?"

Morgie sagged against the car, his face greasy with sweat.

"Whoa . . . hey, now . . . ," Riot said in a voice suddenly punctuated with concern. "Are you sick or something?"

He pulled a handkerchief from his pocket and mopped his face. "I . . . I don't know. Stomach's suddenly all messed up."

She came over and took him by the arm. "You need to sit down?"

Morgie thought about it, then slowly shook his head. "No. It's okay. It's passing, I think . . ."

"You look like death only slightly warmed over."

"Gee, thanks." He belched again, though not as dramatically this time. "Must be something I ate."

They had both eaten exactly the same things, but Riot did not comment on it. Two deep vertical lines were etched between her brows.

"We can stay here for a bit, Morg. Hang out and then start fresh tomorrow."

"No." He began to walk toward his bike, his legs feeling like they were made of overcooked macaroni. "Let's get out of here. We need to get to Asheville."

Riot watched him walk to the quad. He didn't fall, but he didn't look all that stable. When he sat, he thumped down hard into the saddle.

"Morgie . . . ," she began, but he waved her off and started the engine.

"Fine, then," she said under her breath.

They drove away, but the uneasy feelings did not fade with the town of Schulenburg. They passed through La Grange and got all the way to Denverado without seeing a single living person. They saw a few wandering zoms, but only a few. There were other places where it was clear a fight had taken place—each spot littered with those dead whose head or spine injuries either ended their undead lives or prevented them from reanimating. They found more of the strange burns on them.

In each massacre site there was plenty of ejected brass or spent shotgun shell casings, but no guns.

"How many ravagers can there be?" asked Morgie. "I mean . . . they can't seriously be taking all those guns for the zoms to use, can they?"

"God, I hope not," said Riot, looking very scared. Then she turned to Morgie and frowned. "You sure you're okay?"

Morgie dragged a forearm across his brow and looked at the glistening sweat.

"It's just the heat," he said. "I'm fine."

"You sure?"

"Yeah. Totally."

A few miles past the scene of another fight Morgie had to pull sharply off the road. He grabbed a roll of toilet paper from his pack and went scampering off behind a wrecked dump truck.

PART NINE

New Alamo

I do not know with what weapons
World War III will be fought,
but World War IV will be fought
with sticks and stones.

—Anonymous

THE WINDOW GLASS EXPLODED INTO A STORM OF glittering knives. Joe Ledger hooked an arm around Gutsy and yanked her down as death filled the air above them. Gutsy felt some of the shards slice her vest and jeans, and there were tiny detonations of heat, telling her she'd been cut. No way to tell how much or how bad. And no time to care, as a pack of screaming people came pouring into the car wash.

"Kid—get back! Get into the tunnel," cried Ledger as he shoved Gutsy away. "Grimm—*hit, hit, hit!*"

The massive dog uttered a ferocious growl and plowed into the attackers, slashing at them with the spikes that jutted from his heavy armor. Sombra, however, held his ground, growling but clearly too terrified to attack these strange creatures.

The attackers were not shamblers. They wore military uniforms or white lab coats, and a few had on the bland coveralls of janitors. She knew at once that these were the same kind of killers who'd attacked the school. Their faces were twisted into masks of total madness. They were faster and even more wild than ravagers, some carrying weapons like knives, scissors, tree branches, and rocks. One had a chopper torn from a paper cutter, which he brandished like a sword. They screamed terrible, prolonged wails of bottomless hate as they boiled through the shattered windows like cockroaches exposed to sudden light and attacked with a level of mania Gutsy had never seen.

Grimm tore apart the first wave of them, but many more were fighting their way past the razor-sharp teeth of glass still stuck in the window frame. Gutsy scrambled to her feet as Ledger rose to one knee, his big automatic in his hands as he fired and fired. Thunder boomed in the confines of the car wash, and every bullet the soldier fired hit a target, there were so many of these mad killers. Some fell, crippled and bleeding dark red blood, but even they tried to crawl forward to kill.

Gutsy had a machete strapped to her hip that she'd gotten from the general store. The crowbar had been useful, but it was heavy and slow, and she'd always preferred the wide-bladed knife. But as she pulled it free, the weapon felt suddenly inadequate. There were so many of them, and it felt like trying to stop a hurricane with an umbrella. She backed away, edging toward the big double doors to the underground corridor.

The slide locked back on Ledger's pistol, and he reached for a fresh magazine, swapping it in place while backpedaling. Grimm, superbly trained, turned and attacked the infected who tried to take advantage of the brief pause. The new magazine in place, the slide snapped into position, and soon Ledger was firing again. The display of marksmanship was impressive, but Gutsy saw with horror that there were no additional magazines on the captain's belt. Ten of the attackers lay dead and five others were wounded, but there had to be twenty or more still crowding in.

Gutsy turned and looked at the tunnel doors, which were a dozen feet behind them. Ledger and Grimm were holding the line, but if they turned to run, the horde would pour in and overwhelm them before they could get to the tunnel. And even if they somehow managed it, the doors might not hold. The reality chilled her to the marrow.

They were going to lose.

"No!" she growled, and leaped forward, swinging the machete, cutting with the heavy blade. Sombra, confused about what he should do, retreated to the wall and crouched there, tail between his legs, shivering and wretched.

Each blow of the machete did awful damage to reaching arms or howling faces, but cleaving through muscle and bone sent painful shocks up Gutsy's arm. They battled on, and time lost all meaning. Her arms moved, her feet adjusted to drive power into each blow or shifted to yield ground. Breath burned in her throat, and her heart beat like a snare drum.

"Gutsy," roared Ledger, "retreat left."

At first it seemed like a crazy suggestion, because to go left would be to move between the wall and the rusted heap of a delivery van, which was the long way to the tunnel. But then she understood. The van was parked close to the wall, which gave only a narrow alley for the attackers to come at them two or three at a time. The longer way to the tunnel was the safer, smarter choice. Maybe the only possible choice.

All of this flashed through Gutsy's mind, and she began edging that way. The shrieking horde followed.

They're not smart, Gutsy thought as she swung her blade with each sideways and backward step. *They want to kill us so much that they can't plan the best way to do it.*

Even as she fought, Gutsy's logical mind was assessing and evaluating. The intelligence of these creatures was greater than the shamblers—evident by their use of weapons—but less than the ravagers, who could plan and strategize. She also noticed that none of the ones she fought had obvious bite marks. Virtually all shamblers did, because that was usually how they died. Ravagers had some, but not always. These new mutations—if that's what they were—had none.

A killer swung a broken broom handle at her, and as Gutsy ducked, she chopped down on his foot. The thing toppled over and screamed, but whether it was in pain or frustration, Gutsy couldn't tell. Although not badly injured, the fallen attacker caused two more of them to trip over him. Gutsy took one across the back of the neck, and Grimm ripped the other apart. A few feet to the left, Ledger was burning through his last magazine. There were heaps of dead now, but more seemed to be coming out of nowhere, drawn by the noise of combat. They tripped over corpses and crawled forward, compelled by their awful bloodlust.

The only advantage Gutsy, Ledger, and Grimm had was how tight the space was for the fight. If this attack had taken place in the open, they would have been overwhelmed already. Here, though, the infected had to come at them in a half circle, and the floor was littered with their own dead, creating obstacles. Grimm further disrupted things by hurling his bulk against the legs of undamaged killers, breaking bones and dropping them before slashing their throats and faces with his shoulder spikes.

Ledger's magazine was spent, and, without the slightest pause, he rammed the empty pistol into the face of one of the maniacs, kicked another in the hip so that it fell back against two others, and drew his sword with movement fast as lightning. Suddenly the air was filled with drops of red as the attackers seemed to fly apart.

One of the killers dove at Gutsy, but she twisted around and chopped down with the blade. The lunge turned into a fall, and Gutsy smashed down with the butt of the machete.

"Into the tunnel!" roared Ledger as he backed away, losing ground step by desperate step. "Get ready to close the doors!"

Behind them, the big set of double doors stood slightly ajar, and beyond that was the slope that led down from the fake office of the Texas Rose Car Wash to the corridor that ran straight to a secret entrance in the hospital. It was the only possible way out, but they had to get inside and pull those doors closed.

Gutsy had no choice; she had to retreat, but these savage living dead were everywhere. Some were clearly smarter than their fellows, and these few seemed to understand what she was doing. Their howls changed in pitch as four of them tried to circle her. Gutsy swung her weapon with all her strength. Pain bloomed like heat in her shoulders and lower back, and her breath rasped out of her. There was no time to rest.

Then the blade of her machete missed a killer as an infected woman leaned back to *evade* the blow. None of *los muertos* had ever done that before, and even the ravagers were often incapable or unwilling to get out of harm's way. But this female soldier did it, and as a result Gutsy's blade struck the thigh of the maniac next to her and lodged tight in a heavy femur bone. The infected woman grinned like a ghoul, grabbed the handle of the blade, and tore it from Gutsy's grasp with such force that it knocked Gutsy off balance. She fell onto a killer whose skull she'd crushed. The monsters howled in delight and rushed to leap on her.

But something struck the infected woman like a missile, driving her back into the others.

Sombra.

Somehow the coydog had fought past his own terror and helplessness, for her. Or maybe there was only so far the dog part could go before the feral coyote emerged. The coydog's powerful jaws snapped, and the female soldier's reaching arm was suddenly handless.

"*Noooooooo!*" screamed Gutsy. To bite the dead meant that infected blood and tissue were now in the animal's mouth. In Sombra's saliva.

The coydog had reverted to pure predator, shedding its concern for its own life in order to protect the first human who'd shown him kindness. It was an act of both animal savagery and of love.

Gutsy, riding on the edge of panic, snatched up her machete, shook off the dead hand that still gripped it, rose to her feet, and attacked. If her coydog was going to die, then it would not be in vain. She swung and smashed and cut and chopped, and the screaming infected fell before her.

Ledger was fighting now with his *katana*, and the sword was a glittering blur, as if he was painting the air with molten silver. He body-blocked Gutsy sideways, knocking her toward the van, and then stepped in front of her. Grimm smashed into anyone who tried to grab her. Gutsy lost sight of Sombra and screamed.

"Get inside!" roared Ledger. "Try to get one of the doors

closed!" When Gutsy didn't move, he shifted his sword to one hand and pushed her through the open doorway with the other. She stumbled and fell a few feet down the slope, caught the bannister, and ran back up to grab the edge of one heavy door. Ledger backed into the entrance, then stepped aside like a matador to allow Grimm to pass by. There wasn't enough room, however, and one of the dog's spikes slashed a vicious red line across Ledger's thigh. He cried out as blood poured down his leg, but he kept fighting the relentless monsters pressing forward.

"*Sombra!*" wailed Gutsy, but she could not see the dog. The cries of the infected seemed to blow past her like the wind and filled the stone corridor with horror.

It was all Ledger could do to stay on his feet and fight, but he wasn't able to close the door because too many of the infected crowded around him. Gutsy ran back up the slope, chopping with the heavy machete, hitting faces and chests and hips, knocking several of them away from the soldier. It gave her the chance to grab the handle of one of the two big doors and push it shut. It clicked into place, but the other was open, the way blocked by a huge soldier who kept trying to grab Ledger's clothes and hair and wrists.

Then, abruptly, Ledger staggered backward and down as a smoky four-legged body hurled itself over him and through the doorway. Sombra struck Gutsy, and the two of them fell backward down the slope, being brutalized by every inch of the concrete ramp. Gutsy wrapped her arms around Sombra as they rolled. The collision tore yelps from her and the coy-dog, and then the corridor floor punched the air out of her lungs. Grimm jumped over them, skidding on the concrete floor. He scrambled around and started back toward the ramp to help his master, but there was a loud *whooom* as Ledger slammed the other door shut.

There was a moment of stillness and silence.

"Will it hold?" whispered Gutsy.

As if in cruel answer, the mass of the howling killers slammed into the doors. They bowed inward against the locks. The doors held, but dust puffed out from around the hinges.

Ledger didn't need to answer her question. He threw his weight against the door just as the second impact hit. The whole tunnel seemed to tremble. Cracks splintered outward from the hinges.

"Run," he gasped, pushing back against the press of all those bodies.

"Let's go," she said, but then the horror of what he meant hit her. He wanted *her* to run.

"Come on," she pleaded. "We can both make it."

"Not with this leg, kid," he said. "They'd bust through and catch me before I got a quarter of the way up the tunnel."

"Lean on me," she begged. "I can help you."

"Sure, and maybe we'd get halfway there before they swarmed us." Ledger wiped sweat from his eyes. There was a bleak acceptance in his face, and it broke her heart to think that someone who'd fought so long, won so many battles, would simply die down here in the dark like this. He caught her studying him and gave her a fierce grin. "Everybody dies sometime. At least I can buy you enough time to get all the way to the other end. Block it solid. The door there should hold. Forget this tunnel. If things go bad, find some other way to get everyone out of town. Now come on—*go!*"

Gutsy felt the horror of it rise up inside of her. A dozen bad reasons to stay with him filled her mind. Grimm growled softly, and Sombra whimpered.

"I'm sorry," cried Gutsy.

Then she turned and ran.

SPIDER SAT IN A CHAIR IN THE EMPTY STORAGE ROOM. His *bo* was on the floor and his chin propped on his fists as he stared a hole into the middle of his thoughts.

When they'd come back from seeing the two California girls off, he lingered to wait for Gutsy. He didn't mind that they seemed to be taking their sweet time. Being alone was okay with him. Especially now.

He felt strange. Stranger than usual, and Spider generally felt strange. Most of the time it was a matter of feeling like he did not belong in New Alamo. Not in the Cuddlys' orphanage, not in school, not in town. The more people thought he was an oddball, the odder he wanted to become. He was aware that he was unlike anyone he'd ever met—partly because of how he looked. When the town was formed, built on the bones of a detention facility for what were called undocumented workers, the population had been mostly made up of white people, Latinos, and a few Native Americans. Very, very few African Americans, and no one at all in the community with skin as dark as his.

As he sat, he brooded on how everything was changing.

And how those events were changing him. For years he'd trained with the *bo* until he could make the stave spin like a whirlwind. He'd sparred with Alethea and Gutsy, went out into the Broken Lands and fought a hundred mock battles with dead trees, withered cacti, and even old bones set like targets on rusted car hoods. He'd imagined a thousand battles.

Now he'd fought in two actual battles. Actual life and death. The fact that the victims were the living dead didn't matter.

He had killed. He was a killer. A shiver rippled through his thin body.

How did people *deal* with having committed violence? It was a question he couldn't answer. He knew that fighting had done him some harm. Maybe lasting harm. And Spider was afraid that the person he'd been, the person he *liked* being, might have been beaten to death by his own weapon.

He tried not to look at the *bo* on the floor. He did not blame *it*, of course. The staff was only a tool. But looking at it seemed to trigger the most vivid memories and all the feelings associated with those fights. It was like looking at his own guilt.

He wondered if anything could ever make him want to touch that stick again. Maybe he'd break it up and use the splinters for something good. Stakes for new tomato plants. Tools to dig in the dirt, looking for spiders. Kindling to light a happy fire on a cold desert night. Or—

"Help!"

The scream came from far away, bouncing through the

open doors of the fake cabinet, twisted from the concrete corridor that led to the Broken Lands.

It was Gutsy.

Screaming.

Spider exploded from the chair and snatched up his *bo*, running to help his friend.

GUTSY SAW SPIDER RUNNING TOWARD HER.

"No!" she yelled, waving frantically at him. "Go back! Get help!"

Spider's feet outran his ability to understand her words or warning. By the time he got to Gutsy, she grabbed his shirt and, in a voice so ragged she barely recognized it as her own, told him what happened. Then she shoved him back the way he'd come. Spider was confused, but he didn't waste time trying to sort it all out. Instead he whirled around and raced back to town.

Gutsy turned, too. Sombra stood beside her, reading her intent. He began barking at her, scolding her. Warning her.

"No," said Gutsy. Growling out the word. "No."

She wheeled and ran back to Captain Ledger.

38

"WHAT ON EARTH ARE YOU DOING HERE?" ROARED Ledger. "I told you to get to safety. To warn everyone."

"Spider's doing that," said Gutsy as she threw her weight against the door. The concrete around the hinges was crumbling, and the stacks of canned goods were vibrating their way inward. Gutsy shoved them back, trying to toughen the wall, but she knew—as Ledger did—that if the hinges failed, then the crates would not be enough.

"This door's not going to hold," warned Ledger. "Go barricade the far end of the tunnel."

Gutsy looked at the crates that still lined the hall. The wood was pine. Not very strong. But an idea sprang into her head.

"Hold on," she said, and launched herself from the trembling doors. She grabbed a case of canned pinto beans with both hands, turned it, and dropped it. The case landed on the point of one corner and instantly broke apart, sending cans bouncing and rolling everywhere. Gutsy snatched up two slats and chopped the ends into sharp tapers with her machete. She repeated this with several other pieces until she had a small pile of wooden shims.

Watching, Ledger began to grin. "You are one smart freaking kid."

Gutsy took a shim and stuck the tapered end into the crack between door and frame. It didn't slide in easily, but she managed to force it, hammering it in with the butt end of her machete handle. It only went in a couple of inches and stopped, jammed solid.

She grabbed another shim and repeated the action on the far side of the doorway.

"Between the doors, too," said Ledger. "And underneath. Use them like doorstops."

The reinforcement was not going to stop the maniacs from breaking down the door, but it would definitely slow them down.

"Will this hold long enough?" Gutsy asked, but then followed Ledger's gaze to the cracks around all the hinges.

"Crates," he said, and immediately they grabbed crates of food and began stacking them against the door, building row on top of row. He stacked them higher and she added extra rows until there was a slanted wall, like one side of a pyramid. The two dogs barked and snarled at the things outside. There were not enough to cover both of the big doors, but maybe enough to keep the doors from being smashed in.

The pounding on the other side of the doors was getting more furious, and the hinges were grinding their way out of the stone. It was obvious to Gutsy that if they left now, they'd never make it to safety—and a fight midway along the tunnel would be suicide.

They both leaned their weight against a part of one door that wasn't blocked by boxes. With every impact Gutsy could feel the shock wave go right through her. It felt like punches to the heart.

She heard Ledger hiss and looked down to see him tear open his pant leg. The cut from Grimm's spoke was deep and bleeding freely. She glanced at the dog and saw that almost all of his spikes glistened with the dark blood of those howling monsters. Her eyes met Ledger's, and again there was that fatalistic acceptance.

"Yup," he said, "there's a pretty good chance I'm infected."

"No . . ."

Ledger sighed and leaned his head back to rest it against the crates, gritting his teeth each time the killers slammed into the doors. "Be almost funny if that was how I went out after all the stuff I've dealt with."

"God, how can you even joke about that?" cried Gutsy, appalled.

Another massive strike made the wood around one of the hinges crack loud as a gunshot.

"Who's joking?"

Before she could answer, both dogs began barking. They turned toward the long corridor and—to Gutsy's enormous relief—began wagging their tails.

In the distance, way down the hall, Gutsy could see people running. A lot of them.

"Ah," said Ledger without much excitement, "the cavalry."

"*HURRY,*" SCREAMED GUTSY. "THEY'RE BREAKING through!"

As if to punctuate her fears, three of the wedges popped out from between one of the doors and the jamb as the next barrage struck. The top crates were vibrating, jerking inch by inch away from the assault.

The distant figures in the corridor resolved into shapes. Benny was out front, running like crazy, his sword in one hand; half a step behind him was Spider. Other people were coming, too: Karen and some of the reliable men and women from town. Coming fast, but still a long way down the tunnel.

"Gutsy," warned Ledger, "get back. It's giving way."

She spun and slapped her hands onto the crates, trying to hold back what she could. The doors, battered and weary, finally split apart, breaking inward with such force that the shards punched the whole top row of crates off. Gutsy dove for Ledger, knocking the old soldier backward as the crates smashed down on where he'd been standing.

Then the mass of killers slammed forward so hard that half a dozen crates seemed to dance away from the impact. They toppled down, exploding, sending cans of peas and corn and Spam flying everywhere. The dogs were barking louder, but now they were challenging the monsters who were reaching through the gaps with furious hands. Gutsy scooped up several cans and hurled them like baseballs, hitting faces, breaking fingers, but not stopping the attack. Pain meant nothing to these things. She kept up the barrage, though. When she risked a glance over her shoulder, Benny and the others were still a hundred yards away.

The hinges burst from the wall in showers of flying screws and concrete dust. The wall of boxes was halfway down now, and the doors were crumbling into useless splinters. One of the maniacs thrust his head and shoulders through a gap, biting at the air in Gutsy's direction. She snatched up a big can of pork and beans and slammed it down on the thing's head, once, twice. The creature sagged down, plugging the biggest hole. But it thrashed and twitched—not from its own power, but because the others were tearing at it, ripping at one of their own, destroying what was between them and living flesh.

The creature abruptly vanished, sucked back out of the hole and instantly replaced by the head, shoulders, and reaching arm of a female soldier whose face was a mass of recent burns. She saw Gutsy and her face, already crazy, went madder still. There was something in her eyes. It was a light that seemed to glow with an insanity that ran miles deep. Gutsy had never seen anything like this. This wasn't merely hunger but a bottomless need to *hurt*.

The woman hissed like a snake and then began pulling herself through the hole before Gutsy could shake off her shock.

"Gutsy, *get back*," Ledger bellowed as he swung his sword at the woman. The reaching hands grabbed nothing and fell like dead birds to the floor. The woman kept thrusting forward with her stumps, though—a sight straight out of a nightmare. Her face showed no flicker of awareness of her own mutilation.

Ledger grabbed the corner of one of the remaining crates and tried to shove it against the opening, but his leg suddenly buckled. He cried out and fell. The handless woman squirmed the rest of the way through the hole as hands behind her shoved the way clear for more of the killers.

Gutsy grabbed Ledger and pulled him back. The old soldier groaned as fresh blood poured from his injured thigh. Grimm and Sombra kept lunging forward, biting the wriggling infected, tearing at them.

"*Down*," bellowed a voice, and suddenly Benny was there, pushing past Gutsy and stabbing with his sword. Spider was right beside him, thrusting the end of his *bo*. Karen and Sunny-Day Ray crowded past, and soon there was a small army of people battling the killers.

Spider flinched at the sound of the maniacs' bizarre howling. "What *are* they?"

"They're infected," was all Ledger could manage.

There was a huge *crack*, and the doors gave way completely as a dozen of the monsters poured in. They beat at one another, scrambled past the splintered wreckage of the double doors, climbed over the broken crates, and hurled themselves at the defenders in the hallway.

Ten seconds ago, that would have been a slaughter.

Now the creatures were met with swords and staves,

shovels and pickaxes. And then there was another *crack*. Louder and crisper than when the doors fell, and the closest infected to Gutsy pitched backward, his head seeming to disintegrate in a dreadful cloud of red.

"*Down!*" roared a voice, and everyone dropped or huddled to the sides of the corridor as Sam came walking slowly up the hallway. He had a heavy assault rifle in his hands, the stock against his hip, and although he did not appear to pause or aim, every shot killed one of the infected. He fired, fired, fired.

Gutsy did not know how long the fight lasted. Half a minute? A hundred years? All she knew was that the tide turned against the mad killers, and one by one, they fell. The gunshots and the screams faded until there was no sound at all except the echoes that fled away down the corridor or escaped into the morning sunlight beyond the shattered doors.

"God . . . ," breathed Gutsy.

"About damn time," said Ledger. Then he slid down the wall of crates and sat in a pool of his own blood. His smile never quite left his face, even when his eyes rolled up white and he fell over sideways.

Interlude Five

Brother Mercy and Sister Sorrow

FOUR YEARS AGO

THE STRIKE TEAMS HIT AGAIN AND AGAIN AND AGAIN.

Brother Mercy discovered that he had a talent for planning these raids. He identified those reapers who were best at scouting, gathering intelligence, and fighting. He handpicked a few to infiltrate the settlements—going in wearing wigs or hats to hide their tattoos and dressing in the ragged clothes of survivors. They would become part of the community while sending information back to Brother Mercy.

He was still not yet sixteen and was already one of the Night Church's most effective strike team leaders. Mother Rose mentioned him in her sermons. Brother Peter praised him to the other senior staff. His own reapers bragged that they followed his knife. Saint John told him that he was beloved of Lord Thanatos, all praise to his darkness. It made him feel strong and accepted and useful. But it wasn't what made him wake up with a smile on his lips. It wasn't what lifted his heart over and over all day long.

No. That was *her*.

Sister Sorrow—Leafy—had been assigned to his strike

team. He made her his lieutenant, though in truth he shared leadership with her. She was every bit as sharp as he was, and every bit as devious. Together they purified settlement after settlement, sending hundreds of sinners into the darkness.

He was Mercy. She was Sorrow.

He was in no way merciful.

She felt no flicker of sorrow.

They were in love, and the world opened its red mouths to shout in a collective chorus of darkness.

PART TEN

THE ROAD HOME

When the world says, "Give up,"
Hope whispers, "Try it one more time."

—Anonymous

A CITY SEEMED TO RISE LIKE MAGIC OUT OF THE EARTH, an illusion created by the quad rising to the crest of a rolling hill. And Lilah saw a road splitting off from the main highway that would take them there.

"Hold on," she yelled, and then made a sharp turn. The wheels skidded with a shriek, but then caught and the machine shot forward. The side road was cracked and filled with weeds, but they were trampled down, the broken stalks pointing back toward the highway. Lilah figured a swarm had come from the direction of the town, which meant—she hoped—that there were no zoms left there. It was a crazy gamble, but she needed to find something to give them an advantage again. The screaming zoms were still following, and a couple of them were actually gaining on them. Maybe the maze of buildings would offer protection or conceal-ment. Anything was better than a losing race on the open road.

Nix clung to Lilah with small, icy hands.

The city was a battered ruin, with many three- and four-story buildings burned to blackened shells long ago, and now choked with dense cloaks of ivy and kudzu. There was a sign that read WELCOME TO, but the rest was gone, scoured away by fifteen years of wind and rain.

Once inside the town, Lilah made a series of random turns, following nameless streets, careful not to cross her own trail for fear of running into the pack of killers. She passed failed barricades and makeshift shelters that were torn open and empty.

"I don't see them," said Nix, looking behind them. "I think we—"

Lilah made another turn and then slammed on the brakes. The quad's wheels screamed in protest, sending plumes of rubber smoke up behind them as the machine and its trailer began to slew sideways.

Ahead of them, filling this new street, were zoms.

Hundreds of them.

They all turned toward the growl and shriek of the quad. Many of them were wrapped head to toe in kudzu, proof they had been standing there for years. As one they opened their mouths, and a great moan of sudden hunger bellowed outward from their dusty throats. The dead creatures surged forward, tearing at the vines that held them. Some fell as fragile bones broke from the force of their own effort to move after so long. Others collapsed beneath the mass of the dead behind them.

"Back, back, back," cried Nix, but Lilah was already trying to reverse her course, to drive in a tight circle the way they'd come. There were so many zoms, though, and they were so close. The front rank was only thirty feet away. Several of them broke free of the weeds and stumbled forward, reaching with leathery hands. Nix had her gun in her hand, her finger curling around the trigger, but she hesitated. There were so many of them, and the runners had to be inside the city already. There wasn't enough ammunition. Nowhere near enough.

Then the quad bucked and seemed to leap forward; the jolt caused Nix to clutch her hand in surprise, and her finger jerked on the trigger. The gun bucked in her hand, firing a shot that punched through the shoulder of one of the zoms, doing no harm—but worse, the jolt made her lose her grip on the weapon. It fell, bouncing hard enough on the asphalt to kick up sparks, and skittered away.

"My gun!" she cried, but Lilah was already moving too fast.

The quad burned along the blacktop toward the street they'd just turned off, but both girls screeched in horror as they saw the pack of running killers pelting toward them. Lilah jerked the wheel and took the right-hand street, giving the machine all the gas it could take. The mass of vine-covered zoms flooded out into the intersection seconds ahead of the runners. Nix twisted to look back, expecting to see all of them, fast and slow, chasing behind.

But that wasn't what she saw.

She pounded on Lilah's shoulder. "Stop . . . stop for a sec. Look!"

Lilah slowed the machine and turned. And gaped.

A full block behind them was a sight that made absolutely no sense to either of them.

The zoms were fighting *each other*.

It was like watching a riot. The fast ones seemed to have totally forgotten about the two teenage girls on the quad, and were instead hurling themselves at the mass of shuffling dead. Spitting and biting, all the time howling loud enough to scare legions of pigeons and grackles from the empty windows of the burned buildings.

Slow zoms reeled away from their attackers, twitching and convulsing. Some fell; others staggered clumsily into other zoms, or walked into dead cars and brick walls.

"What . . . ?" Lilah began.

"I don't . . . ," said Nix, but that was as far as she could get. Whatever this was, it was beyond the experience or understanding of either of them. But it was a chance.

Nix used the side of her fist to lightly hammer on Lilah's back. "Go, go."

They left the small city, regained the highway, and headed west at high speed.

THEY DROVE AND DROVE.

When the tank ran low on gas, they stopped and filled it quickly and nervously. When something moved toward them in the tall grass, they turned in terror, expecting it to be the fast monsters.

The stalks parted and a cow came ambling onto the road, trailed by a calf. The girls began to laugh with the release of the terrible tension, but it died in their throats. The calf had four eyes and bleated like a screaming child. The mother turned, and they saw that her flanks were covered with fleshy nodules that looked like stubby fingers. Lilah drew her pistol and aimed it at the animals, but Nix touched her arm and shook her head.

The cow and calf, deformed and hideous, bent their heads and began munching the grass. Sickened and scared, Nix and Lilah finished refueling.

Before they mounted the quad, Nix tried the satellite phone. She got static, as if the whole world was dead.

"Nothing?" asked Lilah as she screwed on the gas cap.

"No."

They stood for a moment, looking at the mutated animals.

A soft, cool wind blew out of the north and stirred the grass. In the distance were the blackened bones of a city whose name they didn't know. The cow and her baby munched noisily.

"I thought it would be different out here," said Nix softly.

Lilah wiped her hands on her thighs. "Different than what?"

"Different than home. Back west there were the reapers and Charlie Pink-eye and Preacher Jack. But we beat all of them, and we paid so much to win."

The Lost Girl nodded.

Nix gave a sour laugh and shook her head. "I thought that after war there was peace. Like . . . a real peace. Something that would last. That's what I was hoping for. How stupid am I?"

She turned away and leaned heavily on the quad, head hanging low. Lilah came over and put a hand on Nix's shoulder; then, after a moment, she laid her cheek on her friend's head.

"No," she said in her hoarse whisper of a voice, "it's not stupid. Hope is what we have left."

Nix straightened, and Lilah stepped back. "Hope? What good is that?"

Lilah pointed to the west. "After my sister and George both died, I lived in a cave for five years. Alone. Everyone I ever loved was dead. Murdered. It was just me and my books and the people I hunted and killed. The zoms and the bounty hunters. That was my world. Hope was all I had." She gave a ghost of a smile. "And you know what hope did?"

Nix said nothing.

"Hope sent me you and Benny. You found me. You fought

beside me. Then you invited me back to your town. To your homes. That's where I met Chong. That's when I fell in love. Hope proved that the world wasn't just death and hiding and pain and all that bad stuff. Hope *saved* me." She slapped the metal handlebar. A sharp, hard sound. "Hope isn't stupid, Nix. Hope is the best weapon we have."

She turned and climbed into the quad's saddle. "We're wasting time. Let's go."

Nix lingered a moment, staring at Lilah. Then she climbed on behind her, and they drove west as the shadows chased them, mile after mile.

Interlude Six

The Raggedy Man

TWO YEARS AGO

"WHO ARE WE GOING TO MEET?" ASKED BROTHER Mercy.

He and Sister Sorrow sat on either side of Saint John on the bench seat of the old-fashioned wagon. It was pulled by four farm horses whose harnesses were hung with red tassels dipped in the chemicals that kept the gray people from attacking. A large expeditionary force of reapers accompanied them, some riding far ahead on quads, two hundred more marching in lines a few miles behind.

"I told you already," said Saint John.

"All you said was that he was a prophet of Lord Thanatos—all praise to his darkness."

"And so he is. What else did I tell you?"

"That he calls himself the Raggedy Man," said Sister Sorrow.

"He has *accepted* that nickname," said the saint. "It was first used in a pejorative way by unenlightened sinners."

"Why?" asked both of the young reapers at the same time.

Saint John shrugged. "You'll understand when you meet him."

They were deep in Ohio, moving through ruined and burned

cities. Many tall buildings had bowed to the ground during the last days of man's failed dominion over the earth. Many thousands of the holy gray people moved like ghosts through the ruins or stood watching the reapers pass with unreadable eyes, their mouths moving as if chewing the memory of meat.

"Who *is* the Raggedy Man?" asked Sister Sorrow. "All I've heard are rumors and some tall tales."

"And what have you heard, my dear?"

She hesitated. "That he was the first of the gray people."

"This is truth. What else?"

"That he can speak to them," she said. "That they listen to him."

"Also true. And . . . ?"

"That he cannot die."

The saint's eyes looked thoughtful. "When the dead were called to rise to cleanse the earth and usher the sinners into the blessed darkness, it began with a single man—one whose kiss was enough to begin the great change."

In the world of the reapers, a "kiss" was what they called a bite.

Saint John said, "He is not like any of the children of Thanatos—all praise to his darkness—you have ever seen. He can speak, and he is eloquent in his understanding of god's purpose. He can *command* them. What we do with dog whistles and much effort, he does with a whispered word. With a thought."

Brother Mercy gaped at him. "Really?"

"Really," said Saint John, and gave one of his rare smiles of genuine happiness.

PART ELEVEN

NEW ALAMO

From error to error, one discovers the entire truth.

—Sigmund Freud

DR. MAX MORTON SAT IN A WHEELCHAIR AND SCOWLED at Manny Flores in a way that made it clear he thought the pharmacist was doing everything wrong. Flores ignored the dirty looks. He was used to them, having worked at the hospital for years.

They were in the small morgue in a remote wing of the hospital, rooms kept cold by noisy old construction-site generators, which were among the few machines that still worked in New Alamo. A stainless-steel autopsy table was positioned under lights that also ran on the generator.

Gutsy, Alethea, and Spider stood in a cluster with Benny and Chong in one corner of the morgue. Sam stood silent as a tree against a wall, arms folded, face without expression. Karen and the Chess Players were seated on the only chairs in the room.

Flores stood over the corpse on the table. The body had been stripped down to boxer shorts and lay pale on the cold steel.

"Here's what we know," said Flores. "This man was a soldier at the base. His uniform was damaged but otherwise new and in good shape, and he still wore dog tags. As you can see, he was badly burned, but there's no evidence that the explosion and fire Gutsy saw at the base is what killed him. Mr. Imura's bullet clearly ended him for good."

"So . . . what *did* kill him?" asked Mr. Urrea. "Smoke inhalation from the burning base?"

"An autopsy will verify that," explained Flores, "but I'm not so sure. With smoke inhalation there are typically burns in the nose, including singed nostril hairs and similar blisters around and inside the mouth. There isn't much evidence of that here, though. The burns he has are more consistent with flash burns. I've taken a large number of samples and will process them when we're done here."

Karen asked, "Dr. Morton, do you recognize this man?"

Morton took a long time before he answered, and Gutsy thought he was probably weighing his options, deciding how much to admit. She saw him give a small shrug, and immediately wince at the pain from the bites on his neck and shoulder.

"I may have seen him around," the doctor said evasively.

"Do you have any theory on what killed him?"

"None," Morton said flatly.

"No theories at all?"

"I just said no, didn't I?"

Sam swiveled his head toward the doctor and gave him three seconds of an ice-cold stare. "Answer the lady's question." There was no actual threat in the sniper's words, and even his tone was soft and calm, but Morton flinched as if struck.

"Okay, okay," said the doctor, "I may have *some* ideas, but I want to see the test results first."

Before he could say more, the door opened and Captain Ledger came in. He was pale and haggard, and he leaned on a cane. Gutsy could see the bulge of thick bandages beneath his left pant leg.

"You kids started the party without me," he said.

Karen stood quickly. "Joe, you shouldn't be out of bed. Come over here; take my chair." She took his arm and helped him sit.

Ledger stretched his injured leg out straight and leaned back, laying the shaft of the cane over one broad shoulder. "Just came from Doc Cantu's office."

Raoul Cantu was the town's veterinarian.

"He ran tests on Grimm and Sombra," said Ledger. "And me."

The room became very still, and Gutsy thought her heart was going to burst. Spider and Alethea took her hands and held on tight.

"There's good news, weird news, and bad news," the captain said. Everyone was staring at him. He glanced at Gutsy. "The good news is that Sombra isn't infected."

Gutsy sighed with huge relief. Spider leaned over and kissed her.

"What about his saliva?" asked Benny. "Gutsy said he *bit* some of those things."

"He did," said Ledger, "but there's no trace of active parasites in his saliva or blood. To be on the safe side, Doc managed to give the pooch a pretty healthy dose of antiseptic mouthwash. Not sure how he managed it, but neither he nor the dog was happy about the process. Oh, and, Gutsy, you'd better go make nice with him, because Cantu has three stitches."

"Oh," Gutsy said. "I'm sorry."

"Tell *him* that. Anyway, he's keeping Sombra overnight for observation. Grimm's been cleared, too, though they're both in quarantine for now. Just in case."

"What about you?" asked Benny, nodding to Ledger's leg. He looked scared.

"Yeah, well, that's the weird-news part," said Ledger. "Doc took samples from Grimm's spikes and every possible kind of sample from me. You don't even want to know what indignities I was put to."

"I agree," said Urrea, "we don't."

"The bottom line is that there's no trace at all of live parasites in any of my samples. Dead ones, sure, but no live ones."

Flores looked at Morton, who was stunned.

"I . . . I don't understand . . . ," breathed Morton. "How can that be?"

"Beats the heck out of me," said Ledger. He nodded toward the corpse on the table. "Which brings me to the bad news. I'm beginning to have doubts that this joker here—and the other freak-jobs we tussled with today—are zoms at all."

"But . . . they attacked us," protested Gutsy.

"Sure, but that doesn't automatically make them zoms. Maybe it's some new mutation, or at least new to us." He sighed. "And, frankly, I don't remember *asking* for something else to worry about. We already have shamblers, ravagers, R3's, half a dozen oddball variations out there in the Rot and Ruin—or in the Broken Lands, for you locals—and a bunch of animals going zom, too. I'm not digging this. I am officially weirded out."

"Join the club," said Alethea.

Ford raised a hand. "For the record, I'm way past being weirded and am into full freak-out."

"Seconded," said Urrea.

"Wait, wait," said Gutsy, "does that mean these mutants— or whatever they are—*aren't* contagious?"

"Not sure we can actually say that," Flores said quickly. "All it means is that they can't infect dogs, and that blood transferred from a secondary source like Grimm's spikes isn't directly infectious. We don't know what an actual bite from these things may do."

Ledger reached out with his cane and tapped the dead soldier's foot. "Speaking of which, you run blood work on him yet?"

"I'll start that when we finish here," Flores responded.

"Maybe get in gear with that. I'd like to get my dog out of quarantine sooner than later. Pretty sure Ms. Gomez feels the same."

TÉNÈBRES AND TRÓCAIRE MET WITH THE OTHER
refugees who'd moved to New Alamo. There were twenty-six
of them now.

Trócaire made food for everyone, and Ténèbres went around
to make sure the shutters were closed and the drapes drawn.

The town was quieter now. No gunshots. Fewer screams.

They sat in silence for a long time, eating a simple meal,
drinking glasses of rainwater. Looking at each other. Smiling
and nodding as if they were engaged in a deep conversation.

It was Trócaire who broke the long silence.

"This town is going to fall apart," he said.

The others nodded.

"We don't want to die with it."

More nods.

Outside they heard a man yelling, "*He's infected—he must
have been bitten at the stable. Don't let him near you! Mikey, get
my ax!*"

There were more yells, a scream, and then an awful sound
like someone chopping wet, green wood. After that, the faint-
ness of someone weeping.

"Let's pray," suggested Ténèbres, and they all held hands.

"YOUR TEMPERATURE'S UP AGAIN," SAID ALICE, FEELING her mother's forehead and the side of her throat.

Her mother was buried under layers of blankets, shivering but awake.

"It's nothing," she said. "Just a cold. World's worst timing, but that's all it is."

Alice frowned. "I don't know. Maybe one of your cuts is infected. Let me take a look."

Apart from her injured hand, Mrs. Chung had several small cuts, mostly from splinters and flying glass during the fight.

"I just checked when I was in the bathroom, sweetie. I'm fine. Really, it's just a cold. You go along. I'm sure Gutsy wants to see you." Her smile, despite the fever, was radiant and encouraging.

"Sure, but—"

"Just go. I should try to sleep as much as I can. That's the best way to beat a cold. Sleep it off, and let the body heal itself."

Alice didn't like it, but her mother insisted. "At least let me get you some tea and cut up a few oranges. Vitamin C."

When that was done, Alice kissed her mom on the forehead and left.

Mrs. Chung waited until she heard the click of the front door lock, and then she pushed the blankets away. She sat up and used her splinted hand to pull up the sleeve on her other arm. There were five small bandages there, each taped in place over a cut. The flesh around four of the bandages was normal or slightly pink.

But higher up on her arm, near the elbow, the skin was very different. Although it was the smallest cut, that whole part of her arm was now a dark red. It scared her. She hadn't been bitten—nothing like that—but during the fight she'd been nicked by a splinter of wood smeared with some dark substance. She thought it was oil or grease, because she'd taken the injury near the wagonwright's barn; and she'd cleaned it thoroughly. Several times.

Why was that one cut getting infected while the others were not?

What was that black stuff?

Surely it was only oil. Or grease.

She tugged down her sleeve and pulled up the blankets. Shivering as she did so. From the fever. From the fear.

GUTSY SAT CROSS-LEGGED ON A DESK AT THE SCHOOL, watching as Captain Ledger stumped around on crutches.

"I'm going out first thing in the morning," Sam said. "One of the scouts found a dead shambler a few miles northeast of here. Single pistol shot to the forehead. Very precise, so it could have been Collins."

"Outstanding," said Ledger. "I'll go with you and—"

"You're not going anywhere, Joe," interrupted Sam. "Not with that leg."

"I'm fine. Just a scratch."

"Sixteen stitches isn't a scratch."

"Yeah? Well, screw that."

"You barely healed up from the injuries you got when your chopper crashed, and now you're in worse shape." Sam shook his head. "Maybe for once try not to be a macho idiot."

"You say the sweetest things, Sam. Always captain of my fan club," said Ledger sourly. "But here's a news flash: I'm going. There's no debate on this."

They glared at each other, but it was obvious to Gutsy and everyone else who was going to win the argument.

* * *

As dawn began painting the distant horizon in strips of red, Joe Ledger and Sam Imura prepared to ride out of town on a pair of horses, a day later than they had hoped to. Ledger did a pretty good job of keeping a confident smile on his face, but no one was really fooled. He was sweating with pain as he climbed into the saddle, and sat gritting his teeth as the horse jostled and jangled him. Grimm, still in quarantine, howled so loudly they could all hear him blocks way.

"If we find Collins," said Joe, his face running with sweat, "one of us will come back on her quad. With any luck, Site B will be big enough to evacuate the townsfolk to."

Gutsy looked around at the town, then back at him. "This place already feels dead. Maybe it belongs to them. They can have it."

Her words seemed to leech all the heat out of the day. Even Ledger shivered—though maybe it was a fever from his wound. Gutsy wasn't sure.

She stood with Benny and Chong, watching the two soldiers ride away.

A FEW HOURS LATER, KAREN PEAK CALLED THE GROUP together in an examination room at the hospital. The large crowd that had met in Mr. Ford's classroom a few days ago had dwindled, Nix and Lilah gone to California and Ledger and Sam off looking for Site B.

The body of the dead soldier was now covered by a blood-stained blanket. Dissection tools lay in a bucket of hot, soapy water, which told Gutsy that the postmortem had been performed. Part of her wanted to see what was under the blanket, and to understand the technical process of post-mortem; the other part of her was disgusted by the thought. She saw her friends glancing at the shrouded figure and figured they were having similar thoughts. Well, maybe only the disgust.

Dr. Morton sat on a folding chair next to the table, and Manny Flores leaned on the edge of the table, looking worn out and scared. "First off," he said, "we confirmed that this soldier did not die as a result of a bite or from smoke inhalation."

"Then what killed him?" asked Gutsy.

"A gunshot wound to the chest," said Flores. "He bled to death."

The room plunged into shocked silence.

It was Urrea who finally spoke. "Wait . . . he was *alive*? I don't understand. This man wasn't a zombie?"

"He was not," said Flores. "We also did some spot-testing on the other bodies from the car wash, and none of them are standard reanimates."

"What about the ones at the school?" asked Ford. "The ones dressed in civilian clothes?"

"They're the same as this man," said Flores.

"You lost me," said Urrea. "So, if the car wash attackers weren't ravagers or shamblers . . . what *were* they?"

Flores glanced at Morton. "Doctor, this is your mess. You should explain it."

Morton fidgeted with the bandages on his left arm. When he began speaking, his eyes seemed to stare through rather than at anyone gathered there.

"First," Morton said slowly, "I suppose I need to admit that I haven't been entirely frank with you people about the full scope of the research being undertaken at the base."

"Before you say one more word, let me say this," said Gutsy. "If you don't tell us everything *now*, you're going to have a lot more to worry about than a few zom bites."

Morton almost smiled. "I'm probably going to die and reanimate as one of those things, girl. Am I supposed to be scared by your threats?"

"You should be," said Alethea, and her words hung in the air for a moment. Morton was sweating, but he tried to paste on an expression of professional calm. He wasn't able to sell it, though.

"I *intend* to be frank with you," he said frostily. "The

autopsy confirms what can best be described as a worst-case scenario, which means I'm in as much danger as you. So, in case you think I'm doing this out of the goodness of my heart, think again. I'm a coward; I'll admit it. I don't want to die. I also know that you people need me because I'm useful, and I intend to leverage that. So . . . no more games."

"Then get to it," said Benny.

Morton nodded. "You need to understand that the main base—the Laredo Chemical and Biological Weapon Defense Research Facility—was not created to study Lucifer 113. It existed long before that; it was built even before the Cold War. The base was part of a bioweapons program launched in 1942 as a backup plan if the Manhattan Project failed."

Gutsy heard gasps from Urrea, Ford, and Karen.

"What's the Manhattan Project?" asked Spider.

"It was a top-secret military program," explained Urrea, "launched in 1939 by the United States—"

"—with help from Canada and Great Britain—" added Ford.

"—to develop the first atomic bomb."

"Yikes," said Chong quietly.

"What do you mean by 'backup plan'?" asked Gutsy.

"If the atomic bomb project was a failure, then plan B to defeat the Empire of Japan was to release bioweapons in Tokyo and other major population centers. Because Japan is a series of islands, the hope was that the distance from the mainland would contain the resulting epidemic. That plan, luckily, was scrapped because it was deemed unmanageable. There was no way to guarantee isolation and, therefore, containment. And, bear in mind, this was similar in many ways to what the

Soviet Union was planning when they developed the Lucifer bioweapon. It was intended for use in isolated areas—a base, ships at sea, and so on. In both cases the plan was to let the bioweapon sweep through the population and then the infection itself would die out when there were no more living hosts."

"That's . . . that's . . . ," began Spider, but couldn't finish.

"It's madness," said Morton. "The fact that all of the research and samples of Lucifer weren't completely destroyed when the original plan was deemed too dangerous is proof."

"This is what *you* do, though," said Alethea, "isn't it?"

Morton looked genuinely surprised. "Me? No! My field of research—and everything we did at our lab—was focused on stopping these kinds of bioweapons. We were the shield to the biological sword."

"That sounds very noble," said Ford, "but you also killed a lot of innocent people, so let's wait a bit before we nominate you for sainthood."

Morton gave him a vile sneer, then turned to the others.

"The program begun at our lab during the Second World War was scrapped when the bomb tests proved successful," said Morton. "Unfortunately, that research was, like Lucifer, never completely disposed of. When Lucifer 113 began spreading, we were ordered to investigate whether any of the dormant bioweapons projects might be viable as counter-plagues to stop the infected—including the one designed to exterminate the majority of the Japanese population."

"That's *horrible*," Spider said.

"It's practical," said Morton, then he flicked a glance at Gutsy. "Wouldn't you agree? *You've* always been the practical one."

"Agree about it being practical?" she said. "Sure. But it's evil."

"I'll leave the concepts of good and evil to the philosophers," sneered Morton. "The point is, we soon discovered that a number of these older bioweapons were very useful to us in developing potential treatment protocols."

"None of which actually worked," said Ford. "Like what you did to create the ravagers?"

"That was an accident," Morton said grudgingly. "And yet it wasn't a total failure, because the ravagers are smarter and more humanlike than the shamblers. It was proof that the mental functions of the reanimates could be partially restored."

"Oh, you must be so happy," said Alethea. Morton started to reply, but Gutsy cut in.

"Hold on," she said. "What does all this have to do with this man?" She pointed to the silent body under the sheet.

Morton sniffed. "By the time we learned about the Lucifer 113 variation, we were already dangerously behind the curve, because the designer of that form, Dr. Volker, committed suicide. Various research teams proposed possible response protocols, but when it comes right down to it, all of that was guesswork. Combating disease is, at the best of times, a slow and laborious process. And because we're talking about a genetically modified bioweapon, it requires reverse engineering decades of research. What became clear, though, was that Volker never intended for his Lucifer form to get out into the general public. There were no safeguards built into 113. It was intended for one specific use: he wanted to it to revive the consciousness of the death row inmate Homer Gibbon, leaving that consciousness connected to all five senses, but to completely sever connections with all motor functions. In essence, the intended victim was meant to wake up inside his own inert body following execution via lethal injection. He would be aware of his condition, and remain aware as his body rotted inside its coffin."

"God . . . ," breathed Chong.

"I think we can all agree," said Morton, "that Dr. Volker was psychologically compromised."

No one commented on that.

"During the height of the outbreak," Morton continued, "and before the government tried to limit the spread by dropping nuclear bombs on the areas with the densest populations, one team attempted to fight fire with fire. They released a compound they felt would destroy the parasites that drove Lucifer 113. This counter-weapon was code-named Reaper." He paused and shook his head. "There was no time to test. It was estimated that we were losing upward of three hundred American lives per minute by the time it was deployed."

"Reaper?" murmured Ford. "Are you saying that the Reaper Plague was really this counter-weapon?"

"No. The name stuck, but really what accelerated the spread was the way in which Reaper and Lucifer 113 interacted. Instead of battling each other, the two disease forms combined and mutated into a true pandemic superplague." Morton shook his head again. "It's possible that time, natural mutation, and natural barriers such as rivers and so on might have slowed Volker's plague and kept it from spreading beyond all control, but Reaper amped it up, turned it airborne. And . . . well . . . we all know what happened. It's everywhere. All of us are technically carriers. When we die, the change in metabolism results in the parasite eggs we all carry in our bloodstream hatching. We reanimate quickly."

No one said a word.

"When it was clear how terrible a mistake had been made," Morton went on, "the government sent the last of its resources to bases like ours. We were told—no, we were *begged*—to find a solution. The last message sent by the president of the United States was for the science teams to find a solution by *any means necessary*. The Constitution and Bill of Rights were suspended. In fact, all rights of any kind were suspended. We were the last line of defense in this war."

As he said this, he stared at Gutsy.

"You think we're monsters, Gabriella," he said, and for a moment his voice softened. "But we were trying to prevent the *extinction* of humankind. The government fell. The armies died. Reaper spread around the world. We were the *last hope* of our species. So, you tell me—any of you tell me—what could we have done but do what we did?"

No one spoke for a moment, then Gutsy said, "You could have *told* us. You could have asked us to help. To volunteer."

Morton began shaking his head before she even finished. "Volunteer? To be lab rats?"

"No. To be *test subjects*. To help save the world."

"And why would any of you do that? Why would any of you risk your lives like that?"

"Because," said Spider, "it's our world too. We live here. Our friends are here." He took Alethea's hand. "Our families are here. People would have volunteered. They'd have stepped up if you ever gave them a chance."

Gutsy wiped at her eyes. "If she thought it might help save me, Mama would have been the first in line."

"I'd have done it to keep Sarah safe," said Karen Peak.

Morton shook his head again. "No, no, no. People are afraid. They're selfish. You say this now, but I know we wouldn't have had enough volunteers, and then we would have failed."

"And look at how well you succeeded doing it *your* way," said Mr. Urrea in a voice that dripped with contempt.

"We were doing what we were ordered to do," Morton countered.

Manny Flores cut in. "Look, guys, I tend to agree with all of you, and for two pins I'd feed this piece of garbage to *los muertos*, but Karen called you all in here because of something new we found." He turned to Morton. "Get to the damn point."

The doctor cleared his throat. "*Fine*," he snapped peevishly. "While attempting to find a way to change the function of Lucifer 113, we used many of the earlier versions of the parasite. This research took many forms, including a variety of clinical trials—mostly on animals, of course."

"*Mostly*," said Gutsy in a way that transformed that single word into something obscene.

"Yeah, very successful," Benny said sourly. "We saw some of your test subjects. Nearly had our heads bitten off by a zommed-out gorilla."

"If you expect me to apologize, you can just forget it," said Morton. "We were trying *anything* that had even a whisper of a possibility. Anyway . . . there were other . . . ah . . . *failures*. One of my great fears is that the explosions at the base may have caused the accidental release of some of those stored bioweapons and paracides."

"What's a paracide?" asked Benny.

"Something that attacks and kills a parasite," said Morton. He pointed to the corpse. "We found traces of a very specific paracide in this man's blood. The only possible source of that contamination is from something inadvertently released when the lab blew up."

"Oh crap," Chong said.

"Allow me to explain," said Morton. "Depending on how bad the fire was, most of the bioweapons stored at the base have likely been destroyed; most can't survive outside a living host or some stable medium, and would have been compromised by the heat."

"Most?" echoed Benny. "Not really digging the sound of that."

"No," Morton agreed. "The paracide we found in this man's body is a very specific prion-based bioweapon. Before you ask, prions are misfolded proteins. Very tough, very difficult to destroy. They can survive on virtually any surface, withstand heat, and even survive freezing. We worked with prions because of that natural toughness, but they are not airborne pathogens. We needed something that could be a delivery system for the prions. Something we could use against mass populations of reanimates."

"And that's what this guy was infected with?" asked Spider.

"Yes. It's likely all of the subjects who attacked Captain Ledger and Gabriella here were infected with it, since they all exhibited the same behavior." Morton cleared his throat again. "Understand, this paracide was designed to work in conjunction with a genetically altered version of pertussis—whooping cough. That's the primary delivery system—the infected coughing, spitting, or using a forced exhale."

"The ones who attacked us kept yelling," said Gutsy. "Howling, really."

"Howling projects more than sound," said Morton. "Yelling of any kind carries particles of the paracide in spit or exhaled vapor."

"Then how come Captain Ledger and I aren't infected?"

"I'm not sure," admitted Morton. "By rights, you *should* be. It may be something as simple as neither of you having *in*haled the *ex*halation of the infected."

"So . . . we got lucky?" asked Gutsy.

"In a nutshell," Morton said. "Though I wouldn't count on that a second time. However, this paracide was not intended as a weapon against the uninfected. It was designed to attack and destroy the active parasites comprising Lucifer 113. It was intended for use against the reanimates. It's theoretically possible that it would work against ravagers as well, but that was one of many things we never tested."

"What would have happened to Captain Ledger and Gutsy if they'd been infected but hadn't died yet?" asked Chong.

Morton shrugged. "I have no idea. Our research never got that far."

"What would happen to *me*?" Chong said quietly. "And Sarah Peak? And you, Doc? What would this stuff do to people like us? Half-zoms?"

"I . . . don't know, son," admitted the doctor. "Our research never got that far. We were focused on a weapon of mass destruction against the whole army of reanimates."

"Good lord," said Ford. "What is this paracide?"

"It's called Wodewose 74," explained Morton. "It was a true marvel of genetic engineering. We used transgenics and CRISPR gene-editing technology and—"

"The *point*, doctor," Karen cut in. "They need you to get to the point."

"Fine," snapped Morton. "The reason we stopped that line of research is because when Wodewose 74 and Lucifer 113 interact in the system of an active reanimate, something entirely new is created. The reanimate becomes faster and much more physically coordinated. They reconnect with their motor functions and essentially take control of the body. They no longer crave human flesh, because they are no longer driven to feed the parasites."

"That's a good thing, though, right?" Benny asked.

"No," said Morton, "it's not. Because as the consciousness of the reanimate becomes fully awake, the personality of the original human host is suddenly and totally self-aware. You think each reanimate is aware? That they retain consciousness? That's what many people believe, but it's much more complicated than that. The parasites in Dr. Volker's modified Lucifer 113 bioweapon do indeed keep *some* awareness in play, but only in a very reduced state. Oxygen deprivation, general trauma, and resulting synaptic failure have reduced most of them to near mindlessness. Perhaps even total cognitive shutdown, especially as they age. For the more recently reanimated it's probably more like being in a bad dream. However, Wodewose 74 changes that. It means some of the inert synapses begin firing again, and that brings the consciousness back into partial focus. That realization of what it is and what it has done drives the infected into a state of absolute and uncontrollable anger. Instead of slow, shuffling zombies or deranged, militant ravagers, what we have instead is a growing army of homicidal maniacs."

THE ROOM WAS AS SILENT AS DEATH. EVERYONE JUST stared at Morton.

Finally, the doctor spoke again. "These infected were designated 'wild men.' That's what 'Wodewose' means. Seemed like an appropriate name for something that is driven not by hunger or lust or political ideology but by rage. Pure, unfiltered, unrelenting rage. The only thing these wild men won't attack are others of their kind. When I mentioned that Wodewose 74 was intended as a weapon against the reanimates, I meant just that. Once introduced into the target, the bioweapon spreads very quickly throughout their system. They would pass Wodewose 74 very quickly to any population of living-dead reanimates, and it's possible, even likely, that, given time, all of the zombies in the world would become wild men."

"Which means we'd be overrun and wiped out," said Ford. "We've survived this long against *los muertos* because they're slow and stupid. When a few dozen ravagers came along and organized the shamblers into an army, we barely held them off. Now you're talking about *millions* of these wild men—faster, smarter, much more aggressive, and even able to use weapons . . ." His words trailed off, and he shook his head slowly.

Gutsy felt sick. She looked into the future and imagined a world where all the billions of *los muertos* had become infected with the Wodewose paracide. Eight billion reanimates driven to total madness and unbearable rage by a collision of man-made diseases. Screaming. Filling the whole world with rage.

"Doctor Morton," said Chong, breaking the terrible silence, "isn't there anything that can stop these wild men? Other than actually fighting them all, I mean?"

Morton chewed his lip for a moment. "There's a chance," he said tentatively. "But it's not a very good chance."

"Try us," said Urrea.

"It's . . . something we began working on when the Wode-wose project was active," Morton began. "It's a compound we called Dòmi—the Haitian word for 'sleep'—because it is based on a chemical formula used for centuries in that country that causes a person to go into a calm, trancelike state. And, for the record, people in such a state were called zombies or zonbis. It's where the pop culture word came from, and it isn't really an accurate word for reanimates."

"Who cares?" asked Benny. "Get on with it. How do we make this Dòmi stuff? And will it help us against the wild men?"

"Yes, it will stop them. If exposed to Dòmi, the wild men will simply . . . stop. They may fall down or just stand there, but they will remain inert until the Wodewose 74 in their system finishes destroying the Lucifer parasites."

"Then what?"

Morton shook his head. "I don't know. We never—"

"—got that far," interrupted Alethea. "Right. Jeez."

"Can you make it here?" Gutsy asked. "Or are you going to say that you don't have the right chemicals?"

Morton just looked at her.

"Is the stuff we need at Site B?" asked Benny.

"No," said Morton. "The entire Wodewose and Dòmi projects were conducted at the base. Samples of the active Wodewose paracide were stored in the hot room, but the Dòmi materials are in deep storage. Samples, research notes—all of it."

"And that's all destroyed now," Benny said, sagging back against the wall. He rubbed his eyes. "We can't catch a break."

"How do we *know* it's all destroyed?" asked Gutsy. When everyone looked at her in surprise, she said, "I got the impression from Captain Collins that it was a pretty big underground complex. And you just said it was in *deep* storage. Did you mean actually deep? Like underground?"

"Yes," said Morton. "There are two main upper levels and four sublevels. All of the Dòmi research and samples are down in the basement. Down in sub-four."

"Then maybe there's a chance," said Gutsy.

"How do you figure that?" Ford asked.

"Fire burns *up*," said Gutsy. "Those lower levels might be okay."

"You couldn't get to it," said Morton. "The hot room—the place where many of the most dangerous bioweapons were stored—was on the upper level. The explosions would likely have ruptured that. The air around there must be a toxic soup. You'd need a hazmat suit and probably an armed battalion of crack troops, also in hazmat suits."

"Don't we have some of those suits here?" asked Gutsy.

"Yes," said Flores, "but only a few."

Alethea wheeled around and glared at Gutsy. "No," she said flatly. "I know the look in your eye, and I can read you like a book, Gabriella Gomez. No way are you going out there."

"I never said I wanted to," Gutsy said quickly. Alethea's eyes bored into hers for a long time. Then she gave a single firm nod and turned away.

"So . . . *now* what?" demanded Chong.

"Now," said Karen Peak, "we wait until Captain Ledger and Sam Imura get back. If they find Site B, then we don't need to worry about what may or may not be at the base. We'll have medicine and weapons and maybe a safe place to hide. And, besides, who better to attempt to infiltrate the base to get the Dòmi?"

"And what do we do if they don't come back?" Spider asked.

No one had an answer to that. And no one had anything else to say. The meeting broke up, and, in ones and twos, they all left the hospital. Gutsy was the last to leave. She lingered in the doorway of the examination room, looking at the form under the sheet. For just a moment Gutsy felt as if her mother's ghost was beside her. She looked that way, but there was nothing but a heat shimmer by the window.

Then Gutsy turned away and left.

Interlude Seven

In the Court of the Raggedy Man

TWO YEARS AGO

THE RAGGEDY MAN SAT WAITING FOR THEM ON A throne of skulls.

The throne was on a flatbed truck angled to block the highway. There were no reapers around him, but there were plenty of guards. Those closest to the truck were ravagers dressed in leather and denim, armed with every kind of weapon—knives and swords, pistols and rifles, scythes and axes. Beyond them, and spreading out to fill the fields on either side of the road, were the gray people. Many thousands of them.

Saint John and the two young reapers walked along the center of the highway. Normally it was the chemical soaked into the red tassels each reaper wore that kept the dead from attacking them. Not this time. The gray people merely shuffled aside and watched with dull and hungry eyes as the three uninfected passed.

The three of them stopped fifteen feet from the flatbed. Saint John bowed low, and the reapers bowed even lower, as they had been told to do.

The Raggedy Man was naked except for the torn and filthy

remnants of a pair of ancient blue hospital scrubs. His skin was a bizarre yellowish-gray patchwork of lighter and darker skin divided by deep scars that ran in lines all over him, as if his body had been blown apart and then badly stitched together using parts from every kind and color of human. It was sickening, and reminded Brother Mercy of the creature from a novel he'd read. *Frankenstein*. A living thing made from pieces of the dead.

The Raggedy Man's face was similarly misshapen and scarred. His lips were rubbery, with pendulous strands of bloody drool hanging from them. He had yellow teeth that were sharpened to points, like a shark. His ears were crumpled lumps of gristle, and he had no hair anywhere on his head or body—not even eyebrows or lashes. His eyes glittered like perfect blue marbles, and in those eyes all manner of shadows swirled. Humor and anger, hunger and delight. Those eyes were the worst part of him. They terrified Brother Mercy down to the bottom of his soul.

The saint straightened. "Greetings, my old friend."

"Been a long time," said the Raggedy Man. "I heard you were dead."

"People tell stories," said the saint, shrugging it off. "And there were those told about you. It was quite a spectacular death, as I recall. Your name was on every reporter's mouth."

"I know. Did you see what the *Philadelphia Inquirer* called me?"

"Yes—'The Man Who Killed the World.' Very lurid. All the news services picked it up."

"For once they got the story right."

They beamed at each other.

The Raggedy Man looked at the two reapers. "These are the two hotshots you've been bragging about?"

Saint John introduced them, and again the reapers bowed low.

"They got manners," said the monster on the throne. His diction was rough and his voice coarse, but he had an undeniable air of complete command.

"They have much more than that, Homer," said Saint John. "Between them, they have sent more sinners into the darkness than anyone else except Brother Peter. They are sharp as knives and dedicated to our holy purpose, and I bring them to you."

Homer Gibbon, the Raggedy Man, the man who killed the world, sat back in his throne and smiled a broad, feral, happy smile. "And it's not even my birthday."

Brother Mercy could see tiny worms wriggling between the man's yellow teeth.

PART TWELVE

NEW ALAMO

Faith begins where it ends.
And hope is the first breath taken after everything chokes you.
None of this is supposed to be easy,
broken feathers just make a different flight path.

—ANNE WALSH, "FLIGHT PATH"

"WELL," SIGHED CHONG, "JUST WHEN I THOUGHT I couldn't get more depressed . . ."

They were all sitting around Gutsy's dining room table, Gutsy and her friends and the California kids. The remains of an early dinner lay like debris. Sombra was on a rug by the back door, quietly chewing on a beef bone. Gutsy had liberated him from quarantine, promising to keep him inside her house for at least the next day.

"I learned a while back," Benny mused, poking at his potatoes with a fork, "never to say something as stupid as 'Well, things can't get worse.'"

"No joke," agreed Spider. He had a cup of tea cradled between his palms and stared down into it as if expecting answers to appear there.

Gutsy thought about Alice. On the way back from Misfit High, she'd stopped to knock on Alice's door, but there was no answer.

"Hey, Earth calling Gutsy Gomez," said Alethea, snapping her fingers, and Gutsy jerked, realizing that someone had asked her a question.

"What . . . ?"

"I asked," said Alethea with false patience, "what you thought about this whole Dòmi thing. And these wild men freaks."

Gutsy set down her bowl. "You won't like what I think."

"What exactly is it you think we won't like?" Alethea asked.

"Well," said Gutsy slowly, "I think we need to go out to the base and try to find that stuff. We need to get all of the Dòmi so we can handle any new wild man attacks, and we need to look for some of the stuff Morton needs to make drugs for Chong, Sarah, and the other infected people."

"Sam and Joe are looking for Site B," said Chong.

"Looking for, sure. Doesn't mean they'll find it. Doesn't mean they'll get back here in time. Same goes for Nix and Lilah."

"Sure," Benny said, "but that's two tries at the same time."

"And going to the base would be three. That increases our odds by a third."

"It also increases the chances of getting killed," said Alethea. "It's a stupid plan."

Gutsy shrugged. "Give me a better one that doesn't involve just sitting around waiting."

"At the risk of insulting you," said Chong, "I kinda agree with the whole 'you're crazy' thing."

Spider reached over and clasped Gutsy's wrist. "Please . . . don't even think about it."

Gutsy managed a smile. It was totally fake, but Spider seemed reassured by it. "Whatever, guys," she said to the group.

Benny relaxed a bit. "Though, to be fair," he said, "it *is* kind of a crazy time right now."

"Don't tell me you're *agreeing* with her about going out there," said Chong, alarmed. "I mean, sure, this sounds like one of your classic idiot ideas, but—"

"Nope," said Benny emphatically. "Even *I* wouldn't do this, and I've had some moderately wacky ideas."

"'Moderately'?" Chong echoed faintly.

They stared at Gutsy. She shrugged. "I still think it's a good idea."

"Despite those wild men, regular *los muertos*, ravagers, and every disease known to man?" Alethea wondered. "You need help."

"I'm open to practical suggestions," said Gutsy. "We need to *do* something besides sit here and sulk."

"Sure," said Benny, "we need to keep fortifying the town and wait for Joe and Sam. Going to that base is suicide."

"You don't know that."

"Actually," said Benny, "I kind of do. I went to one with Joe, Nix, and Lilah. It was at Zabriskie Point in California. That's where we rescued Dr. McReady. Oh, and Chong was actually *in* one in Nevada."

"Isn't this a moot point?" Chong said. "The air around that place is basically disease soup. You'd be dead pretty quickly, and probably turn into a wild man."

"Wild *girl*," corrected Alethea.

"Wild girl," agreed Chong. "Or . . . wild woman."

"I could take a hazmat suit from the hospital and . . ." Everyone glared at Gutsy, and the rest of her sentence trailed off. She raised her eyebrows. "Okay, so tell me a better plan."

No one spoke, but Gutsy sat there, arms folded across her chest, steadfast in her opinion.

"Please," begged Alethea, "do not do something stupid here."

Gutsy endured their stares for almost fifteen seconds before she exhaled and nodded. "Okay, okay."

"Promise?"

"I promise."

"On Mama's grave," said Spider, which jolted Gutsy. "Swear it."

After a long moment, she said, "I swear on Mama's grave that I won't do something stupid."

Only then did Spider and Alethea relax, and after a moment, so did Benny and Chong. The conversation resumed, but it was empty chitchat, and soon they all left. Gutsy sat alone in the kitchen, Sombra's head on her thigh, staring at the wall as if the future was painted there for her to see.

GUTSY SNUCK OUT AN HOUR AFTER SUNSET.

The first thing she did was go over to the hospital to steal a hazmat suit. She'd visited Morton before leaving to ask him to make a map of the base. He'd done it reluctantly, though he apparently bought the lie that it was something she was preparing for when Captain Ledger returned. She'd even flattered him, telling the doctor that this kind of assistance would make him a hero in the eyes of the town.

She remembered the look on Morton's face. He was his usual haughty self, and then arrogance gave way to doubt, then fear, and finally a fragile hope.

"And what about you, Gabriella?" he asked. "I know I'll never be a hero to you."

"Yes, you will," she lied. "If you help save New Alamo, then you and I are square."

He gaped at her, eyes wide, fear sweat beading his forehead. "Even though . . . ?"

"Even though," she said firmly.

When she'd drained him of every possible detail, Gutsy folded the map carefully and tucked it in a pocket of her fishing vest.

"Gutsy," said Morton as she turned to go. She lingered in the open doorway as he spoke. "If there had been some other way . . ."

She said nothing.

"I'm sorry," he said, and now the tears fell down his bruised cheeks.

"Sure," she said, and left.

She went home and made thoughtful selections of weapons and equipment, knowing that anything she brought would have to be abandoned because of contamination. Gutsy wasn't sentimental about tools, though. Practicality was often a shield against small hurts.

Then she kissed Sombra and hugged him for a long time. The coydog wagged his crooked tail and whined a little. Gutsy slipped out of the house, quiet as a shadow, went to a section of wall that was deep in shadows, and climbed it, taking her time, making no sound, being sly and careful.

Out in the Broken Lands, she avoided *los muertos* as diligently as she did the roving patrols of town guards.

None of the things she did were, in her estimation, stupid. Risky, yes, and possibly suicidal, but not stupid. So, Gutsy wasn't breaking her word. Or so she convinced herself.

IN NEW ALAMO, ALICE CHUNG RETURNED HOME
from helping deliver food to some old folks. She was bone-
tired and felt icky. The thought of a hot bath, food, and maybe
sitting up reading in the living room with her mom sounded
like heaven.

The house was dark, though, with all the lights out. Mom
must have gone to bed early. Probably worn out from pain.
Those broken fingers looked better today, but the hand was
still really swollen. And her mom seemed to be running a
fever, too.

She tapped lightly on her mother's bedroom door.
"Mom . . . ?"

There was a faint rustle of bedclothes, then a murmur.
"Alice?"

"I just got home. You okay? Can I get you anything? You
want some tea?"

A pause. Then, "No. I'm fine."

"You sure? It's no problem."

Another pause. Longer this time. "I just need to sleep."

Alice stood in the hallway, fingers touching the door,
waiting for more. But there was only silence in the house. She

imagined she could feel pain in the air—Mom's physical pain, and the deeper pain of having lost family and friends in the attacks.

Alice leaned her forehead against the door for a long moment.

"Love you, Mom," she said softly.

Then she went to heat water for her bath.

IT TOOK THREE CAREFUL HOURS TO REACH THE AREA near the base. It wasn't the distance that took so much time, but the staying safe. The darkness was alive with shambling creatures. And with faster ones who snarled and howled and tore at the shadows with teeth and fingernails as if trying to consume the night itself.

Gutsy found a good hiding place a mile from the base, behind the rusted hulk of a Mister Softee truck. She shrugged out of her backpack, removed the hazmat suit, used moonlight to double-check that it was still intact, then pulled it on. She very carefully pulled off strips of duct tape and wound them around the seals at her ankles, wrists, and throat. She'd brought a lanyard to hang the tape roll around her neck. It was the fastest way to seal a tear, Morton had told her. Practical. Then she slipped her vest back on and buttoned it. Last thing she put on was the backpack, which was now empty. The contents—water, some food, and a first-aid kit—were left by the truck. Next to them was a spray bottle of bleach and another of a harsh antibacterial she'd taken from Morton's lab.

Gutsy left her shelter and moved with great care, watching

and listening before drifting from one piece of cover to the next. When she did move, it was in imitation of the slow, awkward manner of the dead. *Los muertos* were rarely triggered by their own kind. Up close, their aggression was nullified by some chemical signature. She used to think it was the stench of rotting flesh, but now she knew better. Morton had told her that the active parasites in the living dead gave off a smell that imitated that of rot. It was the parasite protecting itself from other infected hosts. In a weird way, Gutsy admired that. She knew of plants and trees that used chemicals to discourage insects. Some insects did it too, and since the Lucifer 113 plague was made up mostly from several genetically modified insects, this was a smart design choice.

Motion, though, was different. The dead tended to react to certain kinds of motion. Anything quick, anything that moved with steadiness or speed caused the monsters to want to hunt. Anything that was sluggish or that moved with a broken rhythm was much less of a trigger. Gutsy had long suspected this, but Nix said that Benny's brother, Tom, had taught them to move in ways that kept the automatic response from kicking in.

She used that skill now, becoming, in a sense, one of the dead. It felt strange, like some of the schoolyard games she'd played with Alice and the other kids when they were little. Stop, Go, and Grab. Haunted House.

It was so odd that something like this would recall happier days. When Mama was alive. When New Alamo was the whole world.

When things made sense.

She moved closer and closer to the edge of the pit. Fires

still burned here and there, and there was a pall of black oil smoke hanging like a shroud over the whole area. Parked near the edge was a burned-out Humvee. A sturdy metal tow cable ran from the front end of it over the lip and down into the smoky darkness. The ground at the edge was littered with dozens of sets of footprints as well as hand marks, showing where people had climbed out. Gutsy pivoted on the balls of her feet, studying the ground. From what she could tell, the people seemed to stagger around in aimless circles for a while before abruptly turning and moving off in specific directions.

Gutsy tried to make sense of that. She reckoned that the soldiers were either killed by the blast and reanimated, or killed by all those pathogens released when the hot room ruptured. In either case, they became infected by Wodewose. It was sad. Frightened soldiers climbing out, each of them already infected by the pathogens swirling in the air; then becoming dizzy and disoriented as the bioweapon rewrote the rules of their consciousness and central nervous system. Once transformed, they began to move fast in the direction of the first prey they spotted, living person or undead shambler. She was not as experienced a tracker as either Sam Imura or Joe Ledger, but she was sure this was the story told by the marks on the scorched earth.

Right now, though, the creatures she could see appeared to be shamblers. Had the wild men all run off? Was the toxic cloud *not* filled with the paracide? Two important questions that she did not have answers for.

The cable was tempting and felt like a stroke of luck for her, but Gutsy was too cynical to believe that things were going to be that easy. So, instead of immediately climbing down, she ghosted silently around the edge of the pit, looking down to try and get a sense of the place and matching it with the map Morton drew.

According to the doctor, the base covered a sprawling sixty-three acres underground, with wings jutting out in several directions. A massive section of the roof had been blown up by some catastrophe created by the ravagers, and hundreds of tons of debris then collapsed back into the pit. It lay in uneven piles, the biggest of which rose to within thirty feet of the edge. Desultory fires burned here and there, but they were fading. She had no idea what fuel had kept them burning this long. Possibly stores of natural gas or some kind of geothermal venting, but those were guesses and there was no way or time to check.

The blast seemed to have blown upward from the second of the upper sublevels, tearing a massive hole in the topmost level and the ground. By kneeling and peering through the gloom, though, Gutsy could see under the undamaged portion of the roof, and there were faint glows that were too steady to be fire. Could it be electric lights? If so, then that meant there was still power down there, and that in turn meant a good deal of the underground structure was still intact. As bad as the explosion had been, it could not have destroyed a complex as massive as what Morton described. Her heart jumped at that thought, because it meant that this crazy mission could work.

She completed her circle of the pit and stopped again by the burned Humvee, wondering briefly what happened to whomever had brought it here to try and get survivors out. Had the wild men killed him? Had fumes from the pit overwhelmed him with their mingled diseases and bioweapons? Or had he simply been consumed?

There was no one else around. Not here at the edge, and she reckoned that the newly transformed wild men were the reason for that. They would have attacked any *los muertos*, but where had they gone since then? Some had certainly been among the group that she and Ledger had fought at the car wash. Were there more, or had that been all of them?

"Worry about that later," she told herself. Then she took hold of the steel tow-cable and climbed down into the home of the Rat Catchers.

The place where monsters were made.

THE CABLE REACHED MIDWAY DOWN THE BIGGEST pile of debris, and Gutsy held on fast while she tested the slope to see if it would hold her weight. It did, mostly comprised of broken stone, shattered timbers, and twisted steel beams. She released her grip very carefully and then made her way down—slowly and precariously—to the floor. The hazmat suit was bulky and clumsy, but she managed, and then stood panting on the ground. The glow revealed itself to be emergency lights attached to big battery boxes bolted to the walls. The illumination allowed her to see the openings of several of the facility's wings. Morton's notes told her to follow yellow lines painted on the walls, indicating directions. There was a rainbow of colored lines running everywhere, but she located the yellow ones easily enough. Yellow would take her to the correct rooms, and orange would bring her back. Easy and efficient; just how Gutsy liked it. She did a tap-check of her equipment and hazmat suit, then moved off into the building. The yellow lines took her to a set of elevators—which stood open, empty, and uninviting—and a set of stairs winding downward. She drew her machete and took the stairs.

Gutsy was a scavenger, among many other things, and

had broken into more than one building looking for items to take back to town. She knew how to move silent as a shadow, and how to take stairs at angles to check the corners of each new level. There was a flash in her head as she wondered if Captain Ledger would be proud of how she was handling this—providing he wasn't out of his mind with rage over her being here at all. She also wondered if Alice would be proud of her bravery. Or would she be repulsed by the risks Gutsy was taking?

"Focus," she growled at herself, and even with the muffling effect of the hazmat suit, her voice seemed unnaturally loud in the darkness. It scared her to silence.

She reached sublevel two and peered through the sooty glass window in the steel door of a lab. What she saw sickened her. There had been a slaughter here. The walls, floor, and even the ceiling were spattered with blood that had dried to a chocolaty brown. Pieces of bodies lay everywhere, and several corpses lay in a sprawl—obvious victims of gunfire. One of the shamblers was still alive. Kind of. It was a person who'd obviously died there and reanimated, but was pinned beneath a pair of heavy steel cabinets. That probably was how she died, but the ponderous weight kept her hungry corpse pinned down. The thing's hands clawed with futile persistence at the floor in a vain hope to pull itself free. Gutsy gagged when she saw that the fingernails and much of the skin of each fingertip had been ripped away by days of clawing, clawing, clawing.

The sight of the helpless *los muertos* hurt Gutsy. She knew that this dead woman had been part of something vast and horrible, and that she had to know what was going on. That made her a monster long before she died. And yet there was the other part. The knowledge that the personality of this woman was still in there, even at a greatly reduced level, was horrifying. Able to feel pain and hunger. Able to see and hear. And yet helpless.

Had the woman believed that the work being done at this facility was cruel but necessary? Was this punishment just? Gutsy had no answers.

On impulse, Gutsy opened the door and went inside the room. There was no biohazard symbol on the outside, and the door opened with a simple turn of the handle. The dead thing turned its head and growled at her, and those torn fingers stretched up to grab what was beyond their reach. A few scattered papers rifled, but nothing else moved.

Gutsy drew a push-spike as she walked over to the undead creature. She moved around to an angle where it couldn't grab her, knelt on the creature's upper back, pressed the bloody head facedown, and placed the tip of the spike at the curved depression at the base of the skull. Skin and muscle and tendon resisted, but the sharpened tip punched through and severed the spinal cord. All movement instantly stopped, and the thrashing monster became a truly dead person.

"Sorry," murmured Gutsy, though she wasn't really sure that was the right word. She'd given the woman rest. Peace. Though that word seemed wrong, too. Everything here was a mockery of peace.

Gutsy stood slowly, pulling out the spike. She wiped it on the woman's smock. Someone might still be alive who loved her. Or remembered her. Or she could have been here since the base was destroyed, the consciousness of the person she'd once been aching for death and thinking about the people *she* loved.

The same hell Mama had been in.

"Mama . . . ," she cried. "*Ay, dios mio*, Mama . . . I'm so sorry."

Gutsy moved on through this giant tomb of a place.

PART THIRTEEN

THE LAREDO CHEMICAL AND BIOLOGICAL WEAPON DEFENSE RESEARCH FACILITY

The secret to happiness is freedom . . .

And the secret to freedom is courage.

—THUCYDIDES

GUTSY CONTINUED FOLLOWING THE YELLOW LINES.
Going deeper. She was relieved that so little of the complex
was damaged down on the lower levels.

Because the hazmat suit she wore was completely sealed,
her body heat had nowhere to go, turning her into a walking swamp. So much sweat ran down her legs that her feet
squelched inside the boots. But she didn't dare open the hood
and take a sip of water or let a breeze in.

Everywhere she looked there were signs of panic and violence. An open doorway surrounded by bullet-pocked walls.
Blood splashed high from the force of opened arteries. A few
corpses with head wounds. A headless man dressed only in
boxer shorts. They were evidence of small battles lost, where
both the living and the dead had wandered off, recruited by
default into the Night Army. Or, perhaps, the wild men.

The yellow lines ended at a massive metal door set with
an airlock. The door stood open, propped by a leather swivel
chair. Gutsy stopped and stood looking at a message someone
had written on the wall in blood:

GOD FORGIVE US

The airlock was set into a concrete wall reinforced with

plates of steel. Morton's notes included a method to bypass the lock, but it wasn't necessary. She left the swivel chair in place to make sure the door would remain open.

Directly inside was a kind of mudroom, with clothes hung on pegs and five brand-new and undamaged hazmat suits. They were of better quality than the one she wore, but she didn't dare change.

The mudroom led to a much smaller airlock that was similarly blocked open, this time with a small metal trash can. Gutsy stepped over it, placing her feet deliberately to avoid noise. The suit itself rustled a bit, but there was nothing she could do about that except pay attention to the room, listening for sounds, watching for movement.

Morton had warned her about the facility's biohazard alert system—something he called a BAMS unit. He'd explained that this was a bioaerosol mass spectrometer, which was a device that could detect infectious particles in the air. There were BAMS units positioned throughout the facility. As she stepped inside, one of the units mounted above the inside of the door began flashing a red light and— exactly as Morton had warned her—two ferocious jets of steam hit her from either side, and a third blasted down on her head with such force that it drove her to her knees. The steam jets, Morton said, were filled with a strong combination of antibacterial, antiviral, and antifungal agents, as well as some kind of solvent like bleach. It blasted her for ten seconds and then abruptly stopped, leaving her gasping.

She struggled back to her feet, trembling and scared.

"Keep going," she urged herself. "Don't stop."

Gutsy moved from beneath those spray heads into a

much larger room. She had expected to find a laboratory, but it was really more of a combination clerical office and storage unit. Rows of desks lined one side of the big room, and rank upon rank of heavy metal cabinets faced them across a narrow walkway. The cabinets each had a number stenciled on them, 001 through 012. Morton had been very specific about what things he wanted from cabinets 003 and 009.

Four emergency lights cast the room in a dirty yellow wash that pushed the shadows into the corners but did not dispel them. Gutsy didn't trust those shadows, but time was ticking away; so she threw caution to the wind and began moving fast. Morton's notes told her where to find a durable foam-lined cooler from a stack of them against a back wall. They were each marked with a biohazard symbol like those that could be found on abandoned trucks from the Centers for Disease Control that were everywhere in the Broken Lands, on walls all through this complex, and even on the hazmat suit she wore.

She hooked a foot around another swivel chair and pulled it over to the cabinets, set the cooler on it, opened the top, and then reached for the handle of 003.

A sound made her stop, as still as a statue.

It was not a growl. Not a moan. Not even the scuff of a shambling foot.

The sound was the cold, sharp, precise click of someone racking the slide on a pump shotgun.

"DON'T SHOOT," CRIED GUTSY WITHOUT TURNING. Her body was rigid with fear.

There was a scuff of a shoe on the concrete walkway behind. She didn't know what to do. Most *los muertos* couldn't use a weapon, but if this was a ravager, then she was going to die very badly.

The silence stretched, and Gutsy strained to hear something—*anything*—that might give shape and meaning to what was happening.

"Who are you?" she asked.

Another scuff. Closer. And now Gutsy could hear the person behind her breathing. It was soft, rapid, and pitched slightly high. She didn't know for sure, but her gut told her it was probably a woman.

"My name is Gabriella Gomez," she said.

There was no reply, but the breath paused for a moment.

"My friends call me Gutsy."

Nothing.

"I'm from New Alamo."

Silence. Cold sweat beaded all over Gutsy's face and ran down her body inside the hazmat suit.

"Look," said Gutsy slowly, "I'm going to turn around. I'll do it really slow, okay?"

It took all her courage to raise her arms very, very slowly out to the sides and then turn.

There was a rustle of clothes as the person moved suddenly.

"I'll *kill* you," said a terrified voice. A woman's.

"I'm not one of them. I'm not infected," Gutsy said, forcing her voice to sound reasonable, controlled. Telling the woman, not begging for her life.

She kept turning. So slowly.

There she was, half in and half out of a pool of yellow light. A hazmat suit hid her in baggy whiteness that was speckled with drops of red. The shotgun was some kind of military model, with a pistol-grip handle and a second handle on the pump. The weapon shook in the woman's hands. Her whole body trembled visibly.

"I'm not infected," repeated Gutsy slowly.

The shotgun barrel was pointed directly at her face.

"Why are you here?" demanded the woman.

Gutsy had no idea what kind of answer would be safe. Her brain raced past a score of possible responses, discarding each for one reason or another. Finally, she settled on the truth.

"Dr. Morton sent me."

There was a sound like a snarl. "Max is dead," snapped the woman. "Everyone's dead."

"No!" Gutsy said quickly. "Dr. Morton is in town. He's hurt, but he'll be fine. He sent me here."

"In town? New Alamo is gone."

"No, it isn't," said Gutsy. "We were attacked, but we won. We're okay."

It wasn't exactly true, but Gutsy wanted to calm her down. They stood only four feet apart, but Gutsy had no illusions about being able to take that shotgun away. She once read that most shotguns have a trigger pull-weight of about four pounds, and there was probably half of that on the woman's finger already.

"I can prove it," said Gutsy.

The shotgun wavered for a moment, then the barrel steadied again. "How?"

"I have a note from Dr. Morton. Do you know his handwriting? It's in my bottom left vest pocket. I can show it to you."

The woman seemed to consider this for a few moments.

"Do it slowly, or so help me, I'll kill you," she said. "Don't try anything stupid."

"Believe me," said Gutsy earnestly, "I don't want to get shot."

She kept her right hand out to the side and used two fingers of her left to slowly dip into the pocket and pull out the folded piece of paper.

"See? Just a piece of paper."

The woman gestured with the barrel. "Open it up and put it on the cooler. Good. Now turn around and face the cabinet. Hands on your head, fingers laced. Don't move."

Gutsy followed each direction with deliberate care. As she stood facing the cabinet, she heard the crinkle of paper as the note was lifted. Then there was silence for a moment, which was broken by a sob.

"He's alive," cried the woman. "Oh my God, he's *alive*."

ALICE CHUNG FETCHED BUCKETS OF WATER FROM THE stove three times to keep the bath hot. Each time she sank back into the tub, soaked a washcloth, and lay back with it over her eyes.

Their house was just inside the wall, and workers had built a gigantic scaffolding of pipes as a platform for repairing it. She could hear men and women climbing and clanging. There was a huge boom crane up there and she had no idea how they'd managed to get it to the big flat wooden deck. Wouldn't they need a crane to lift it? Alice smiled, thinking that Gutsy would probably know how it was done. Gutsy knew stuff like that. She was so nuts-and-bolts. Always had been.

Alice smiled, re-wet the rag, and sighed.

Thinking of Gutsy Gomez made her smile, but even as she did so, there was an odd feeling to it. As if the smile did not quite fit. Flirting with Gutsy the other day was fun. A lot of fun, really. She'd had her eye on Gutsy for a long time, and had hoped the girl would nerve up and ask her out. But, tough as Gutsy was, she never seemed to find the guts to try.

Then there was that kiss. The first one. Alice knew that

if she hadn't made the first move, then the sun would burn to a cold cinder before Gutsy ever did.

There was a heavy *caroooom* as the boom crane placed another crushed car onto the wall. It made the whole house shake and sent ripples across the surface of her bathwater. Alice understood why they had to work all day and night, but it annoyed her too. Mom was hurt and resting, and this wasn't going to exactly rock her to sleep.

For a moment Alice sat up and looked at the closed bathroom door, chewing her lip, debating whether to dry off and go check or let Mom sleep. She listened for a sound, a word of complaint, a call.

There was nothing.

The house was silent and the only noise was from the work outside.

She settled back into the water, refreshed her rag, found a comfortable angle for her head, and thought more about Gutsy Gomez. Were they an official thing? It was impossible to tell. Not with everything going on. Alice liked Gutsy but was far from being in love. Flirting with her—*kissing* her—had been almost a whim. Gutsy's response, though, surprised her. The way Gutsy looked at her, the way she held on to her hand with so much strength. Did that mean Gutsy was farther along the path to something serious?

Maybe.

Alice wasn't sure how she felt about that. Even if things were normal in town, she was the furthest thing from impulsive. She didn't want to rush anything. Not romance. Not relationships. Not anything.

Not even her bath.

She smiled and let out a long sigh.

Alice was asleep in minutes, and she slept a long time. She slept for much too long.

THE WOMAN'S NAME WAS SERGEANT ANGELA HOLLY. She was a lab technician, in her midtwenties, with brown skin and very dark brown eyes that were jumpy and filled with terror. She and Gutsy stood a few feet apart again, but now the shotgun hung loose in Holly's left hand as she reread the note.

"I thought the ravagers killed everyone," she said. "Or the wild men. Both, I guess."

"It was close," admitted Gutsy. "Glad to meet someone alive down here."

"Things fell apart, and I've mostly been hiding."

"Alone?"

Holly hesitated, and her eyes shifted away. "Not at first. There were ten of us. But the others mostly got sick. One by one. We had to . . . we had to . . ." She couldn't finish, and Gutsy didn't need her to.

"You said the others 'mostly' got sick," Gutsy said gently. "What happened to the rest?"

All Holly would give in reply was a fierce shake of her head. "I hid. I kept waiting for someone to come and take charge. No one did, though. Not even the captain."

"Collins?"

Holly beamed with relief. "You know her? You're a little young to be a nurse, and you're definitely not a soldier."

"My mom worked for Dr. Morton. I was, um, kind of apprenticing with him. I met Captain Collins a couple of times."

"Is the captain okay?" asked Holly, seeming to accept the apprentice lie.

"She was the last time I saw her," Gutsy said, sidestepping what would certainly be an ugly truth.

Holly set the note down on the cooler. "What about town? Tell me what happened."

"Sure," Gutsy said, "but would you mind putting the gun down?"

Holly glanced down at it and grunted. "Oh. Right. It's empty anyway." She leaned it against a cabinet.

"Empty . . . ?" echoed Gutsy.

"It was all I had," said Holly. "If you turned out to be a ravager or wild man, then I guess I'd be dead."

"You could have used it as a club," Gutsy suggested, but Holly didn't comment. So, Gutsy said, "Look, I'll be happy to tell you everything, but Dr. Morton wants the Dòmi stuff. Wild men tried to get into town through the secret door at the car wash. Do you know about that?"

"The door? Sure."

"Good. The wild men are going to be a problem because a huge wave of *los*"—she stopped and switched from the town nickname for the dead to the word Morton used— "reanimates is going to hit us. The Night Army. If the wild men infect them, then they'll just overwhelm us."

Holly nodded. "That's what we've always been afraid of,"

she said. "Ever since Homer Gibbon escaped and started organizing the ravagers. He's like a god to the reanimates. He destroyed this place. I figured he'd have wiped New Alamo off the map."

"Not for lack of trying," said Gutsy. "But, look, Morton is hurt. He's been bitten. We have people looking for Site B to try and get the supplies he needs for his treatment, but he sent me here to get the Dòmi stuff."

It was only partly true, but Angela Holly kept nodding as if it was all reasonable. "You came all the way from New Alamo?" She shuddered again. "You're out of your mind. Those *things* are out there."

"I was careful. Look . . . why don't you come back with me?"

"I . . . I'm okay down here."

"Really?" Gutsy asked frankly. "How much gas do you have left for the generator?"

Holly's eyes shifted away again. "Enough, I guess."

"How much is 'enough'?"

"Another week. Maybe more."

"And then what?" asked Gutsy.

"Well, by then most of the reanimates will have wandered off. I figured I'd risk opening the south exit, load up a Humvee, and drive out to Site B."

Gutsy stared at her.

"Whoa, wait—you have a vehicle that *works*?"

"Of course we do," Holly said. "Humvees, Strykers, Fast Attack Vehicles, some of those deuce-and-a-half trucks. They're in the motor pool on sublevel one. But we can't get there from here because part of sub-one collapsed. We have to go up to the main floor and then take stairway F to get there."

"How do you know that hasn't collapsed?"

"I've been there. Just to make sure, you know? But there are too many reanimates out there, so I came back down to wait." She paused and frowned. "You seem surprised, but how else were you going to get the Dòmi back to the lab? Didn't Doc Morton tell you to take a jeep or Humvee?"

"I, um, don't know how to drive," Gutsy admitted. "But, look, we need to get moving. Will you help me get the stuff on Dr. Morton's list?"

Holly seemed indecisive, but then nodded. "Sure."

Gutsy picked up the list again and moved to cabinet 003. She dialed in the code on the manual lock, opened the cabinet, and began removing small plastic devices, each marked with a code of mixed numbers and letters matching Morton's list. Gutsy knew that these were flash drives, which she'd heard about but never seen before. It was still hard to believe that vast amounts of information could be stored on such tiny devices.

"Do you have any, um, computers?" she asked. "Doc wanted one. A lap one."

"No problem," said Holly, as if that was nothing. "We can grab a couple of laptops."

Something occurred to Gutsy. Sergeant Holly was only about ten years older than she was. "Were you *raised* down here?" asked Gutsy.

"Oh, sure," said Holly. "My folks were both staff here. I went to a local school until the outbreak, and then grew up in the base with the other kids."

"Wait . . . *other* kids?"

Holly met her eyes for a moment, then looked away. "Of course there were other kids."

The word "were" hovered in the air, and Gutsy did not want to pursue it. They finished packing the thumb drives into the cooler and Gutsy stepped over to cabinet 009, but Holly touched her hand.

"Wait a sec," said the sergeant. "These units run off a generator, but to transport we'll need to keep the stuff cold. Let me get some ice packs." She hurried across the room to a big gray metal box that, when opened, exhaled a frosty breath of refrigerated air. Holly removed four blue plastic bricks and brought them back. "These will keep the samples secure for six hours."

Gutsy took one of the blue bricks and almost dropped it. The brick was made from plastic but was as solid as ice. She watched as Holly placed the other bricks securely in the cooler and then added the one she held. They turned to cabinet 009. Despite looking identical to the others, this one hissed open, and icy mist wafted out.

Inside there were rows and rows of small, clear vials filled with liquid that ranged in color from lemonade yellow to pumpkin orange. Most, though, were a golden hue, and each of these was marked with DM, which had been on the list.

Dòmi.

"Is that everything?" Gutsy asked.

"I think so."

"Then let's go. We need to—"

A sound cut her words to silence. They both spun toward the door. Outside in the hallway there was a noise so strange, so alien, that it chilled Gutsy to the bone. Not a moan, or a yell, or a howl.

This was much, much worse.

"Oh God . . . ," Holly breathed as she backed away from the open airlock. "Oh God, they found us."

The sound that floated through the polluted air was the high, sweet, evil laughter of children. And it chilled Gutsy to the bone.

Interlude Eight

Brother Mercy and the Raggedy Man

TWO YEARS AGO

SAINT JOHN LEFT THE TWO YOUNG REAPERS IN THE care of the king of the dead.

They remained with him for over a year, becoming his apprentices, as they had once been apprenticed to Brother Peter and Saint John.

It was a strange time. On one hand, they were required to sit and listen to the Raggedy Man ramble on and on about his plans for the world. Much of it was incoherent, though, and the dead king would throw out references to people and things from the old world that Brother Mercy did not understand—Sith Lords and *CSI* and supervillains and cable news. He laughed a lot, even though he was often the only one who understood the jokes.

However Brother Mercy privately wondered if the rambling was some kind of test, because the Raggedy Man's eyes were always sharp and alert. He always seemed to be enjoying some enormous private joke, and occasionally threw out comments or questions that required a good memory for things that had been said. Brother Mercy and Sister Sorrow learned to be very alert, and in their private moments often went over the details to make sure they would not be caught short.

It was clear that the Raggedy Man was not as educated as Saint John, but he was highly intelligent and very sly. Much more subtle than he appeared. It would be to his great peril, Mercy knew, to underestimate this creature.

After the first few weeks of merely being with the Raggedy Man, Brother Mercy finally summoned the courage to ask, "How can we be of service to you?"

The king of the dead grinned his wormy grin. "I was wondering when you'd stop being so afraid of me and get 'round to asking that."

The reapers shared a glance. So this *had* been a test.

As if he could read their minds, the patchwork king said, "You kids are supposed to be sharp. Fine. Let's see how sharp. Here's what you're going to do for me. First, you're going to start recruiting more of you breathers."

"For what reason, lord?" asked Sister Sorrow.

"Because I'm going to need a strike force. Call it special ops. Reapers like you can go places my ravagers can't. So, you are going to recruit and train as many as you can. Make 'em kneel and kiss the knives, or whatever it is you do. They need to be one hundred percent loyal—or they're lunch for my friends over there." He jerked a thumb toward the hordes of the dead.

"We can do that," promised Sorrow. "What else?"

The king leaned forward, elbows on rotted thighs. "There are some towns out there. Small cities, fortified camps. Strong ones. I could take 'em down by force of numbers, but I don't want to waste my people doing it. Saint John tells me you kids have a real talent for cracking those kinds of places open from the *inside*. Well, that's what I want you to do for me."

"Which towns?" asked Mercy. "Where?"

"There's a bunch. Freetown, right here in Ohio, is where we'll start. Then we'll work our way up to the big enchilada."

"Do you mean Asheville in North Carolina?"

"Yeah. We'll take that, too. But I have a very personal score to settle with a couple of places in south Texas. A military base where they tried real hard to kill this ol' boy." He touched his patchwork skin. "We're going to take that, and a juicy little town a few miles away called New Alamo."

PART FOURTEEN

THE ROAD TO ASHEVILLE

The question is not, Can they reason?

nor, Can they talk?

but, Can they suffer?

—JEREMY BENTHAM, WRITING ABOUT THE NATURE OF ANIMALS

THEY STOPPED FIVE MORE TIMES THAT DAY.

Morgie hated that he was slowing them, but he couldn't help it. Whatever this was made any flu or cold he'd ever had feel like nothing by comparison. He had the shivers but no fever, and it felt like there were ants crawling around in his stomach.

Even so, they made it all the way to Beaumont, staying well away from the dangers of Houston. The town was as empty and ghostly as the others had been, but everywhere they looked it was clear people *had* lived here until recently.

"You think the swarms chased them off?" Morgie asked. After some bland food—a bowl of rice and chicken broth made from stores found in an abandoned house—he was feeling a little better.

"Ah," said Riot, "the zombie speaks."

"I'm not a zombie, thank you very much."

"Yeah? You run into anyone who doesn't know you and they'd quiet you quicker than a chicken on a June bug."

"I'm fine."

"Whatever." They were in a big house that had clearly been occupied by a family both before and after First Night. There were pictures on the wall that showed two people smiling at their wedding; a picture of the woman holding a tiny baby as the man beamed down at her; another of them with a four-year-old girl and another baby; and so on, all the way to what looked like grandkids. The furniture was old and patched but clearly cared for, and except for recent dust, the place was clean. Riot walked slowly along the hall looking at the pictures. Morgie, seated on the couch with a blanket around him, followed her with his eyes. She stopped and touched one photo that showed the mother of the family standing with her daughter, who held a sleeping infant.

After a moment Riot took the framed picture down from the wall and stared at it, and Morgie wondered what was going on in her head. Riot had originally been raised by her birth father, who'd gotten custody following a divorce. Riot's mom had been a drug addict and was plagued by mental problems. Then, during First Night, her mother had been found and rescued from a gang by a man who called himself Saint John. Although Saint John had been a violent mass murderer and serial killer, he'd been kind to Riot's mom, and to a bunch of orphaned children she had tried to protect during those first wild days after the dead rose and all sense of law and order crumbled.

Riot's mother became "Mother Rose," and the children became the very first reapers in what would become Saint John's Night Church, all of them dedicated to what he believed was his holy mission to exterminate all human life. Saint John believed that the zombie plague was god's way of cleansing the world, removing a race that had failed to live up to what their god wanted of them. As Saint John saw it, anyone left alive was doing so in direct opposition to god's will. His reapers slaughtered tens of thousands of people, and planned—once all the killing was done—to take their own lives in an orgy of suicide. Riot's father had died, and Riot was taken and raised by this new and even more twisted version of her mother. By Mother Rose.

It hurt Morgie to know this, because he'd come from a loving home, and Riot never had a chance to know what that was like.

"Riot . . . ?" he asked softly.

She stiffened, gave a last lingering look at the picture, and hung it carefully back on its hook, straightened it, and brushed dust from the glass. Then she turned, pasting on her usual sardonic expression.

"Yeah, I heard you, son. I guess the people here packed and run off." She walked over to the living room window, which had been modified with light-blocking shutters on the inside. The doors were reinforced, too, set with panels of sheet aluminum. Loopholes had been cut through the walls, each covered with a leather flap for privacy, but easy to use for shooting without opening a window or door. "They fixed this place up smart, and looks like they had time to do it right. I 'spect the other houses round here will be the same. They *lived* here, maybe for years. Then they left, and in a right hurry, too."

"How can you tell that?"

"They left behind stuff they would have taken if there'd been time. I checked around. There's some bedding missing, and some clothes, but if they had time, they'd have taken the cots in the closet and medicines from the bathroom. And in the kitchen pantry, there are cans of stuff missing, but sacks of rice, flour, and cornmeal are still here. Nah—they left fast and just took what they could carry."

She sat down on a threadbare overstuffed chair. Since arriving, she'd stripped off the heavy body armor and carpet coat, and was now in jeans and her leather vest, which she wore over her bare skin. Morgie, sick as he was, had trouble not staring at her. He loved the way she was made. Lean and muscular, with broad shoulders and narrow hips, and long legs made for running. Or dancing. He wondered if, had the world been different, she might have been a dancer. There were a couple of people in town who'd been dancers before First Night, and they had the same athletic grace.

But the world had not been that kind to her. Riot's tanned skin was marked with pink and white scars, and there were permanent lines etched around her mouth that should have been laugh lines.

"I don't get it," said Morgie. "What's the *point* of all this? Of these swarms? Of these ravager monkey-bangers herding them like cattle and attacking towns? It can't be just for food, because they left all those dead people behind."

Riot shrugged. "Beats me." She cut him a look. "How are you feeling?"

"Okay."

"Let's say we try that again, and you give me a straight answer."

Morgie ate some more of the soupy rice. "Better than I did."

"But—?"

"But not all that good. And it's freaking me out, because it came on all of a sudden."

She thought about it and shook her head. "I don't even know how to guess at this," she admitted. "You grew up in Mountainside, on a mountain in the middle of California. We're in Texas. Different everything out here—different animals and plants, different things to be allergic to, different mutations everywhere we look. Maybe there's different kinds of flu viruses out here."

Morgie said nothing to that, because what she said was pretty much what he was most afraid of. Back home, the doctors in town managed to scavenge or make some antibiotics for bacterial infections, but they had no real way of making effective antiviral medicines. Luckily, Mountainside was a closed community, so it was mostly a matter of people handing the same strains back and forth, and after fifteen years most people were immune. Or close enough.

Not out here.

Captain Ledger had told them all stories of how diseases—old ones running rampant with no hospitals to combat them, and new strains—killed more people than the zombies ever did. Rotting corpses in rivers and lakes, new diseases born from the wild mutations, and strains made stronger by groups of survivors misusing the antibiotic and antiviral drugs they found. Measles, mumps, whooping cough, rabies, and dozens of other diseases stalked the Rot and Ruin like invisible armies.

Since leaving home, Morgie and the others had been exposed to thousands of zombies in a prison, to mutated animals, to a dying soldier, and to a polluted landscape that was warping—season by season—into something out of a nightmare.

"You better be careful yourself," Morgie said.

"I never get sick," Riot replied, but then he saw something flicker in her eyes. A flare of awareness that he was sure he understood. The previous night they'd held each other for hours. They'd kissed and touched. If he was sick, then . . .

Riot cleared her throat, got up quickly, and took the map from her pack. She spread it out on the dining room table and bent over to study it. Morgie watched her, studying how the lines around her mouth stretched tighter.

"I think we should take it easy tomorrow," she said without looking up. "Try for Lake Charles, Louisiana. That's only sixty miles, and all along Route 10." She paused. "We can stop as often as you need, no problem."

"Sure," said Morgie. "Whatever."

The house was secure, the windows and doors shut, shutters secured, and curtains drawn, but it seemed to him as if there was a cold wind blowing through the spacious rooms. It smelled of sadness and loss.

Or maybe it smelled of memories.

Stop it, he scolded himself. *Deal with it, or this is going to kill you.*

PART FIFTEEN

NEW ALAMO

Strength does not come from physical capacity.

It comes from an indomitable will.

—Mahatma Gandhi

GUTSY WHIPPED HER MACHETE FROM ITS SCABBARD as shadows filled the airlock opening.

"Oh God, oh God, oh God . . ." That was all Sergeant Holly seemed able to say, and with each repetition her voice lost more of its force, becoming emptier.

Despite what Gutsy knew had to be the source of that childish laughter, she wanted the shadows to be different. At that moment she would have given almost anything for the shapes out there to be adults. Even if they were wild men and this would be where she died, that would be better than what she actually faced.

Gutsy stepped toward the airlock, raising her machete as if it weighed ten tons.

"We have to get out of here," she said, but there was no answer.

The shadows outside capered like demons as the laughter increased.

"Are they wild men?" Gutsy asked in a fierce whisper.

Holly swallowed audibly and gave a single, weak nod. "Wodewose was . . . it was . . . designed for adult brain chemistry. Wodewose works on the reanimates, not the living.

Those kids were already infected by the Lucifer pathogen in the air, and that made them turn. With kids, it . . . it had a different effect. We never expected it to affect neuroplasticity and neurogenesis. Wodewose crosses the blood-brain barrier. It would do all kinds of damage to any developing neurosystem, but we never studied how the mutated form would affect children's brains. They're so different—still growing and changing at that age. The brain doesn't fully form until age twenty-five. These kids died down here, reanimated, and then were exposed to Wodewose. We never did studies on something like that. If we had, then we'd know the pathogenesis of this and . . ."

Holly rattled on and on, explaining too much, trying to hide her fear behind the science while at the same time using the truth of that same science to chip away at her defenses. Gutsy had no idea if any of what Holly said made sense, or if she was totally losing it.

"Those . . . *things* out there," said the sergeant in a ghastly whisper, "they're from here. They're *ours*. They're the kids who were born down here. Now they're wild men. Wild kids. Whatever."

Gutsy and Holly were near the back wall, more than fifty feet from the open airlock. The shadows still moved, making distorted monster shapes, but so far none of the children showed themselves. "How many of them are there?"

Sergeant Holly shook her head. "I don't know."

From the laughter outside, Gutsy figured that there had to be at least half a dozen, maybe more.

"Why aren't they coming in?"

Holly pointed to the BAMS units above the door. "The

steam jets are toxic. Three of them chased me in here a few days ago, and . . . well, you know. Now the others stay outside. Waiting."

Gutsy hefted her machete. "Is there any other way out of here?"

"No."

She thought about something she'd read in at least a dozen novels. "What about air vents? Can we crawl through them?"

Holly shook her head. "Of course not. This is a biohazard station. The air ducts are small, and there are half a dozen filters. There's no subfloor or electrical access tunnels. Nothing we can crawl through. The airlock is the only way out."

Gutsy grabbed Holly by the arm and pulled her toward the cooler. "You take that," she ordered. "Follow me. We're going to head straight to the stairwell. I'll . . . I'll do the fighting." Her voice broke for a moment at the thought, but she firmed it up. "You follow." Gutsy waved her hand in the sergeant's face, making her flinch. "Hey, are you listening?"

"Yes, yes . . . ," Holly gasped. "I just don't know if I can do this."

"It's that or die," said Gutsy. "You can't stay down here forever, you know." She picked up the cooler and thrust it at her. "Don't drop it."

Gutsy moved toward the airlock, gripping her machete, ready to do awful things. The laughter rose and rose, as if the infected children knew that she was coming. There was a cruel delight in their voices. A dreadful anticipation.

She inched her way toward the door, glancing up at the BAMS unit, not sure if it would spray her again. Sweat ran down her entire body, soaking her clothes, and it felt icy despite the humid hazmat suit.

There were soft, sneaky scuffling sounds outside as the laughter faded away. Like children playing a monstrous game of hide-and-seek. She glanced back to see that Holly was directly behind her, holding the cooler by the handle and clutching the knife to her chest like a crucifix. Gutsy, despite her doubts about God and religion, prayed in that moment. Reciting the prayers Mama taught her when she was little. The prayer to Mary, begging for help.

Be with us now and in the hour of our death . . .

Gutsy was crying as she stepped out into the hall. She sobbed aloud as the children rushed toward her, reaching with tiny hands, smiling with small mouths. Laughing. Grabbing.

What happened next was monstrous.

GUTSY CLIMBED THE STEPS. STAGGERING BENEATH the unbearable weight of what she had done.

Her hazmat suit was covered with blood. Her mind was lost in horror.

Her legs went through the motions of lifting her step by step. Her left hand grabbed the handrail and pulled the weight of her guilt up and up. The machete, dripping, dangled from her right, the tip banging like a dull church bell on the edge of each step.

Somewhere behind her, Sergeant Angela Holly followed.

It took forever to climb those steps.

Back in town, Alice Chung moaned in her sleep and turned onto her side, sloshing tepid water onto the floor. Had anyone been there to hear her moan, it would have sounded like someone in pain. Not physical pain, but something caused by a hurt that ran miles deep.

In the other room, her mother moaned too. Very softly.

Miles and miles away, far from New Alamo, the Raggedy Man slept.

He did not sleep the way the living did. Nor did he stay perpetually awake like his billions of shambling children. But every now and then he fell slowly into a stupor, his ugly head sagging down onto his patchwork chest, his hands going slack in his lap, as still as dead tarantulas. His breath—such as it was—faded to the faintest of whispers.

His eyelids did not close, though. They stayed open, and the eyeballs, milky and dusty, stared at nothing. Rubbery lips, caked with dried blood and utterly slack, hung open. A fly landed on his chin and walked over the torn skin and onto those lips, nibbling at tiny flecks of uneaten meat.

Homer Gibbon's tongue, gray as a worm, flicked out and caught the fly, pulling it in, pushing it toward teeth that ground it to paste. At no time during this did the Raggedy Man wake. He slept, and dreamed dreams that were painted in shades of black and red.

WHEN THEY REACHED THE LOWER OF THE TWO MAIN
floors, Gutsy and Holly stopped in the stairwell doorway,
keeping back to remain in shadow. The mound of debris that
reached up to the dangling steel cable was right there, less
than two dozen paces away.

But it might as well have been on the far side of the moon.

The whole mound and much of the ruined top floor
swarmed with figures that moaned and howled and tore and
bit. Wild men. She had no idea where they'd come from. Other
rooms, other floors, maybe drawn by the sounds she'd made,
even though Gutsy had tried to be quiet. Or had something
else triggered them? There was no way to know, and no time
to figure it out.

And then she understood.

The wild men were not looking for her. All their rage was
directed upward, and by leaning out, Gutsy could see that
the upper edge of the big pit was thronged with hundreds of
shapes. *Los muertos.* A swarm of them must have come upon
the base, drawn by the smell of living flesh. The wild men,
after all, were not dead. Not the ones here in the base, at

least. They had been transformed by the paracide spread by the clouds of toxic smoke.

The living dead packed the rim of the pit, moaning with impossible hunger, and there were so many of them that the mass behind pushed those in front over the edge. They fell by the dozen, raining down onto the slope or smashing themselves on the concrete floor. Gutsy flinched as she heard bones shatter and meat burst apart. Some hit the sides of the heaped debris and bounced or rolled and then struggled to their feet, unconcerned with any injuries. Soon so many were falling that they landed not on broken concrete or twisted metal but on the bodies of other living dead.

The wild men, true to their name, went into a frenzy as the dead fell among them.

They surged forward, leaping on each zombie, biting and tearing at them with savage ferocity, sparing only those who transitioned quickly to wild men. The ones who, for whatever unknown quirk of biology, turned more slowly were simply torn to pieces.

At first Gutsy thought that it was just being close to their victims that turned the living dead into wild men, but then she saw that the paracide was also active in the bites. She was terrified, but at the same time found a splinter of twisted admiration for the science behind Wodewose. There were so many ways the howling carriers could infect *los muertos*— saliva, their own blood, skin-to-skin contact, breath. They had clearly been engineered to be perfect delivery systems for this counterplague. It also made Gutsy understand why Wodewose had been shelved. It was *too* dangerous. Too overwhelming.

The fight she watched proved that. It should have been

unequal, because there were only about twenty of these frenzied mutants and dozens of *los muertos*. But the wild men were so much faster. They were much more coordinated in their attacks, too, bashing aside reaching arms and tripping the living dead before falling on them.

Some of the wild men were dragged down, though, buried under piles of the zombies, but even as they were torn apart they bit their attackers and howled and spat their infection at the reanimates. A few of the dead fell back, and Gutsy could see their bodies begin to twitch. The Wodewose paracide worked with unbelievable speed. Within a minute of the first wild men exposure, zombies began rising and turning on their own kind. Others, turned by spit from the howls, turned even faster. Seconds.

The fight was getting worse as more and more of the shamblers fell over the edge, and Gutsy realized that this must be a swarm. One of the big ones Benny and his friends had seen. She saw a few ravagers fighting their way along the rim, trying in vain to push their mindless charges back. She saw one fall, pushed over the edge by the weight of bodies. He pinwheeled his arms as he dropped, trying to avoid a jagged spike of broken steel and failing in a gruesome way. He landed on a seething mass of shamblers, bounced, rolled, and then sprawled at the feet of two of the wild men, who fell upon him instantly.

This fight was different, though. Even with the hard fall and sudden attack, the ravager rolled away and got to his knees as he drew a pistol. He fired six shots, hitting the two wild men in the chest and face. They fell, but the gunshots drew the attention of the others, and a pack of them ran howling toward the ravager. He emptied his pistol into them, dropping another three, but then the rest swept over him like a tidal surge. He went down with a roar of anger and fear. Then he shrieked like a wounded fox as they bit him on the hands and neck and face.

The wild men cast him aside and ran howling in search of fresh prey. After a few seconds, the ravager began to twitch. As the spasms racked him, he struggled to his feet and tried to stop the wild jerks of his limbs, tried to stand or walk normally. The ravager fought back, even to the point of punching his own face and chest and legs as if he could force them to obey. Then a series of terrible cramps hit him in the stomach and he caved over, vomiting explosively. As he dropped to his knees, his face, by pure chance, pointed toward the open stairwell. He stared into the shadows as if he could see the two young women crouched there.

Gutsy had looked into the eyes of the ravagers before, and all she'd seen was a lingering intelligence but no trace at all of humanity.

Not now, though.

The ravager blinked over and over again as if trying to clear his eyes, and—impossibly—the rage was gone, replaced by pain and . . .

Awareness.

Yes, that was it. In that moment, the ravager seemed somehow aware of what it was. Completely aware. Terribly aware. He looked at his filthy hands, stained with old and new blood. He plucked at his clothes—leather and chains—and touched his torn face. All the time his eyes stared into the shadows.

He spoke a single word.

"Please . . ."

Close as she was to him, there was too much noise to hear the word, but she saw the shape of his mouth. She knew what he meant.

Here, in the middle of a battle between two kinds of living dead and mutated wild men, one former ravager was—for the moment—a person again.

But then the Wodewose won the internal battle and the ravager crossed fully over. He seemed to forget about the two women, and when the next zombie fell, he turned and attacked it. Spreading the paracide.

"Let's *go*," urged Holly, pulling at Gutsy's arm.

Gutsy allowed herself to be pulled backward, then she turned and hurried down the stairs to sublevel one, along a complex series of empty corridors and up a remote stairway far away from the fight. They emerged in a huge room filled with vehicles—dozens and dozens of them. Humvees and trucks of all kinds. Some were on jacks or lifts, or had their hoods open beneath chain hoists from which transmissions or engine blocks hung. Some sat on blocks, their wheels gone, and many were nothing more than hulks stripped down to skeletons for parts.

But in rows against the farthest wall were at least forty vehicles squatting on good tires, facing a massive roll-down door made from reinforced steel. Holly said that there was a long tunnel on the other side, and that she could open the door from any of the vehicles. The exit was four miles past the base, hidden among the abandoned houses of a dead town.

They moved through the big room among dozens of

silent, rotting corpses and thousands of shell casings. There had been yet another terrible battle here. They crept between the lines of vehicles, Gutsy in front, her machete ready. Nothing moved down here. Everything truly felt dead.

"Some of the staff got out," whispered Holly, as if reading her mind. "But I don't know if they were already infected by Wodewose or one of the other pathogens released by the explosions." She stopped by the first vehicle in the line—a tan Humvee—grabbed the door handle, and opened the door. Gutsy knew cars of all kinds, but most as silent metal shelters to get out of the rain or cold when out scavenging. The first working engine in her entire experience was the quad Nix and Lilah took.

The Humvee was big and looked solid. About fifteen feet long, covered in sturdy metal armor, with an ugly brute of a .50-caliber machine gun mounted on the top.

"Do you know how to fire that thing?" Gutsy asked.

"Ha! Not a clue," said Holly. "I'm a lab tech."

"Great," Gutsy said under her breath as she took the cooler and put it in the back seat. Holly climbed in behind the wheel, and Gutsy walked around to get into the passenger side. They closed and locked the doors. The engine started with a throaty growl, and Gutsy studied everything Holly did to adjust mirrors, put on a seat belt, fix the orientation of her seat. And Gutsy filed it all away in her library of a brain.

Holly took a breath, exhaled, and put the car in gear, then drove forward slowly. She did not have to do anything special to activate the big security door, and it began to rumble up as the Humvee approached—it obviously had its own generator. Gutsy braced herself, terrified of the possibility of a tunnel filled with some type of swarm.

All that waited for them were shadows.

Holly flicked on the headlights and drove forward with an awkward jerkiness that proved just how unskilled she was at driving. The Humvee moved, though, and after a few hundred yards the sergeant's confidence increased, and she picked up speed. By the time they emerged into the gray light of an early dawn, the machine was ticking along at forty miles an hour. Gutsy was breathless, sitting with her feet braced and her hands clamped to a bar set inside the door. She'd never gone anywhere near this fast before, and she did not like it one little bit.

The hidden entrance was inside a big industrial warehouse, and Holly drove out into the street, turned to the north, and found a highway.

"We'll have to go the long way," she said. "Don't want those things to see us."

"Works for me," said Gutsy, maintaining her death grip on the frame.

The Humvee settled onto the cracked and weedy blacktop, and it seemed like Holly pressed the accelerator nearly to the floor. Gutsy watched in horror as the speedometer climbed from forty to fifty and higher, all the way to sixty-five miles per hour. An insane speed.

Far over to her right she could see the faint glow of the last fires from the pit, but it was nearly obscured. By *los muertos*.

"Wait a sec," said Gutsy as she fished a small but powerful pair of binoculars from her vest. "Slow down. I need to see this."

Holly rolled to a stop, letting the Humvee idle quietly while Gutsy stood up and trained the glasses on the creatures in the distance. It was not a swarm. That was far too small a word for what she saw crowding around the pit. Stretching off toward the south and east was a sea of the living dead. Not hundreds or even thousands but tens of thousands of them. So many of the hungry dead.

An army.

This was what Captain Collins had warned them about.

The Night Army, in all its unstoppable force, was marching on New Alamo.

She thumped down into her seat and began beating on the dashboard. "Drive, drive, *drive!*"

Holly put the Humvee in gear, and it shot forward.

"Faster," cried Gutsy, but Holly couldn't hear her over the engine's roar. Gutsy repeated it. Not meaning to scream but unable not to.

PART SIXTEEN

THE ROAD HOME

"Hope" is the thing with feathers—
That perches in the soul—
And sings the tune without the words—
And never stops—at all—

—EMILY DICKINSON, "'HOPE' IS THE THING WITH FEATHERS"

THE QUAD STOOD ON A RIDGE THAT LOOKED DOWN
on a wide plane littered with black smudges of soot where
towns used to stand. Many of the roads were choked with cars
or thoroughly overgrown with weeds.

A swarm of living dead—all shamblers—was making
its way up the slope with the patience of the undying. Lilah
checked the magazine in her pistol for the eighth time, and
it still held only four rounds. That was all they had between
them: four bullets, against a horde of as many as five thousand zoms.

"We have to go," said Lilah, her voice filled with dread.

"Let me try again," Nix said as she fiddled with the sat-
phone.

"It doesn't work," growled Lilah. "You've tried it a hundred times. Either it's broken or those satellites are dead. But
we need to get moving, or *we'll* be dead."

"Just let me try one more time."

The relentless dead climbed toward them. Even moving
slowly, they seemed to devour the distance.

Nix fiddled with the dials and even jiggled the phone.

"We have to *go!*" cried Lilah.

Then Nix froze. "Wait."

"Wait for what?"

"I thought I heard something." She pressed the speaker to her ear. "I heard something. I swear it."

"It doesn't matter what you hear, we need to—"

There was a burst of high-pitched static, and then a voice spoke. "—*come in, caller,*" it said. "*This is a military channel. Please identify yourself . . .*"

The girls stared at the device, almost too startled to speak.

"*Repeating, this is a military channel. Please identify yourself.*"

Nix clicked the button. "My name is Nix Riley, I'm from Reclamation, California. We're in trouble and we need help."

PART SEVENTEEN

THE FALL
OF NEW ALAMO

I am determined to sustain myself as long as
possible & die like a soldier who never forgets what
is due to his own honor & that of his country—
Victory or death

—WILLIAM B. TRAVIS, LAST COMMANDER OF THE ALAMO

62

"I DON'T UNDERSTAND WHAT I'M LOOKING AT," said Alethea.

It was just past two in the morning, and the stars shone down on two points of light that bounced along the ground.

"It's coming really fast," said Spider. "Could it be one of those quad things? Hey, maybe the girls are back already."

"Can't be them," said Alethea. "It's way too soon."

They watched the lights come closer. It was weird for them to see anything move that fast. Way faster and brighter than a lantern on a mule-drawn wagon, or even a solar-powered flashlight carried by a rider on a fast horse.

Other people started gathering around them, watching. The adults, especially those in their middle thirties or older, pointed and yelled in genuine surprise.

"No, it's a *truck*, I think," said one. "It's an actual darn truck! And it's driving fit to beat the devil."

The sound of it rolled ahead of the oncoming lights and reached the watchers on the walls. They all ran to meet the vehicle. Everyone was excited but armed in case this was some new trick by Captain Collins and her Rat Catchers. Benny stood, sword drawn, next to Karen; Alethea had Rainbow

Smite ready. A few people leveled shotguns or pistols at the vehicle, which slowed to a skidding, sloppy halt just outside the gates. The passenger door popped open, and a figure stepped out, hands raised.

"No, it's me! It's Gutsy!"

SAM RODE IN FRONT TO SCOUT THE TRAIL, BUT THEN he suddenly reined in his horse and raised a clenched fist in the military signal to stop.

Ledger waited, and then Sam waved him up. They stood in the shadows of some pine trees and looked down the slope to a small group of industrial-looking buildings just off the left-hand side of the road. Both men pulled out their binoculars.

The moon was so bright that they could easily see that the weeds in one spot along the side of the road had been battered down, leaving a gap about five feet wide. They glanced at each other, and Ledger felt a flare of hope ignite in his chest.

They tied the horses to the trees and crept down the slope, making maximum use of cover. As they drew close, they saw that the weeds were newly crushed, and that running past them were the unmistakable tire tracks of a quad.

"This is it," said Ledger quietly, but with obvious excitement in his voice. "This has to be Site B."

They studied the buildings and saw neither cameras nor motion sensors. Everything was still. So they approached the nearest structure, sticking to corner angles to reduce visibility of them from windows.

The tread marks of the quad's fat rubber tires led them across the dusty and overgrown parking lot, but they ended, unhelpfully, at an ordinary-looking steel garage door with a few nondescript trucks parked near it. The fiction they sold was that this was some minor factory in the middle of nowhere, and everything was business as usual. At least, that had been the cover story before the dead rose.

Sam kept watch with the sniper rifle while Ledger tried the big roll-down door and the smaller standard door beside it. Both were sturdily made and locked solid. It wasn't necessary for either of them to speculate on whether this was merely a front, or that beyond the facade there would be a much more sophisticated entrance, possibly a steel hatch or airlock. Instead, Ledger went to work on the exterior door. Picking locks was something any special ops soldier knew how to do, though this lock was particularly tricky. It took him nearly fifteen minutes to tease the tumblers into the right angles using a set of lock picks he always carried. The door clicked, and both men fanned back as it swung open.

No shots. No alarms. No movement.

"A very cliché movie line keeps playing over and over in my head," murmured Ledger.

"Oh? Which one?"

"I have a bad feeling about this."

"Ah," said Sam. "Me too."

They grinned at each other and shared a nod.

They went in, very fast and very savvy. Two soldiers who had done this a thousand times. Fighters who'd survived everything a fractured world could throw at them.

* * *

The horses waited with their stoic equine patience as the door swung silently closed behind their riders. They munched grass and dozed beneath the stars. They only stirred and began to whinny when the muffled sounds of gunfire raged from inside the building.

The animals began to panic when they heard the horrible screams.

THE GATES WERE OPENED TO ALLOW THE HUMVEE to roll inside. A crowd of people surged around the vehicle, staring at it as if it was something out of a dream. Everyone knew about the little quads, but here was a powerful military vehicle.

Gutsy no longer wore her hazmat suit, having instructed Sergeant Holly where to stop to pick up the strong disinfectants left outside for just this purpose. The suits were now in a plastic bag in the back, soaking in germ-killing chemicals.

Karen Peak, Alethea, and Spider reached her first.

"You *promised*!" yelled Alethea. "You swore you wouldn't do anything stupid."

"I didn't," snapped Gutsy. "But I don't have time to argue. We have to get this stuff to Morton."

She pulled the cooler out of the back. As she did, a lot of hostile eyes flicked to Sergeant Holly. Gutsy could hear the murmurs start and then spread like wildfire.

"She's from the base . . ."

". . . she's one of them . . ."

". . . Rat Catcher . . ."

". . . scientist . . ."

"...monster..."

Gutsy thrust the cooler into Spider's hands, whipped out her machete, and wheeled on the crowd. "Anyone lays a hand on her, I'll cut it off and feed it to my dog."

That stopped the murmuring and the movement toward where Holly still sat.

"This woman helped me get stuff we need to fight what's coming."

"She's a monster," yelled a big man as he came pushing his way through the crowd. His face was scarlet with fury. "Those people killed my Mary..."

Alethea shifted into his path and touched his chest with the fat end of Rainbow Smite.

"Don't," she warned.

The big man glared past her and then down at Alethea. His furious eyes filled with tears. "They killed my Mary," he said again in a voice that was suddenly small and lost. They were the same words, but they came close to breaking Gutsy's heart.

Gutsy reached out and gently pushed the baseball bat down. She looked up at the man, who towered more than a foot over her.

"Mr. Howard," she said in a measured voice, "I know how hurt you are. You *know* that I know. You came to Mama's memorial. But listen to me now. Please. Things are worse than you know. We aren't just facing *los muertos*. Not anymore. Not even just them and the ravagers. There's something else coming. Something called wild men. A different kind of infected. They're faster. Smarter. And they are definitely coming here. Soon." She pointed to the cooler. "The stuff Sergeant Holly helped me bring here is the only thing that might give us a chance. I need you—and everyone—to leave her be. Same with Doctor Morton. Judge later, but right now do what I ask, or everyone will lose . . . everyone." She stepped a little closer and lowered her voice, speaking only to him. "*Please*."

A big sob broke in his bull chest and he nodded, turned away, and shambled back into the crowd. Other people put comforting hands on his shoulders. No one else made a move toward Holly.

Gutsy looked around at the people of her town. Then she took the cooler back from Spider and raced toward the hospital.

MORTON AND FLORES WERE WAITING FOR HER, already alerted to her dramatic return.

"Did you get it?" cried Morton. "Tell me you got it."

Gutsy set the cooler down on the now-empty autopsy table. Morton struggled to his feet and peered in as Flores removed the top. The doctor nearly fainted.

He turned to Flores. "You see? I *told* you she would do it. Remarkable young woman. Truly remarkable."

The pharmacist nodded to Gutsy. "He made me get everything set up because he was convinced you'd bring this stuff. I've been mixing a nutrient-rich stabilizer. Mostly horse dung, but we have a lot of it."

"Really?" she asked.

"Yes," said Morton. "The engineered prions will bond to the organic material, and that will allow it to last much longer. Days without refrigeration."

"We have people making more of the stabilizer," said Flores.

Gutsy glanced dubiously at the cooler. "What good will all that stabilizer do if we only have a little of the Dòmi?"

"Prions are small," said Morton, tapping the cooler's lid

with a fingernail, "and there are a lot of them in here. Mixed correctly, we could create a few tons of weaponized Dòmi."

"*Tons?*" Gutsy gasped. "That's great! We can throw it in batches off the wall once the wild men infect *los muertos*. If we time it with the way the wind's blowing, we can—"

"Are you mad?" cried Morton. "We need to get out of this town as soon as possible. Right now."

"But why? We have the Dòmi. You said the wild men will infect or destroy all of the undead, and that Dòmi will stop them." Gutsy was furious. "That's why I went to the darn base. What am I missing?"

"Use your brains, Gabriella," snapped Morton. "Yes, the Dòmi will work, but we don't have any kind of delivery system to regulate how we use it. Once Wodewose eliminated the parasites, we would then introduce mass quantities of Dòmi to shut down their aggression. And that's if it worked as intended. Remember, this project was shelved before we'd done any major field testing. This is theory. Dòmi was never intended to be used in areas with active communities of uninfected people. If the Raggedy Man's army is infected by the paracide, there could be half a million or more wild men scaling the walls. If we had fifty times as many able fighters as we do now, and each had automatic weapons with an unlimited supply of bullets . . . we'd still lose."

Gutsy stared at him. Stunned. Gutted.

Into the awful silence, Morton said, "We need to abandon the town. Tonight or first thing in the morning. Do you know if any wild men followed you? Are they already coming here?"

Gutsy shook her head numbly. "No. We were going so fast. I kept looking back, but I didn't see any the last few miles."

Morton frowned. "Maybe they wandered off. There are plenty of reanimates out there to distract them. Even so, we need to evacuate the town and head for Site B."

"Which is where, exactly?" asked Flores. "You said you weren't sure. Captain Ledger and Mr. Imura could be out on a wild-goose chase."

"No," said Gutsy quickly, "the lab technician who drove me here—Holly—says she knows exactly where it is, and from what she said, it's one of the spots you told Ledger and Sam about."

"Excellent!" Morton cried. "Then we need to evacuate New Alamo and get there. With the materials and equipment in that lab, we can mass-produce Dòmi. Mind you, we'd still need a stabilizer of some kind. Something moist enough for the Dòmi to bond with, but heavy enough to be usefully directed once we come up with a delivery system."

Gutsy stood there, staring hard at the doctor. "At the base," she said slowly, "the staff there were infected by Wodewose that was in the air from the blast. Wouldn't Dòmi spread, too?"

"As I said, Gabriella," said Morton impatiently, "it *could* spread everywhere in time. We can't rely on chance. Wind patterns are unpredictable. Bioweapons, and event counteragents, have to be directed."

Gutsy stabbed a finger toward the west. "Then we need to figure something out. I saw a whole swarm of *los muertos* being infected by wild men. That swarm could be on its way here right now. Thousands of wild men."

Morton paled. "Save my soul! Listen to me: the Dòmi will work, but we don't want to be around when the wild men collide with the Night Army. Dòmi is a superquick-onset counteragent. The original plan had been to lure swarms of reanimates into remote areas and then deliver the paracide, via airburst. That would take over the reanimate hosts, and by the time the wild men found their way to any populated area, the more extreme symptoms—the shrieking and murderous rage—would have worn off. The older reanimates would simply collapse, and the new ones would likely starve to death. In either case, that plan won't work if this town becomes ground zero for the Dòmi release. We'd be caught between the monsters. New Alamo is built to defend against the unthinking dead, and it can barely do that. The wild men would overrun our defenses and sweep through the town."

"What choice do we have, though?" Flores begged. "The wild men are bringing Wodewose with them. Believe me when I say that we do not want to be here when that happens."

"Site B is our fallback," said Morton.

"Okay, okay," said Flores, "but what if Captain Collins is still *at* Site B? She'll never let us in."

"Captain Ledger and Sam Imura might already be there," said Gutsy. "They might have gotten in and stopped her."

"Sure, and the wild men will all suddenly become our friends and we'll sit around and sing 'Kumbaya,'" mocked Morton. "You're insane, girl."

"The world's insane," she replied. "At least we have hope."

GUTSY RAN BACK TO THE GATE AND FOUND THE Chess Players there, grilling Holly. Alethea and Spider seemed to be referees, but the mood of the crowd had turned ugly again.

"Stop it," snapped Gutsy, stepping between Holly and the others. She pointed the way she'd come. "We don't have time for this crap. The Night Army is coming, and so are the wild men. We're about to get crushed between them. We have to get ready to fight." Before anyone could speak, she added, "And we need to think about going back to the base."

"*Back?*" said Karen. "Are you out of your mind?"

"Didn't you hear what I said before? There are other vehicles back there." She thumped the Humvee's hood. "More trucks like this one. All sorts of stuff."

"And weapons," added Holly, trying to sell her own usefulness. "We have more guns than you'll ever need—small arms, automatic rifles, rocket launchers, grenades, even flame throwers. We have a whole stock of weapons. Probably a couple million rounds of ammunition, too. All of it's in the armory, which is right next to the garage."

Alethea said, "And how exactly do we get all that stuff

without catching every disease known to man?"

"We have more hazmat suits at the hospital."

"Five more," said a nurse in the crowd. "Six, including that one you stole."

"Borrowed," Gutsy corrected. "And Holly has one. Which means six people can go with her back to the base and bring back seven vehicles, and a lot of weapons."

"There are hazmat suits at the base, too," said Holly. "In the garage. They were for people coming into the facility during a biohazard lockdown. They won't be contaminated."

That kicked off a buzz of excited conversation, during which Karen, the Chess Players, and Gutsy's friends closed around her.

"Even with a lot of guns," said Karen quietly, "we can't stop all of those wild men and shamblers."

Gutsy prompted Holly to explain where Site B was. Then Gutsy said, "We have to evacuate, and we should do it *before* those things get here. Like, now. Everyone should pack only what they can carry, and we can head right out. We need to do it on foot, because it'll take too long for us to shuttle with cars and trucks. I don't think we'll be able to get a whole fleet back here in time. So, the farther we are from town, the better. We can set rally points so the cars can find us. Then they can take the old and sick people, and little kids, while the rest of keep walking. It's about twelve miles, so we can get to Site B a couple hours after midnight."

"The east gate is the best exit," said Ford. "We can get out there and then turn north along the highway."

"Good," Chong said, "but what happens if the Raggedy Man has some ravager spies and sees us leave?"

"What about the tunnel?" asked Spider. "It comes out at the car wash, and that's pretty far from town. There's a lot of supplies down there, too, so if people brought wheelbarrows and carts with them, they could load up as they leave."

"I like it," said Gutsy.

"We need to set those rally points," said Urrea, and he named several places where people could gather that would give them easy access to either the east gate or the hospital. Several others joined the discussion to work out details.

She heard Benny mutter, "This is the world's most insane plan." But then he stepped up and said, very loudly, "This is how we stay alive. Come on—let's move."

"Who are you to tell us what to do?" demanded one of the townswomen, Mrs. Gray, who ran the feed store. "You're not even *from* here."

"Well, lady," said Benny, "I'm here now. And I sure as heck don't want to die here. So, if you have a better plan to stop about a million infected from turning New Alamo into a breakfast buffet, let's hear it."

There was silence.

"Didn't think so."

Mr. Urrea and Mr. Ford stepped up and stood on either side of Gutsy. Karen Peak joined them and, surprisingly, so did the big man, Mr. Howard. That seemed to break the resistance.

Within minutes the plan was in motion. Spider, who was the fastest runner, zoomed off to the hospital to fetch the hazmat suits. By the time he returned, the Chess Players had located five adults willing to head to the base and drive vehicles back. Everyone suited up and the Humvee left at top speed, with half the town on the walls watching in a grave silence.

As soon as the truck vanished into the dusty distance, Karen took charge of the packing for the planned exodus.

Benny and Chong, accompanied by the armored hound Grimm, went to the hospital to start collecting medical equipment, and Spider hurried back to the orphanage to warn the Cuddlys and make sure the other kids packed.

That left Gutsy and Alethea momentarily alone.

"Whew," said Alethea, wrinkling her nose.

"What?"

"Girl, you stink."

"Gosh, thanks," Gutsy said. "Maybe I'll take a long soak with bath balm and get my nails done. Take the rest of the day off and read a book."

"Hey," said Alethea, adjusting her tiara, "just because it's the end of the world doesn't mean there isn't such a thing as self-care and personal hygiene."

Despite everything, Gutsy laughed.

It didn't last, though. She turned and looked in the direction of the east wall. Alethea followed the line of her gaze.

"Alice?" she asked.

"I should check on her. Help her pack."

"I'll go with you."

They headed off to Alice's house.

PART EIGHTEEN

THE ROAD TO ASHEVILLE

For the Angel of Death spread his wings on the blast,
And breathed in the face of the foe as he passed;
And the eyes of the sleepers waxed deadly and chill,
And their hearts but once heaved, and for ever grew still!

—LORD BYRON (GEORGE GORDON),
"THE DESTRUCTION OF SENNACHERIB"

67

THEY REACHED THE SERPENTINE EXPANSE OF Douglas Lake, still following I-40 but rarely going above twenty-five miles per hour. They made stops, though after a while they both felt hollowed out, with nothing left to give to the demands of the sickness.

They passed through Wilton Springs, pulled off the interstate and circled around to the 440 Truck Stop, which sat at the edge of a vast, mountainous forest. The truck stop's diner was deserted, half of it crushed nearly flat by the body of a yellow-and-black Bell Jet Ranger helicopter. The serial number—N90090—was readable, but most of the machine was either scorched black or rusted to a reddish-gray.

Mile marker signs on the side of the road told them they were only sixty-three miles from Asheville.

"Well," said Riot wearily, "that's something."

Morgie nodded. "I guess."

Riot glanced sharply at him and started to say something, but a fit of coughing stole her words. Morgie held out his canteen and she took it, still coughing.

Sixty-three miles. A few hours, even at reduced speed. They'd be there tonight.

To Morgie it felt as if they had been driving forever, as if the distance to where they'd left their friends was ten million miles, and the distance to home in California was incalculable. He and Riot were sick, weak, and exhausted, and so tired of riding. Every part of Morgie hurt, from the bones in his butt to the teeth in his clenched jaws. The diarrhea and vomiting were constant, and he felt like his whole body was made from wet tissue paper; anything could tear him apart.

They parked their bikes behind a massive tractor trailer that squatted on eighteen flat tires. When the engine noise died away, the world once again became a place of eerie quiet. In the sheltered cleft of a couple of smashed semis they made a camp. Morgie fell asleep right away and dreamed that he was home. Not in the new town of Reclamation but in Mountainside, before Benny ever left. In his dream, he and Benny and Chong were sitting on the steps of Lafferty's General Store, each of them with a small stack of unopened packs of Zombie Cards. They were tearing open the wax paper and sorting through what they had, swapping doubles, making shrewd trades.

"Hey, look at this one," said Chong. He held up a card for them to see, and on it was a zombie with wild hair, dead eyes, and jagged teeth biting a terrible red chunk out of Nix Riley's throat.

Benny laughed. "That looks like Morgie," he said brightly.

Chong snickered. "*Morgue* Mitchell," he joked.

"I got a good one too," said Benny, and the card he held up actually showed Morgie. But the image was of Riot standing over him as he lay facedown in the dirt, and she was about to drive a steel sliver into the back of his neck.

"Oh, cool," said Chong. "I'll trade you my extra Captain Ledger card for that."

"Sure," Benny agreed. "I have doubles. Morgie's always getting killed."

They both laughed at that as if it was a joke.

The zombie Morgie on the cards—both cards—began growling so loud that the dreaming Morgie could actually hear it. It was a low, deep, steady growl. He turned away from the sound and rolled right off the counter, slammed into the cracked red vinyl seats of the row of stools, and then crashed painfully to the floor. He woke in confusion and pain.

And froze, because waking up did not stop the growls.

It did, however, *change* them. Awareness transformed the snarls from the guttural moans of the living dead to the steady, aggressive roar of engines.

"Someone's stealing our quads!" he yelled as he scrambled to his feet. Riot snapped awake and swung her legs over the edge. By the time her feet hit the floor, she had her slingshot out and was fishing for a ball bearing. Morgie snatched up his bokken.

Weak and sick as they were, they ran for the door, tore it open, and rushed out, ready to fight the thieves.

They were wrong, though.

The quads sat in the shadow of the big truck. The roar of motors came from up the road. Not quads, either.

A line of motorcycles was burning its way down the center of the blacktop.

Motorcycles.

Ten of them. And riding each were figures—male and female—dressed in soiled leather set with studs and chains.

Their faces were harsh and discolored, more dead than alive.

They were *ravagers*.

Morgie and Riot flattened out on the ground and peered under the truck as the bikes thundered by. The lead biker was a brute of a man with enormous arms that were so over-packed with muscles that he looked deformed, apelike. His face was equally simian, with stiff orange hair and a filthy beard in which leaves and bugs were stuck. He had guns and knives sticking out of holsters and pockets, and a huge scythe strapped to his bike so the big curved blade arched over his head. A name was painted in silver script on the bulbous fuel tank of the Harley.

DEATH ANGEL

The other bikers were also fierce, but none were as mas-sive or as unbearably terrifying as Death Angel.

The wooden sword in Morgie's fist felt ridiculously fragile and useless. Beside him, Riot lowered her slingshot, letting the steel ball roll out. If it came to a fight, they were never going to beat that inhuman monster or his people. Never in a million years.

The bikes passed so close to the semi that the two teens could see the tread on their tires and the mud-caked boots on the foot pegs. Morgie and Riot clung to each other's hands, knowing that death was one tiny moment away.

But the bikes rolled on, leaving behind a cloud of dust that hung like a pall over the parking lot. Morgie and Riot dared not move until the sounds of the bikes dwindled and then faded. Silence blew like a winter wind beneath the big rig, chilling them and the whole day.

Slowly, very slowly and carefully, they got to their feet,

still holding hands. They stood there, weak and sick and trembling. Never before in his life, not since the world expanded for him beyond the walls of his town, had Morgie Mitchell ever felt this young. This small.

This helpless.

DAWN WAS A PALE PROMISE ON THE HORIZON when they wheeled their quads outside and continued on their way.

"Asheville today," said Morgie. His voice sounded weak and fragile even to his own ears. Riot just shrugged. "Look . . . we're both sick, and getting sicker. If Asheville is still there, then there will be doctors. Hospitals."

She nodded weakly.

They plunged into the woods, following a road that was badly overgrown. The forest was vast and lush, and no attempt had been made to keep it from reclaiming the highway that cut through it. Only the movement of zombie swarms had trampled down the tall weeds and crushed some of the persistent shrubs that grew out of the many cracks in the asphalt. Where young trees stood, the marks of the swarm simply went around them.

"How many do you think came through here?" asked Morgie, studying the massive swath the shamblers had cut through the overgrowth.

Riot shook her head. "Way too many."

They rode on.

Several miles in, they rode along the French Broad River,

which was a brilliant blue ribbon laid haphazardly through the forest. Sunlight sparkled on the rippling water and birds bobbed near the bank, watching the quads with unreadable eyes. Morgie had an irrational desire to stop his bike, strip to the skin, and dive into the water as if it was some healing bath that could wash away the red rash and all of his other pains, inside and out. He gazed longingly at it as the miles rolled away beneath his tires.

I should never have left home, he thought. *Never.*

As if in reply, the blisters on his skin seemed to all flare at the same time. It was like being spattered with hot cooking grease, and he hissed. The pain was so sharp, so sudden, that it sent a wave of nausea through him and he had to stop, jump off the bike, and throw up.

Riot stopped to wait. It did not take Morgie long, but he walked down to the river's edge and plunged his face into the clear, pure water. Despite the day's heat, the water was shockingly cold, and he kept his face under for as long as he could. Then he leaned back on his heels, sputtering and gasping as water sluiced down under his carpet coat and body armor.

"You alive down there?" called Riot.

Morgie grunted. "Define 'alive' . . ."

He splashed a few handfuls of water on his face and over his hair, then got up and climbed shakily back to the road.

They drove on, moving more slowly now since both of them were so out of it. They made frequent stops. Neither could keep down any food. Morgie felt like he was more asleep than awake. Or, maybe, more dead than alive. The drone of the motor was muffled, as if he was going away, deeper into his own dark thoughts.

Neither of them was paying much attention, and had no warning at all when a pair of motorcycles burst from the woods to their right. Riot screamed as the lead bike slammed into her quad.

"Riot!" screamed Morgie as the big motorcycle knocked her quad right off the road. Two wheels lifted, and the whole machine canted over and rolled down the hill. Morgie saw Riot tumbling on the slope a few feet away, having either dived or been thrown free from the quad. Even so, the force of her fall sent her bumping and churning down toward the water.

Out of the corner of his eye Morgie saw something rushing at his face, and he threw himself sideways as the blade of a farming scythe slashed through the air where his neck had been. He fell out of the saddle, and the quad kept rolling until it smashed into a pine tree. Morgie hit hard, tried to tuck and roll, bungled it because it was all happening too fast, and instead flopped hard onto the weedy asphalt. The air left his lungs in a whoosh, but he forced himself to twist again as the wheel of Death Angel's bike roared past, inches from his face.

Morgie scrambled up, coughing weakly as he did so, fighting pain and nausea. The bike that hit Riot was twenty feet behind him, and Death Angel was turning his for another run. That gave Morgie only a scant few seconds. Run, help Riot, or fight. Those were his choices, and none was good. Only one made any real sense, though.

He ran to his quad and tore the bokken from its holder, and instead of waiting for Death Angel to come at him, Morgie charged the monstrous ravager. The killer grinned as if amused by the attack and he gunned his bike with one hand while raising the scythe with the other. It was a testament to the biker's massive strength that he could handle the cumbersome tool as if it was a small hatchet.

"This is my meat," he bellowed to his companion. "Get the girl. I want to hear her scream."

The second biker dropped the kickstand, got off, and ran down the hill.

Morgie swung his wooden sword just as Death Angel's bike seemed to leap forward and the wicked blade cut a glittering arc through the air. Morgie did not try to block the blade, nor did he try to smash the muscular half-zombie. Instead he put every ounce of his strength and all of his speed into a diagonal downward strike to the bike's front wheel. The impact sent shock waves up his arm with such force that the sword's handle shivered itself from his grip. Morgie fell sideways, but the blow had done its work. The scythe missed again, and the wheel slewed around on the trampled weeds, ruining the forward momentum of the bike. Death Angel was launched from the seat and crashed down hard on the road, sliding nearly four feet on his chest and hands. The scythe fell across Morgie's waist.

He grabbed it and propped it on end to help him stand. He hoped the biker was dead or crippled, but as soon as that thought formed in his head he knew that it was ridiculous. This wasn't just a zom . . . it was a ravager. Half alive, half dead, all monster. Nearly unkillable. And before this one had transformed, he'd been something else: huge, with overdeveloped muscles and the look of someone who had always been a brute, a causer of pain, a taker of lives.

Death Angel got to his feet. The impact with the road had torn his clothes and ripped flesh from his palms, chest, and right cheek. Blood that was a strange mixture of black and red—not blended at all, streamers of both colors—ran from the torn flaps of his flesh. He pointed a finger at Morgie and grinned to show lots of yellow teeth.

"I was going to turn you, boy, but now I think I'll bust you up and let you watch Mongo and me turn the little chickee into an all-we-can-eat buffet. How would you like that?"

A scream rose from the bank of the river, but Morgie could not see what was happening with Riot.

"I'm going to kill you," promised Morgie, but even he could hear how weak his voice sounded. His body was tired from days of illness, and even if Morgie had been at his best, this man looked unbeatable. He had no illusions of this being a David-and-Goliath situation. Even so, he had to try. Morgie took a threatening step toward the big man.

Death Angel did not flinch or show the slightest concern that he was unarmed while Morgie had the scythe. Instead, his ugly grin widened to a jack-o'-lantern leer. Behind him and all around the scene of the confrontation, the woods seemed to break apart as more ravagers stepped out of the shadows with weapons in their hands, and behind them, shambling with relentless hunger, were the living dead.

There were so many of them. Too many. One quad was wrecked, the other damaged. Riot was screaming, and Morgie knew that this place, this moment, was the end of all the things he'd done, and all the dreams he ever had.

He raised the scythe anyway.

MORGIE CHARGED THE RAVAGERS AND THE ZOMBIES. He swung the scythe as if it could somehow sweep away all of the dozens of creatures who had come from this trap to kill and devour him. Death Angel laughed and ducked backward, and the force of Morgie's swing whipped the blade across the necks of two zombies, instantly decapitating them. It was a cut so powerful and so effective that it shocked him.

Then the tip of the blade buried itself into the chest of a ravager and stuck there. The killer cried out, more in outrage than pain, grabbed the handle near the blade, and tore the scythe from Morgie's grasp. The ravager staggered back, completely run through, tugging at the steel and cursing.

Two of the shamblers lunged at Morgie and tripped over the front wheel of the fallen Harley. They collapsed in a heap and four others fell over them, piling up a mound of thrashing dead inches from where Morgie stood. In another place—maybe at the harvest festival at home, with actors dressed as zoms—this would have been laugh-out-loud comedy. Here it was merely unreal, as if pernicious monsters were playing a game to mock his inevitable and horrible death. Morgie had always feared the living dead, but until that moment he'd never actually hated them. Now he did.

He hated every single one of the rotting, lumbering, insatiably hungry creatures. He wanted to chop them up and burn the pieces.

Morgie whirled instead and ran to find his bokken. In stories, heroes made a glorious last stand, killing so many of their enemies that grand tales would be told about it for generations to come. But these enemies would not tell any tales, no matter how many he killed. He could fill the underworld with their corpses, and the story of it would still die right there on a lost road in an empty corner of the Rot and Ruin.

He snatched up the weapon, turned, and swung as one of the ravagers came at him with a pickaxe in his dirty fists. Morgie ducked low as he swung, evading the attack while smashing the sword into the killer's knee. The leg buckled and Morgie darted sideways, not needing to do more to a crippled opponent when there were so many others.

Riot screamed again, but this time it sounded more like rage than pain. Morgie wanted to look, to see if somehow she was managing to fight, maybe to escape, but another zom came at him and he swept its reaching arms to one side and kicked it hard in the hip, driving it backward against Death Angel. The big biker bashed the thing away and drew a pistol from his belt.

"I'm gonna make this—"

And that was all the monster said. If there was more, the words were lost beneath the huge and ugly roar of a heavy caliber machine gun.

But that was impossible, Morgie thought. He turned, the world swaying sickeningly around him, as soldiers—*soldiers*—

came running out of the forest. He slipped on blood and fell, hitting his head against a tree. The world spun sickeningly around him and everything seemed to be painted in all the wrong colors. Gunfire orange. Blood that was red and black. The green of the immense forest. And the mingled green and gray and brown of uniforms. Then it all went very, very black.

PART NINETEEN

THE FALL OF NEW ALAMO

Turning and turning in the widening gyre

The falcon cannot hear the falconer;

Things fall apart; the centre cannot hold;

Mere anarchy is loosed upon the world,

The blood-dimmed tide is loosed, and everywhere

The ceremony of innocence is drowned;

The best lack all conviction, while the worst

Are full of passionate intensity.

—WILLIAM BUTLER YEATS, "THE SECOND COMING"

ALICE WOKE IN THE TUB, SHIVERING. THE WATER WAS ice-cold now, and her skin was pruned. She got out, dried off, and hurried into underwear, pajamas, and a thick robe. The house was still but not quiet. She put her ear to her mom's bedroom door and heard the rustle of sheets.

Alice went to the kitchen, put the kettle on, took an orange from the basket on the table, sliced it, and arranged the pieces on a plate. There were a few ibuprofen tablets left, and she put the bottle in her robe pocket and went down the hall with the plate and a teacup. She tapped lightly on Mom's door and turned the knob.

"Mom?" Alice whispered as she came quietly in. "How are you feeling? How are your hand and the cuts?"

Her mother was in bed, the covers pulled high, only a small lantern lit on the dresser, the flame turned low.

"I have some pain pills," said Alice, putting the plate and cup on the night table. "But you need to eat something first."

Her mother moved and groaned a little. It made Alice sad that she was in so much pain. As she set the tray on the night table, her mom reached out and touched her wrist.

"You okay?" Alice asked gently.

The touching fingers curled around her wrist. Mama felt cold, and Alice glanced at the window to see if she'd accidentally left it open. The days were hot, but the nights were often frigid. The curtains stirred in the breeze.

"Hold on," she said, "let me close the window before you catch your death."

The circling fingers tightened.

They locked around Alice's wrist in a powerful, unbreakable grip.

"Ow! Mom, don't, you're hurting me—"

Her voice cut off as her mother sat up in bed. The covers fell away, and Alice saw that the sleeve of her mother's left arm—the one with all the cuts—was torn to rags and soaked with blood. But in the lantern light the blood looked too dark. Nearly black.

The truth rose up above her like a vast wave: Mom had been hurt at the wagonwright's place when it was overrun by ravagers and shamblers. The monsters had been beaten back, slaughtered. Their blood was splashed everywhere. On the walls. On the splintered doors. Everywhere.

And that's where her mother had been scratched. But how much more than a drop of *los muertos* blood did it really take?

"Oh my God," Alice breathed.

The grab turned into a pull as her mother opened her dead eyes and stretched her dead mouth wide and lunged forward with awful, snapping teeth.

AS GUTSY AND ALETHEA WALKED QUICKLY THROUGH town, they saw people running from house to house, yelling for friends and neighbors to start packing. Riders on horses galloped up and down the streets, spreading the news. Most people jumped right to it, running to gather belongings and loved ones; but some just stood there, watching everything unfold around them as if what was going on didn't matter to them. Was it some kind of shock, Gutsy wondered, or had those people plain given up?

The two girls hurried on.

The big tower crane above Alice's house creaked as it swung slowly around.

"Why are they still bothering to do that if we're all bugging out of here?" Alethea asked.

Gutsy shook her head. "If there are ravager spies, they'd get suspicious if we suddenly stopped reinforcing the walls. Those guys up there will be the last to leave, and they'll block off the tunnel on the way out."

Alethea grunted. "Okay, that's pretty smart."

As they approached the corner near the Chung house,

Alethea slowed. "Look," she said "I'll hang back a bit. You know, in case you two need to get all kissy-face."

Gutsy flashed her a smile and hurried up the block. The house was neat and tidy, with a manicured lawn and lovely flower beds in which something bright and fragrant was always blooming. A pair of big live oaks stood vigil on either side of the walkway, and there were bird feeders hung from a dozen limbs.

Gutsy was embarrassed to realize that she really *did* stink to high heaven, but there wasn't time to do anything about it now. She needed to see Alice. She needed a tiny bit of normal, a small piece of undamaged ground to stand on. Even if for only five minutes.

She took a deep breath and knocked.

Which is when she heard Alice Chung scream.

"ALICE? *ALICE!*" GUTSY YELLED AS FEAR SHOT THROUGH
her. There were more screams, but no actual answers. Gutsy
pounded on the door.

"Mama . . . no!"

Gutsy stepped back, braced herself, and then kicked at
the door with the flat of her foot. It shuddered, but the strong
lock held.

"Alethea!" she bellowed, but Alethea was already running
down the street, her bat ready.

"*Los muertos*?" demanded Alethea. "Wild men?"

"I don't know. Alice is in trouble. Help me."

"Move out of the way," Alethea said, shoving Gutsy to one
side as she lashed out with her own kick. And still the door
held. She kicked again, and again.

Gutsy snatched up a rocking chair and hurled it through
the window, smashing the glass and tearing the curtains off
their rods. She used the blunt side of the machete blade to
knock the last jagged fragments out of the frame, and Alethea laced her fingers so Gutsy could step up and jump inside.
Gutsy immediately turned the lock on the door and opened it
for her friend. The living room was weirdly neat and pristine

except for the broken glass. The two girls ran down the hall to the largest bedroom, near the kitchen. The door was open, and there were cries and moans and thumps of a kind Gutsy knew too well.

She paused for an awful moment in the doorway, staring at the horrific scene.

The room was in shambles, with the mattress overturned and bloody sheets cast on the floor. The bedside table had been knocked over, taking the sturdy lantern with it. The flame was still lit, though, and cast everything in the room in a shadowy yellow glow.

Alice, holding a broken chair as a shield, cowered in a corner. Pawing and clawing at the chair was her mother.

What had been her mother.

Mrs. Chung wore a torn nightgown. Her black hair hung in sweaty strands, and she growled like some feral thing.

"No!" cried Gutsy, and the growl stopped as the dead woman slowly turned toward the two girls in the doorway. The face—which had looked so much like Alice's—hung slack and rubbery; her dark eyes were dull and faded to a dusty gray. Mrs. Chung opened her mouth and uttered a moan of endless, aching hunger as her twisted, broken fingers reached for Gutsy and Alethea.

Into that tableau, Alice screamed out three words. A demand, a plea, filled with such raw emotion that it punched Gutsy in the heart.

"Don't hurt her!"

Those words were like a chain that jerked Gutsy backward in time to her own bedroom two weeks ago. To waking into horror as Mama reached for her to kill her. It had been too big to deal with, too broken to fix, too wrong to ever understand. Now Alice was going through the same nightmare.

Mrs. Chung staggered forward, snarling with need. Gutsy raised her machete.

"Noooo!" Alice flung the chair away and came up off the floor, driving forward with the intensity of the unhinged. Not at the monster in the room but at Gutsy. She tried to wrench the machete away even as the creature pawed Gutsy's shirt and hair.

Suddenly Alethea grabbed Mrs. Chung by the arm, swung her violently around, and sent her flying toward the bed. The dead woman struck the footboard and crashed over onto her face. Then Alethea spun and tore Alice away from Gutsy.

"Sorry about this," she said, then released her grip and punched Alice in the stomach with all of the strength she owned. The punch lifted Alice onto her toes, drove every bit of breath out of her lungs, and dropped her. Alice collapsed into a fetal ball and turned red and then purple.

Gutsy whirled as Mrs. Chung climbed to her feet and came at her again. The machete was in Gutsy's hand. One stroke and the fight would be won. But what would witnessing that strike do to Alice? Could she bear that? Silencing Mama had nearly broken Gutsy, and that had been with a spike, not a brutal machete.

So Gutsy dropped her machete and stepped into the dead woman's charge, parrying the reaching arms hard enough to spin Mrs. Chung off balance and then kicking the back of her knees. The sudden bend made the woman sag and fall, and Gutsy took the weight and spun her back. Mrs. Chung crashed down onto the floor. Gutsy jumped on top of her and pressed her face into the area rug.

Alethea, too experienced to stand and gawp, snatched up a pillow and pulled it over Mrs. Chung's head, with the pillow against her face and the back of the pillowcase pulled down behind her head. It was a common technique in New Alamo, something everyone learned. While Gutsy held her down, Alethea took the two corners of the case, pulled them back, and tied a tight knot at the base of the woman's skull.

Then she yanked a second pillow off the bed, tore the case off, spun the cloth into a rope, and handed it to Gutsy, who bound Mrs. Chung's hands behind her back. Gutsy cut the remainder off and similarly bound her ankles. When that was done, Alethea sat down with a thud against the dresser while Gutsy crawled over to Alice.

Mrs. Chung thrashed and moaned, but was otherwise helpless.

"I'm sorry," she said softly, brushing hair from Alice's face.

Alice was breathing, but in gasps and coughs. Her face was filled with pain, and her eyes and nose were streaming. Gutsy reached for her, needing to hold her, to try and comfort her.

Alice resisted her pull. Fought her. Shoved her back. She spat ugly words and screamed for her mother. But Gutsy gathered her up anyway. Endured the words that stuck like knives and held Alice with all her strength.

"I'm sorry," she whispered as Alice's struggles slowly disintegrated into awful sobs. "I'm sorry."

GUNFIRE ERUPTED TO SHATTER THE MOMENT.

Alethea and Gutsy turned to each other.

"It's starting," said Alethea in a hollow voice.

"Can't be," Gutsy countered. "Even running full tilt, I don't think the wild men could have gotten here this fast. Something else is going on."

"Stay here," ordered Alethea as she shot to her feet, snatched up her bat, and ran out into the hall. Alice and Gutsy stared at the bedroom window but could not see anything.

"No more, no more, no more," said Alice in a small, cracked voice.

Gutsy threw a despairing look at the shrouded, thrashing Mrs. Chung, then pulled Alice up, led her into the hall, and closed the door.

From outside they heard Alethea yelling, "*Gutsy—you better get out here.*"

Gutsy did not want to leave, but what choice did she have? "Look," she said to Alice, "I need to go see what's happening. Come with me."

"I can't," cried Alice, horrified. "Mom needs me."

It made no sense, but sense did not matter.

"Okay, okay," said Gutsy. "Stay here, though. Go into the kitchen. Get something to protect yourself. Don't go back into your mom's room. You hear me? Don't do it. I'll be right back."

Outside there were more screams, and the sound of running feet. Gunshots cracked continuously. Gutsy kissed Alice and ran out of the house.

Karen Peak raced along the wall, gun in hand. One of her senior guards, Primo, saw her from above and waved her up. She climbed a ladder.

"What's going on up . . . ?" she began, but then looked over into the fields beyond and her words fell away. Everyone had been worried about what might be coming at them from the east.

But this . . .

She stood and stared into the east, looking at what everyone on all the walls was already seeing. The pale light of a billion stars shone down on a sea of figures moving across the fields. Shamblers, driven by ravagers.

She looked down at the newly rebuilt walls, at rows of sharpened wooden spikes that had been angled against attack, at trenches filled with flammable materials, and fortified sniper posts. The preparations had seemed so smart, so strong.

Now they seemed foolish. To stop a few hundred ravagers, yes. To stall an attack by a thousand, or even two thousand, shamblers, yes. Maybe even to defeat packs of wild men. But here, under the light of the cold stars . . . she did not see a few hundred, or even a few thousand.

She saw an *ocean* of the living dead. Tens of thousands.

Maybe more.

Karen felt her body turn numb, and the hand that held her pistol sank to her side. Her fingers went slack, and the Glock fell unheeded to the walkway, where it lay totally useless in the face of what was coming.

This was the Night Army. Come to devour them all.

As soon as Gutsy stepped into the street, she knew that things were really bad. She could smell smoke, and saw dark clouds of it obscuring much of the sky. People were running everywhere, some carrying their hastily packed bundles. Others ran in the opposite direction, heading home to grab a weapon, a suitcase, or a loved one. There was no sign of Alethea. Gutsy ducked as someone fired a shotgun, but in all the confusion, she couldn't see who fired, or at what.

Alethea came running toward her, ducked low in case there was another shot. She pulled Gutsy behind a low stone wall in the neighbor's front yard.

"What's happening?" Gutsy demanded.

"What's happing is everyone's losing their darn minds, that's what's happening. Jimmy Maynard is shooting at everything that moves. And I saw Dave Sanchez and his two older sons go running away from the wall. Ollie Sanchez had a big bottle of something, and he's totally drunk. They were all laughing." Alethea shook her head.

"Can you blame them?"

Alethea's eyes were cold. "Yes, I can. *You're* not losing it. I'm not. And Spider . . ." She stopped as if realizing that Spider wasn't with them. "Crap. He's back at the Cuddlys. Hey, are you all right with Alice for a few minutes? I need to go get him. If this is going to be as bad as it looks, we should all be together."

"Go," said Gutsy, giving her a little push. "I'll be here. I need to see to Mrs. Chung."

"See to her?" Alethea said, glancing in the direction of the house. "You're going to silence her in front of Alice?"

"What's the alternative? Leave Mrs. Chung like that?"

"Alice is strung out, Guts. She'll never forgive you. It won't matter to her mother, but it will destroy Alice if she sees you do that."

"She has to understand how the world works," said Gutsy, her tone pleading.

But Alethea shook her head. "What Alice needs right now is love." She gave Gutsy a brief, fierce hug, and then she was gone.

A scream tore the air from the other end of the block, and Gutsy started in that direction to see what was happening.

She never got there.

A sound—weird and loud—made her look up. There, far above her, was the boom of the tower crane, and from it dangled a crushed Ford pickup truck. The ponderous weight swung wildly on the end of a steel cable, but instead of angling toward the wall, the truck was only a dozen feet above Alice's house. Gutsy saw three people working the lines and pulleys to operate the crane. They were young, not much older than her, and she recognized two of them—the boy in the cowboy hat and the girl with the red ponytail and baseball cap.

They were shouting as they fought to control the swinging boom. Shadowy figures climbed up the scaffolding, and Gutsy could see that they were ravagers.

"Hey!" she cried. "Watch out!"

The two seemed unable to hear her over the sounds of fighting, and then there was a mechanical groan of pain, and suddenly the truck was falling. The cables holding it whipped back like scalded snakes, and five thousand pounds of mangled steel smashed down onto the back of the Chung house. Smashing through the roof, exploding the cinder-block walls outward, kicking up a plume of dust and debris.

"Noooooooooooo!"

Gutsy ran into Alice's house but skidded to a stop. The truck—a dark blue F-150—had landed squarely on the kitchen roof and smashed it down, blocking the entrance from the hall. Gutsy whirled and ran outside and around to the side yard. The back door was crushed out of shape, and both windows were smashed. A fire flickered inside, and Gutsy began screaming Alice's name.

"Help . . ."

The voice came from inside the kitchen. Faint but it was there. *Alive*.

"Alice, are you hurt?"

"I . . . I can't move . . ." came the weak reply. "My legs . . ."

It galvanized Gutsy, who grabbed a piece of broken board and used it to knock away the jagged teeth of glass still in the left-hand window; then she grabbed the sill and, with a grunt, pulled herself up and into the destroyed kitchen. The whole front of the truck had punched down with such force that the bumper shattered the dining room table. There were deep cracks in all the walls, and a lantern had been smashed, spilling oil in fiery tendrils along the floor like the claws of some vast dragon.

"Gutsy," cried Alice, but it took Gutsy a moment to find her in that all that dust and smoke. But there she was, pinned against the stove with a yard-high mound of debris humped across her legs. Her face was scratched and bleeding, and there was a look of wild panic in her eyes.

"*I can't feel my legs.*"

ALETHEA RAN TOWARD THE CUDDLYS' ORPHANAGE, zigzagging through the streets, cutting down alleys, hopping backyard fences, and trying to avoid people. There was more panic now than when the shamblers and ravagers first attacked the town. More than the tunnel fight. It was as if people had reached the limit of how much fear they could take.

Or maybe they'd seen the size of the army about to smash into New Alamo.

She wished those two old soldiers would get their butts back here.

She wished that Sergeant Holly would come back with a convoy of trucks filled with guns. Or a fleet that was somehow big enough to take everyone far away from here.

She wished that time would roll itself back just two weeks. To when the worst trouble was getting caught reading by candlelight by Mrs. Cuddly. Kitchen duty had seemed like a dire punishment then. Now she would trade all of this for thirty years of kitchen duty. Heck, she'd clean the orphanage bathrooms with a toothbrush and be happy about it.

Time, stubborn and mean-spirited, kept moving forward.

She reached home and ran inside.

But no one was there. Not the Cuddlys, not any of the kids. Not Spider.

She stood in the empty bedroom between the rows of beds, and suddenly a great sadness swept through her. She looked at each tightly folded sheet, each properly fluffed and squared pillow, and in a flash of absolute clairvoyant certainty knew that no one would ever muss those beds again. The whole place had the feeling of an empty box, filled only with memories.

Spider's absence made her feel as if he was not only gone from the building but gone forever. Like he was already dead somewhere.

Alethea wanted to cry. She wanted to crawl onto Spider's bed, curl up with her head on his pillow, and cry until some form of permanent darkness came for her. The bat was heavy in her hand, and she almost let it fall.

Almost.

Alethea raised the bat and looked at it. On the handle, drawn in a delicate hand, was a tiny black spider. It was something that appeared one morning after the fight at the wall. Spider pretended he knew nothing about it, but Alethea understood, and she had a deeper insight into it now.

"Always you and me," she said aloud. It was an old, old thing they used to say. When one of them was sick. When one or the other was in trouble. When times were bad.

Always you and me.

Poor grammar, but a perfect sentiment.

She touched the little spider and smiled. Then she took a deep steadying breath, turned, and went out. She went to the wall, looking for her brother.

* * *

One block away, Spider moved quickly and silently through the shadows. He'd been to Gutsy's house, but Alethea wasn't there. No one was there. The Cuddlys were gone too; they must have already gotten the other kids packed and out. They were sharp, those two.

Spider then checked the hospital, but Mr. Flores said they hadn't seen her. The pharmacist was still working on mass-producing the Dòmi despite the general hysteria as the staff packed all of the supplies and equipment they could manage while at the same time prepping the wounded for evacuation. It was a madhouse. Spider wanted to stay and help, but he needed to find Alethea. A premonition of disaster seemed to whisper her name in his ear.

He'd been to the wall and searched all of it, but his sister wasn't anywhere. He asked people in the street. Some of them just ran past him. Two people chased him away as if he was a shambler. Then he saw Joanie Cantu from school running toward the wall with an armful of fresh splints and bandages.

"Hey," he called, "have you seen Alethea?"

"Yeah," yelled the girl as she ran past. "She was outside Alice's place."

"Thanks!"

He tore along the street.

Alice's words hit Gutsy like a flight of arrows, each striking hard and deep.

"Don't move," she said, trying to force calmness into her voice. "Just wait until I get this stuff off you."

"Why can't I feel my legs?"

"Something must be pressing on the nerves," said Gutsy. "It'll be fine. It'll be okay."

She tore into the debris, tossing away pieces of lath and pine studs and sheet-metal roofing and nameless chunks. She saw blood before she found Alice's trapped legs.

There was a lot of it. Too much of it.

She worked faster still and cleared everything away until she saw what held Alice down. It was a six-foot-long piece of broken roofing beam. It was angled so that one sharp corner pressed down across the tops of Alice's thighs, cutting into the skin. Blood ran and pooled. There was no way to tell how bad the cuts were, or if one or both legs were broken. Panic kept whispering the worst in Gutsy's ears.

"I have to lift this beam," she said. "It's going to hurt, Alice."

"I . . . I . . ."

"Alice, take a breath," said Gutsy. "A deep breath, and when I lift, let it out. Scream if you have to. But I have to do this right now."

Alice's face was white with shock and pain and her eyes twitched with terror, but she nodded. She took that breath.

Outside there was a massive, heavy sound that shook the whole house and made the crashed truck shift and groan. Dust fell from what was left of the ceiling, and through the big hole overhead, Gutsy could see vast clouds of smoke, veined and lit from underneath with the red of fires.

She looked around for something to use as a lever, but none of the laths were sturdy enough to bear the weight. She was going to have to try and lift it herself.

"What's happening?" Alice demanded in a reedy, terrified voice.

"Focus on this," said Gutsy tersely. "Brace yourself."

Gutsy straddled Alice's pinned legs, crouched, wrapped her arms around the heavy beam, and lifted. The wood was thick and solid, designed to support the rainwater tank on the kitchen roof. The carpenters who'd put it in place a year or so after the dead rose had done their job very well. The beam had been shaped from the heartwood of a telephone pole, and Gutsy knew the math. Utility poles weighed thirty pounds per cubic foot, and the beam was a foot square. She used the strength of her thighs, her core, her lower back, and her wiry arms, and pulled.

The moment the timber began to move, Alice Chung felt her legs. She felt every nerve ending, every inch of them. She screamed so loud it seemed to shatter what was left of the kitchen. Gutsy, straining, screamed too as she heaved the beam up and walked it back, inch by inch. Black poppies blossomed in front of Gutsy's eyes, then turned a bright red. She forced herself to stare through them down at the floor, seeing Alice's knees, then her shins, her sneakers . . . and finally the floor. With a cry she let the beam drop. It smashed down with a shudder.

Gutsy darted forward to examine the deep cuts on Alice's legs. They were very bad. Worse than she thought. Alice was still screaming as the pain threatened to overwhelm her. Gutsy had no first-aid kit with her, realizing with horror that she'd left it in the Humvee.

So, instead she whipped off her belt and wrapped it around Alice's right upper thigh, cinching it tight to stop the bleeding. That tore a new shriek of pain from Alice, but Gutsy had to endure it.

"I have to stop the bleeding," she said, once more forcing her tone to sound infinitely calmer than she felt. Alice's screams dwindled to whimpers but spiked again as Gutsy buckled the tourniquet in place. The cut on her right thigh was the worst, and Gutsy was worried about the amount of blood Alice had already lost.

Alice's left leg was still bleeding profusely, and Gutsy had no second belt. So, she pulled out her small lock-knife, flicked the blade into place, and began cutting strips from the hem of Alice's pajama top. She used the widest strip for the second tourniquet, since wide strips did less damage to nerve endings and blood vessels. She inserted a broken piece of wood into a loop in the strip to allow her to turn it like a dial, using the torsion to exert pressure on Alice's upper thigh. Luckily the blood was only pumping, not shooting out in jets, which she hoped meant that no arteries were severed.

Once the second tourniquet was in place, Gutsy fumbled for Alice's hand and told her to hold it, repeating it until Alice gave her an actual spoken answer instead of a hysterical nod.

"You're doing great," Gutsy said. "It's going to be okay."

The gunfire outside made a liar of her, and they both knew it. Gutsy wondered where the heck Alethea was, and feared for her friend. She leaned over and kissed Alice's flushed cheek.

The next step was to bandage the wounds so that direct pressure would further stop the bleeding and allow her to remove the tourniquets. She cut more strips off Alice's top—some for bandages, and some for padding. Soon, she realized, Alice would be wearing just pajama bottoms and a thick tank top, but modesty was a luxury that had no place in a crisis.

The cuts looked horrible, and there were little pieces of

cloth punched into each by the beam's passage through the pajamas. That was something she'd need to take care of later to avoid infection. Now, all that mattered was keeping Alice from bleeding to death.

Alice was panting, though, and her eyes were glassy with shock. Gutsy got up and hurried into Alice's bedroom, grabbed a pillow and blanket off the bed, and came back and draped the blanket over her. It would keep her warm, and serve as makeshift clothing. She tucked the pillow under Alice's head.

There were more sounds of fighting outside in the street, and Gutsy wanted—*needed*—to go see what was happening, but she simply could not.

Gutsy knew she had to do more than this if Alice was going into shock. Ideally, she would have liked to carry her to the bedroom, but she didn't want to risk moving her for fear of restarting the bleeding. So, she kicked enough debris out of the way to clear the floor near the stove, then helped Alice lie flat. Then Gutsy dragged the beam end over and gently—very, very gently—raised Alice's ankles and placed them on the solid wood. She rushed back into the living room and came back with both couch cushions, carefully inserting them under Alice's calves to take the strain off her knees and thighs. It was still uncertain whether one or both legs were broken, but the fact that Alice didn't scream when her legs were lifted was a hopeful sign.

"Alice," she said, "I need you to stay like this, okay?"

Alice nodded. She was either unable or unwilling to speak. Her color was still bad, and she was sweating. Cold sweat, too, so Gutsy got a big decorative macramé blanket and draped it over her. Once that was done, Gutsy took the wooden torsion bar from Alice's hand and gradually eased the tension while keeping her other palm on the bandage, feeling for the warmth that would bloom if heavy bleeding began again. It did not, and Gutsy exhaled a ball of tension, taking it as a good sign.

There was a heavy thump against the front door.

"That's probably Alethea," said Gutsy. "I'll let her in. Don't move."

Gutsy headed for the door, but before she got there it flew inward, the lock tearing from the hinges, splinters filling the air.

It was not Alethea.

It was a ravager. He was big and broad-shouldered, and he had a pump shotgun in his hands.

Gutsy had no chance at all.

PART TWENTY

THE ROAD TO ASHEVILLE

If we really think that home is elsewhere
and that this life is a wandering to find home,
why should we not look forward to the arrival?

—C. S. Lewis

MORGIE WAS LOST IN DARKNESS.

He was not entirely unconscious, though. He could feel his body. Feel the wrongness of it. The pain in his head and back. The heaviness of his limbs. The sickness in his skin and in his stomach. It was as if getting bashed against the tree had done something strange to him. Disconnected his mind from his body in almost every useful way, leaving only the ability to feel pain.

And to hear.

As he lay there, he listened to voices. Men and women. A few scattered gunshots. The swish of wind through the leaves. He was on his back, staring up at the blue sky above the road. The tall trees seemed to bend forward to look down at him.

Then he heard more voices.

"Oh God, is he . . . ?"

Was that Nix? No. Riot? *Yes*, he thought.

"No, he's alive," said a stranger's voice. "There's a pulse."

"Who are you?" Morgie asked, or thought he did. Morgie's consciousness went away before the question was answered and came back to a different part of the conversation.

"What's that all over his skin?" demanded someone. A woman, Morgie thought. Talking to a man. Both strangers.

"Oh no, don't touch him. Look. Oh my God . . ."

"She has it too," said the man, and there was something in his voice. Urgency, surprise. And fear.

Morgie tried to speak, tried to explain that the rash on his skin was nothing. An allergy, maybe. Or something they ate. He tried to make his mouth move to say the words, but the connection did not stretch that far. All he could do was feel and hear.

He went away again. And again.

He heard the woman say, "August, they have it. They both have it."

"Have what?" cried Riot weakly from somewhere off to Morgie's left. He reached for her, for her hand. Found it. Her fingers were so cold, but they curled around his with desperate force.

"Who . . . who are you?" Morgie managed to get out.

"Sergeant August Porter," said the man. "Third Rangers, second platoon, long-range patrol out of Asheville."

"Ashe . . . Asheville?" Morgie tried to smile but couldn't. Tried not to cry, and failed. "We . . . made it . . . ?"

"If you kids were trying to get to Asheville, then you made it." A face came into view above him. A soldier. Sergeant Porter. August. "Help is on the way. Can you tell me who you are? Where you come from?"

"Reclamation . . . ," whispered Morgie. "We . . . we were looking for Captain . . . Ledger . . ."

The other soldier's face now appeared. A black woman in her twenties. "*Joe* Ledger?" she asked. "You came all the way from California?"

"Y . . . yes . . ." His voice was ghostly thin. "How . . . how's— Riot?"

"Is that your friend's name?" asked August. "Riot?"

Morgie told them who they were, what they'd seen, and why they had come. He told them about New Alamo, about the swarms of zoms. He told them as much as he could. A fit of coughing interrupted him, and he tasted blood on his lips. He heard the other soldier speaking rapidly on a walkie-talkie. He heard her mention New Alamo, and Benny, and Captain Ledger. The rest seemed to fade out as his brain kept trying to fall into darkness.

Riot's fingers were still wrapped around his, but her grip was noticeably weaker, and she hadn't said a word for a while. Morgie used his free hand to fumble for August's hand.

"What . . . what's wrong . . . with us?" he asked.

There was a pause, and it lasted so long that Morgie thought he'd floated away again. But it wasn't that. It was merely that August was steeling himself to answer his question. When the young soldier spoke, there was deep horror and sadness in his voice.

"Those burns," said August, "the sickness you've both been feeling . . . it's not plague or anything like that."

"What . . . what is it?" Morgie managed to say.

Then August said the terrible words.

"It's *radiation sickness*," he said. "You've both been exposed. It's . . . bad. God, I'm sorry, but I think it's really bad."

That was all Morgie could hear. It was all he could bear to hear. He stopped trying to speak. Stopped trying to reconnect. Instead, he let himself fall.

And fell for a long, long time.

He fell forever.

PART TWENTY-ONE

THE FALL OF NEW ALAMO

Sometimes even to live is an act of courage.

—Lucius Annaeus Seneca

76

THE RAVAGERS WERE ON THE WALLS.

They left a trail of dead behind them. Bullets and arrows rained down on them as they rushed for the outer row of stacked cars. Then, as they clustered at the base, the stones began falling.

They fell. Two more. Five. Ten. Twenty.

But there were so many more, and with snarls of hunger and fury, they began to climb.

Far above them, Karen Peak leaned out, taking careful aim, and fired, fired, fired. She was a good shot, and even with smoke and noise and fear, she knocked a climber down with nearly every shot. Ravagers leaned into the wall to avoid the falling bodies, and then, like roaches, they kept coming.

God save us, Karen thought as she reloaded.

"They're on the wall!" The cry rang out, louder than gunfire, louder than the moans of thousands of *los muertos*. It was Karen Peak's voice, the words screamed out with such ferocity that Alethea could hear how it tore the lining of the woman's throat. *"They're on the wall!"*

A shocked moment passed, and then another voice repeated the cry.

And another.

Then ten more. A dozen.

"They're on the wall!"

Some of the voices were filled with panic. Some with anger. Some of the defenders wept as they took up the cry. People down in the street began shouting too.

"They're on the wall!"

Alethea yelled it too. She heard the same hopelessness in her voice that burned in every other voice.

And then a new and much more terrible cry rang out from behind her.

"They're in the streets!"

She whirled and saw that somehow, impossibly, a mass of shamblers was lumbering through the streets. People scattered in blind panic, dropping the hastily packed bundles and suitcases, fleeing in all directions. No longer running toward carefully selected exit points. Within seconds the escape had become a rout.

Alethea turned and ran. What good was defending the wall if the enemy was already inside? She hustled to the ladder and climbed down as fast as she could. A shambler clamped cold fingers on her ankle when she was still five feet from the ground, but Alethea swung her bat one-handed and the creature fell away, its head shattered.

She reached the ground and heard high-pitched screams, turned, and in horror saw a group of children being cornered by the dead. Their parents were nowhere to be seen. With a growl, Alethea charged, swinging her bat in short, vicious, powerful arcs, hitting faces and chins and chests as the dead turned to meet her. The creatures fell like straw men in a hurricane blast. Some crawled at her, dragging broken bodies; others lay still, the last of their unnatural life crushed out of them.

She stood between them and the four kids. The whole neighborhood seemed to be falling to pieces. Alice Chung's house was only two blocks over, but Alethea knew she couldn't get there. Gutsy and Alice would have to defend themselves. Gutsy could, Alethea knew; but as much as she liked Alice, the girl wasn't strong in the same way. Alice's strength was her kindness and her compassion. She wasn't a natural fighter. Alethea didn't think Alice could go on fighting without it eroding her.

As it had been eroding Spider.

Thinking about how these monsters were hurting everyone she loved made Alethea very, very angry. When her rage was this intense, fatigue and everything else seemed to melt away. She swung her bat, and the monsters went down.

One after another.

"They're in the streets!"

Benny and Chong heard the terrified cry. They were in the general store, helping the old owner pack canned goods into a big cart, ready for the exodus out of New Alamo. The cry stopped them for a moment.

"No," said Benny under his breath, despair sharp as a knife, "no, no, no—it's *too soon.*"

Grimm began growling, and his whole body tensed as he turned toward the door. The teens dropped the cans they held and ran outside, snatching their weapons from where they'd placed them next to the door. The shouts were coming from the northeast corner of the town. There were yells, screams, and gunfire.

"Chong," Benny said, grabbing his friend's arm, "we're out of time. Get to the hospital. Start the evacuation. Tell everyone to get to the rally points."

"Benny," said Chong, "those shots are coming from the east gate. We can't send people there."

Benny cursed. "Okay, *everyone* has to get to the hospital. That's our only rally point now. The tunnel is our best hope. Go tell everyone you can. Then make sure the tunnel's still safe. Take Grimm with you. If people don't listen, let him bite a few of them. That'll work."

"Wait, where are you going?"

Benny stepped away and drew his sword. "To help," he said, and then he was running.

"Good luck!" yelled Chong. "Don't die!"

"Not a chance," Benny shouted back. Though as he ran his snarky comment felt like tempting fate.

Chong ran back into the store and had to push the owner into taking the cart and heading directly to the hospital. People were pouring out of their homes, but few of them carried their belongings, and fewer still were heading toward the rally points. He yelled at them. He shoved them. He even had to threaten one stubborn young man who wanted to stay in his house with his wife and two little kids.

"You'll die in there," Chong pleaded. "They're already in the streets."

The man's wife gathered up the kids and pushed past her husband. The man stood for a moment longer, though, looking around at his house. At his life. Then the man looked at his wife, holding their little ones as she went out into the madness, and there was a visible change. He did not suddenly swell into a towering hero, but he picked up a wooden chair and smashed it to pieces on the floor. He picked up one of the legs and hefted it, feeling it become a weapon in his hand. He gave Chong a brief look—as much fear as courage—and then followed his wife outside.

It hit Chong very hard. The man was not a fighter, but he would have to fight. He was not a killer, but he was likely going to have to kill. It made Chong's heart go out to him, but it also reminded him of the version of himself who'd been a bookish, gentle, nonviolent teen only two years ago. Now he was older, scarred, with the memory of blood on his hands and a body warring with infection.

He wanted to sit down on the couch in this now empty house, put his face in his hands, and cry. He needed to do that.

Instead he took a deep breath, and—with his bow and arrows—went back out to the war. Grimm followed close behind.

There were fresh yells coming from the eastern wall, and Benny angled that way. Those screams had contained rising notes of panic. Not mere warnings but sheer terror.

Looming inside the wall was the big tower crane that had been used to restack the cars.

"Oh my God," Benny cried, looking up.

High above he saw two figures on the crane, working the levers that turned the giant boom. There was a guy in a cowboy hat and his girlfriend, with hair as red as Nix's. Benny had seen them around town, two refugees who'd been brought in after the first siege. A dozen yards below them, climbing with the agility of apes, were several ravagers.

Benny cupped a hand around his mouth to shout a warning to them, but the night suddenly took on a new shape, something fierce and feral and insane. As the ravagers climbed all the way up, the boy walked toward them. As he did so, he took off his hat, and with it came his mop of blond hair. The girl did the same, plucking off the baseball cap and red wig, laughing as she did.

Beneath their hats, bared now to the glow of fire and the cold starlight, were scalps shaved smooth and covered with elaborate tattoos. The teens dug into their pockets and removed strips of red cloth and began tying them to their ankles and wrists.

The teenagers up there were *reapers*.

THE BIG RAVAGER POINTED HIS SHOTGUN AT GUTSY and pulled the trigger.

There was a blast so loud it seemed to tear the world apart, but the buckshot missed her. Every single pellet tore into the ceiling as the ravager suddenly pitched backward, bellowing in surprise. A shape appeared out of the shadows behind him, and there was a whirl of brown hardwood as Spider spun his *bo* and brought the end down on the monster's skull.

"Gutsy!" he yelled, and leaped over the body, but something pushed past him, a gray streak that flew straight for Gutsy.

"Sombra!"

And the coydog was all over her, licking her, pushing himself into her, against her, seeming to be everywhere at once. Then he stopped and began barking at her, scolding her for locking him up. Gutsy hugged him but looked at Spider.

"Alice is hurt," she blurted, then in a few fast sentences told him what happened. They went into the kitchen, and Spider dropped to his knees to examine Alice's legs. He knew a lot about first aid, maybe more than Gutsy did, and she watched his face, seeing his immediate and deep concern.

Alice was half asleep, faint and weak from blood loss.

Spider felt for her pulse, then rose and pulled Gutsy aside. "We need to get her to the hospital. I think she needs blood."

"To the hospital?" gasped Gutsy. "How? It sounds like a war out there."

Spider winced and nodded. "It *is* a war. They're inside the walls. Not many, but enough. I think maybe there was another tunnel after all. I don't think the walls are going to hold. The hospital is the only rally point left. We need to get Alice there, get her treated, and then get out through the tunnel while there's still time."

Dull thumps kept coming from the bedroom, and although Alice was out of it, she flinched each time, nightmares connected to the truth.

"She can't walk," said Gutsy. "We need a cart or a wheelbarrow."

"Okay, wait here," Spider said, and was off like a shot. He was back in less than two minutes with the Carnovskys, a couple who lived a few doors from the Chungs. They were greengrocers and hurried up with a red wheelbarrow spattered with vegetable stains.

"We were about to head to the rally point," said Mr. Carnovsky. He looked around. "Where's her mom?"

"Turned," said Gutsy. It was a simple but deeply ugly word. Mr. Carnovsky murmured a brief prayer.

Mrs. Carnovsky rushed over to examine Alice while Spider, Gutsy, and Mr. Carnovsky cleared a path for the wheelbarrow. There was another of those deep groans of metal. Sombra began barking furiously. Gutsy and Spider went outside and stopped dead in their tracks. Behind the house, on the platform of the tower crane, two teens and three ravagers were pulling at cables.

"Wait . . . are they . . . are those two kids working *with* the ravagers?"

It was impossible, but that's what it seemed to be. Instead of raising another car, they had hooked the cables to cars already on the wall. And the teens no longer wore their hats. Instead, Gutsy saw bald, tattooed heads. Suddenly she understood. These weren't refugees. They were the strange killers Benny and Nix had talked about, who'd attacked the towns in Central California. It seemed impossible that they could be out here, but here they were. Gutsy simultaneously understood what happened with the truck. It hadn't slipped from the crane; it had been dropped deliberately. An attack. Which explained why the teens hadn't come down to see what happened to the house it had fallen on.

And she also realized what those reapers and their ravager allies were attempting to do. The hooks, the cables . . .

"They're going to tear down the wall!" The words exploded from her, and suddenly Gutsy was running, charging the crane. Spider and Sombra were at her heels, and then off to her left she saw another figure charging the scaffolding, too.

Benny.

He had his sword in his hand and was bellowing at the reapers. Cursing them. Daring them to come down and fight.

Gutsy changed direction and ran into the house. "Can you take Alice to the hospital? I have to go. Something bad's happening, and—"

"*Go*," shouted Mrs. Carnovsky. "We'll look after her."

Gutsy grabbed her weapon and ran.

Far above, the reaper boy leaned over and looked down at the teenagers and dog approaching. He said something to the girl, and they both laughed. The ravagers laughed too. They were fifty feet above the ground, and the hooks were already in place. If they could exert enough leverage, then the whole section of wall would collapse into the town, opening a clear path for invasion and slaughter.

The reapers and ravagers hauled on the cables and heaved on the pulleys, throwing all their weight against the big boom. The wall creaked; metal screeched. A single car at the very top canted over and fell, crashing down to explode in a storm of jagged metal, plastic, and glass.

Gutsy and the others dodged and ducked and came up running. They leaped over debris and jumped for the pipe bars of the scaffolding. Gutsy briefly thought about doing something to destabilize the scaffolding, but there simply wasn't time. And it probably would be suicidal anyway. No, what she had to do was stop them. So she sheathed her machete and climbed.

Benny circled around, looking for the easiest place to climb where he wouldn't be seen.

The ravagers and reapers saw them coming but didn't bother to draw their blades. Instead they labored at the crane with renewed vigor. The wall of cars trembled. Pieces broke and fell, and from beyond the wall Gutsy could hear a terrible noise—the voices of uncountable *los muertos* moaning with hunger. She climbed as fast as she could. There was a chance—slim as a razor—that the walls could still keep the dead out. Ravagers and reapers could climb, but the masses of the shambling dead could not.

Down below, and throughout the town, she heard people shouting, *"Rally point! Get to the rally point!"*

It sounded like a plea, a prayer, and a war cry all at once.

The stacked cars trembled again, and a second vehicle toppled over. It fell past her, less than two feet away, and then struck the ground below. She prayed Sombra was smart and quick enough to get out of the way.

Then she was there, at the lip of the platform.

One of the ravagers saw Gutsy scrambling up and yelled to the teenage girl, who was closest. She let go of the cable and drew her weapon. It was a machete. Spider was always better at numbers, and Gutsy wondered what he would make of the statistical probability that the reaper would be armed with a machete too. No gun, no ax. A weapon identical to Gutsy's own.

The platform itself was larger than the scaffolding on which it stood, which meant that Gutsy had to lean away from the pipes, grab the decking, and then do a kind of chin-up to get over. It was a tough enough challenge without having to worry about a killer with a heavy blade. But she had to go for it. She twisted, tensed, and then sprang for the lip of the deck. Her hands were small but hard and strong, and she caught the hardwood decking, and for a moment her legs swung out over a sheer drop.

Then, with a grunt of effort, Gutsy began to pull herself up. Even with all the noise of the battle and the metallic groans of the crane and the wall, she heard the footsteps as the reaper girl ran toward her.

Gutsy swung sideways, hooked a leg over the lip, and, with a surge of raw power, pulled herself up. The girl was ten feet away, whirling her machete in a figure eight, building speed and power for a killer blow. She brought the machete up, over, and down in a vicious butcher's chop—but Gutsy was already rolling like a log toward her. Instead of trying to stand or draw her own blade, she hurled herself at the older teen's shins. The impact knocked the girl's knees straight, and the reaper crashed down hard on her butt, driving her tailbone against the unyielding boards. Gutsy wasted no time and scrambled onto her, hitting the girl in the nose, the eye, the lips, the throat. The reaper girl's face seemed to break apart in a spray of red.

"*No!*" bellowed the reaper boy in alarm. "Sorrow—I'm coming!"

It was an odd thing to say, and he said it as if Sorrow were the girl's name.

He drew two long-bladed fighting knives from hidden sheaths under his baggy shirt and rushed at Gutsy, slashing down as soon as he was within reach, aiming for her neck. Gutsy tried to swing around and grab her machete, but she knew there was no time.

Suddenly a line of silver cut the air and intercepted the blades, which rebounded with a sound like a ringing bell. The shock of it threw the teen back, off balance. Benny Imura crouched on the edge of the platform, teeth bared in anger.

The reaper girl yelled, "Mercy—the boy with the sword. It's him—it's *Imura*." Her voice was thick with pain but also laced with hatred bordering on hysteria.

Benny blinked in surprise at hearing his name and raised his *katana* in a two-handed defensive posture. The young man's eyes went wide as he looked at Benny. Seeing him, his face, his weapon.

"You," breathed Brother Mercy, and loaded that one word with bottomless loathing.

Benny blinked. He'd never seen this person before, and had no idea why the reaper should seem to hate him personally, but he didn't really care. What mattered is that this guy was a reaper. Right here in New Alamo, and clearly working with the Night Army to sabotage the town's defenses. As the reaper charged him, Benny raised his sword and rushed forward, hungry for the fight.

A hand grabbed Gutsy's vest, jerking her backward, and she spun as she fell, turning to see a ravager clutching at her. She drove the heel of her palm into the center of the thing's forehead, jolting the killer. Then Gutsy kicked him in the groin and head-butted his nose, and as the ravager staggered back, Gutsy fell hard but back-rolled and came up with her machete in her fist.

Now the three ravagers came at her, one pulling a hatchet from his belt, another with a length of chain to which small nails had been welded, and the one she'd hit, who stooped to pick up a length of pipe.

The bald girl groaned and got to her knees, bleeding and dazed. She fumbled for her machete, which had slid away and hung, handle-first, over the edge of the platform.

Gutsy was trapped in the moment, uncertain how to fight three ravagers and this girl, who may have been hurt but was clearly not out of the fight. Benny and the reaper were battling on the far side of the platform, and Spider was still climbing. Sombra, left down on the ground, was barking and snarling in helpless fury.

Gutsy had two choices: run and hope she could climb down to safety, or defy the overwhelming odds of the reaper girl and the three ravagers.

"This is *my* town," she yelled, and charged.

A RUNNER CLIMBED UP THE RAMPS TO THE TOP OF THE wall and found Karen Peak.

"There was a tunnel," he said breathlessly. "It was in one of the houses near the east wall. We think forty or fifty shamblers got in, plus a dozen ravagers. But I think we got them all."

Karen clapped him on the shoulder. "Are you *sure*?"

"Billy Dow and the Dominguez sisters have teams going through that whole part of town, so, yeah, I think we got them."

Karen turned back to the fight on the wall. More than half the defenders had answered the cry to head to the rally point. They were holding it against the climbers, but there were still so *many* monsters out there.

"What should we do?" asked the runner.

But Karen did not have a quick answer. If they deserted the wall, then the dead would swarm over before the town could be evacuated. If they stayed to fight, they would all die defending their home. She looked around as if for answers, but every door seemed to be nailed shut.

Alethea dropped the last of the shamblers with a mighty overhand swing that left a corpse with almost no head. Then she pushed the kids into a bunch and began herding them toward the hospital. It was the safest building because there were guards, more rooms to hide in, and—as a fallback—it had the escape tunnel.

"To the rally point!"

So many people were yelling it that even some of the kids took up the chant without knowing what it meant.

She was already exhausted. Huge blows with the bat were easy at first, but with every swing, Rainbow Smite seemed to gain another ten pounds. Pain lanced through her sides, and breathing felt like inhaling fire. Stopping for a rest, though, was impossible.

She ran, and the children ran with her.

The Chess Players made their way up to the wall, puffing and sweating. They each had long poles and stood shivering in the chilly wind. They were terrified, and each was acutely aware of the years, the arthritis, and the weakness that was the dreadful gift of old age.

"Funny," said Ford, in a way that meant it wasn't going to be funny at all, "but after all this talk of wild men, I kind of figured it would be them."

"Yeah," Urrea agreed.

"Not that I *want* a horde of wild men."

"No. Of course not."

They watched the army of the dead move forward with a hideous slowness. They both knew it was because the shamblers did not move fast, but it had a strange mockery to it, as if the dead had all the time in the world to consume this town.

Which, of course, they did.

GUTSY FEINTED RIGHT AND DODGED LEFT, DUCKED, and chopped down on the foot of the closest ravager. The blade cut through shoe, skin, and bones, and the strange red-black ravager blood welled out. The ravager bellowed, and in an insight of crisis, Gutsy realized that they actually *could* feel pain. All of *los muertos* actually felt pain, because that was how the parasite worked; that was Volker's sick design. The dead could see, hear, feel, smell, and touch, but could not do anything about it. At least, the shamblers could not. The ravagers not only felt pain, they could scream *in* pain. But, being zombies, pain did not stop them, though damage did slow them. This one tried to rush her, but his maimed foot gave out and he fell.

Gutsy rose fast and drove her shoulder into the killer's side, knocking him toward a second ravager. She stepped on the back of the one she'd injured and swung at the third ravager, who was taken completely by surprise.

Her blade missed his head and instead clanged off the chain he carried as a weapon. Gutsy's momentum sent her crashing into the monster, knocking him backward with such force that he had to take a step to catch his balance—except that he was at the edge of the platform, and there was nowhere to step. His arms windmilled for a frantic second, and several nails welded to the links of the whirling chain caught Gutsy's vest. As the ravager fell, the chain jerked her toward the edge. She screamed, dropped her machete, and grabbed one of the steel cables with both hands. She swung out over the edge with the full weight of the ravager pulling at her. Her vest tore open, spilling the many useful things she carried for all eventualities. All, but not this one.

"Spider!" she wailed as her hands began to slip, but her friend was still nowhere to be seen.

When hands suddenly caught her and pulled her back, they were not the brown hands of her best friend. These hands were pale and diseased, and they grabbed her leg to pull her toward a mouth full of snapping teeth. It was the ravager who'd been knocked down by the injured one. He clung to her legs, his weight pulling her down while at the same time he tried to climb high enough to take a bite.

Gutsy hung between two deaths—the unforgiving ground if she fell, and the monster's teeth below.

Benny thought he had an easy fight—a long sword against knives—but the teenager he fought was fast as a scorpion. The young man danced away from the *katana* time and again, parrying thrusts and cuts with his knives as if *they* were the superior weapons and not the ancient blade of the samurai.

Benny and the reaper dueled there on the platform, steel ringing on steel, both of them moving with quick, small steps, darting and lunging.

The reaper reminded Benny of someone else he fought

last year. A young reaper not much older than this one, but who had a harsh, unsmiling face. Brother Peter, the right hand of Saint John. They'd fought a duel while both reapers and Benny's friends watched; at the time it seemed a foregone conclusion to everyone that Brother Peter would win. He was the more skilled fighter, the protégé of Saint John. Benny was barely an apprentice to a deceased master, his brother.

What Benny learned that day was the skills Tom taught him ran deep, but the second layer of training he had gotten from Captain Ledger ran deeper still. Not the elegance of combat or the nobility of the samurai but something else Benny had gotten from Tom. An animal cunning. During that fight Benny had actually allowed Brother Peter to cut him, gambling that the cut he allowed would be damaging but not fatal. He used the moment of that cut—the certainty that Brother Peter would take the obvious opening—to deliver a killing blow.

It was not as stupid a move as everyone watching thought it was. Even then, Benny had been sure he would kill the killer and thereby save his friends from the reaper master's deadly knives.

Now he fought someone who was every bit as good as Brother Peter. Another master of slaughter.

The blades rang and clanged; they sliced the air and whistled like strange flutes. Playing their song of death.

Sister Sorrow crawled toward the edge of the platform, reaching out a trembling hand toward the handle of her machete. Blood dripped from her nose and mouth, and her head felt like it was full of bees. She wanted that knife so she could chop the little witch into pieces and then feed them like treats to the gray people.

Then the blade simply vanished.

It moved on its own out over the edge and was gone. Stolen from her as if by magic. Sister Sorrow threw herself flat in a vain hope of catching it as it dropped, but her flailing hand closed on empty air.

Gutsy's hands slipped on the steel cable, and the braided wire tore at her palms. Her arms ached abominably, and her shoulders seemed to ignite with fire. It was ten times worse than lifting the roof beam off Alice.

She tried to kick at the ravager who held her leg, but the killer gave a savage jerk and pulled himself up and then darted forward to bite her calf.

Pain—like nothing she'd felt before—exploded in her leg, and Gutsy screamed.

Brother Mercy fought Benny Imura back and forth across the platform, each of them gaining and losing ground, taking and yielding the advantage. It was a more evenly matched contest than he had any right to expect. Was Sister Sorrow right? Was this the one who'd fought and killed Brother Peter? The Imura who defeated Saint John of the Knife? How was it possible? That boy was out west, in California.

Brother Mercy shuffled back out of range and paused for one moment as he spoke the name.

"Imura."

The dark-haired boy paused, his sword raised, shock in his eyes.

"It *is* you," said Brother Mercy. "You are the great sinner, the despised of god. It's *you*."

Benny Imura lowered his sword for a moment. "Yes," he said. "But don't bother to tell me who you are. 'Cause I really don't care."

"I am the servant of Lord Thanatos—all praise to his darkness. I am the herald who has made the path smooth for the chosen of god. The Raggedy Man will devour this town, and I will be at his left hand as he marches on to wipe Asheville from the face of the earth. The Night Army, with all of its holy gray people, its ravagers, and my battalions of reapers will crush the American Nation into blood and dust. And then they will hunt all of you down. The living, the sinners. They will sweep like a tide across this continent."

Benny Imura raised his sword.

"Whatever," he said, and then his blade was a flash of silver fire.

Gutsy swung her free foot and kicked down, catching the ravager in the face over and over again in a frenzied effort to dislodge the teeth clamped around her calf. She stamped and stamped, screaming shrilly, until she broke his jaw and seeded the air with his rotted teeth. But still the monster held onto her ankle, hurt but by no means stopped.

And then a hand reached down and clamped strong fingers around the shoulder of her canvas vest.

It was a dead hand and she looked up into the face of another ravager who knelt on the edge of the platform. She was being pulled into two directions now. Death played tug-of-war with death, and she was the fraying rope.

* * *

Sister Sorrow tried to rise, needing to rejoin the fight, but she couldn't. Something held her fast to the deck planks, and at first she could not understand what it was.

She placed her palms flat against the boards and gave a great heave, and that's when she felt it.

The pain.

If pain was a word that fit.

There was a white-hot immensity of sensation in her stomach, and somehow it held her to the boards. It was some kind of sorcery, some strange magic, and her mind fought to understand it.

Then whatever held her was gone, and she was rising, surging backward onto her knees. She froze then, as if kneeling in prayer as she stared down at her stomach. Her lips formed two words, but there was no sound.

Red mouth.

For so it was. An enormous one had opened in her stomach, and she could feel a corresponding one on her back. As if an invisible blade wielded by a demon hand somehow passed through her. She looked at the planks, but there was no blade anywhere to be seen.

Then something rose up over the edge of the platform. A face. Young, dark, with a lot of hair and eyes that were not at all like a demon's. They were kind eyes, and so very sad.

A boy clambered up onto the platform. He had a long *bo* tucked through the back of his belt, and in his hand was a machete.

Her machete.

As the whiteness of pain ebbed, a bright clarity opened

in Sister Sorrow's mind. This boy had seen the handle of her weapon as he climbed up. He'd taken it, and as she lay down to try and catch it, he'd driven the blade up between the boards. Into her.

She tried to say that, despite being a sinner, she thanked him for the gift he'd given her: sending her into the eternal darkness where Lord Thanatos—all praise to his greater darkness—was waiting to enfold her. Sister Sorrow wanted to say all of that. Needed to.

But she had no voice left. There was no breath left in her. She felt herself go . . . to fade. The blessed darkness wrapped its gentle wings around her, and she was gone.

Brother Mercy parried the sword, lunged with one knife, and whipped out with the other, but as he did so he saw something that tore a terrible cry from him.

He watched Sister Sorrow topple forward like a broken doll and then roll off the platform, vanishing into the darkness below.

His scream was so big, so filled with despair, that it made Benny Imura pause and step back. The scream tore a huge hole in the night, and for a moment there was nothing except that sound.

Spider crawled over the edge and onto the platform, winded, bloody from stabbing the reaper woman. Then he saw Gutsy and tore across the boards. He dropped the machete and pulled his *bo* free from his belt, swinging it at the ravager who clung to the edge of the deck. The staff hit solidly, knocking the zombie forward. The killer started to fall, but his fingers caught in the pockets of Gutsy's canvas fishing vest. The impact tore the bottom third of the vest away, dropping the ravager onto the one clutching her ankle. The shock broke his grip, and both ravagers plummeted to the ground. However, the initial downward tug on Gutsy's vest nearly broke her grip. She managed to hold on, even though blood welled from between her clutching fingers.

"Gutsy," Spider cried as he used his *bo* to try and snag the cable. The angle was impossible, though. "Don't let go."

"Spider," she yelled, "push me."

"What?" he yelped.

"Push me. Make me swing. Come on, do it . . . I'm slipping."

Spider looked terrified, but he changed his grip on the staff, leaned out, placed the end against her hip, and pushed. It made her swing about a foot away, but on the return, she didn't come anywhere near close enough to the platform.

"Harder!"

Brother Mercy made a guttural sound of raw hatred and attacked with renewed ferocity, driving Benny back step by step.

Benny realized that he was too close to the edge and abruptly threw himself at a right angle, tucking into a roll and coming out of it running. He stamped down, pivoted to arrest his momentum, and met Brother Mercy's charge.

Their blades met again and again.

Gutsy knew she was going to fall. There was no strength left in her arms. Everything was numb, except for where it was on fire. She thought of Alice down there, hurt, needing her. Had the Carnovskys gotten her to the hospital? Would that even be enough? Gutsy had no idea how bad Alice was hurt. She hated herself for not staying with her. For not caring enough for her.

Except that wasn't true, and on her deepest practical level, Gutsy knew that. Stopping the crane meant saving the whole town. If the reapers and ravagers had torn down the wall, then nothing Gutsy could do would save Alice. Or any of the people she cared about.

As she swung through the night she felt the strength in her hands fail at last.

Benny parried the knife strokes again and again and again.

Then he shifted in and blocked them both at the same time, catching the reaper in a double attack. Benny held the contact for a fragment of a second and lashed out with a kick that caught the older teen on the inner left thigh.

Spider dropped his *bo* and heard it bang and clang all the way down through the network of scaffolding, but he didn't care. As Gutsy swung toward him he saw her bloody, swollen hands open. He lunged and caught what was left of her vest and her T-shirt and flung himself backward.

He fell onto the planking, and Gutsy landed on him. Part of her did. Her legs were still over the edge, kicking in midair.

Spider clawed at her, trying to pull her up before her weight could pull him down. They hung there, on the balance of life and death.

* * *

Benny pressed his advantage, kicking again and catching Brother Mercy's right wrist hard enough to send a knife spinning off into the darkness. He slashed with the sword, but the reaper was not even close to finished.

Brother Mercy ducked, rolled, and bounced up onto the balls of his feet, springy as a dancer, as he shifted his remaining knife to his right hand. He dropped into a fighting crouch, and then suddenly seemed to lose interest in Benny. Instead he stared, slack-jawed, at something else. Then the reaper gave a small cry of obvious terror, spun around, and leaped off the platform.

Benny, startled, ran to the edge and saw the reaper, nimble as an ape, climbing down. As soon as the killer reached the ground, he ran for the eastern wall and began to climb.

The urge to chase him was incredibly strong. Reapers fighting along with the Raggedy Man? Benny wanted to catch Brother Mercy and force some answers out of him. But a sound made him turn, and he saw Spider trying to keep Gutsy from falling over the edge.

Benny ran over to them, dropped his sword, grabbed Gutsy and Spider with one hand each, and hauled. He was not a big teen, but Benny Imura was all muscle, and his weight, leaning backward, did the trick. Spider fell flat on his back and Gutsy literally rolled the length of him, narrowly missing his face, to collapse beside him.

She clutched her torn hands to her chest, weeping from exhaustion.

Spider lay there, panting, staring upward at the smoke clouds that obscured the sky.

Benny knelt beside Gutsy. "Pull up your pant leg. I saw one of those freaks bite you."

"No, he didn't have a good angle; just a bruise. I'm fine."

There was only steel in Benny's eyes and in his voice. "Show me."

Gutsy licked her lips, hoping what she'd said was true. She pulled up her pant leg and angled her calf toward the glow of the distant fires. The skin was badly bruised, but there wasn't a single drop of blood.

Benny and Spider visibly relaxed.

"Jeez, Guts, you have really weird luck," said Benny, straightening. "From all the crazy stuff you do, like going out to that base and coming back with a whole skin. You're either totally out of your mind or you have an angel on your shoulder."

"Both," Spider suggested.

Gutsy merely shrugged. Benny offered her a hand and helped her up. The three of them stood for a moment, looking over the wall toward the mass of the dead slowly advancing on New Alamo.

Spider pointed with his *bo*. "Guys . . . *what is that*?"

OUT IN THE FIELD, BEYOND THE WALL, SOMETHING moved. The light from burning sections of the wall painted it in yellows and oranges, but even with that glow it took the three of them a while to understand what they were seeing.

It was a truck.

Not driving. Not something from the base, but a massive flatbed being pulled along the road by what looked like a thousand *los muertos*. They were yoked like oxen and moved with the steady, unbreakable, tireless stride of the dead. In the center of the flatbed was something that looked like a giant chair. Or throne. And upon the throne was a giant of a man. Dozens of ravagers stood around the throne, firelight glinting on rifle barrels, axes, and swords. And behind the truck, spread out like an ocean, were a million shambling monsters. An army so vast that it was lost in the distance.

"Oh my God," Benny breathed.

None of them had to ask what they were seeing. Not anymore. Now they understood.

Homer Gibbon, the Raggedy Man, king of all the world's hungry dead, had come to New Alamo.

THE MASS OF ZOMBIES SEEMED TO BULGE OUTWARD as if the vast body of them took a deep breath. Then the bulge broke free as a group of about a thousand of them seemed to rush forward faster than the others. They did not walk but actually ran, and for a moment Gutsy was confused. Were they ravagers? Or the faster *los muertos*? The R3 mutations? She'd thought there weren't many of them. Certainly not *this* many.

But as they neared the wall, firelight bathed them in brightness, and Gutsy could see that these were not *los muertos* at all. Nor were they ravagers or wild men. They were *living* people. Dressed in black clothes with red tassels attached to ankles and wrists. Their heads were shaved and elaborately tattooed, and each of them carried a weapon—scythe, ax, sickle, sword, or pitchfork.

"Reapers," gasped Benny. "So *many* of them."

Fires sparked to light among the reapers, and, with mounting horror, Gutsy and the others watched as they threw bottles set with flaming rags at the walls. The bottles, filled with alcohol or fuel, exploded and sheets of flame shot up, driving the defenders back from the edges of the wall.

Hundreds of the bottles arced high, landing on the ramparts or falling into the town. Houses next to the wall caught fire at once. Several of the firebombs exploded on the crushed roof of Alice's house, and in seconds it was burning.

The gunfire from the walls diminished to a few sparse, desperate shots as most of the defenders deserted their posts.

"What do we do?" asked Spider. "We can't stay here."

Gutsy looked up at the crane, wishing she knew how to operate it. Wishing there was time to learn. The thought of using it to drop cars onto the reapers was compelling. Benny glanced up, too.

"Yeah," he said, as if reading her mind. "I wish we had catapults, too."

"Let's go," said Gutsy, turning away. "We need to get to the rally point. We need the Dòmi, and we need to get out of here."

"We should have left right away," said Spider. "As soon as you and Sergeant Holly got back."

"I thought we'd have a little more time," Gutsy said helplessly.

They'd just reached the edge of the platform when the night was split by a new sound. Gunfire, but different. It was a harsh, heavy *rat-a-tat-tat*.

"That's a machine gun," Benny cried as he ran back to the other side. He pointed. "*Look!*"

Out in the troubled darkness were uncountable flashes of orange flame seeming to come out of nowhere. Then two massive spouts of flame shot out, sending tongues of fire toward the reapers. The screams of the burning killers rose louder than any sound so far that night. The illumination from these streams of fire chased back the darkness, and the three teens stared in shock as four vehicles smashed their way through the ranks of *los muertos*, firing machine guns and flamethrowers.

"It's Holly!" cried Spider.

Gutsy stared, her heart torn. The people who'd gone to the base had survived and returned.

But . . . with only four vehicles.

Not nearly enough.

THEY CLIMBED DOWN AND RAN TO THE WEST GATE, which had been cleared by the flamethrowers, but as the vehicles raced inside the surviving reapers charged, backed by many thousands of the dead. It took everyone's strength to close the gate in time.

Karen called bucket brigades up to douse the fires on the wall so they could continue defending the gate.

Sunny-Day Ray climbed out of one vehicle—it was called a Stryker Dragoon, a massive eight-wheeled monstrosity with a huge gun mounted on top.

"Where are the others?" she asked.

Sunny-Day Ray shook his head. "We got swarmed and had to split up. Not sure if the others made it, but they didn't make it here, that's for sure. We wouldn't have either, except for that big Bushmaster up there." He pointed to the gun. "Don't matter if it's a ravager or a shambler, 'cause that thing plum tears them all apart. Flamethrower's pretty goldurn handy, too."

He looked around and frowned. "You evacuating the town?"

"Trying to," said Benny.

"Looks to me like you left 'er too late."

"No kidding."

"Work faster," said Holly. She and one of the other drivers were handing out automatic rifles and bundles of loaded magazines to the people clustered around. "We saw a lot more coming."

"We can hold them off for a while with these," Spider said, pointing to the big machine guns mounted on the vehicles. "Can't we?"

Holly and Sunny-Day Ray both shook their heads. "You ain't been out there, Spider," said the old man. "You ever heard the expression 'between a rock and a hard place'?"

"Sure, but—"

"You seen the rock already. That big mook on that throne? That's the Raggedy Man."

"We know."

"Well, what you don't know is it weren't them zombies made the convoy split up."

"What do you mean?" asked Spider, but Gutsy clutched his wrist.

"He means the wild men are coming."

"No," said Sergeant Holly. "The wild men are already here."

BROTHER MERCY TRIED TO FIND THE REST OF THE
strike team that had infiltrated the town with him and Sister
Sorrow. He found only Brother Cactus and Sister Moon. The
rest were scattered, doing their assigned tasks. He told the
two he found about seeing the wild men. They were aghast.
They knew about Wodewose from the ravagers who'd been at
the base. It was a great evil to those half-zombies. None of
them had known that wild men would be here. Right here.

"We have to get out of here," he said urgently. "Forget this
cursed town. Let the wild men have it. We need to get outside
and turn our army back."

Brother Cactus looked past him to the empty street.
"Where's Sister Sorrow?"

The sneer was replaced by a mask of such deep hate that
the others recoiled. "She's *gone*," he said. "Into the darkness.
Now come on!"

They swarmed up the eastern wall, scaling the tires and
bumpers and door handles of the stacked cars until they
reached the walkway. There were only a few guards left over
here, and the reapers cut them down.

Below, in the field outside, the first of the ravagers and

the rest of Brother Mercy's strike team reached the wall. They hurled grappling hooks over the top of it and began to climb. Brother Mercy leaned out and waved them back.

"No!" he called down to them. "Go back. *Go back!*"

They stared at him in confusion. There was too much noise, too many things happening at once, and Brother Mercy knew that this army was going to fail. The gray people—the sinless dead who were beloved of Lord Thanatos, all praise his darkness—could not stand up to the wild men. The Raggedy Man and some of the ravagers had told tales about this new threat. A single one of the howling madmen could begin an infection that would sweep through the king of the dead's shambling army. Even the ravagers were vulnerable. Taking this town of sinners was not worth the risk, and the Raggedy Man did not know the wild men were coming. That they were nearly here.

Brother Mercy sheathed his knife, took hold of a grappling line, and slithered down the outside of the wall. The other reapers followed, silent as ghosts.

84

GUTSY AND HER FRIENDS RAN TO THE WEST WALL AND climbed to the gate. A few ravagers and reapers, along with several hundred shamblers, had attacked that side of town, but it was more of a diversion, drawing resources away from the main assault on the east gate. Now those same attackers were themselves being attacked. How soon before the Wodewose infection reached the larger army on the other side? And then what?

Gutsy stared in horror as the wild men overran the living dead, attacking the shamblers and ravagers, but also tearing down the reapers with relentless savagery. Mad howls filled the night.

The undead had no chance. Not only were they attacked with hands and teeth but their bodies were assaulted by Wodewose spat at them or delivered through bites. Within moments the living dead began twitching and thrashing as a second war was fought in their bloodstreams—paracide versus parasite. A few of the more recent reanimates actually screamed in very human voices as the disease swept through them, awakening parts of their brains, reconnecting them to the realization of what was happening. Driving them insane within seconds.

It was horrible to see.

But the fight was not entirely one-sided. The reapers, seeing and understanding that something terrible was happening to their undead allies, mounted a sophisticated defense. They were all excellent fighters—as Gutsy had just learned—and while the wild men could use clubs and stones as weapons, the reapers had skill and cunning. They met the attack, often putting themselves between the wild men and the living dead. Blades flashed, and bodies fell.

The fight shaped itself that way, with the reapers learning from success. They formed a curved wall around the uninfected shamblers. Some of the ravagers stood behind them, firing pistols and shotguns at the wild men.

"I don't know who to root for," mumbled Benny.

"Us," said Spider.

"Right now," Gutsy said, "those reapers are slowing down the wild men, and the wild men themselves are shifting the focus away from us. Maybe that's the break we've been praying for."

"I could use a better break," said Benny. "Like a fleet of American Nation helicopters and a hundred pounds of pills for Chong and Sarah and the others."

"Yeah," said Chong, who'd caught up with them moments before. "That would be nice, wouldn't it?"

Gutsy gave a dry laugh, then said, "Benny, maybe you and Chong should get over to the hospital. Make sure Morton and the stabilizer stuff get out."

"What about you?"

"Spider and I will do what we can to get everyone to the

hospital rally point. We need to get them outside and heading to Site B before those monsters stop fighting each other and remember us."

Benny abruptly held out his hand. "See you on the other side, sister."

She paused for half a moment, then shook his hand. "See you there, brother."

She hugged him and Chong and watched them run off.

KAREN KNEW IT WAS ALL FALLING APART.

The plans and preparations, the fortifications and the careful selection of who should defend what—it all seemed pointless now. There *was* no way to prepare for this. Two armies, each created by a different warped science, were coming now to exterminate what was left of the living.

New Alamo was going to die, and she knew it.

Though it hurt her to do it, she went to where the huge old air raid siren stood on a corner of the wall. It was operated by a crank, and as she wound it around and around, the voice of doom woke up. The banshee wail rose high and floated out across the town. Other sirens, one on each corner of the wall, picked up the shriek.

Evacuate.

Nearby, a handful of defenders paused in their work of reloading guns and throwing rocks and stared at her. She saw their faces, saw the hopelessness there. The dread of what was going to happen.

Karen released the handle, and the siren began to fade away.

"Go on," she said. "Save yourselves. Save your families. I'll stay here."

One of them, a tall man who'd brought his family to America all the way from Ecuador in the weeks before the outbreak, stepped toward her.

"What about Sarah?"

She smiled at him. "Josué . . . get your family. Take Sarah with you. Her pills are in the blue backpack in the living room."

Josué lived two doors away from the Peaks. He looked pained, torn. He did not want to desert his post, but he had a wife, two grown children, and three grandkids.

"I . . . ," he began, but words failed him.

Karen gave him a brief, fierce hug. "Tell Sarah that I love her very much. Tell her I'll try to find her. If I can."

The last three words were as thin and false as they both knew them to be.

Josué nodded and hurried toward the ladder. Of the eight other defenders on the wall, only two others went. Both had families.

The rest, some single, some whose remaining family members had died in the two recent attacks, stayed. They looked at one another. There was so much fear, but there was also acceptance. She saw how acceptance firmed their chins and straightened their spines.

As one, they turned back to the wall.

All around the town, other defenders were making the same choices. Some going. Some willing to stay and fight.

And die.

GUTSY, SPIDER, AND SOMBRA RAN TOWARD THE EAST
gate. The evacuation siren had been wailing for what seemed
like forever, but now it wound down, the blare fading as if in
despair.

Halfway to the gate they met Sunny-Day Ray, who,
already old, seemed to have aged another twenty years. He
was soaked with sweat and splashed with mostly black blood.
He saw them and began waving them back.

"No," he cried, "we're losing the wall."

"What about Karen and everyone?"

"She ordered them all to the rally point," the old man
panted. "I'm going to try and get out the gate with the other
vehicles. Those machine guns might give us a chance to break
through and protect your backs while you get moving to Site B."

Spider looked past him. "Did you see Alethea?"

Sunny-Day Ray nodded. "Saw her shepherding a passel of
kids toward the hospital."

Gutsy started to turn, then stopped as she heard several
spaced gunshots from high on the gate. She cupped her hands
around her eyes and peered through the smoke and shadows
and saw Karen still there, holding a handgun, taking careful

aim, and firing. Again and again. Gutsy started to run in that direction, but the old man caught her by the arm in a surprisingly strong grip.

"No," he said.

"She'll die up there. She needs help."

There was a sad smile on Sunny-Day Ray's face. "She's helping *us*. Buying us time."

"She can still—"

"Listen to me, Gutsy," he said. "We'll try to pick her up on the way out. That's *my* plan."

But as he spoke, the gun fell silent, and the top of the gate was obscured by smoke.

"God save our souls," said the old man. "You kids better run. And I mean right now."

Spider and Gutsy, their hearts breaking, turned and ran. Sombra lingered a moment longer and wagged his tail at the old man, and then he, too, fled.

"WHY ARE YOU STILL *HERE*?" DEMANDED BENNY AS he and Chong burst into Dr. Morton's lab, a nearly frantic Grimm at their heels.

The injured physician and Manny Flores both looked up from their work. They were haggard, pale with fright, and sweating badly, but Morton looked more dead than alive. His skin was a grayish green, and sweat rolled down his cheeks. All around them were boxes and bags filled with the fertilizer-based stabilizer. Heaps of the smelly manure were drying under a row of lamps.

"I thought it had to be moist in order to bond with the Dòmi," said Gutsy.

"Only slightly moist," explained Flores. "We've already treated most of this stuff and have been drying it out so it's lighter to carry and easier to disperse."

"Someone said they would be bringing a cart for all of this," said Morton irritably. "But they haven't come back yet."

"Is it true those things are in the town?" asked Flores, his eyes jumpy with fatigue and terror.

"Some got in," Benny confirmed.

"Wild men?" Morton's voice was nearly a screech.

"Not yet," Benny said quickly, and then explained what was happening outside the walls and watched the words hit the two scientists like a series of punches. "So, we need to get out *right now*."

"We still need that cart," cried Flores. "Otherwise all of this is for nothing."

"I'll find one," said Chong, but paused at the door. "Will this Dòmi stuff actually work?"

Flores glanced at Morton, who also paused, and then he nodded. "It will work best if the reanimates are already infected with the paracide."

"What if regular people breathe it in?" asked Benny.

Morton shook his head. "We just don't know. Our tests never—"

"—Got that far, right. Got it." Benny went to a table, took a trowel that was stuck in a pile of the Dòmi-treated manure, and began shoveling it into one of the many bags prepared for that purpose.

"What happens when the reapers get exposed to Wode-wose?"

"Probably nothing," said Morton. "Captain Ledger and young Miss Gomez were exposed and were not turned, so we can assume that it hasn't mutated into a threat to regular humans."

"It would drop you," said Benny.

"We don't know what it will do to me, or to Mr. Chong or Karen's daughter. It could drive us mad, or kill us, or do nothing at all."

Benny raised a heap of stabilizer. "Well, at least we have magic horse poop. . . ."

Morton ignored that. "We also don't know what the effects of Dòmi will be on ordinary humans. Or on reanimates who have not yet been exposed to Wodewose."

"Swell," said Benny. "But it will stop those wild men . . . right?"

Morton looked down at his work, avoiding Benny's eyes.

"Hey—*right?*"

"Once the reanimates are infected with the paracide," said Morton slowly, "then even the smallest particle of Dòmi should shut down their aggression . . . or at least in theory."

"In theory," Chong said. "Swell." He took a breath, then said aloud to himself, "Go get a cart, Lou Chong. Don't think about all the ways you could die tonight. Nope, don't do that at all."

He left. Grimm trotted behind, armor clanking.

Benny looked at Morton. "Okay, be straight with me, Doc. Even though you never did tests, you're still a scientist. You must have a theory. What's going to happen if he gets exposed to the paracide or the Dòmi? Just tell me."

Morton shook his head. "I really *don't* know. I know *I* don't want to risk exposure. And if you care for your friend, keep him away from it too."

"How do we do that if you guys find some way of spraying this magic poop all over the wild men? How do I keep Chong safe then?"

"Maybe tie him up. Or . . ."

"Or *what?*"

"Or use that sword and end it all for him, Mr. Imura," said the doctor coldly, his eyes finally meeting Benny's. "Given what could happen, that might be the greatest kindness."

There was a rattle in the hall and Chong appeared, pushing a big laundry cart with canvas sides.

"Perfect," cried Flores, and immediately began grabbing bags of the stabilizer. Despite his injuries, Morton tried to help. It was clearly agony to do it, and for a moment Benny was content to let him suffer. But then he took a heavy bag from Morton and pushed the doctor gently toward the door.

From somewhere outside they heard a man yell in a voice raw with terror.

"They're inside the walls. Oh God, the wild men are here!"

A chorus of awful howls filled the night.

"We're out of time," said Morton.

AS GUTSY AND SPIDER RAN, THEY COULD HEAR THE howls. First outside the walls, then high up on them, and within moments, inside the town. Far away, outside the gates, there was a burst of heavy-caliber gunfire punctuated by screams so twisted that it was impossible to tell if they were from dying wild men or the small group with Sunny-Day Ray and the vehicles. Of Sergeant Holly there was no sign.

Sombra ranged ahead and twice stopped short, the hairs on his back bristling. Each time Gutsy and Spider faded sideways and hid in shadows as packs of wild men went running past. They were a mixed bag now, some of them clearly from the base and others looking much older and more weathered—converted shamblers. There were a few converted ravagers, too, though now they carried their guns like clubs instead of ready to fire.

Gutsy kept pulling Sombra close, trying to become invisible in the dark. The coydog trembled in her arms.

Then, when the last howls vanished down a side street, the three of them ran on.

"They're not heading to the hospital," whispered Spider.

"So far," Gutsy said, and was immediately sorry she said

it. Those words seemed to offer up a challenge to the spirits of bad luck.

As they passed a store, Gutsy slowed to a stop. The sign outside read:

NOTIONS & NOVELTIES

"What is it?" Spider asked.

Instead of answering, Gutsy ran inside. Most of the stock were handmade toys, scavenged stuff like old board games, party supplies for the town's many small festivals, and the one thing she hoped to find. Something no one fleeing this catastrophe would ever think to pack. She picked up a box and showed it to Spider.

"Fireworks?" he asked, confused, but immediately a smile blossomed on his face. "Yes!"

Without having to say a word to each other, they gathered armfuls of the fireworks, some of which were decades old. They piled a lot of them in the middle of the floor and then dumped other stuff on top. Paper and anything that would burn. They worked fast as Sombra looked on with canine interest. While they worked, Gutsy set some items aside, and they began stuffing their pockets with smaller things like M-80s and TNT Poppers, items neither of them would normally go anywhere near. Not since Jillie Cooper blew off three of her fingers playing with them five years ago.

Gutsy searched her undamaged pockets, produced an old metal lighter, and lit the longest of the fuses. They grabbed a few additional fireworks and fled. They were half a block away when the night of the apocalypse turned into a New Year's Day celebration. There were loud bangs and pops and *rattle-tattle-tattles* and whistles and whooshes.

A large pack of wild men came running at the sound, shrieking at the noise as if challenging it, the way one barking dog will try to outbark another. Another pack ran to join them, and another.

The shadows behind them seemed to disintegrate into an ocean of sparks, and then the whole of the storefront leaped outward and upward in a massive explosion. Individually the fireworks were dangerous, but together they were deadly. The blast plucked fifty of the killers off their feet, tore them to rags, and flung them like burning embers in all directions.

Gutsy and Spider, keeping to the shadows as they ran, saw a dozen more small packs of wild men tearing along toward the noise and light.

Running away from the hospital.

Gutsy set up several more fireworks—a kind called 16-shot cakes—in curbside flowerbeds and propped them at an angle to fire back the way they'd come. Spider took the lighter and ignited the fuses. Then they continued running. By the time the fuses hit the powder, they were a block away. Each cake began firing shot after shot into the air, bursting in party colors above the town. Drawing the ears and eyes of the wild men with each loud pop and stunning light.

BENNY, CHONG, AND THE SCIENTISTS REACHED THE storeroom that hid the entrance to the tunnel, but they had to fight their way through crowds to do it. The hospital corridors were choked with people, some carrying bundles, others empty-handed and barely dressed. If it wasn't for the steel spikes bristling from Grimm's armor, no one would have let them pass. As it was, the refugees flattened themselves against the walls, sometimes three deep. The dog walked ahead, growling at everyone, followed by Chong pushing the cart, Flores supporting Morton, and Benny walking with his *katana* unsheathed.

When they reached the entrance to the tunnel, Benny drafted four strong-looking men to help carry the laden cart down the short flight of stairs, ordered Grimm to stay with Chong, and then ran ahead.

It took what seemed hours to reach the far end of the corridor, but when he got there, he was gratified to see that the Chess Players were there. They were grouping the refugees together, making sure each group had a copy of the map and knew where to go.

Benny ran along, catching up to several groups.

"Everyone be quiet out there," he said. "Take only what you can carry, and if you have to run, drop everything except your weapons. Everyone who can fight watches the people directly in front. Don't look back. Just keep going. No one goes east, because that's where the shamblers are coming from. No one goes west, because that's where the wild men are. Follow the map north-by-northeast to Site B. There's enough moonlight to guide you. Sunny-Day Ray and the convoy will try and keep the attack at the gates, to make it look like we're doing a last stand. Then they'll take off due south to try and lead the reapers and zoms that way."

"Wait," cried one of the storekeepers, "they're *leaving* us?"

"No," Benny assured him. "My guess is they'll go south until they're completely out of sight of anyone chasing them, then split up and circle around to meet us on the road to Site B. That's the smartest play. Don't worry; they'll come for us."

In the distance Benny could heard the roar of the Bushmaster and other machine guns. The fact that the convoy was still fighting was a good sign.

What he didn't immediately understand, though, was the fact that there was a pretty impressive fireworks display erupting over the town.

"Has to be Gutsy," he said aloud, and knew it to be true. Somehow it seemed like something that clever girl would do. It made him like her even more.

GUTSY AND SPIDER REACHED THE HOSPITAL AND SAW that the entrance was completely jammed with people. Gutsy climbed onto a big metal trash can and balanced on the rim as she scanned the crowd, looking for Alethea, Alice, Benny, or Chong.

She saw the tiara first. Sparkling with reflected light, nestled in wild chestnut hair.

"*Alethea!*" she called, yelling through cupped hands. Spider yelled even louder, and Sombra began barking. Alethea did not hear them, though.

It was a full-on panic now. Civility was gone. Gutsy saw a grown man shove two children out of his way so he could squeeze into the entrance. A woman was swinging a golf club at him, missing, and hitting other people around her. On the floor, shoved against the wall, an old couple clung to each other, their faces bloody, their eyes streaming tears, and no one even paused to help.

Alethea had her back to the wall next to the tunnel entrance, and Rainbow Smite in both hands. A knot of children clustered around her. Two men, both of them bruised and bleeding, lay dazed on the floor, and for a moment the frenzied exodus ground to a shocked halt. Alethea's eyes blazed with terrible fury. One of the children had a badly bleeding nose and he had his arms wrapped around Alethea's thighs.

Gutsy could read the scene—one or both of the injured men had done something rough and violent to try and get into the tunnel first. That had been a mistake. Another man tried to shove Alethea out of the way, and she rammed the fat end of her bat into his stomach with such force that it lifted him off the ground. He dropped to his knees, face purple, and she kicked him away. Her hair was wild and her eyes wilder, but her tiara was still in place.

"Kids go in next," she roared, "*then* adults. Anyone else shoves a kid out of the way and I will murder them right here and now."

One man—a big hulking fellow who Gutsy recognized as a wall construction worker—laughed at Alethea and told her to get out of the way. He emphasized the demand with a very ugly comment about her weight.

The hardwood tip of a fighting staff *tokked* him on the top of the head hard enough to stagger him. He dropped to his knees, and then the *bo* swung around and stopped less than a quarter inch from the tip of his nose. The man gaped and his eyes stared down the length of the staff to a pair of intense green eyes.

"You heard the princess," said Spider. Sombra took a step past Spider and bared his considerable teeth.

The big man had nothing to say. The kids fled into the tunnel. Alethea and Spider flanked the door, and the congested knot of people transformed into a steady flow.

Gutsy edged over to Alethea. "Where's Alice and the Carnovskys?"

Alethea shook her head. "Sorry, Guts, I haven't seen them."

She took her group of kids and ran into the tunnel.

Gutsy and Spider stayed outside and made several trips deeper into the hospital to drive stragglers toward the tunnel. Gutsy looked for Alice in every room, too, but didn't see her anywhere. The tide was slackening now, kindling a fragile flame of optimism in her. She had no idea how many people had gotten out. Not all, of that she was sure. Some would have been hunted down by either the dead or wild men. Some were probably hiding, convinced they could wait it out.

Where was Karen Peak? Had she gotten out with Sunny-Day Ray and the vehicles? Or had she fallen with the town, the last defender of the New Alamo?

And . . . where was Alice?

The flame of optimism in her heart flickered and offered no comforting warmth at all.

"Gutsy," said Spider, "*listen.*"

She pulled herself out of her own thoughts and heard the sounds. Howling.

Coming from inside the hospital.

AT THE FAR END OF THE TUNNEL, BENNY STOOD AT THE exit, guiding the fleeing citizens out through the car wash and into the night. Many were weeping as they fled into the darkness. Away from the only home they knew and toward the uncertainty of Site B far to the northeast.

Alethea came through with a bunch of little kids and herded them along, her bat clutched in one fist and her other hand darting out to touch each of them as they ran, tallying them. It was an automatic thing, unconscious. For all her bluster, Benny suspected she had a big, gentle heart. He prayed that she would survive this. Her and those kids. Seeing them gave him hope but also deepened his fear.

"Where's Gutsy and Spider?" he called.

"Coming," was her only reply. He peered down the tunnel but could see nothing except shadows and debris.

Not far away, the town was beginning to burn. There were still explosions and yells and even a few scattered gunshots, but most of the fighting was distant.

"God, I wish Joe and Sam were here," he said to himself. It was not the first time he'd said or thought that. It had become a mantra for him, and he kept hoping the two soldiers would appear as if by magic—as they had during the siege of New Alamo.

Where *were* they? Had they found Site B? Or had they encountered an overwhelming force of zoms or wild men out there in the Broken Lands?

"Come on," he said to the people, "hurry. *Hurry*."

The last of the refugees were sorted into groups and sent on their way. Morton and Flores still waited, though, because Benny wanted to provide them with his own protection. Chong and Grimm stood with them, all of them silent and frightened. Even the big dog looked small and lost.

Morton limped over and pulled on Benny's sleeve. "We have to go," insisted the doctor. "We have to go right now."

Benny swatted his hand away. "Gutsy and Spider are still in there."

Morton got up in his face, furious and terrified. "We're trying to save *thousands*. Don't be a sentimental fool. Do you want to get us all killed? Do you want your friends to have died for *nothing*? Let's go now."

Gutsy and Spider barricaded the door that led to the hall with every piece of heavy furniture and file cabinet they could find. The howls were louder, and definitely coming their way.

"Will that hold?" Spider asked, but a split second later the whole fortification shook with unbelievable force. Howls seemed to punch through the barrier as if mocking its ability to keep the wild men out. The mad killers rammed it again. And again.

Gutsy looked around, but there was nothing else they could use to reinforce the barricade. Sombra barked at it but then retreated, whining as pieces of furniture toppled down.

"Maybe it'll hold for a few minutes," she said, but the words tasted like the lies they were.

She pushed Spider toward the tunnel entrance.

"Let's go."

They pulled the false cabinet closed behind them, but Gutsy did not for a minute think it would fool the wild men. At best, it would slow them down for a bit. Maybe long enough for her and Spider to get to the car wash and barricade that door too. If Site B was really there, then the townsfolk would need the better part of the night to reach it.

The tunnel was long and empty now, and they ran past tons of food and supplies that she ached to take with her. Canned goods, bottled water, kerosene for lamps, and boxes of military rations. All of it useful. All of it going to waste now.

Behind them the sound of the howling wild men grew louder, proof that they'd broken through the barricade. They would be in the tunnel soon, and then there would be no way to stop them. The doors at the far end hadn't been properly repaired after the fight in the car wash. There hadn't been time. And they didn't hold the wild men back the last time anyway.

There was renewed pounding, and Gutsy turned in horror.

"They broke into the office," Spider gasped. "They're at the tunnel door. How'd they know it was even there?"

How indeed, Gutsy wondered. Was it possible that one or more of them somehow, despite disease and madness, remembered the hidden tunnel? It might explain why that group of them had attacked her and Ledger at the car wash.

Maybe they had some primitive reasoning powers. That ter-rified her, because it meant the fleeing people could have walked into a trap.

No, she told herself. If that had happened, she would have heard the sounds of fighting. But that didn't help her right now. The wild men were going to break into the tunnel. That was inevitable, and from the fury of their attack on the door, it would be very soon.

Too soon.

Please, she begged silently, *we just need a little more time.*

They kept running, but Gutsy felt something tugging at her mind, wanting her to stop, to turn and go back. She fished for what it was. Something she'd seen . . . ?

Then Gutsy suddenly stopped and stood there, looking back the way they'd come. Spider ran another dozen paces before he realized that he wasn't being followed. He wheeled around.

"What's wrong?" he demanded. "Why'd you stop?"

"Kerosene," she blurted so loud it made Sombra bark in alarm.

"What about it? We can't carry lamp oil."

"No, no," she said quickly, and began running back.

Confused, Spider followed.

The rows of big plastic containers of kerosene were close to the tunnel entrance. Gutsy skidded to a stop, grabbed two of the containers, and dragged them to the base of the short stairs. Then ran back for two more.

"Help me," she yelled, but Spider was already there, reach-ing for a pair of the red jugs. They worked fast as Sombra barked and danced excitedly around them. Within seconds they had a mound of the containers. Gutsy fished in her pockets for several of the M-80s, the big and very dangerous firecrackers. Each of them was a small red cardboard tube, about an inch and a half long, a fuse extending from the side. According to the writing on the tube, each contained three grams of pyrotechnic flash powder. Despite being used at celebrations, they were in no way toys.

Which is what Gutsy counted on.

She knelt and began fitting the M-80s under the edges of the kerosene containers. Spider saw what she was doing and immediately joined her.

"How many should we use?" he asked.

"All of them."

The pounding was getting louder, and the false door was shuddering in a dangerous way. As they finished, Spider took one of the containers and removed the cap. Gutsy did the same, and they backed away together, leaving a very wet double trail as far as the kerosene would reach, which was about two hundred feet. They dropped the empty jugs. Sombra ran far down the tunnel to escape the noxious fumes. Gutsy and Spider pulled their shirts up to cover their noses and mouths.

The door continued to tremble and shudder.

"You have your lighter?" asked Spider.

She held out her hand to show him. "Get ready to run," she said.

"I'm ready."

With a mighty crash, the tunnel door exploded inward and a horde of the wild men came pouring into the tunnel.

"I'm sorry," she said as she clicked the lighter and knelt

to touch the small flame to the end of the kerosene trail. Yellow flame shot away from her, racing like some hellish demon toward the mound she and Spider had created.

They raced as fast as they could down the long tunnel. The howling mob of wild men boiled out of the hospital and chased them.

The fire outran them all.

It reached the mound, and suddenly the world was unbearably loud and unbearably hot. A shock wave of superheated gas punched both ways along the tunnel. By the time it reached Gutsy and Spider, they were more than halfway down the length. It didn't matter. The blast picked them—and Sombra—up and hurled them viciously away. They shrieked as they flew through the air.

Gutsy heard Sombra yelp in pain as he hit a wall of boxes, but she could not see him. Or Spider. Her vision was seared to bright white and intense black. She felt herself hit. And land. All of the air in her lungs was knocked out of her, and there didn't seem to be anything left to breathe.

"I'm sorry . . . ," she gasped again.

And then the world burned to a tiny cinder and winked out.

BENNY IMURA HAD NO CHANCE AT ALL.

He didn't even understand what was happening until a giant's fist composed of fire punched him in the face. The blow staggered him, knocking him out of the mouth of the tunnel and ten feet into the car wash. He slammed into Chong, who went down hard beneath him.

Benny lay sprawled, dazed and stupid with pain and shock.

"Get. Off. Me."

The three words were punctuated with gasps of pain. It took Benny a few seconds to understand what the words meant, and longer to realize who was speaking.

Then he rolled to one side, coughing and groaning.

Chong lay like a starfish: arms and legs spread wide, and his whole body looking flattened. Benny managed—somehow—to get to his hands and knees. He looked back at the tunnel mouth, seeing smoke curling out of it as if from the end of a shotgun barrel.

"What . . . ?" he tried to say, but a full sentence eluded him.

Flores came running over and helped him up, then saw to

Chong. Neither of them was badly hurt, but both were shaky and bruised.

"What happened?" Chong wheezed.

Then he stiffened. They all did. They'd been waiting for Spider and Gutsy.

And now . . .

"Oh my God," said Benny in a faint and horrified whisper.

PART TWENTY-TWO

ON LOST ROADS

If quick, I survive.

If not quick, I am lost.

This is "death."

—SUN TZU

93

GUTSY FELT PAIN AND WAS CONFUSED BY IT. HOW could a dead person feel anything?

Then terror swept through her as she remembered that the Reaper Plague kept the original personality awake and aware even after the body reanimated.

Ay dios mio! Estoy muerto!

Then, suddenly, she felt something wet on her face. Warm. Moving.

And it smelled awful.

Gutsy flinched away, bashing at it, afraid it was one of the wild men. Her flailing hand hit something that yielded. A sharp yelp of pain and fear filled the air.

A . . . *yelp*?

Gutsy opened her eyes. It was like lifting ten thousand tons. She stared through tears, grit, and dust into a pair of smoky gray eyes.

"S-Sombra . . . ?"

The coydog was hesitant because she'd just hit him, even if by accident, but he was there, trying to help her, his tail wagging nervously. He began licking her all over for the sheer joy of her being alive.

Actually alive.

Gutsy wrapped her arms around him and pulled the scared and skinny animal into a fierce embrace. He whined and wriggled, licked her and barked.

A voice behind her said, "Are we dead?"

Gutsy let Sombra go and turned to see a thin, trembling shadow rise from the debris. Spider was covered in ash, and his T-shirt had been nearly torn away. He leaned on his *bo* and looked at her with eyes that were dull with shock.

"We're alive," she said in a hoarse voice she barely recognized as her own.

She bent forward and vomited. Spider came and wrapped his arms around her and held her while she did. Then Gutsy straightened, dragged a forearm across her mouth, and together they staggered toward the car wash. Sombra, following, whined continuously, his tail curled between his legs.

"Gutsy!"

A voice came echoing through the ruined tunnel, and Gutsy and Spider looked up and saw Benny Imura running full tilt toward them, his gleaming sword in his hands.

"Gutsy," he cried. "Spider . . . what the heck *happened*?"

Spider just pointed the way they'd come. The far end of the tunnel was gone, blocked entirely by fallen debris, burned cases of food, and half the ceiling. The blast had done more than ignite their mound—it had exploded all of the remaining containers of kerosene, and clearly something else that was stored there. The detonation had been too large, too powerful for just a few hundred gallons of lamp oil and a handful of fireworks. Gutsy pulled a wrapper from one of the fireworks out of a pocket and handed it to Benny.

"*You* did that?" he marveled.

"Seemed . . . practical."

Benny laughed and gave her shoulder a squeeze. "You're really something, Gutsy Gomez."

She gave him a strange look. "We're supposed to be kids."

"The world's supposed to make sense," he said. "Life's supposed to be fair. Isn't that what the grown-ups all told us? And yet . . ."

"Yes," she said. "And yet."

Gutsy took a steadying breath and slapped dust from her clothes, looking around. "What's happening outside?"

Benny pointed back the way he'd come. "Everyone out," he said. "At least everyone who came to the rally point. We broke them into groups and gave them maps. Alethea got out too; she's leading one of the groups. Morton and Flores are right outside with Chong. We have all that Dòmi stuff mixed with horse poop in a big cart. We were just waiting on you."

"Benny," she asked, "did you see Alice in the hospital? Did she get out?"

But he looked uncertain. "Maybe. She was in a wheelbarrow, right? I saw a couple of people pushing injured folks in them, but there was so much going on . . . I'm not really sure."

"It's okay," said Gutsy. She took another breath, forcing back the pain she felt in every cell of her body. "Let's go."

She and Spider limped after Benny, but as they went the shock began to ebb and she could feel adrenaline in her system, giving her some strength, sharpening her vision. That was a costly benefit, though, and at some point she would have to pay for it. There was an end to strength and stamina, and Gutsy just prayed that what was left for her would be enough to get to safety.

Chong stood in the tunnel mouth, an arrow fitted to his bowstring. He lowered it when he saw who was coming toward him. "What *happened*?" he demanded.

"Gutsy blocked the tunnel," said Spider.

"How?"

"Fireworks."

They left the car wash and joined Morton and Flores, who were visibly nervous. Grimm and Sombra wagged their tails and sniffed each other. Flores pointed toward town, and they all turned.

The entire sky in that direction glowed with a thousand shades of orange and red, and hands of flame reached up to scratch at the roof of the world. Inky black clouds twisted and roiled above the conflagration. There were howls carried on the wind, but they were not howls of hunting. These were shrieks of dying. It was as if a chorus of demons sang a lament for the death of New Alamo.

They stood, struck by the horror of it all. The entire town was on fire. Every house, every building. It could not have been from the tunnel explosion, though that probably added to it. It was as if the devil himself had decided to make New Alamo part of his domain. Now and forever.

Spider wept openly. Flores kept shaking his head as if unable to accept it.

"We have to go," said Morton, but his voice lacked emphasis, as if even he, monster that he was, mourned the loss of this place.

It took so much for Gutsy to turn away. Somewhere out in the vast fields around the dying town was the army of the Raggedy Man. The fire and explosions might have distracted him and drawn every eye, living and dead, but soon the hunt would begin again in earnest.

"Yes, we have to go," she said. "We don't belong here anymore."

As she turned away, she caught Benny's eye. "Fifteen," she said.

"Sixteen," he replied. It was a conversation that made perfect sense to them, in a world that made no sense at all.

BROTHER MERCY STOOD BY THE OPEN EAST GATE. Bloody, flash-burned, furious, and brokenhearted.

Once the hated Imura and his friends were gone, he'd returned to the crane to find Sister Sorrow. He released the other reapers to hunt for any sinners still hiding in town, and for the wild men. There were dreadful fights in the street, with the reapers protecting the gray people and the ravagers and sending any of their own holy infected into the darkness lest this strange new disease spread.

They killed hundreds of the wild men.

But neither they nor Mercy found Sister Sorrow. There was only blood on the ground in the place where she'd landed after that long fall. Red-smeared footprints led away from the spot.

"Leafy," he murmured into the empty night, "I'm sorry. I tried to keep you safe . . ."

The part of him that was still the Hated—the battered child on the pilgrim's road—was still clutching that broken clamshell, still fighting for the girl with autumn leaves in her tangled hair.

But Leafy was gone.

Sister Sorrow was gone.

Just as Mother Night and Brother Peter and Saint John were all gone. Killed by Imura and his unclean kind. They had polluted his life, darkened his skies, and burned down the Night Church.

He had never felt more alone in his entire life.

A few houses were burning, but most of the town still stood. It defied him and defied god, as if saying that it had endured everything since the End and would outlive this, too.

"No," murmured Brother Mercy.

He walked across the street, stepping over corpses, feeling the last of his love and hope die within him. A general store was filling the street with its burning light, but the fire was not spreading. Even as he approached, the roof collapsed, and the force of it extinguished all but some peripheral fires.

"No," repeated the reaper.

He bent and picked up a stick that lay partly ablaze. He saw that it was an old hockey stick. The plastic blade had mostly melted, and small fingers of fire danced along the wood handle. Brother Mercy tore off his shirt and wound it quickly around the burning end. He stuck it back into the fire until the shirt was burning. Then he raised it and turned, walking from house to house to house, entering open doors, touching his torch to chairs and beds and curtains. Setting it all alight. Creating out of New Alamo a funeral pyre for Sister Sorrow.

For Leafy.

For love.

THREE MILES AWAY, ALONG THE ROAD TO SITE B, Alethea was trying to keep the fleeing people of New Alamo alive.

"Run!" she screamed, shoving the refugees forward.

Pale-faced figures seemed to materialize out of the shadows, reaching with dead hands, biting the air with dead mouths, filling the night with moans of endless hunger. People cried out and ran in all directions, avoiding one set of clutching hands only to run into another.

Alethea swung her baseball bat at every pale face she saw, but so many people needed her all at once.

You can't save them all.

The words flashed through her head and broke her heart with their truth.

Then she was moving. Rainbow Smite rose and fell, shattering wrists and knees and necks. The dead fell. People fell too, crying out in agony as gray teeth bit into their flesh.

As Alethea fought, some of the panicked people shook off their despair and rallied. A few. Not all. They used whatever weapons they carried. Some did not have weapons and used fists or rocks they picked up.

She saw Amos Gunderson, the town farrier, fall, his throat spurting blood.

She saw Isabella Sweetwater use a golf club to batter two teenage zombies away from a stroller that was filled with babies orphaned during the two previous attacks. Isabella had to be at least eighty, but she swung the club like a brutal warrior, grunting and snarling.

She saw Mr. Ford—who Alethea had not even realized was with her group—kneeling on the ground, one hand clutched around a wrist that was bleeding heavily. Their eyes met, and she saw a deep hopelessness there, a realization that the old Chess Player knew this was his end. Despite all of that, he managed a smile as he struggled back to his feet. He tore off his scarf, wrapped it around his wrist, picked up the antique sword he'd brought, and went back to the fight.

Alethea's bat seemed to move without conscious thought, and Alethea felt herself shifting inside, in her head, even in her muscle memory. There had been so many fights since the first ravager attack that battle seemed to define her. She was *of* this, not just *in* it.

She fought and killed. Fought and killed.

The shamblers crumpled beneath her onslaught, and even as she bashed and smashed, Alethea seemed to view herself from a distance. Where was the sassy queen of snark who loved nothing more than to sprawl on the summer grass with Spider and Gutsy? Where was the princess of New Alamo who made everyone, even adults, jump? Where was the girl who loved life? Who was this person? Grief for who she had been and would never be again stabbed at her.

And yet she fought on.

Then, suddenly, there was a shrieking agony in her leg, and Alethea was falling. A shambler, its legs broken, had crawled up behind her and clamped teeth on her calf. Terror was a huge black wave that wanted to smash down on her as she used the butt of the baseball bat to hammer at the dead face. Bones and teeth broke, and it fell away; then she got to one knee and chopped down, ending the thing.

Her fingers shook with the palsy of dread as she patted her leg. Her jeans felt damp, but when she held her fingers up to the starlight there was no blood on them. She was not infected.

Could she believe that? Could it even be true, with all of the other things that were falling apart? Was this the setup for another of the world's cruel jokes?

She got to her feet and limped back into the fight.

Mr. Ford was still on his feet, and Alethea saw Mr. Urrea battling his way to his friend's side. The two old writers grinned at each other like a couple of kids, as if this being the end was a joke that only they understood. These were not happy smiles, though. They were jack-o'-lantern grins, and it frightened Alethea. They shifted around, standing back to back, and their antique blades whistled and thudded.

Alethea moved around the edges of the fight, trying to stop the shamblers before more of them attacked. And then, just like that, the fight was over.

She whirled, looking for another enemy, but there was none left to fight, Not where her group stood weeping and bleeding and fighting for breath. Far off to the east and west and south there were sounds of fighting. And when she looked toward New Alamo, all she could see was a pillar of fire. Nothing close, though.

"Are we . . . safe?"

It was Mrs. Sweetwater who spoke. She leaned on her golf club, hunched over and clearly in pain.

Alethea almost laughed. She almost said no. Instead she raised a trembling hand and adjusted her tiara.

"We're alive," she said.

Then a massive explosion from town turned night into day for several seconds. Alethea saw that her group was on a slight incline—not high but enough to let her see a wide swath of the flat lands around the dying town. She could see for miles, and what she saw nearly tore the heart out of her. All she could see was war. Death and pain and loss and suffering. There was nothing else *to* see.

Ford and Urrea came and stood with Alethea, leaning on each other. They both looked as pale as the walking dead. Alethea could see how frail they were; something she'd known before but never really accepted.

"Oh my God," said Urrea faintly. He was not commenting on the general carnage but was instead looking toward the southwest. Toward where the main army of the dead was still smashing up against the town. Between that and the spot where they stood was a mass of hurrying figures. Ravagers and . . .

Reapers. All of them with knives and scythes and other deadly blades.

"They're coming for us," said Ford. "They're coming this way."

The light from the explosion faded and darkness fell again, once more hiding the oncoming band of killers. They were less than a mile away. They would here in minutes.

Alethea looked around at her people, old and young. A few fighters left among the adults. Not enough for this, though. Not nearly enough. There was no chance at all.

Urrea placed his hand on her shoulder. "Get everyone out of here. You know the way to Site B, princess. Go."

"What?"

He raised his weapon and laid it over his shoulder. "We'll lead them another way. Ford and I will buy you some time."

"As much time as we can," Ford agreed. They were still smiling, but the smiles were like pictures hung crookedly.

"That's crazy," Alethea fired back. "We *all* need to—"

Ford held out his wrist and pulled back the scarf. The bite was deep, and there were already black lines of infection running jaggedly from the wound.

"Last chapter for me," the old writer said, trying to make a joke of it.

"No," pleaded Alethea, "we can find Mr. Flores or Doc Morton and get you—"

"There's no time," said Ford. "I can already feel something happening in here." He touched his heart, and then his head. "And here."

"Crazy old goat," Urrea muttered.

Alethea grabbed Urrea's arm. "Make him come with us."

But he took her hand and gently—firmly—pulled it away. He tugged at the collar of his shirt and leaned down to show his shoulder. She saw the bite, and her knees wanted to buckle. Tears filled her eyes, broke, and fell as a sob was punched out of her.

"No, no, no, no, no . . . *NO!*" Her bat fell into the dirt, and she buried her face in her filthy hands.

Urrea knelt beside her and took her in his arms. Ford placed his hand on her back.

"All stories end, Alethea," Urrea said gently. "Even for old fools like us."

"You have to go," said Ford.

The two old men took Alethea's arms and raised her to her feet. Ford handed her the bat. The world was breaking around her, and death was coming. She did not want to run anymore. Did not want to fight.

"We love you, princess," he said. "You and your friends. But you need to leave."

Urrea stroked Alethea's cheek and kissed her forehead. "Let us do this for you. Let all we've been through *mean* something."

She looked at him. At Ford. And saw their resolve. Their acceptance.

She kissed and hugged them both, and then she staggered back. Caught her balance. Tears blurred the world, but she found the best path.

She and the survivors ran away.

The first time Alethea looked back, she saw the Chess Players watching her.

The next time she looked back, the old writers were hurrying away to the northwest. They were making noise, clanging their weapons. Being heard by the killers who chased them. Leading death in the wrong direction.

The last time she looked back, Ford and Urrea were out of sight.

She and her people ran. Quickly and quietly. Into the night. She never saw them again.

THEY PUSHED THE CART FOR MILES IN THE DARK-
ness, lit by moonlight and guided by stars. Gutsy led the
way, because she knew the Broken Lands better than any
of them. Sombra was with her, sniffing the ground, darting
out into the shadows to investigate noises and returning
quickly. Grimm stayed with Benny, guarding him and the
Dòmi.

There was a cluster of small buildings on a high hill, above
which rose the rusted skeleton of an old cell phone tower.

"Wait here," said Gutsy. "Rest while I go up and take a
look."

Chong and Benny collapsed on the ground beside the
cart, which they had muscled over the rough terrain. They
didn't dare use the main road, because it was evident from
thousands of scuffed footprints that it was how a big part of
the Raggedy Man's army had come to New Alamo. It was too
big a risk if they used that route, in case more were coming,
or the clever reapers might follow to try and chase down
refugees.

Gutsy stood at the base of the tower and took a deep

breath. The adrenaline rush was fading and she had never in her life felt this exhausted, but resting was not a possibility. Not now, and probably not for hours. Site B was still many miles away, and they had to move fast. So, she took another breath, set her jaw, and climbed.

The tower was very tall and the wind was whipping out of the west, making the structure creak threateningly, and the whole thing swayed like a willow. She had to force herself to continue to climb, praying to Mama, the Virgin Mary, and every saint whose name she could remember not to let the tower fall.

There were a lot of different kinds of dishes up there, which she knew from people in town were for different kinds of service for handheld phones—similar, she assumed, to the satellite phone Nix and Lilah had. Most were weather-battered and covered in bird droppings. A few had become nests for insects.

She had to climb above the cluster of dishes to see, and was immediately sorry she did. It wasn't just that the elevation offered a more comprehensive view of the utter destruction of her home. No. What jolted her, what nearly knocked her from that precarious perch, was what she saw moving through the darkness.

From that bird's-eye view, she saw two masses of figures on the march. Far to the west, coming from the direction of the destroyed base, were more of the wild men, hidden by the ancient ruins of small towns. Not as many as before—Gutsy wondered how many had been destroyed in the fires—but enough. Sixty or seventy of them. Running erratically toward the northeast, loping sometimes on two legs and occasionally on hands and feet, like misshapen dogs. It was an ugly sight. Terrifying.

But much worse was what she saw to the east. She thought she'd understood how massive the Raggedy Man's army was when viewed from the crane platform. But she was wrong. Very, very wrong. She'd half-joking referred to it as an army of a million, but now she was sure that's what she was seeing. There were so many of them that it was as if the entire surface of the desert moved. Too many of the walking dead to count. They moved like a tide, a mass at least two miles wide and many miles long, shambling with inexorable slowness in the same direction the refugees had gone.

Here and there she saw ravagers and reapers—and she could identify them by the way the moonlight glittered on their weapons. She figured the teen Benny had fought was down there. He didn't seem the type to have been caught helpless when the town burned.

Gutsy forced herself to look toward the northeast. Off in the distance, spread out in the night, she saw dozens of small refugee groups picking their way through lands most had not walked since the dead rose. Her heart sank, because none of them were very far ahead of her own group. They should have been. They should all be halfway there by now, but they were not. Fatigue, fear, confusion, and perhaps infighting had slowed them. The night fought them by making each footfall treacherous and uncertain. The people of New Alamo were struggling against their own survival.

The night breeze brought both distant howling and the soft pleading of hungry moans. They were all following the refugees. All of them heading on what was clearly a collision course to Site B. Or, worse, to a point before anyone could reach the hidden place. If the doors were still locked, then the land in front of that last bastion of hope would be a killing ground. Gutsy and everyone she knew would die there.

And no one would ever know.

A SUDDEN GUST OF WIND NEARLY FLUNG GUTSY from the tower and she clung to it, crying out in sudden fear as it leaned so far over she thought it would fall. From below she heard Spider and Benny cry out too.

"I'm okay," she called, though that was in no way certain.

Mama, please . . . , she begged. *Help me.*

The wind did not stop blowing, and in fact, seemed to intensify. It picked up dust from the desert floor and whipped it at her, stinging her skin, half blinding her.

Help me, Mama . . . please!

For just a crazy and impossible moment she thought she smelled something on that wind. A familiar scent of flowers and spices, like Mama's kitchen when she was cooking. It was the second time since Mama died that Gutsy had smelled it. It made her think of her mother's spirit, released from its troubled envelope of infected flesh, going home. As if her cries for Mama's help were being somehow answered.

But if there was a message from beyond the grave, its meaning was lost on her. And that was maddening, because she could use any help she could get. Even a hint.

The wind blew past her, though, taking those beloved

smells away in the direction of the Raggedy Man's vast army. The tower creaked, but it did not fall.

Gutsy climbed down and rejoined the others. Her legs trembled, and she was happy to be back on solid ground. She quickly explained what was coming.

"We have to get everyone to go faster," she said. "A lot faster."

They set out at their top speed and soon overtook the rearmost of the refugee parties, urging them to hurry. The fitter young men and women from that group were sent as runners to find other groups and pass the word. Soon the whole mass of them were moving at a near run. When someone lagged behind, pairs of survivors flanked them and half carried them. Wheelbarrows and carts with goods were dumped out so older people and little children could ride instead.

It was not orderly, and it was not nearly as fast as Gutsy knew they needed to go.

Behind them the howls of the wild men could be heard, rising in intensity, becoming even more savage as the creatures caught the scent of their prey. What Gutsy didn't know was if that meant they could smell the fleeing townsfolk or if they'd discovered the massive army.

"Keep going!" she cried.

She and Benny formed the rear guard of the group, with Grimm and Sombra flanking them. As they ran, they had a conversation without words. It was a look of truth. It said, *We're not going to make it.*

It was not a statement of insecurity or resignation. Just an honest appraisal of the situation. There were miles to go to reach Site B. Even if the doors stood open and waiting for them, they both knew there was simply not enough time to get there.

Gutsy set her jaw. If she was going to die, then she'd die. Maybe she and Sombra could hold the monsters off long enough to allow *some* of the people to survive. Maybe they'd at least get Morton and the Dòmi to Site B, which would allow for the possibility of a counterattack. A slim chance of survival for what was left of the human race.

If she could do that, then dying may not be so bad.

And Gutsy was sure that was what she'd read in Benny's eyes as well. She did not want or need to be a hero, but if she died, then Gutsy wanted her life to matter.

BROTHER MERCY STOOD ON THE EDGE OF THE RAGGEDY
Man's mobile flatbed. The king of the dead was leaning forward, head craned as he looked around, rotted hands clutching the arms of the throne.

"Did you kill them all?" he demanded.

Brother Mercy pointed. "No, lord. Look there."

They stared in mutual horror as sixty or more of the wild
men came howling across the field toward the front rank of
the seething mass of shamblers. The young reaper put a silver
whistle to his lips and blew a high, shrill note, which caused
scores of reapers and ravagers in the army to turn and look.

"There!" he cried. "My reapers, my brothers and sisters—
kill them. Kill them all."

The ravagers immediately turned and began shoving
the shamblers back, beating them with clubs—not to injure
but to direct. As they did that, the reapers swept forward.
Engines roared, and a dozen quads came whipping around
from behind. The rest ran, knives, axes, and bows in hand.
The leading archers fired, and arrows shot through the night,
the deadly points catching silver sparks of cold moonlight.

The whole front rank of wild men went down.

But the rest, undaunted, came howling on.

Gutsy and Benny paused at the crest of a hill, the first of a series that rose into the distance. Each had their binoculars out and watched the battle begin.

"They have quads!" Gutsy cried.

"I know. That's how we got them," Benny said. "We stole four from the reapers in Nevada. It's how we beat Saint John's army to California in time to mount our defense."

Seeing the machines—even after having been up close to them—still managed to send a thrill of unreality through Gutsy. It was as if the past had somehow broken through a wall into her present. In the last couple of weeks, the entire fabric of reality had been fractured.

Benny gave a harsh, sour laugh. "I don't know who to root for here," he said.

Then the night was split apart by a new sound. Flashes of light and harsh pops filled the air, and for a moment Gutsy had the irrational notion that someone had borrowed her idea for using fireworks. But within seconds she realized that this wasn't the case, as there was a sound of heavy engines buried beneath the pops.

Then she saw them: two Stryker Dragoons came bumping over the desert floor, the big Bushmaster machine guns firing toward the masses of reapers.

There was no sign of the other vehicles.

She looked over her shoulder and saw that the refugees had moved a considerable way along the path in the direction of Site B. They were no longer climbing over the landscape but had gone to the road and were using that. What had been a poor choice earlier was now the only choice. The enemy already knew where they were, so staying off the road didn't matter except its flatness allowed the refugees to move much more quickly along the path of least resistance.

The big guns kept firing, and Gutsy looked back again. Would they be able to slow the armies down? How far was it to Site B? Three miles? Four?

Sunny-Day Ray fired and fired while Sergeant Holly drove. The Stryker's big diesel engine growled like a dragon as she plowed forward, using all-wheel drive to conquer the terrain. The dense hardness of the steel body was a battering ram, smashing through shambler, ravager, reaper, and wild man alike, but the impacts still sent horrific shock waves through the interior. Below the Bushmaster was a nest of anti-tank rocket pods, and Ray shot these into the masses of killers, blasting them apart. Each detonation created a massive fireball that hurled burning bodies high into the air, but as devastating as they were, they were not enough. Nor could the Bushmaster fire enough rounds.

As the Strykers plowed through the crowds, the last of the rockets fired. The heavy wind whisked away the clouds of smoke. Fires burned here and there on patches of dry grass, and in places it was beginning to spread.

A minute later the machine guns themselves fell silent.

Trailing smoke from empty barrels, the war machines kept lumbering forward. But powerful as they were, the sheer mass of the enemy was too great. The vehicles slowed . . . and slowed . . .

And then they stopped, unable to push farther through the thousands of tons of tissue and bone. Not even hardened steel and heavy tires could manage it. The shamblers and ravagers pounded on the doors and tiny windows. Gutsy heard a few desperate pistol shots.

After that, nothing.

The two teens stood on the hill, able to see a large swath of the field in the moonlight. Everything was black and white—even the blood.

"The reapers are taking out all the wild men," said Benny. "I guess that's good for us."

"Is it?"

"Sure," he said. "They're a lot faster than the zoms."

Gutsy raised her machete and pointed. "No, wait. There are more wild men over there."

They both studied a new spot of violent movement off to the southwest. A knot of shamblers were attacking others of their kind. Gutsy could not see how that started, but she could see it spread. First a handful of wild men were biting *los muertos*, then ten. Reapers came running, summoned by Brother Mercy's whistle and shouts from ravagers, but by the time they got there, a dozen shamblers had been transformed.

Then it was two dozen.

It was like watching a stone dropped into water. Ripples of infection radiated out from where those first wild men had attacked. This is what the Raggedy Man and Brother Mercy had tried to stop. It was what they feared. It was so strange a concept that creatures such as they could fear anything. And yet there was panic in the shrill bleats of the whistle. Panic in the waving arms of the king of the dead. Ravagers with guns turned their weapons on the infected, cutting them down. Others waded in with axes and clubs, aiming to cripple and kill what had been their own shock troops.

One by one these defenders of the army of the dead were attacked, overwhelmed, dragged down. The ravagers rose again as wild men. Gutsy could not see what happened to the reapers. It was all becoming so frenzied. The Wodewose was spreading faster than any wildfire. It was unstoppable now, and they knew it. The Raggedy Man was howling in rage, but now there was a note of fear in his voice. The area of infection was a hundred yards from where he stood, but the wave was coming.

The end was coming. His vast and unbreakable, unconquerable army of the dead was about to be swept into the dustpan of history, replaced with millions of screaming infected. Mad beyond control, each of their bodies a battleground more fierce than the one on which they stood.

Brother Mercy was calling his reapers back, no longer trying to fight the infection but to provide a wall of fighters between the wild men and Homer Gibbon. Ravagers kept up a continuous barrage of small-arms fire, and the wind stoked the burning grass.

"We need to get out of here," gasped Benny, backpedaling. "Right now."

Grimm howled and then took off after Benny, who began running.

Gutsy, however, lingered. She was not really watching the spread of infection. Something else had drawn her eye. It was the smoke from the burning grass. It blew across the fields, at times obscuring the flatbed. The breeze whipped it through the struggling monsters.

Once more she thought she smelled the scents of Mama's kitchen. Just for a moment, there and gone.

Then she, too, turned and followed Benny.

THEY RAN AND RAN. BOTH OF THEM LOOKING BACK to see if they'd run far enough. But each time the killers were closer. The wild men on one flank, the mixed army of reapers and zombies on the other, and, directly behind, the melee where monsters were fighting one another.

Then once, when Gutsy and Benny looked back at the same time, they saw that all their fighting and planning and struggles to survive were for nothing. The mass of conflict had moved so much closer and within it, they could see him.

The Raggedy Man on his throne, pulled by all the dead.

As if he could somehow sense the eyes on him, the king of the dead turned slowly and looked out over the sea of bloodshed, straight at them.

Gutsy and Benny stood on the hill, panting, drained of hope. The others came and joined them. The two dogs sat near their masters, heads lowered, tongues lolling. Sombra whimpered softly. The hill was bare, dusty dirt, and, painted in bright moonlight, they were as visible as black flies on a whitewashed wall. The Raggedy Man slowly raised one arm, extended a crooked finger toward Gutsy, and grinned like the monster he was. Whatever strange connection he had with his army was in full force. Many thousands of them turned away from the commotion, abruptly disregarding the threat of the wild men, and immediately began moving forward. A fierce, dry wind whipped sand at the oncoming tide of death, but the zombies did not pause, did not even blink.

That same wind blew past Gutsy, rifling her clothes, whipping her hair, making the canvas sides of the laundry cart snap and pop. Chong sat down heavily, head sunk between his shoulders. Gutsy looked at him, watching how the freshening breeze stirred his black hair. It was blowing steadily out of the north. She remembered thinking only a few moments ago that it was as if the wind itself had betrayed them and was trying to slow their escape.

And yet . . .

Impossibly, unexpectedly, Gutsy caught a smell on the wind. Just for a second. It was not of pinyon pines or creosote bushes, nor the stink of blood and fire. This breeze smelled of flowers and spices. It smelled like Mama's kitchen. There was nothing in that blighted place to account for those smells. Nothing. But Gutsy knew what it was and where it came from. The stiff wind carried it not as a weapon of betrayal, no. It was a gift from someone very far away.

"We need to run," Morton wheezed, his voice sanded raw by the horrors of the night. Gutsy looked at him—at each of them in turn—and then closed her eyes and turned once more into the wind.

"Mama," she said. "Oh, Mama, *muchas gracias* . . ."

And she smiled.

"She's lost it," complained Morton. "Her mind's snapped.

Come on, boys, we need to go right now. Those monsters will be here in five minutes or—"

"*The wind*," Gutsy said, cutting him off.

"Wind?" sputtered Benny, frightened and impatient. "Who *cares*, Guts? We have to . . ."

Benny's words died as if the wind had snatched them away. He stared at her, past her to the fires that were already being fanned by the wind. He stared at the struggling wild men, ravagers, reapers, and shamblers. His lips formed words without sound.

A single word. Repeated over and over.

Gutsy nodded and spoke it aloud.

"Dòmi."

They stared at each other, and now he, too, smiled. The kind of smile only the truly desperate would smile. It matched her own.

"I know that look," said Chong, looking accusingly at Benny. "You two just had a really, really, really bad idea."

"Really bad," agreed Spider, recognizing the smile Gutsy wore.

100

"WE NEED TO GET OUT OF HERE," MORTON YELLED, his voice thin and high with terror.

"We need a better vantage point," murmured Gutsy. Benny tapped her and pointed to a big old billboard a hundred feet up the road. It had the faded face of a smiling man holding up a piece of fried chicken, promising that it was going to be *dee-eee-licious*. The two of them went over and circled it.

"There's a ladder over here," she observed, pointing to a set of rusted metal rungs nearly hidden in shadows.

"Perfect," said Benny.

"Perfect for what?" Flores demanded. "You think we can hide from them up there? They already saw us."

Benny pulled Chong to his feet. "Listen, man, you need to get out of here. You and Spider; get Morton and Mr. Flores out of here. Get the research stuff to Site B."

"We can't get the stabilizer out of here in time," protested Flores. "The cart's too heavy."

"Yeah, but if we leave it and just run," said Spider, "then we lose our only shot."

They all flinched as a few bullets, fired by ravagers far down the slope, struck the billboard. They were wild shots, but it proved the closest of them were already in range. Time was boiling away.

All around them the wind howled louder than the wild men, roaring like a gale. It was as if the night itself had become so furious that it wanted to shriek as the drama entered its final, bloody act.

Dr. Morton tried to pull on the cart. "What are you idiots doing? We have to—"

"Shut up and listen," Gutsy snapped as she hurried to the cart and grabbed a heavy bag of the stabilizer. "The Dòmi is already mixed in, right?"

"You know it is. So what?"

She reached down, tore a handful of grass out of the ground, and threw it at the doctor. He put a hand up to block it, but before he did, the wind whipped it away. Morton blinked at her, still confused.

"You said we needed a delivery system, right?"

Morton stared for a moment, and then his eyes went wide. "My God . . ."

Flores got it too, but he frowned. "It won't work yet. Not against *los muertos*."

"I know," said Gutsy. "We need to let the wild men win."

They all looked at the billboard.

"Up there," said Benny.

"What if the wild men don't reach you first?" asked Spider.

"Shamblers don't climb," said Gutsy, "and the reapers don't have guns. They'd have to climb the ladder one at a time, and we'll have the advantage."

Chong shook his head. "Not against the ravagers," he said

sharply. "They'll pick you off from the ground."

As if to emphasize his point, another bullet struck the billboard ten feet above their heads.

"We're out of other options," Gutsy said determinedly. "You're plan B. Now go, before we lose even this chance."

Chong and Spider looked horrified. Flores was dubious and frightened. Only Morton was anxious to go.

"Let them try it," he said quickly. "It might work."

Flores gave him a look of utter contempt, but then he turned and shoved the cart toward the slope down to the paved road. Morton hurried after, limping and weak. Spider gave Gutsy a fierce hug and then turned, wiping tears from his eyes. He ran to catch up and threw his weight against the cumbersome cart, too. Gutsy ordered Sombra to go with Spider, and Benny told Grimm to protect Chong. Both dogs looked at each other and then ran to stand with Gutsy and Benny.

"Wait," Gutsy said and ran over to the cart. She reached in, took two heavy bags, and tossed them to Benny before taking two more for herself. "Let's go have some fun."

Benny grinned. "You're even crazier than I am."

101

"I'LL TAKE AS MUCH AS I CAN CARRY TO THE TOP OF that billboard," Gutsy said quickly. "When the wild men get close, I'll throw the Dòmi up into the wind."

"You mean *we'll* throw it," Benny corrected.

She gave him a hard, steady look. "You do know what's probably going to happen, even if I succeed, Benny. You should go help the others. You can keep them safe. You're a better fighter."

"And you're smarter and maybe weirder," he said, walking toward the ladder. "You want to go up first, or me?"

The monsters were coming. Wild howls filled the night to one side of the road, and ungodly moans tore the air everywhere else. The flatbed with the Raggedy Man was less than three hundred yards away.

There was no time left for debate. Gutsy took a firm grip on the bags of Dòmi-infused dried manure and began climbing. It wasn't easy; she had to hold the bags with one hand and climb with the other. The rungs were old and rusted, and they creaked under her feet. Benny was right behind her, and she could hear him grunting with effort.

Up and up they went. Gutsy thought about Spider and

Alethea, about the Chess Players and Karen, and about Alice. She would never see any of them again; of that she was certain. This was a true suicide mission.

But if it worked . . .

Up and up. A stray shot burned through the air, sounding like a furious bee, five inches from her face.

Just climb, she ordered herself. *No matter what happens, just climb.*

The wind was getting worse and worse, as if it was turning into some kind of summer hurricane. Pieces of debris whipped past. The breeze was so weirdly strong it nearly plucked her from the ladder. She dropped one of the bags, and it clipped Benny's shoulder, almost knocking him down.

"Sorry!"

"Climb," he bellowed back.

A roar made them both whip around to see a group of reapers—at least a dozen of them—zooming at them on quads, blades out. Gutsy hurried and reached the top rung.

"Gutsy," Benny yelled, "take this."

Gutsy turned and saw him holding up one of his bags. She leaned down and took the bag, hoisting it and her remaining bag onto a narrow catwalk at the top of the ladder. Then she took Benny's other bag and gasped as he immediately began climbing back down.

"What are you doing?"

"Stick to the plan," he yelled. "You're not the only one with really bad ideas."

Benny let go and jumped the last few yards, landed in a crouch, pitched forward, and rolled back to his feet to slough off the force of the impact. As he straightened, he whipped his sword free and took a stance at the base of the ladder while reapers on quads raced toward him.

The wind suddenly howled louder than ever, sounding almost like a teakettle.

And then the entire group of reapers, quads and all, exploded.

It happened at once. Something seemed to streak through the whistling wind and strike the second quad in the pack, and then a massive fireball snatched them all off the ground and hurled them into the night. The sound of it was titanic, and a shock wave punched into Benny and Gutsy and knocked them flat.

They lay there, dazed, completely stunned by what had just happened. Gutsy's logical mind was already trying to make sense of it, conjuring a dozen different possible explanations, but all of them were wrong.

A second shriek split the air, and something smoky and gray blew past them and slammed into the front rank of ravagers just as the killers opened up a fresh barrage of automatic gunfire. The explosion seemed even bigger and louder than the first.

The shock wave loosened Gutsy's grip on the catwalk and she began to fall, but her hands darted out just in time to grab the uprights of the ladder. Her momentum was plummeting, though, and she slid down toward the ground at an insane speed. She braced the inside arches of her shoes against the pole and they acted like brakes, so hitting the ground was merely painful instead of crippling. Gutsy flopped over onto one side and looked at the trails of gray smoke lingering in the sky being pulled apart by the wind. She had no idea what was happening. The world refused to make sense. But then she followed the smoke trails back to their source. What she saw froze the whole night into something impossible.

She saw two figures standing on the crest of the next hill. Two men, each with a shoulder-mounted rocket launcher in their hands.

Two bruised, battered, and bloody old soldiers.

THE RAGGEDY MAN RULED THE NIGHT. THAT'S HOW
he saw it, even though things were not going according to his
well-laid plans.

To one side of his flatbed, the wild men were destroying a
huge chunk of his army. In front of him, someone was using
rocket-propelled grenades to kill his ravagers and reapers.
Somehow the people of this bloody town had outfoxed him,
made a fool of him. Lured him into a trap.

He snarled and spat into the teeth of the wind.

"You may be smarter," he said very softly, "but I'm stronger. You watch."

He raised his hands, and the entire mass of the army,
nearly eight hundred thousand of the living dead, surged
forward. The reapers and ravagers still held the line
between him and the wild men. The Raggedy Man was wise.
He understood something of this new threat from things
he'd learned and overheard while a prisoner of the research
base. He knew about Wodewose, and seeing it here, as a
terrible reality, sweeping through his beloved dead, was
horrifying.

Would it do the same to him? If all it did was to wake

up the brain of the undead, how would it work on someone whose brain was already fully alive?

Part of him wanted to jump down from the flatbed and wade into the sea of wild men, to prove to himself and to everyone that he was invulnerable. He was the king of the dead. He could no longer be killed. Not by anything.

Another part of him wanted to flee. Let Wodewose take the million he had here. What was that to him? He had seven billion more dead he could call. Everyone who had died since the plague began, every man, woman, and child on the face of the earth who'd fallen to the Reaper Plague, belonged to him. He would find some way to make them better fighters. See if he could wake up enough of their minds to let them handle guns. Or . . .

"Reapers!" he bellowed, and when some of the children of Thanatos ran to him, Homer Gibbon pointed to the wild men. "Burn them. Burn them all. Set fire to the gray people and shove them into those maniacs. Set fire to the grass. Burn every one of them."

The reapers ran to obey, and within moments fires began igniting all along the lines of battle. The wild men, driven by a madness more powerful than any fear of harm or death, ran at the reapers and the burning zombies, and they, too, burned.

Then the Raggedy Man turned back to the small knot of survivors by the billboard. He watched a squad of reapers zoom toward them on quads.

And then he saw the burst of flame from another hill, and the streak of gray, and the massive explosion that picked up the quads and hurled them in all directions, most of them with reapers still gripping the handlebars with burning hands.

There was a second explosion, and Homer stood at the edge of the flatbed and stared through the night. Two teenagers at the foot of the billboard, and two older men with RPGs. They looked like soldiers, and their hands moved with practiced ease as they fitted new rockets into their weapons.

"Kill them!" roared the king of the dead. "Tear them apart and bring me their hearts!" The mass of zombies and ravagers surged forward, some of them stumbling, others beginning to run because he willed it. Focused now, because he drove them. The greatest assault force in the history of Planet Earth, toward the figures on the hill. Let them fire their little RPGs. Go ahead. There weren't enough bullets or bombs in the world to stop the Night Army.

"Kill them all," he whispered. "Leave nothing. No trace they ever lived. Do it!"

103

THE MEN WERE BLOODY, SOILED, WEARING TATTERED clothes.

"*Joe* . . . ," breathed Gutsy, totally stunned.

"Sam!" yelled Benny. Grimm howled in delight and ran like a puppy toward his master. Sombra ran, too, sniffing and prancing and barking. Gutsy and Benny followed, hugging the big men, staring at them in frank amazement.

"How? I mean . . . *how*?" demanded Benny, unable to frame a better question.

"We found Site B," Sam said simply.

"But . . . but . . . what about Captain Collins?" asked Gutsy. "Wasn't she there?"

"Sure," said Ledger, "she was there."

Gutsy looked from him to Sam and back again. "Didn't she try to stop you?"

Ledger touched a bloody bandage wrapped around his chest. "She *tried*," he said in the coldest voice Gutsy had ever heard.

And that's all he said. It was enough.

Gutsy and Benny exchanged a look.

"Jeez," Benny said.

"We've got bigger fish to fry," said Sam. "The dead are coming."

They looked down the hill. The first waves the Raggedy Man sent had been destroyed, but there were still countless more behind.

"What the heck are you two numbskulls doing here?" asked Ledger. "I saw Chong and Spider and the eggheads hot-footing it down the road with a laundry cart. Why are you two not with them?"

Gutsy explained her plan very quickly. Sam looked doubtful, but Ledger began smiling.

"Jeez, guys," he said, "you two don't lack ambition."

"But we won't have time," said Benny.

Despite the heavy wind, they could hear a voice, and when they looked in that direction, they could see the Raggedy Man himself striding toward them, not a hundred yards distant. Reapers and ravagers flanked him, and hell followed him.

"How many of those rockets do you have left?" asked Benny.

Ledger shook his head. "Not enough for all of that."

And yet he did not look worried. Not nearly as much as he should be.

Ledger looked up at the billboard and then at the approaching wall of death. "I like your plan," he said.

"Really?" asked Gutsy.

"No. But it's what we have."

"Even though it involves us dying before we can make it work?"

"Remains to be seen, kiddo," said Ledger. "Let's see what Sam and I can do to slow these bad boys down a tad."

"'A tad'?" Gutsy echoed. "By the time the wild men infect enough of the army, we'll be long dead."

"Maybe," said Ledger. "And maybe not. Look—half the wild men are burning, and five times as many zoms. It's cool. . . . Sam and I have been in worse situations."

"No, we haven't," said Sam.

"Work with me here, man," said Ledger. His jokey manner was completely at odds with the reality of the moment.

"Joe—" Gutsy began, but he pointed to the billboard.

"You two get back up there. Do it now."

"But—"

"No time to argue. Go."

Benny took Gutsy by the elbow and pulled her away. They went to the other side of the billboard, and then every part of the plan fell apart.

A figure came racing out of the shadows, a glittering knife in each fist. It was the reaper, Brother Mercy, screaming a single word that didn't make sense to either of them.

"Leafy! Leafy!"

The first cut caught Benny completely off guard and he staggered back, blood erupting from a deep slash across his shoulder. He fell, his sword dropping to the grass as Brother Mercy jumped over him and slashed at Gutsy.

Then the Raggedy Man's ravagers opened fire on Ledger and Sam.

LEDGER DOVE ONE WAY AND SAM THE OTHER, EACH
of them grabbing one of the dogs and pulling them down as
bullets filled the air like a swarm of hornets.

Grimm, trained for combat, stayed low, flattening out in
the tall grass, but Sombra panicked and tried to get up. Sam
yelled at him to obey, but the coydog tore free and ran.

Ledger rolled down behind the crest of the hill, drew his
sidearm, and began firing into the oncoming mob. There were
at least twenty armed ravagers, though not all of them had
guns. Ledger fired from forty feet away, one hand steadying
the other wrist as he took fast, careful aim. With every shot
one ravager went down, but not every shot was fatal. Some of
those who fell struggled to get back up again.

Sam rolled down the hill, then got up and ran in a fast
zigzag pattern to the hilltop behind, where he and Ledger had
left their gear bags. The fight was too close for the grenade
launchers, so he tore the bag open and pulled out an M4, pivoted, dove, rolled, and came up with the stock of the weapon
tucked into his shoulder. He opened up on the ravagers, careful of his friend and the armored mastiff.

* * *

Gutsy backpedaled fast and felt the whoosh as the reaper's blade sliced the air an inch from her face. Then Sombra was there, leaping at the killer, mouth opened to bite.

But the reaper checked his swing and stabbed at the dog. The thrust missed the coydog's throat, but the wicked edge slashed a deep red line along Sombra's breastbone. The animal yelped in pain and fell hard on the ground, right on top of Benny.

That gave Gutsy a fraction of a second to whip her machete out of its scabbard just in time to parry Brother Mercy's next vicious cut. Steel met steel with a sound like a ringing bell, and a shock shivered all the way up her arm. The reaper's blow was so powerful that it nearly tore the machete from her hand.

Behind him other figures moved. Ravagers with scythes were hustling up the hill, grinning as they saw Benny struggling to get up.

"*Benny!*" Gutsy yelled, but then her warning turned into a cry of pain as Mercy slashed again, opening a burning line across her midriff. Only her fast reflexes kept the cut from going deep. Even so, blood welled and ran down her stomach. She wheeled and ran ten paces, then turned again, setting herself for his charge.

For a moment Brother Mercy paused, looking at Benny with unfiltered loathing, but then his eyes—and the full weight of his hatred—slammed back to Gutsy.

"Leafy," he said again. "You stole her from me."

Leafy?

With a jolt of insight, Gutsy realized that this was the female reaper she'd fought on the crane platform. And with the realization came a strange dual reaction. On one hand, she needed to stop this madman, even if it meant killing him. But on the other, he'd lost someone he clearly loved. It drove a splinter of genuine empathy into her heart. It made him less of a monster and more human. More like her. How would she feel if she thought Alice was dead? How would she react if she faced the person who'd killed her?

And yet . . . this young reaper had been working that crane. He had dropped the truck on the roof of the Chung house. If Alice was dead, then he had killed her as surely as if one of his knives cleaved her beautiful heart.

The wave of empathy Gutsy felt was there, but now a bigger, blacker wave of pure hatred rose up in her own heart. The air in front of her eyes seemed to blossom with black flowers, and she heard a terrible roar fill the air as some beast howled with a fury beyond speech, beyond control. Gutsy heard it and knew it to be her own cry, torn from the darkest place in her heart. She charged Brother Mercy, slashing with her machete in a series of strikes so fast they were blinding. They beat at the reaper's knives and he stumbled back in surprise, her unbridled ferocity overriding even his own.

Benny heard the shriek of fury as he got to his feet and drew his sword. He knew who it was, but not really the why of it. Maybe it didn't really matter. What did was that it put steel into Benny's trembling legs. It made his feeble hand grip the sword handle with real strength. He yelled his own war cry, the one taught to him by his brother, Tom.

"Warrior smart!"

And he rushed to meet the ravagers.

* * *

Sam Imura burned through a full magazine and swapped it out with the smooth ease of someone who'd stood on a thousand battlefields, large and small, and fought a legion of enemies before this. Those enemies were all dead.

So, too, were these. The fact that it was an army of the dead that closed in on him seemed like some kind of ironic, cosmic joke. He felt his lips carve into a feral grin as he fired and fired and fired.

"You!" roared a bass voice, and Ledger turned fast—but not fast enough—as something smashed into him. It felt like being hit with a cannonball, and he fell backward, but tucked and rolled and came up on fingers and toes, staring at the thing that had hit him.

It was a human head.

The blank, empty eyes of a zombie stared into his own. The mouth opened and closed once and then was still forever. Ledger raised his eyes and saw who threw the grisly object.

The Raggedy Man.

Grimm rose to his feet and began to charge, but Ledger growled a word of command. The king of the dead was toxic, the source of all the plague in this broken world. This was the monster whose first bite started a chain reaction that killed nearly everything Ledger ever loved. His wife and child. Most of his friends. This man had destroyed everything that was beautiful, replacing it with pain and ugliness.

Ledger rose and stood his ground, letting the king of death come to him.

"Come on, Homer, haul your wormy butt up here," he taunted. "Let's dance."

The zombies and ravagers and reapers closed in, but the Raggedy Man snarled them back. "This one is *mine*."

Gutsy hammered at Brother Mercy with unrelenting force, but he blocked every strike. Then he twisted aside and kicked her in the stomach. If she hadn't seen it coming and began to turn, it would have crippled her, but even so it exploded in red hot pain and sent her staggering backward.

She almost lost her machete again, but managed to hold on to it and even bring it up as he slashed first right and then left.

It was immediately obvious he was a much better fighter, far superior because he was trained and she was not. But he attacked as if he was aware of that—too aware. He slashed and chopped with a kind of arrogance born of a belief that he would win, that such an outcome was inevitable. He even teased her, cutting her here and there with quick, shallow cuts. Making her hurt. Making her bleed. Trying to humiliate her, to teach her a lesson before he killed her.

Gutsy wasn't there to be schooled.

She saw movement behind him and yelled, "*Now!*"

And something moved with the speed of the wind. Gray and ugly, battered and covered with blood, it struck Brother Mercy's left leg, clamping teeth around the base of his thigh. The reaper screamed and stumbled, and Gutsy Gomez taught *him* a lesson with the edge of her machete.

He fell with a look of deep and profound surprise on his face.

His lips formed a word, or tried to. Then he collapsed back onto the grass and lay still. Sombra stood over him, chest heaving, blood dripping onto the ground, eyes blazing.

* * *

Thirty feet away, Benny Imura fought the ravagers. He looked like a ghost from an old manga—bled pale and wild-eyed—but he moved like a dancer, his body blurring, his sword a whisper of mercury on the wind.

Several times ravagers tried to circle him and attack from his blind side, and each time there was a *crack* as a bullet from Sam Imura's gun spoke with deadly eloquence. Together, the Imura brothers fought as if they had done this a hundred times before.

Gutsy turned and saw Ledger squaring off against the Raggedy Man.

"Oh my God," she gasped. Homer Gibbon was indestructible. The unkillable lord of death. No matter how tough the soldier was, the Raggedy Man was worse.

Joe Ledger let Homer Gibbon swing first. He was ready for it, his weight on the balls of his feet, knees bent, hands loose and ready. The former serial killer was no fool, though. He swung a big, hard left, but it was a fake, and he immediately drove an uppercut to Ledger's stomach that would have doubled the older man in half.

Had it landed.

Ledger clubbed it aside with a snort of annoyance and counterpunched a left-right-left to the zombie king's face. The blows were blindingly fast but did not lack power. Ledger was a master fighter. Possibly the best combat specialist left on earth, and one of the best of all time. There was a reason he had survived this long.

The Raggedy Man fell back a step. He was not in pain, but he turned and spat a broken tooth onto the dirt.

"Oo'ho, look what we got here," he said. "You're a real schoolyard tough guy, ain't you?" He began walking in a wide circle around the old soldier.

Ledger said nothing but turned with the monster.

"You the big bad boy who organized these Happy Meals and taught 'em to fight?" asked Homer.

"No, they seem to be pretty good at whipping your ugly butt without me."

Gibbon suddenly darted in and struck at Ledger's throat with stiffened fingers. The soldier leaned back and snapped out a kick that cracked something in Homer's knee. The king of the dead staggered. Ledger feinted right and shifted left and kicked the monster again, this time in the face. Before Homer could fall, Ledger cupped the back of his head and punched him four times in the face with crushing force, breaking bones and splitting the patchwork skin. Then he spit in Homer's face and kicked him in the chest to send him sliding five feet down the hill.

The reapers and ravagers gasped and then surged forward, but Homer Gibbon shouted them back. Grimm stalked in a rough circle around the two combatants, his spikes gleaming, eyes blazing, daring any of them to interfere. Gutsy and Sombra edged forward, uncertain how—or even if—they should do anything.

Homer got to his feet, damaged but truly unhurt. He was no more able to feel pain than any zombie, and even if he could, all that would have done was make his desire to literally devour this man all the greater.

"I'm going to enjoy—" he began, but Ledger leaped from the hill and hit him with a devastating right cross that spun the monster around in a complete circle. Ledger squatted over Homer, picked him up, and locked one brawny arm around the creature's throat.

"Listen to me, worm meat," he said in a fierce whisper, "if I wanted you dead, you'd already *be* dead. You think just because you started this that you're *actually* unkillable. Yeah, I know you've been blown up, cut up, and sewn back together, but that was because the people who did that wanted to study you. I heard they tried hard to kill you once they realized you could talk to the dead. Guess they didn't try hard enough to end you. Well, I'm here to tell you that I *do* know how to put you down for good. Don't believe me? Just look."

He dragged the monster back to the top of the hill, limping as the wound in his leg—torn open now from his jump— threatened to cripple him. It did not matter to Ledger. He needed Homer to see what was happening out in the dark.

"See that?" he murmured in Homer's ear, turning him to face the mass of his zombie army. "That's your kingdom. That's your Night Army. That's your *future*."

Homer Gibbon stopped struggling and stared.

Beyond the front ranks of his army there was a boiling, thrashing fury of movement. The plague of paracide infection from the wild men had spread beyond anything the Raggedy Man thought possible. Exponential. Faster than a wildfire. Not stopped—or even slowed—by the walls of flames.

Where there had been thousands of wild men, now there were hundreds of thousands. More than half of his army had become his enemies.

With a howl of rage Homer drove an elbow back into Ledger's stomach, catching him off guard enough to break his hold. The Raggedy Man shoved the soldier back and spun, raising his arms. The reapers and ravagers and shamblers who'd been watching the fight—more than a hundred of them—moved forward.

"Then if I die, you go with me," he growled. "*Everyone*. We'll kill them all before those wild things take us. See if we don't."

Joe Ledger backed away a few steps, waving Gutsy back too. Benny and Sam broke off their battles and ran to join them, chased by killers both living and undead. The dogs retreated, and they stood in a tight knot as the mob closed in. Gutsy looked up at Ledger to see how a hero prepared himself to die.

Ledger's face was tight with pain, but there was no defeat in his eyes.

Then there was a strange sound. A squawk of static, like the sound the satellite phone had made when Nix was testing it. Ledger raised his hand and touched something Gutsy hadn't seen before—a small black device fitted into his ear. He pressed it.

"Well, it's about darn time, Top," said Ledger. "Been trying to keep these freaks entertained until you got here. Go weapons hot. It's a target-rich environment. Let's rock and roll."

"What's happening?" demanded the Raggedy Man. "Who are you talking to?"

Ledger looked at Homer Gibbon. "You have your army, sport. Turns out it just so happens I have one of my own."

Suddenly there was a sound like a thousand cats screeching all at once, and Gutsy looked up in wonder to see that the stars were obliterated by dozens of lines of mingled fire and gray smoke. Not dozens—*hundreds*. They scratched like matches and arced down into the fields where the wild men and the living dead struggled for dominance. They struck, and the world was transformed from moonlit night into sun-bright day. The combined detonation of five hundred Hellfire missiles was the loudest sound Gutsy had ever heard.

She screamed and clapped her hands to her ears.

Then she whirled to see a flight of nightmare locusts rise up from over the horizon. She knew the word but had only ever seen broken husks of these things.

Helicopters.

From one side of her sightline to the other, the sky was filled with them.

Wave after wave of them. Firing missiles as they blew the dreams of the Raggedy Man into burning ruin.

Some, faster than others, flew over the field and opened up with machine guns, chasing down the ravagers and reapers. Others skirted the edges and dropped cannisters that exploded into massive clouds of flame.

Gutsy looked at Ledger and Sam and Benny. They were all grinning. She understood. Nix and Lilah had gotten through to someone. Maybe Benny's other friends, Morgie and Riot, had reached Asheville after all. And maybe Ledger and Sam had made a call for help from Site B.

Or perhaps all of that happened. Maybe, just once, the stars aligned in the direction of hope instead of extinction.

Homer Gibbon screamed in rage and horror as his dreams

burned. There was a ravager near him, and he tore the creature's rifle from its hands and swung it toward the small group of humans on the hill.

With a movement too fast to follow, Joe Ledger drew his pistol and shot the Raggedy Man in the head. Six fast shots that blew all of the dark dreams from the mind of the king of the dead. The body of Homer Gibbon stood for one moment longer and then crumpled.

"You stole the world from us," said Ledger quietly, "and we're officially taking it back."

The reapers stared at the beloved of Lord Thanatos, and the sight of him dead broke them. They scattered like leaves, and the fiery wind chased them. They tried to outrun the helicopters, but they could not. Ledger yelled to them to stop, pleading with them to throw down their weapons, to give up. To live.

Some did. A little more than half. The choppers did not fire on those who'd given up. But so many of the reapers were too far gone along the path to the shadows to which they prayed. Even as they ran, they shook their weapons in defiance to the machines that represented the hated world from before their god raised the dead. Gutsy watched in horror and wondered if such a death somehow filled those defiant reapers with joy even as the bullets found them. In a strange way, she hoped that it did.

A pair of Black Hawk helicopters dropped down low and hovered a dozen yards above the hill, doors open, machine gun barrels pointing down at the ravagers and shamblers circling the four humans and two dogs. The guns roared.

THE NIGHT WAS DARK AND FILLED WITH FIRE AND blood.

But even the darkest night is burned away by the light of a new day. The sun, half blinded by smoke, peered in horror over the horizon. In its glow, Gutsy and Benny held on to each other, leaning like a pair of old people, as they made their way along the road to where the refugees from New Alamo waited. Toward Site B.

There was a mass of people in the weed-choked parking lot of a small industrial complex. The door to the main building was open, and the two horses Sam and Ledger had ridden out on were tethered there, munching grass as if there had not been a war raging a few miles away.

Chong and Spider ran to meet Benny and Gutsy. They hugged and wept, and everyone spoke at once. Trying to make sense of it.

Then Alethea was there, pushing everyone aside and wrapping her arms around Gutsy in a bear hug so fierce it nearly broke bones. Then Alethea pushed Gutsy back, alarmed by the bloody bandage wrapped around her torso.

She straightened her tiara and gave Gutsy a frank up-and-down appraisal. "Well," she said, "*you* look like crap."

Gutsy laughed, but then she glanced around. She saw Sarah Peak clinging to Mr. Howard.

"Where's Karen?" asked Gutsy. "Did she make it out?"

Alethea's smile flickered, and she shook her head. Gutsy felt like she'd been punched. "Where are the Chess Players?"

Tears broke from the corners of Alethea's eyes. "Mr. Ford . . . and Mr. Urrea . . ."

This was worse. Now Gutsy felt like she'd been shot through the heart. Her knees began to buckle, but Spider caught her.

"Have . . . have you seen Alice . . . ?"

Alethea did not look away. Her love for Gutsy was too real for that. But she could not speak the words. Instead she bent at the waist and crumpled slowly to the ground. Rainbow Smite fell from her hand and rolled a few feet away.

Gutsy felt the world tilt and the ground collapse under her. She screamed as she fell. Spider grabbed her and knelt with her, holding her. Alethea crawled to them, and they wrapped one another up, sobbing and screaming.

"Please," Gutsy begged, but there was no answer. Some prayers cannot be answered.

Not for so many. Not for Alice. Not for Karen or Urrea or Ford, or for Sergeant Holly or Sunny-Day Ray. Because this was war, and war was hungry. It was unfair, and it loved to hurt.

Gutsy buried her face in the hollow of Alethea's neck and wept.

EPILOGUE

One

The winds, so fierce the night before, faded, and a sky of absurd and tranquil blue owned the day.

Medics came to apply dressings, set bones, save lives. Sombra received eighteen stitches, and Gutsy was given twenty in a straight line from left hip bone to right. Benny had a bunch of his own, as did the two older soldiers. Only Grimm was unharmed, thanks to his armor. The big hound looked tired and seemed older, though, as if deeply weary with war.

Maybe, thought Gutsy, this would be the last war for all of them. But she didn't think that was really true.

Two

Gutsy's plan for using the windstorm to spread the Dòmi was never put into practice.

At least, not that night.

Over the next days, helicopters chased packs of wild men and seeded them with the Dòmi-laced stabilizer. The wind of the rotor wash spread the treatment over them, and the wild men stopped running. Stopped fighting. Stopped howling.

They stopped entirely.

Those who had been shamblers before the Wodewose corrupted them stood silent and then fell. Without the parasite driving their motor cortexes and other functions, their bodies simply died.

More helicopters arrived from the American Nation. Monstrous Chinooks and Ospreys came and brought doctors, medicines, and help. It was as if the past had invaded the present with mercy. Once they'd breached Site B, Ledger and Sam found a communications room and made contact with California—only to find that Nix had already gotten through and that help was coming. Then Ledger called Asheville, and once more found that the military was mobilized, with every available chopper already on the way to New Alamo, thanks to Morgie Mitchell and Riot. The two fleets of choppers flew fast, moving from refueling point to refueling point, racing to get to New Alamo in time.

Only just in time . . .

Three

There were reunions at Site B.

One of the helicopters—painted with the sunrise symbol of the Nine Towns of Central California—landed, and two slender figures emerged. One was tall and had hair as white as snow. The other was shorter and rounder and had fiery red hair and a lot of freckles. They saw Benny and Chong at the same time the boys saw them.

"Nix!" yelled Benny, and he ran as fast as he could toward her.

"Lilah!" cried Chong, and pelted after him. For once in

his life, Chong outran Benny. Lilah and Nix met them halfway, and they collided with hugs and kisses and laughter and tears.

Gutsy and her friends sat on a picnic table, watching the reunion. Despite everything, Gutsy smiled to see their joy. Alethea took her hand and squeezed it.

The four California kids came over, and there were more hugs and tears.

"Hey," asked Benny brightly, "I guess that monkey-banger Morgie actually made it to Asheville. Riot, too."

The smile on Nix's face faltered. "They made it," she said.

"Where are they?" Chong asked, looking around. "Did they come with the army? I haven't seen them anywhere . . ."

His voice trailed off because Nix's eyes were bright with wetness.

"Hey, whoa," said Benny, "what is it? What's wrong? Where *is* Morgie? Where's Riot?"

"They . . . they took the fastest route," began Nix in a fragile little voice. "They did everything they could to get to Asheville in time. They wanted to help, you know?"

She paused and wiped at her eyes. She tried to say more but couldn't. She just put a hand over her mouth and shook her head.

So, Lilah said it. "They drove too close to Houston," she said.

"So what?" asked Alethea. "Did they get bit or something?"

"No," Lilah said. "There was some kind of radiation thing. A power-plant meltdown. They made it to Asheville, but they were sick."

"*How* sick?" Benny demanded. "Come on, Lilah, how bad are they?"

Lilah just looked at him. Then tears rolled down her cheeks too.

"Oh . . . my God . . . ," Chong breathed.

Benny sat down hard on the edge of the table and put his head against Nix's chest.

No one said a word for a long time.

Four

Every day after the fall of the Raggedy Man, Gutsy and Sombra went out looking for Alice. Alethea had seen her during the exodus, her eyes empty of everything but hunger. The girl Gutsy loved had been staggering awkwardly on badly broken legs, but there had been no time to quiet her. Gutsy looked for her every morning. Every afternoon. Well into each night.

Alethea and Spider volunteered to help. So did Benny and Nix and the others. Ledger offered too. Gutsy said no.

On the fifth day Gutsy came back just as the sun was setting fires in the western sky. She did not speak to anyone. She went into the tent that had been set up for her by staff from the American Nation. Gutsy stayed in there all night and most of the next day. Sombra sat outside and would not let anyone come close. When the moon rose, the coydog howled. After that day, Gutsy no longer went out looking for Alice.

Five

There was more to the story. Mysteries solved. Answers given.

Asheville had never been destroyed, but it had been attacked. A team of reapers had staged a series of systematic sabotage missions in the capital of the new American Nation. They destroyed all of the cell towers in the region, blew up two electrical power plants, and set off bombs in the communications center. The town went dark, unable to reach the rest of the national network.

By the time the power was back on and communications restored, the Raggedy Man had launched attacks on a dozen smaller towns and countless settlements. No one had any estimates of the loss of life, but it was staggering.

When Ledger and Sam had reached Site B and forced their way in, Bess Collins tried to ambush them. The small group of soldiers stationed at the site fought hard to keep it. They fought the wrong enemy, though. Sam and Ledger had taken more heavily defended places than that. Five of the eight soldiers had surrendered after the others and Captain Collins had died in the fighting. They each claimed they were just following orders, which did not work well with anyone.

The rescue operation was overseen by a pair of old friends of Ledger and Sam—a grizzled old man named Bradley Sims, known to everyone as Top, and a brawny fiftysomething ex-marine from Orange County with the improbable name of Harvey Rabbit, known as Bunny. They had been part of Ledger's special ops teams for decades.

Even so, it had been way too close.

Six

Dr. Morton found everything he needed at Site B to make pills. His ability to almost miraculously improve on the formula did not go unnoticed. After all, he was now a patient who required those drugs. They let him work and gave him plenty of assistance, but he was never thereafter allowed into any lab or hospital without a military escort.

A transport came and took him away to Asheville, where Dr. McReady, the brilliant researcher who had led the fight to cure the Reaper Plague, had her main facility. With Wodewose and Dòmi and the bulk of all the research, there was talk of an actual cure—for Sarah Peak and Chong and all the infected. And, of course, for Dr. Max Morton.

Seven

Captain Ledger found Gutsy sitting in her tent one morning. He stood there studying her, his eyes unreadable.

"Are you going to sit there forever?" he asked.

She shrugged.

"People need you," he said.

"No one needs me," Gutsy said. "I did what I could, but I'm done."

He came in and squatted down. Sombra allowed it.

"Listen to me, Guts," he said softly. "You look like crap."

"Thanks."

"No, you need some food and a shower and some air."

"I'm fine," she said, and looked away.

"No," insisted Ledger gently, "you're *not*. Listen—I get that you likely feel that you somehow let Alice down, that it's your fault she died. Thinking that is natural. We humans tend to take out the knives and stab ourselves when things are really bad. You're looking at the champ of that."

She said nothing.

"Here's the thing: you did more to save New Alamo than anyone. You want me to go over it point-by-point to explain why I—and everyone else—thinks that?"

"Just leave me alone."

"No, I won't be doing that. Your friends out there won't either. And pretty soon they're going to get tired of this vigil or whatever it is." He rubbed some old scars on his face. "But they're going to need Gabriella *Gutsy* Gomez. That smart problem solver, the one who figures things out. And you know why they'll need you? Because you *do* figure things out. You look at the clockwork and understand what makes it tick."

"I did everything I could do, and look what happened."

"I get it. You lost your mom, and now you lost Alice. You are gutted, empty, broken. I really get that," he said.

She shook her head. "If you came in here to give me a pep talk, it's not a very good one."

"Look, we're all children of the storm lands," said Ledger. "We're all marked. We're all scarred, inside and out." He leaned forward and gave Gutsy's shoulder a slow, firm squeeze. "What matters in the end is what we choose to become when the world rips apart who we've been. So, tell me, Gutsy Gomez: Who are you going to be?"

Instead of waiting for an answer, the soldier got slowly to his feet, knees popping. He lingered in the opening of the tent and gave her a sad, weary smile. But it was a smile nonetheless.

Eight

Three weeks after the fall of the Raggedy Man, Benny Imura and Gutsy Gomez sat on the same picnic table, looking out at the endless wastes of the Broken Lands. She looked southwest, to where New Alamo had been. He looked northwest, toward his home in Central California. Sombra lay with his head in Gutsy's lap.

"You sure you don't want to come with us?" Benny asked.

"I thought about it," she admitted, "but no. Thanks, though."

"So, what are you going to do? Go live in Asheville?"

Gutsy bent down and plucked a stalk of sweetgrass and put it between her teeth. "For a while. Alethea and Spider want to see it. I guess I do too."

Benny turned to look at her. "See it, or live there?"

"I don't know," she said. "Yet."

He nodded, and they watched a fleet of clouds sail across the sky.

"What about you?" she asked. "Back home to California?"

"I suppose."

"To see it, or live there?" she asked, smiling.

"I don't know either."

Sombra's leg twitched in his sleep as if he was running from something. He uttered a small whine. Gutsy stroked his head, and he settled down to a more restful slumber. Like Gutsy, his stitches were out. And also like her, he would wear a scar for the rest of his life.

"Tell you one thing," said Benny, "there are still a lot of zoms out there. Billions of them. Dr. Morton says that there's no way to even be sure the ones in other countries are the same. Different mutations, exposure to different chemicals and weather conditions. All that. Could be stuff out there the Wodewose and Dòmi won't touch."

"Yeah," Gutsy said, "but there could be whole communities out there, too. Intact, I mean. People who stayed safe. On islands and mountains. Or people who found their own cures. It's a big world. Who knows what's out there?"

Benny nodded. They glanced at each other, their gazes lingering.

"I might want to go take a look," said Benny.

"Yeah," said Gutsy. "I was thinking the same thing."

A cloud passed in front of the sun, for a moment darkening the day, but then it moved on. They watched the shadow move across the field and then vanish into the unknown distance. Like a traveler wandering down a lost road.